❧ Praise for *Knightley Academy* ❧

"Steam-punky, subversive, and enthralling!"
—Tamora Pierce

"A fabulously enjoyable tale, brimming with humor,
suspense, and swordplay. I found myself wishing
I could attend Knightley Academy!"
—Kaza Kingsley, author of the bestselling Erec Rex series

"Terrific fun! Knights-in-training, a looming war,
and white-knuckle subterfuge made for a great read.
Can't wait for the next one!"
—Dean Lorey, author of the Nightmare Academy series

"If only regular school could be as much fun as the
academy. . . . Violet Haberdasher has a way of
capturing the wonder and joy of learning something
new that really grabs readers."
—Kidsreads.com

"For those longing for a new Harry Potter,
. . . be just the thing."
. . . s Literature

ALSO BY VIOLET HABERDASHER

KNIGHTLEY ACADEMY

THE Secret Prince

A KNIGHTLEY ACADEMY BOOK

VIOLET HABERDASHER

ALADDIN

NEW YORK LONDON TORONTO SYDNEY NEW DELHI

This book is a work of fiction. Any references to historical events, real people,
or real locales are used fictitiously. Other names, characters, places, and incidents
are the product of the author's imagination, and any resemblance to actual events
or locales or persons, living or dead, is entirely coincidental.

ALADDIN

An imprint of Simon & Schuster Children's Publishing Division
1230 Avenue of the Americas, New York, NY 10020
First Aladdin paperback edition July 2012
Copyright © 2011 by Robyn Schneider
All rights reserved, including the right of reproduction in whole or in part in any form.
ALADDIN is a trademark of Simon & Schuster, Inc., and related logo is a registered trademark
of Simon & Schuster, Inc.
Also available in an Aladdin hardcover edition.
For information about special discounts for bulk purchases, please contact Simon & Schuster
Special Sales at 1-866-506-1949 or business@simonandschuster.com.
The Simon & Schuster Speakers Bureau can bring authors to your live event. For more
information or to book an event contact the Simon & Schuster Speakers Bureau at
1-866-248-3049 or visit our website at www.simonspeakers.com.
Designed by Lisa Vega
The text of this book was set in Bembo.
Manufactured in the United States of America 0612 OFF
2 4 6 8 10 9 7 5 3 1
The Library of Congress has cataloged the hardcover edition as follows:
Haberdasher, Violet.
The secret prince / Violet Haberdasher. — 1st Aladdin hardcover ed.
p. cm.
Sequel to: Knightley Academy
Summary: Fourteen-year-old orphan Henry Grim's schooling at the prestigious Knightley
Academy continues, as he and some friends discover an old classroom filled with forgotten
weapons, which lead them into a dangerous adventure.
ISBN 978-1-4169-9145-8 (hc)
[1. Orphans—Fiction. 2. Knights and knighthood—Fiction. 3. Secret societies—Fiction.
4. Boarding schools—Fiction. 5. Schools—Fiction.] I. Title.
PZ7.H11424Se 2011
[Fic]—dc22
2010038855
ISBN 978-1-4169-9146-5 (pbk)
ISBN 978-1-4424-3605-3 (eBook)

To the Philomathean Society—
For barefoot fencing matches in the library and nights spent pondering life on Gothic rooftops. For jokes in Latin, and human chess, and scholars' gowns worn in earnest over impeccably cut suits and fashionable dresses. Sic itur ad astra. Of this I am certain: In Philo, the spirit of Knightley Academy lives on.

ACKNOWLEDGMENTS

There is a dreadful yet necessary page in every novel where the author must break character long enough to thank the people responsible for the book's existence. And so, in lieu of a simple "thank you for being awesome," I have decided to bestow honorary knighthood upon the following:

My crack team of agents, editors, and publicists: Mark McVeigh, Ellen Krieger, Paul Crichton, Bernadette Cruz, and Jason Dravis.

Those friends who insisted on staging a late-night reading of *Knightley Academy* and recording it for posterity: Emily Kern, Abbey Stockstill, Alec Webley, Thadeus Dowad, Jith Eswarappa, Saad Zaheer, and Paul Mitchell.

And these people of the Internet: Paige Harwood, Karen Kavett, Kayley Hyde, Liane Graham, Erica Sands, Kaleb Nation, Jennifer Levine, Alex Bennett, The SchneiderKnights (Kaeli, Sean, Matt, Sasha, Grace, Hayley, Claire, and Ninja), Adam and Rohan (for the, um, tassels), Julia DeVillers, and the Group That Must Not Be Named.

1

DOWN THE ALLEYWAY

In a rough-and-tumble, not-altogether-respectable neighborhood south of Hammersmith Cross Station, wedged between darkened taverns and foggy docklands, sits a rambling bookshop with cheery red shutters.

For most of the year a tiny old lady minds the shop, frowning in concentration as she knits stocking caps for no one. But should you pass this shop and find the dusty windows scrubbed clean, or the door decorated with a sign advertising deliveries, you would find someone else behind the counter of Alabaster & Sons, Purveyors of Rare Books Since 1782—to all appearances, just an ordinary teenage boy, bent intently over a detective story. But appearances can be deceiving.

* * *

In the pale gloom of the unusually cold January afternoon when our story starts, the roads are desolate, but their emptiness is not due entirely to the dreadful weather.

As you have probably heard or read or suspected without quite knowing why, sinister things indeed were happening up north, and in those dark days, fearful rumors were more common than holiday cheer.

But where there is suspicion there is also doubt, and some people still pretended that nothing was the matter. After all, appearances have to be maintained, especially by those looked to as an example. "Let the superstitious servants worry!" the aristocracy scoffed from the comfort of their elegant town houses.

After all, it wasn't as though there were proof to any rumor.

"Wot's in the boxes, then?" The tall dangerous-looking boy sneered, taking a step forward.

"Jus' deliveries." The boy called Alex whimpered, feeling the cold, slimy wall of the alleyway against his back, blocking his escape. "Please. I ain't got money, an' I need this job."

The dangerous-looking boy's eyes narrowed, and his

two hulking friends laughed, their fists already raised. "Will yeh be needin' both yer arms fer that job o' yours?"

Alex paled.

"Or," the sneering boy continued, hoping that no one could hear his stomach rolling with hunger as he withdrew a knife from his tattered jacket, "both yer ears?"

Henry Grim shook his head in mock disgust as his best friend demolished a strawberry tart in two enormous mouthfuls.

"Oh, very polite," Henry said. "Be glad that Rohan isn't here. He'd perish from the shame."

Adam swallowed thickly and wiped his mouth with his coat sleeve. "What? They're good."

"Well, of course they're good," Henry said in exasperation. "Sucray's is the best bakery this side of the river. Come on. I wasn't really supposed to leave the shop unattended . . ."

"Right, because someone might be having an emergency that only a rare encyclopedia can cure."

"It's the Code of Chivalry, Adam." Henry sighed. "I gave my word to Mrs. Alabaster that I'd mind the shop."

"It's *boring* in there," Adam complained. "I can't wait for term to start."

"Next week," Henry said, reaching into his jacket pocket for his keys. "And at least save me *one* of the tarts."

Adam opened his mouth, frowned, and stood absolutely still.

Henry shot his friend a confused look, and then realized that Adam was on to something. The road on which they were walking was too empty, and altogether too quiet.

Adam cocked his head in the direction of an alleyway up ahead. Faintly they could hear scuffling and muffled whimpers.

Henry nodded and put a finger to his lips, trying to move silently over the icy cobblestones. He knew that it wasn't Sir Frederick—that it couldn't be—not with their former professor's face plastered on hundreds of faded posters advertising a handsome reward for any information that led to his capture.

But even though he knew it was impossible, for a moment Henry hoped for the chance to confront Sir Frederick. For the chance to, somehow, fix everything that had happened last school term.

His heart hammering nervously, Henry peered around the corner.

It wasn't Sir Frederick. But then, he'd known it wouldn't be.

Down the dingy alleyway, past a pile of wooden crates, stood three huge boys, their clothes in tatters. They formed a menacing circle around Mr. Sucray's delivery boy, Alex, who was curled into a ball on the ground.

Less than a year ago it would have been Henry at the center of that circle, resigned to enduring whatever bullying or punishment his tormentors had planned.

But so much had changed since then.

"You there!" Henry called with false confidence, blocking the alley's only exit. "What do you think you're doing?"

The largest of the boys froze, a battered Sucray's cake box in his hands. Alex, still on the ground, coughed and moaned. "Wot d'you want?" the hulking boy growled.

"I want you to give Alex back his packages and get out of here," Henry said calmly, even though he was unprepared and terrified and knew that if it came to a fight he'd lose.

"You ain't no police knight," the boy sneered, nodding at the braid and crest on Henry's jacket.

"Not yet," Henry allowed, lifting his chin and

performing an impression of Rohan's posh accent. "But my father is, and he's waiting in our automobile just outside the shop." Behind him Henry heard Adam snort.

The bullies in the alley looked at one another in defeat. Grumbling, they abandoned their perilous game and stomped toward Henry and Adam with murder in their eyes. Henry held his ground as the leader edged past.

Wordlessly Henry took the box of tarts from Adam and thrust it into the boy's chest.

With a sneer the boy grabbed the parcel and slammed his fist into Henry's mouth. Henry didn't flinch, even though he tasted blood.

Adam gulped nervously and flattened himself against the wall as though he rather hoped he could disappear.

"I ain't afraid o' no rich brats," the boy jeered, and then took off running, his cronies following suit.

Letting out a breath he didn't know he'd been holding, Henry wiped a smear of blood from his lip.

"Let's go down the creepy alleyway," Adam muttered. "Oh, yes, what a wonderful idea. Then we can confront a trio of murderous bandits and get ourselves punched in the face."

Henry chuckled at Adam's reaction, and then winced,

touching his fingers to the fresh split in his lip.

"You okay, mate?" Adam asked.

"No," Henry said, and then because he couldn't resist, "I really wanted that last tart."

Down the alleyway Alex coughed and stirred.

"You all right?" Henry called.

"Yeah, you're not dead, are you?" Adam asked.

Henry sighed. Just once it would be nice if Adam *didn't* say the first thing that popped into his head.

"What hurts?" Henry asked, kneeling next to Alex and checking the boy for injuries. At Knightley they'd learned a semester of medicine for situations precisely like this one.

"My head," Alex mumbled. "An' my foot."

Henry and Adam helped Alex hobble to the bookshop, where they took a closer look at the boy's injuries. One eye was entirely black and nearly swollen shut. There was a lump on his head that hopefully wouldn't cause a concussion, and his right ankle was sprained.

"Have those lot given you trouble before?" Adam asked, perching on the counter while Henry held a cold compress to the boy's ankle.

"Not me," Alex said, shaking his head. "But I seen them about, an' I know wot they're up to. Supportin' the

Nordlands an' goin' to rallies down at the docks instead o' workin' honest jobs."

Henry and Adam exchanged a look. And at that moment a crowded omnibus rattled past the storefront.

Adam glanced at the clock, swore, and scrambled for his coat. "How'd it get so late?" he asked.

Henry shrugged. "Guess we lost track of time, what with the bookshop being so *boring* and all."

"Oi, you know I have to be home in time for supper or I'll never hear the end of it," Adam said, edging toward the door.

"See you later," Henry called. The jingle of bells answered him as the shop door shut behind Adam, and Henry sighed.

It was wonderful that Adam could visit over the holiday, that they were only a half hour's ride apart, while the rest of their school friends were spread out all over the country. Even so, every time Adam left, scrambling tardily after the departing omnibus, Henry was still sad to see his friend go.

At school they were roommates—Henry, Adam, and proper, perceptive Rohan. And while an afternoon playing cards in the bookshop was nice, it wasn't the same as their late-night exploits or illicit fencing bouts with Frankie, the headmaster's rebellious daughter.

"What are you doing?" Henry asked, turning around as Alex tried to wedge his swollen ankle back into his boot.

"I've got a delivery," Alex said helplessly. "It has t' be tonight. Some posh party up the Regent's Hill."

Henry closed his eyes and took a deep breath. He'd just *had* to go down that alleyway, hadn't he?

"Put your boot down, Alex," he said. "I'll make the delivery."

That was how Henry found himself hurrying along the frost-covered cobblestones, carrying a stack of parcels tied with twine. He wore his old falling-apart boots, since he was trying to save his good pair for school. The cold had seeped in through the soles, and he kept slipping over icy patches and having to pinwheel his arms to stay upright.

This was not, Henry thought wryly, one of his finest moments.

Regent's Hill was one of the city's wealthier neighborhoods, and Henry caught glimpses inside the town houses as he passed by. No doubt many of his classmates were spending their holiday on these very streets, in town for the city season, expected to make polite chaperoned conversation with giggling schoolgirls and to endure five-course dinners that involved at least five different forks.

For once he was glad to be different.

Henry shivered and tucked his chin deeper into the layers of his school scarf, longing for the crackling fire that warmed the parlor above the bookshop, and for the mystery novel propped on the edge of his favorite armchair, two chapters remaining. He wondered if he'd get back to their flat before Professor Stratford returned from his tutoring job, and he wondered if the professor would worry if he didn't, and he wished he'd remembered to leave a note.

Well, he hadn't. And anyway, it wasn't as though Professor Stratford were his guardian. Henry had never been adopted. He had simply left the orphanage the moment he was old enough, and had looked after himself as best he could. And as much as he enjoyed sharing the flat above the bookshop with his former tutor, a little voice in the back of his head wouldn't let him forget that all of his school friends were spending their holiday with their families—adopted or otherwise.

Somehow, without Henry's noticing, it had begun to snow. Thick flakes landed on his coat and hair.

Finally Henry reached the address Alex had given him. He stared up at the town house, briefly watching the shadows of partygoers pass behind the lighted windows before he descended the shabby out-of-the-way stairs to the basement.

He knocked, and a maid took her time opening the door.

Her eyes narrowed. "Whatchoo want?"

Henry held out the parcels. "Delivery from Sucray's," he said.

"'Bout time," the girl said, and sniffed. "Cook's been askin' after them pettyfours fer an hour." The way the girl spoke reminded Henry of his days working at the Midsummer School, where he'd been piled with extra chores by other members of the serving staff. But enough time had passed since then that Henry was no longer afraid to speak up.

"I'm sorry for the inconvenience," he said, "but would you mind showing me where to put these?"

"All righ', come inside, then," the girl grumbled.

Henry eagerly brushed snow from his coat and hair and followed the girl down the warm hallway, pulling off his wet scarf along the way.

"Cook!" the girl shrilled. "The cakes're here." She pushed open the door to a cinnamon-scented kitchen and spun around to grumble at Henry some more.

"Don' touch nothin'," she warned, and then her eyes widened as she took in the braid and crest on Henry's school coat. "Yer not a delivery boy."

"Never said I was," Henry replied, placing his parcels on a table and holding out his chilled hands to the warmth of the nearby stove.

The girl glared, but then thought better of it and flounced away, grumbling to herself.

Cook, a gray-haired old woman who was all chins, opened the parcels with a dangerously glittering butcher's knife and peered inside. "Everythin' looks in order," she said, presumably to Henry, although she hadn't thrown so much as a glance in his direction. "Warm yerself fer a minute more an' then be off."

"Yes, ma'am," Henry said reluctantly, thinking of the long trudge back in the snow. It was moments like these when he wished he hadn't signed his name to the Code of Chivalry after all, when he wished he didn't go *looking* for trouble in all the worst places.

"*Maureen!*" A haughty voice shrilled, and Cook stiffened.

"'S the mistress," Cook hissed in warning.

Henry edged around the curve of the stove, trying to be inconspicuous.

"Honestly, Maureen," the lady continued, descending a staircase in the far corner, all emerald skirts and disdain. "I have been ringing for the desserts for ages, and clearly there is a very good reason as to why I have had to disengage myself from my guests to inquire after them personally."

"Yes, mum," Cook said with a curtsy. "They've only just arrived."

"Only just?" the lady carried on in disapproval, having reached the bottom of the stairs.

Henry grimaced, because suddenly he knew whose house this was.

Frankie's dreadful grandmother Lady Augusta Winter stood, hands on her hips, daring her serving staff to account for the late delivery.

"I'm sorry, madam," Henry said, stepping out from the nook behind the stove. "But the roads are slicked with ice, and it's snowing again—" Henry broke off with a sigh.

Grandmother Winter squinted at him and frowned. "Mr. Grim," she began, "might I ask what you're doing in my kitchen?"

"Delivering cakes, ma'am," Henry said, feeling his cheeks color with embarrassment.

"And why are you delivering cakes, Mr. Grim?"

"A street gang accosted the delivery boy. I ran them off, but he was injured, and I—er, I volunteered to come in his place." Henry looked up, cringing still.

Grandmother Winter had always made him feel as though everything he said were entirely wrong, and no matter what he did, there was no redeeming himself for the fact that he had grown up in an orphanage.

"How heroic of you," she said coldly.

"Yes, ma'am." Henry bit his lip and then winced as the split began to bleed again.

"Perhaps, since you have saved the day, you would like to join the party."

Henry tried not to let horror show on his face as the kitchen staff gawked in his direction. He was certain that the only reason Grandmother Winter wanted him to attend the party was so that he'd embarrass himself or so that she might do it for him.

"Actually, I should be going."

"Nonsense. I insist," Grandmother Winter said, extending her arm. "You shall escort me back upstairs."

It wasn't a question. Henry gave a small bow and, with a sinking feeling, did as he was told.

2

LORD HAVELOCK'S WARNING

I'm ever so glad you came to my grandmother's soiree," Frankie murmured, staring up from beneath her fluttering eyelashes at the object of her torment.

"Yes, well," the boy said gruffly, desperately looking for someone—anyone—who might come to his rescue. "My uncle brought me. I didn't have a choice."

"And did he choose those darling spectacles for you as well?" Frankie asked, trying to hide her enormous grin behind the delicate china pattern of her teacup. "I couldn't help but notice how very nicely they disguise the squintiness of your naturally beady eyes."

"And I can't help but imagine spilling my cider all

over that silk dress of yours." Fergus Valmont's glare was murderous from behind his new spectacles.

"Please do," Frankie said, giving Valmont a wide smile. "I detest this dress. It's a perfectly horrid shade of pink, don't you agree? 'Puce.' The word alone sounds like cat sick."

"I can think of other things that remind me of cat sick," Valmont muttered.

"How could you say such a thing?" Frankie fake gasped, her blue eyes mocking. "Really, Mr. Valmont, there's no need to bring up your personal hygiene."

Valmont made a strangled noise and gripped his cider so hard that his knuckles turned white.

It was too easy, having a go at Valmont at her grand-mother's party, where the rigid constraints of society forced him to simper and play chivalrous. Because as much as Valmont pretended to have changed toward the end of last term, as much as he had lain off torment-ing Frankie and her friends, she didn't believe for one moment that he actually had changed.

Valmont's uncle had made him promise to be nice, and although he wasn't quite as horrible as he'd been in those first few weeks at the academy, Valmont had insulted Frankie and her friends one too many times for her to forgive and forget now. Henry could spend a hundred more evenings playing chess against Valmont in the first-year common room. It didn't mean that *Frankie* had to like the smarmy little arse-toad. Unfortunately, it wasn't nearly as fun as she'd hoped, tormenting Valmont at this wretched formal party.

Frankie glanced around the second-floor parlor, a converted ballroom festooned with lavish holiday decorations. Dozens of impeccably dressed gentlemen and demure ladies were engaged in polite conversation. It was even more miserable than the Maiden Manor School for Young Ladies—well, until she'd decided to get kicked out. That part, at least, had been gratifying.

Frankie wasn't used to attending her grandmother's holiday soirees. Before her father had become headmaster of Knightley Academy, they had avoided the city during the social season, preferring instead the shabby comfort of their dilapidated old manor house. But now, for the school's sake, Lord Winter had to keep up appearances. Frankie spotted her father in the corner by a potted fern, deep in discussion with Lord Havelock, Valmont's strict uncle, who taught military history at Knightley.

"You've got to be joking," Valmont muttered as a

hush fell over the room and everyone tried very hard not to look at all interested in who had just arrived at the party.

Frankie turned, not bothering to appear disinterested. Grandmother Winter stood imperiously in the doorway, and at her side, looking as though he desperately wished to be anywhere else, was Henry Grim. He wore his formal school jacket soaked from the snow, a wrinkled shirt spattered with blood, and a pair of old boots. His brown hair, just long enough to be impertinent, stuck damply to his forehead, shading his eyes.

"How perfectly dashing," Frankie overheard the mindless Miss Swann whisper to her giggly friend from a nearby settee. "Perhaps he has just saved the life of a poor street urchin in peril!"

Frankie snorted, certain that Henry had done no such thing. And just because Henry *was* sort of dashing these days didn't mean that Miss Swann had to giggle over him with her friend. They didn't know the first thing about him!

"Excuse me," Frankie said, abandoning a relieved Valmont.

Henry was still standing uncertainly at Grandmother Winter's side when Frankie reached them.

"Hello, Mr. Grim," Frankie said, bobbing a demure curtsy for her grandmother's sake.

Henry bowed and, with the faintest hint of a smirk, ventured that he hoped Miss Winter was having a pleasant holiday.

Frankie wondered how much more of this ridiculously stilted behavior she would have to endure.

Finally, after an excruciatingly drawn-out silence, Grandmother Winter cleared her throat and announced that she had best return to her *respected* guests.

After Grandmother Winter had gone, Frankie grinned. "You used the wrong bow," she said. "I hate to break it to you, but I'm not a foreign prince."

"Did I really?" Henry asked, his forehead wrinkling in anguish.

"No," Frankie said, snorting. "I was joking. Come on." Henry followed Frankie across the room, acutely aware of judgmental glances and conversations that went hastily silent as he passed. "By the way," Frankie began as she led Henry to a window seat, "did you know that your lip is bleeding?"

"Er, right," Henry said. "I got punched in the face."

Frankie burst out laughing and then quickly glanced toward the partygoers, afraid of their reaction. But no one seemed to have noticed. "Sorry," she said. "Go on. You were punched in the face, and then you arrived at my grandmother's formal party—I'm assuming uninvited—to tell me about it?"

"You've guessed it," Henry said with mock disappointment. "And now that my quest is fulfilled, I'll be going."

Frankie shot him a look.

Henry sighed, suddenly serious. "I was playing cards with Adam in the bookshop—," he began.

"And *he* punched you in the face? I wouldn't think he could reach," Frankie interrupted.

It was true. Henry had fast become the tallest boy in his year, much to his horror. He was having to scrape to afford a new uniform for next term. "Do you want to hear what happened or don't you?" he asked.

"No, I do," Frankie said contritely.

And so Henry hastily explained about the boys down the alleyway, and Alex's being injured, and how Grandmother Winter had discovered him half frozen, huddled against her kitchen stove. Frankie was shaking with laughter by the end of it.

"It isn't funny," Henry said. And then he raked his fingers through his hair and admitted, "No, it is. You're right."

"Why on earth did you go down that alleyway in the first place?" Frankie asked, still teasing.

"The Code of Chivalry. Helping those in need and all that."

Frankie raised an eyebrow, not believing for one moment that Henry would be so quick to rush into unknown danger just because of the Code of Chivalry—the same code that Henry, Adam, and Rohan had broken countless times over the last school term.

"Shall I remind you of the time we plastered Valmont's textbooks shut?" Frankie asked. "Or, how about that time we snuck into the armory so Adam and I could fence? Or pretty much every time you left the window cracked so I could climb—"

"All right," Henry said. "It wasn't just because I felt obligated to help. Satisfied?"

"Sir Frederick?" Frankie guessed.

Henry nodded. "I keep thinking he— No, it's ridiculous."

"Keep thinking what?" Frankie asked.

"That he's out there, waiting for us. Wanting revenge. Brooding over what we—what *I*—cost him."

"So you went down that alleyway because you thought it could have been Sir Frederick *waiting* to jump out and get you?" Frankie asked, surprised at Henry's stupidity. "For someone supposed to be so clever—"

"Forget it," Henry said angrily. "I shouldn't have said anything. It's not as though I'm meaning to track him down."

"I know that. But you shouldn't . . ."

"Shouldn't what? Worry? Never mind that there's a war coming and no one will listen to us, that Adam and I were nearly expelled, that Rohan actually *was* expelled? Or never mind that there's a madman who tormented us for half a school term who's out there somewhere, probably wanting revenge? Or never mind that I took an oath to serve and protect, and just because I'm a first year, I should walk right past trouble I can stop and go memorize a textbook instead?"

When Henry had finished, Frankie stared at him, wondering when her sweet, eager-to-please friend had become so frustrated. Of course she'd been caught up with quite enough of her own dramatics last term, what with Grandmother Winter suddenly and unexpect-edly coming to stay, putting an end to Frankie's free-dom. And then she'd nearly been sent off to a foreign reformatory. . . .

"That's not what I meant," Frankie snapped. "You shouldn't have to feel so responsible for everything all the time, is all."

Henry laughed hollowly. "I *have* to be responsible," he admitted, more honestly than he had intended. "There's no one else to do it for me."

"Am I interrupting?"

A shadow fell over the window seat, and Henry looked up.

Fergus Valmont glared down at them. His evening wear was expensive and elegant, his blond hair slicked back with obvious care, and his shoes polished to a glossy shine. Perched on his nose was a pair of thin spectacles, their oval lenses catching the light.

"Nice glasses." Henry smirked.

"Shut up, Grim." Valmont meant it as a threat, but it came out sounding like a whine.

But then, at least Valmont was calling him Grim now, a vast improvement from the beginning of last term, when Valmont had called Henry and his roommates servant boy, Jewish boy, and Indian boy.

"If you don't want me to talk, then why did you come over here?" Henry asked.

"To commend you on your stylish formal wear." Valmont's lip curled.

"Look," Henry said, "I didn't mean to come here. I didn't even know there *was* a party."

"Then what are you doing here?" Valmont asked.

"What happened to playing nice?" Henry returned.

"Uncle gave the condition that I had to be nice to you and your friends only *at school*."

"That personality of yours is a real winner," Frankie noted under her breath, but Henry overheard and tried not to laugh.

"If you don't feel like being nice, then I don't feel like telling you why I'm here," Henry said.

"Oh, come on. It's pathetic," Valmont snarled. "We all know you've got some demeaning little job as a dishwasher, and Lady Winter brought you up here during your break so everyone could have a laugh."

"That's not true, Valmont," Henry said icily.

"What's not true?" Valmont challenged, his blue eyes boring into Henry's brown ones. "That everyone's having a laugh at your expense? Because they are."

Henry took Valmont's challenge, rising to his feet and glaring down at his long-standing nemesis. Back at the Midsummer School they'd been the same height, but these days Valmont's forehead barely reached Henry's chin.

"Is that why you failed the Knightley Exam, Valmont?" Henry asked. "Because you were too proud to admit that you needed glasses?"

Valmont paled.

Henry realized with sudden regret that he'd struck a nerve, that Valmont truly had needed glasses—the way he'd always sat in the front row of military history, as though it were a prized, rather than a dreaded, seat.

"I'm sorry," Henry mumbled, but the damage was done.

With a sneer Valmont emptied his mug of cider down the front of Henry's shirt. "Oops," Valmont said, his voice filled with venom rather than apology. "How terribly clumsy of me. I seem to have ruined your best shirt."

Henry looked down at his dripping blood-spattered shirt. "Hallway. Now," he spat, daring Valmont to refuse.

With a reassuring smile in Frankie's direction, Henry—with Valmont—marched past the throng of partygoers, past the curious stares and accusing whispers.

"What is your *problem*?" Henry demanded as they

filed through the doorway and onto the lavishly wall-papered landing. "I *said* I was sorry."

"You take *everything*," Valmont accused. "Miss Swann hasn't shut up about you ever since you arrived at the party. She thinks you're so brave and handsome, upholding justice like a real police knight."

"That's what I *was* doing, Valmont," Henry snarled, and then gestured toward his shirt. "This isn't *my* blood."

Valmont's eyes widened in surprise, but then he shook his head, as though trying to dislodge Henry's explanation. "Whatever, Grim. I just thought you should know that you're out of your league."

"With what?" Henry asked in exasperation. "Fighting you? Because the boys this afternoon were a lot bigger than you are. Or are you talking about *Miss Swann*?"

Valmont's cheeks reddened. "I'll thank you *not* to talk about Miss Swann."

"I don't even know who she is! This is absurd." Henry shook his head, baffled. What good did it do them to chase after girls when they weren't yet fifteen, when they were stuck at Knightley and restricted from female visitors, with Frankie as the only girl around?

"You take everything I want," Valmont accused.

It was the old grudge again, back to their days at

the Midsummer School, when Henry had been the first boy in five years to pass the Knightley Exam. Of course, the reaction to *that* hadn't exactly been the honor and glory that was supposed to come with breaking the so-called Midsummer Curse. Especially because Henry had been a serving boy at the time, and no one even knew that he could read, much less that Professor Stratford, the school's English master, had been secretly tutoring Henry at night.

"I don't do it on purpose," Henry returned. The two boys glared at each other, hands balled into fists, each daring the other to make the first move.

Suddenly, without warning, Valmont's hands shot out and shoved Henry squarely on the chest.

Startled, Henry stumbled backward. The soles of his old boots were worn down, and he slipped on the polished floorboards. Henry desperately grabbed hold of the banister, his heart hammering. Less than a step behind him, the stairs angled sharply downward.

"Trying to kill me?" Henry asked casually, fighting to stay calm.

"I—er, I—," Valmont stuttered, terrified at how far it had almost gone.

"Forget it," Henry said, throwing up his hands in

disgust. "This ends *now*. I'm not going to threaten you with the horrors my friends and I could plan for you back at school, and I'm not going to warn you again. The next time you pick a fight with me over anything less than life or death, I'll—"

"Ah, Mr. Grim," someone said icily from the doorway.

Henry gulped. "Sir?"

Lord Havelock glowered at Henry, somehow even more intimidating with the absence of his master's gown and tweeds. "Perhaps you are not aware of how to behave in such polite company, so let me enlighten you." Lord Havelock glared at Henry with his signature Havelook of Doom. "Come with me."

Henry stared at his head of year in horror. It was just his luck to get into trouble with a teacher during the winter holiday.

"Yes, sir," Henry whispered.

Lord Havelock pushed past Henry, disappearing down the dark thin staircase. Henry, with a backward glance at the broadly grinning Valmont, followed.

Lord Havelock whirled on Henry at the bottom of the stairs, his dark eyes hard and glittering. "Do you have any idea how dangerous that was?"

Henry flinched at Lord Havelock's closeness—at the graying stubble on Lord Havelock's sunken cheeks, the stench of moldering tobacco that seemed to come from his pores.

"I wasn't the one pushing people down staircases," Henry said, his voice cracking nervously.

"In here," Lord Havelock said, grabbing a fistful of Henry's shirtfront and dragging him into an alcove that led to the servants' quarters below stairs. "Now explain yourself."

"Explain what?" Henry asked, puzzled.

"Am I wrong in supposing that you wish to attend Knightley Academy, Mr. Grim?"

"No, sir."

"And am I wrong in supposing that you are aware that not everyone wishes to have students such as yourself at the academy?"

"I'm aware, sir."

Lord Havelock gave Henry a significant look. "Must I remind you that many such people are upstairs, and have just witnessed your behavior?"

Henry stared at Lord Havelock in surprise. "Well, no. I—I mean—," Henry stuttered.

"You mean what, exactly, Mr. Grim?" Lord Havelock

asked silkily. "To jeopardize your hard-won place at Knightley? To make Lord Winter and myself look bad in front of our peers? Or to pursue a schoolboy grudge I have tried my hardest to put to an end?"

Henry sighed. He just couldn't win. "*Valmont* dumped his cider down my shirt, sir."

"It was provoked, I'm sure," Lord Havelock returned.

"Is that all, sir?" Henry asked.

"So eager to return to the company of your improper little lady friend, Mr. Grim?"

"No, sir," Henry said, staring at his shoes.

"Look at me when I'm talking to you," Lord Havelock commanded.

Henry caught his breath and stared up at his head of year.

"I don't know what you were doing this afternoon, and I don't care to," Lord Havelock continued, "but before you return to school, let me make one thing clear: You are not, under any condition, to do anything foolish with regard to the events of last semester. Do you understand me?"

"Not fully," Henry admitted.

"Looking for Sir Frederick would be a severe violation of the Code of Chivalry," Lord Havelock clarified.

Henry blanched. "I wasn't looking for Sir Frederick," he muttered.

"You were looking for trouble. It's the same thing," Lord Havelock snapped. "You forget that *I* vouched for you and your friends at the hearing last term. That *I* took the blame for your foolishness."

"And *you* forget about the Midsummer Curse," Henry said, trying to keep his voice calm and even. "I know what you tried to do, rigging the exam."

Lord Havelock's eyes narrowed. "You are quick to accuse, Mr. Grim, but slow to produce proof to back up your claims." Lord Havelock paused, letting the barb dig in before resuming his lecture. "A lesson for you, Mr. Grim: Intending an action and doing it are far from the same thing. Until you are right there, with the choice in front of you, you can only guess what you might do, and what your character might be. Are you hero or coward? Often you will guess wrongly."

Henry frowned. Was Lord Havelock talking about Sir Frederick or the fight with Valmont or the Knightley Exam the previous May? Henry puzzled over this for a moment in that cool dark annex, with the merriment of the party clattering above him.

"They haven't chosen a new chief examiner for the

coming year," Henry said, carefully watching Lord Havelock's face to confirm his suspicion. He'd guessed correctly. Emboldened, Henry asked, "I don't suppose you'd be wanting your old position back, sir?"

"It is to everyone's advantage, not just my own, that troublemakers are watched carefully," Lord Havelock returned. "And you, Mr. Grim, are trouble."

It *was* rather starting to seem that way, Henry thought dejectedly, whether he meant to be or not.

3

KNIGHT AT
THE STATION

Henry straightened his uniform as he stepped off the clanging omnibus outside of Hammersmith Cross Station. All the way to the station, he'd felt the other passengers staring at his pressed gray trousers with the first-year yellow piping down the sides, his yellow-and-white-striped tie, and his dark blue formal jacket, a bit worse for wear, done in a military cut with brass buttons, white braid, and the school crest over the right breast pocket, bearing the silhouette of an old-fashioned knight with a lance, seated upon a prancing horse.

It hadn't mattered that he'd kept his boxy stiff-brimmed ceremonial school cap hidden in his lap, or that he'd nearly blocked the aisle with the corner of his largest suitcase, which had stubbornly refused to fit anywhere else. Everyone still treated him with respect. Old men still doffed their caps as they passed. Little children still pointed excitedly. He didn't think he'd ever get used to it.

Henry waited until the omnibus had gone before putting on his cap and checking Rohan's old pocket watch. There was plenty of time before the ten o'clock train to Knightley Academy, Avel-on-t'Hems, departed from platform three. With a sigh he picked up his suitcases, wondering for the fifth time that morning if he really *did* need quite so many books.

It was old Mrs. Alabaster's fault, really. She'd given him a massive parcel of dusty old mystery novels at Christmas, an unnecessary present that had made Henry feel guilty for getting her nothing in return. He couldn't just leave the books behind in the flat for her to find, abandoned and unappreciated. And so Henry gritted his teeth against the weight of his suitcases as he staggered into the station.

Hammersmith Cross Station, the main railway in the city, was a tremendous, arched thing that rather resembled an overfrosted wedding cake. Grandiose moldings clung to the soaring ceiling, and the marble floor echoed horribly, turning the whole place into an overwhelmingly loud, crowded tunnel.

Along the walls rows of brightly colored carts sold everything you could imagine, from tiny mechanical toys to garish souvenirs to newspaper cones of fresh-roasted chestnuts. Henry bought a cone of nuts and ate them absently, watching the crowd surge past. Despite the ache in his shoulders from his heavy suitcases, and despite the more than occasional curious glance in his direction, Henry couldn't help but smile. In just a few hours he'd be back at Knightley Academy, sharing a triple room with his best friends, spending his evenings playing chess in the common room, and trying not to laugh over Professor Lingua's abysmal Latin pronunciation in languages.

Finally he was going *home*. Or at least the closest thing he had to one.

Henry crumpled the newspaper cone into a ball, and his heart hammering excitedly. And then he caught sight of the headline crushed in his fist.   FFLING AFFLIC   IN NORDL   MENTAL   LUM.

Henry smoothed out the page so that he could properly see the article, even though he already knew what it said. The story had haunted him for two days, ever since he'd come across it over breakfast: During a routine inspection of a Nordlandic mental asylum, more than a dozen inmates were found to have had their tongues split down the middle, which had rendered them incapable of speech. There was no explanation for this procedure, and no record of it in the patients' files. It was simply a mystery, and yet another troubling occurrence done under the terrifying leadership of Chancellor Mors.

His throat suddenly dry, Henry tossed the newspaper page into the nearest rubbish bin. Just six months before, he'd dismissed all of these rumors as preposterous gossip from reporters desperate for a story. Six months ago he wouldn't have believed it. But now, with what he knew of the Nordlands, with what he had seen during the Inter-School Tournament at the Partisan School, stories such as this one worried him deeply.

"Not the wisest place to stand, son," a man's voice said kindly.

Henry looked up, startled. A police knight winked at him before giving a salute, which Henry quickly returned.

"No, sir. I don't imagine it is," Henry said.

The police knight furrowed his brow, and with a sinking feeling Henry realized why. "I know you," the police knight said. "You gave that guardian of yours quite a scare on Saturday night." Henry's cheeks flushed with embarrassment.

When he'd returned home after Grandmother Winter's party, it had been much later than he'd anticipated. And of course he'd forgotten to leave a note. He'd hoped that Professor Stratford wouldn't worry, but Henry had found the professor frantically accosting a police knight outside the flat, insisting that his ward was missing, and demanding that a search party be formed. His ward. Right.

By the time everything had been straightened out and Professor Stratford had stopped shooting Henry troubled, searching looks when he'd thought Henry wouldn't notice, it had been past midnight. Professor Stratford had left the following morning to get settled into his old rooms in the headmaster's house at Knightley Academy, and to prepare his lessons as Frankie's tutor.

Henry had spent the last two days moping around the flat, mortified that his good deed of delivering Alex's parcel had caused such a fuss.

"Yes, sir. I know," Henry replied a moment too late. "And I'm awfully sorry if you were put to any trouble. Everything's sorted now."

The police knight gave Henry a friendly pat on the shoulder. "No harm. I remember being your age. I was always bunking off to play cricket."

"Right, cricket," Henry said, forcing a smile.

The police knight dropped his voice to a conspiratorial whisper. "Or at least that was the excuse I gave my family. Her name was Caroline, she worked in a hat shop in Baker's Green, and she had eyes like emeralds."

Henry's smile tightened uncomfortably.

"It's been such a long time," the police knight continued. "And then she went and married some banker. Had four kids . . ." The police knight's expression turned to one of sadness, and his eyes glazed over as though he were no longer staring at Henry, as though his mind were very far away indeed.

"Ah," Henry said politely. "I see."

The police knight didn't respond.

"I'd, er, better be going, sir. I have a train to catch."

With a hasty salute Henry picked up his bags and wound his way through the crowded station, noticing a few other boys dressed in their Knightley uniforms as he neared platform three.

When Henry reached the platform, the conductor was

already clanging his handbell. "All aboard! Ten o'clock express to Knightley Academy, Avel-on-t'Hems."

Henry walked to the end of the platform, remembering from last term that yellows were in the last two cars. It was strange how so many of the faces on the platform were familiar to him now. But even stranger was how, among the blandly supervising butlers and awestruck little brothers, there were at least a dozen young ladies, their lovely faces crumpled with despair as they clung desperately to the arms of their departing suitors.

Henry nearly laughed aloud at the uncomfortable expression on one of the older boys' faces as he extracted himself from the arms of a very determined young woman in a preposterously plumed hat. *For pity's sake,* Henry thought. *It's not as though we're going off to war!*

And yet the girls persisted, remaining on the platform to wave their handkerchiefs at the departing train.

Henry heaved his bags into the last car as the whistle shrilled.

"Oi, where have you *been*?" a familiar voice demanded indignantly.

Henry grinned. "I had to say good-bye to my lady friend. Tell me, do I still smell of her imported perfumes?"

"No. You reek of something else," Adam replied

merrily. "Come on. Rohan's meeting us at school, and Edmund's saving a compartment."

Henry gladly followed Adam down the cramped corridor as the train lurched out of the station.

"Do you like it?" Adam asked, patting the back of his head, where he always pinned his yarmulke. This one was bright yellow.

"Very, er, yellow," Henry said diplomatically.

"That," Adam said, throwing open the door to a compartment, "is exactly what I was going for."

It was afternoon when the train pulled into Avel-on-t'Hems station, and the sun was casting long shadows from the bare branches as the boys climbed the hill to the school.

Knightley Academy was just as rambling as Henry remembered. It sprawled awkwardly over its two dozen acres, featuring a nonsensical array of styles—innocent wooden cottages topped with turrets; a tiny castle with what looked suspiciously like a thatched roof; flying buttresses; trailing ivy; and a staggering amount of chimneys, which Henry suspected were more decorative than actually useful. Thankfully, the hedge maze had been abandoned after it had refused to grow more than waist high. Not so thankfully, it had been replaced by a massive rock garden complete with brightly colored boulders.

Henry and Adam were still laughing over the rock garden when they reached their room. The door was open, although this took a moment to register, as it was not a very noticeable sort of door. Barricading the doorway, however, was a very noticeable and rather precarious pile of luggage.

"Henry? Adam? Is that you?" a voice called from inside the room.

"Rohan?" Adam asked.

"Naturally," Rohan replied briskly. "It seems we've gotten our bags, but as you can see, they've been unceremoniously and inconveniently dumped in our doorway."

Henry frowned at the suitcase tower. "What if I pushed that bag on the top? Could you catch it?"

"I doubt you can reach—," Rohan protested.

There was a muffled *thwack!* that didn't bode well.

"You alive in there, mate?" Adam called.

"Barely," Rohan groaned. "Next time you're about to toss a valise at my head, I could do with some warning."

"Warning," Adam said helpfully, giving Henry's book-filled suitcase a shove.

By the time the three boys had managed to maneuver their luggage out of the doorway, Adam's tie hung wildly askew, and Henry's school hat had been trodden on.

As the boys unpacked their things, they traded stories of their holiday. Rohan had been in the city for a few days, but his parents had returned to their manor in Holchester when his mother caught a cold. Adam had been stuck at home with his sisters when he wasn't hanging around the bookshop.

"They've taken up *knitting*," Adam wailed, shoving a dozen rainbow-hued yarmulkes into his desk drawer.

"You might want to save that drawer for school supplies," Rohan suggested.

Adam shrugged, and then piled last term's notebooks on top.

Henry laughed. He'd missed his friends terribly.

And with the troubling newspaper article forgotten, Henry hung his formal jacket in the shared wardrobe and told Rohan what had happened at Grandmother Winter's holiday party.

4

HEADMASTER WINTER'S SPEECH

Even before the bells sounded, signaling half an hour until supper, Henry's stomach was grumbling with hunger. But, then, it was his own fault; he'd forgotten to buy a sandwich to eat on the train. Edmund had offered to share his, but Henry had declined out of politeness, an act that he was sorely regretting.

Henry, Adam, and Rohan joined Edmund at the first-year table, on the end closest to the High Table. All across the Great Hall, boys were waving to one another, yelling out greetings, and inquiring after one another's holidays.

"All right, Grim?" James St. Fitzroy asked, sliding into the seat on Henry's left.

Adam and Rohan exchanged a look.

"What?" James asked, frowning. "Is the seat taken?"

"Henry's left-handed," Adam said patiently.

James sighed and turned to Henry for confirmation.

"Sorry," Henry said. "I could swap with Edmund, though, if you'd prefer."

Edmund, who was on the end, shook his head. "Absolutely not. I like this seat." A telltale corner of Edmund's mouth twitched.

"Oh, very funny," Henry said.

"I don't mind," James put in quickly, passing the salad bowl. Henry gratefully forked a pile of salad onto his plate, marveling at how different everything felt from last term, when the other first years had gone to great lengths to avoid him and his roommates. But, then, what had Henry expected, when Theobold, the resident bully of their year, had disapproved of him so thoroughly? Toward the end of last term, though, the other boys had seemed to tire of Theobold's imperious orders. And even Valmont had begun to resent his position as Theobold's second-in-command, since, back at the Midsummer School, he'd had cronies of his own to order about.

"Hey, wasn't that bloke at our hearing?" Adam said,

nodding toward the High Table and tucking his napkin into the neck of his shirt in the way that irritated Lord Havelock no end.

Everyone turned.

There were a few new additions to the staff, but Henry quickly realized whom Adam meant. One of the trustees from their expulsion hearing sat next to Professor Stratford at the High Table. He was young-ish and nervous-looking, with a pair of wire-rimmed spectacles that had slipped down his nose. He and Pro-fessor Stratford were deep in conversation.

"Do you think he's the replacement head of second year?" Rohan wondered.

"I hope!" Edmund said. "It's either him or Lord Muttonchops over there." An old man who rather resembled a basset hound with alarmingly bushy whis-kers glowered down at them from the seat next to Pro-fessor Lingua.

At that moment a door hidden in the wooden panel-ing swung open, and Headmaster Winter hurried into the dining hall, late and out of breath. He fumbled hast-ily with his cravat as he took his place behind the lec-tern. Above his head, carved into the mantel of the vast fireplace, was the school motto: *A true knight is fuller of bravery in the midst, than in the beginning, of danger.*

The headmaster ran a hand through his patchy ginger and gray beard, composing his thoughts while the students quieted in anticipation; Headmaster Winter's speeches were rarely long, and were frequently amusing.

"I do hope the salad hasn't gone cold whilst you boys were waiting for me to choose a cravat," the headmaster said. "I really was baffled—red or green, you know. Not an easy decision." The boys looked at one another, wondering if Headmaster Winter truly had gone mad over the holiday.

"Especially," the Headmaster continued, "when one is color-blind and cannot tell the difference between the two."

"But, sir?"

The students and staff turned to see who had spoken. It was Jasper Hallworth, a big, booming second year. He rose from his seat at the second-year table. "Sir," Jasper continued, "that cravat is blue."

"Ah, is it?" Headmaster Winter peered down. "Bless my soul, it *is* blue. So you see, boys, sometimes we must present the truth to those who may be too blind to see it—or to those who do not know that they are blind to it, even if they are in a position of great authority." The headmaster paused significantly, and Henry frowned, certain that Headmaster Winter had known all along what color cravat he was wearing.

"In any case I would like to welcome you all most sincerely to the start of a new term here at Knightley Academy. There are two new additions to the staff: Sir Robert, who will be taking over as medicine master and head of second year students." The headmaster paused as the youngish gentleman from the hearing ducked his head in acknowledgment. "And Admiral Blackwood, who has returned from India to resume the long-vacant post of drills master." The gentleman with the enormously bushy whiskers surged to his feet and saluted.

Confused, the boys returned his salute, half of them standing, all of them at different times. Adam still had his napkin tucked into his collar, which made Henry snicker.

"I'll have that again, gentlemen. In unison," the admiral boomed.

The boys snapped to attention and saluted sharply this time. Adam hastily balled his napkin into his fist, his cheeks bright red.

"Well met, gentlemen," pronounced Admiral Blackwood.

Headmaster Winter grinned and winked conspiratorially at the students before continuing. "As you boys have no doubt surmised, there will be a few changes to the curriculum this term, all in the name of progress. After all, who knows what the turn of the century may bring—and it never hurts to be as prepared as the laws may let us, even when such preparations may seem unnecessary.

"Despite some alarming setbacks, last term was a good one, and I expect this one to be even better. I also expect it goes without reminding that you have all signed the Code of Chivalry, a code to which you are required to adhere without—ahem—*creative* interpretation. Welcome back to Knightley Academy. May the dreary weather make you thankful for school to be in session once again!" The headmaster took his seat at the High Table amidst enthusiastic applause and much whispering.

Henry took a thoughtful sip of his cider and considered the headmaster's eccentric speech. A war was coming. That much was clear. A war that could no longer be ignored, that their professors no longer denied with such conviction as they had just six months earlier.

But the Longsword Treaty still prevented students

from being trained in combat, which meant that whatever changes the headmaster planned to make to the curriculum, he had to work around that restriction.

Still, at least the headmaster was doing *something*, for Henry remembered all too well that day last term when Headmaster Winter had come to their room and informed the boys that without proof that the Nordlands had violated the treaty, there was nothing to do but sit and wait.

When Henry, Adam, and Rohan passed the common room on their way back from supper, Theobold was holding court in an elaborate thronelike chair by the fire.

"And what does *he* know, really," Theobold drawled. "He's just some *academic* with a family title who hasn't a clue what he's doing running this school. I don't know why your uncle listens to him. But, then, I suppose taking orders runs in your family."

This last part was directed toward Valmont, who had just brought Theobold a threadbare footstool. Valmont scowled but stayed silent. Theobold kicked off his boots with a sigh, one of the shoes thwacking loudly into Valmont's shin.

Henry winced in sympathy.

"Oi, Henry, are you going to stand out there all night?" Adam asked, creaking the door to their room back and forth.

"Sorry. Right," Henry mumbled. For a moment he felt sorry for Valmont, but the moment quickly passed. After all, it *was* Valmont.

But still, a nagging voice in the back of Henry's head reminded him, *no boy deserves to be bullied, no matter how horrible he might be.*

Trying to put the matter out of his mind, Henry closed the door to their room and loosened his school tie. Before he could slip the tie out of his collar, a soft knock sounded at the window, followed by a lot of muffled shushing.

Rohan, with a withering look at Henry and Adam, opened the window just a crack and announced, "I did so hope to make it through the first day of lessons before committing an expellable offense."

Frankie's face appeared at the window. "Come on, Rohan. Be a sport. You know you've missed me terribly over the long holiday."

Rohan gave a rather long-suffering sort of sigh.

"Let her in, Rohan," Henry said. "You know Lord

Havelock never comes this far down the corridor."

Rohan pushed the window open.

"*Thank* you," Frankie said disdainfully.

"But, miss, surely you can't be meanin' to climb through the window?" a worried girl's voice announced.

"Of course I am," Frankie patiently explained. "It's the only respectable way. Walking through the first-year corridor would be entirely improper." Frankie climbed deftly through.

"But, miss—" A girl appeared at the window—plain, slightly plump, and about sixteen.

"Well, go on." Frankie gestured toward the girl. "Be gallant young knights and help her."

Henry and Adam managed to coax her through the window.

She looked around, her eyes wide and frightened. "We're in a boys' bedchamber," she whispered.

"If you stand in the part with the desks, you can pretend it's a classroom," Adam said helpfully.

Rohan buried his face in his hands.

The girl, it turned out, was Frankie's new chaperone. Frankie pulled her into a corner and whispered furiously, clearly reminding the girl exactly what would happen if she told anyone where they'd gone. When Frankie had finished, the girl stoically plopped herself in the corner, pulled a piece of sewing from her pocket, and ignored them.

"Do you know anything about the new professors?" Henry asked, once they'd settled in to play cards.

Frankie shrugged. "Father hasn't said much. Although it's a pity about Sir Robert."

Rohan frowned. "How do you mean?"

"He's a knight detective," Frankie said. "Top of his year at Knightley. One of the youngest knights ever appointed to the board of trustees." Frankie tidied the stack of discarded cards and dropped her voice to a dramatic whisper. "He was investigating those gruesome docklands murders and was horribly injured. Nearly died. He's supposed to be home resting, but he convinced Father to let him take the position of medicine master."

For a moment no one spoke.

"Well, that's heartbreaking and all," Adam said, breaking the silence, "but the real question is, is he evil?"

Everyone burst out laughing.

They played a few more hands of cards before Rohan yawned pointedly. "Getting rather late, isn't it?" he said.

"Lights-out isn't for another thirty minutes," Henry said with a glance at his pocket watch.

"Yes, well, half an hour until lights-out is still late," Rohan said.

Henry bit his lip. Ever since Rohan had returned from his expulsion last term, he'd been passionate about following the rules. Henry was certainly sympathetic, but it didn't change the fact that Rohan's behavior was driving him mad.

"I *am* a bit tired, miss," Frankie's chaperone, Colleen, called from the corner.

"I wish she'd quit," Frankie murmured. "It's horribly annoying to drag her around with me."

"Pardon, miss?" Colleen called.

Frankie smiled sweetly. "I was just saying that we should bring cake with us tomorrow night."

Colleen gasped. "But, miss, surely you can't want to come back again tomorrow?"

"Tomorrow and tomorrow and tomorrow," Frankie said with a grin.

After Frankie left, the boys changed into their pajamas and climbed into bed. Henry stared up at the ceiling, thinking how, for the first time in a long while, he felt as though he were home. The flat above the bookshop was cozy enough but had given the curious impression of being empty, despite the clutter of furniture and the teacups that Professor Stratford abandoned on armrests and windowsills.

Even after the terrible incidents of last term—or perhaps because of them—it felt wonderful to be back at Knightley Academy with his friends. Henry fluffed his pillow and tried to fall asleep, but it was no use.

"Adam, you awake?" he whispered.

Adam snorted sleepily and kicked at his covers.

"Listen, Henry, can I have a word?" Rohan whispered back.

In the faint moonlight slanting through the window, Rohan's expression was shadowed, making his frown seem even more troubled.

"What's the matter?" Henry asked.

"I just . . . I'm not certain that being friends with Frankie is necessary."

"Friendship has nothing to do with necessity," Henry pointed out. "You become friends with someone because you want to."

"Well, last term we didn't have a choice." Rohan paused significantly. "But *this* term we do."

"What do you mean?"

"We're not outsiders anymore. James and Derrick are perfectly respectable, and quite friendly. We should be sitting in the common room with our classmates, not boosting ladies' maids through our bedroom window."

"If it means so much to you, go ahead," Henry snapped, and then felt instantly ashamed. "I'm sorry. I didn't mean it."

"Well, I *did*," Rohan whispered fiercely. "I didn't come to Knightley to separate myself from my peers. No one's sabotaging us anymore. We can be normal. We can *fit in*." Henry heard the yearning in his friend's voice and realized it was different for Rohan. He'd been raised the same as their classmates, been brought up with private tutors and expensive toys. Rohan only *looked* like an outsider, and clearly he was tired of being one.

"Just because the other students are being friendly doesn't mean we can fit in," Henry returned. "After everything that happened last term, how can you think that we'd ever be the same as everyone else? *You* were poisoned and expelled. *They* played cricket."

"Well, I *wanted* to play cricket, but no one asked."

"Fine. Next hour free, I hope you do and have a sparkling good time," Henry whispered crossly. "Good night."

Henry stared up at the ceiling, a horrible feeling in

the pit of his stomach. Did Rohan truly resent being their roommate? He knew that Rohan and Adam hadn't always gotten along, but, then, Adam *could* be massively frustrating.

"Henry," Rohan whispered urgently.

"What?"

"I didn't mean it like that."

"How did you mean it?"

"I just thought we could be friends with the other boys. All of us. Well, maybe not Frankie, but, to be honest, she won't be coming round much longer."

Henry didn't reply.

"She has a chaperone now," Rohan continued. "You might not know what that means, but I do. She's nearly sixteen. What will her suitors think if she's climbing through our window?"

"It's her choice."

"It doesn't reflect well on any of us," Rohan said. "What girls will accept our courtship if they think we're spending our nights with someone else, or if they imagine us to be the sort of boys who willingly let girls compromise their propriety?"

Henry frowned. He was relatively certain no girls would be interested in them either way.

"Just think about the future," Rohan whispered in a maddeningly superior tone. "And see if what I'm suggesting wouldn't be the best option over time."

Henry fell asleep still unsure what exactly Rohan meant—about everything.

5

THE NEW
PROFESSOR

A thin layer of snow coated the grounds the next morning. Henry groaned and rubbed the sleep from his eyes, glimpsing a weary, gray morning that looked the way he felt. He'd forgotten how very early they were expected to wake up at school.

An insistent peal of bells sounded from the direction of the chapel. Adam curled into a ball and clamped his pillow over his head.

Rohan was already fastening his cuffs by the time Henry mustered enough enthusiasm to crawl out from beneath his warm blankets. "Snow's already melting," Rohan said with a tentative smile.

Henry smiled blandly back. No doubt Rohan was hoping to be chosen for cricket during that afternoon's hour free.

With a sigh Henry pulled the blanket off Adam. "Up," he said. "Chapel."

Adam moaned and swatted Henry away uselessly.

"It's snowing," Henry said enticingly, knowing that Adam loved snow.

"Is it?" Adam, suddenly wide awake, dashed to the window. His face fell. "It's only a bit of leftover frost. Already melting."

Even though the snow was mostly slush, that didn't stop Theobold from lagging behind to relace his boots outside of chapel that morning. Henry watched as Theobold smuggled a handful of slush into the chapel, which he slid down the back of Edmund's collar.

Edmund yelped, disrupting the prayer, as every head swiveled in his direction. With a muttered apology he sunk down low in the pew, his face bright red.

Theobold bit back laughter as Edmund shivered through the service.

At breakfast Henry heaped eggs and toast onto two plates.

"Couldn't afford meals over the holiday?" Valmont asked through a mouthful of bacon.

Henry snorted. "At least *I* don't insult people's manners with my mouth full of food," he said, passing the second plate to Edmund, who had just run breathlessly into the dining hall.

"Thanks," Edmund said, sliding into the seat next to Henry and fastening the cuffs of a dry shirt. "I thought everything would be gone."

James, who was having only a blueberry scone, reached for the saltshaker. He fiddled with it for a moment, while staring wistfully at the eggs, and then put it back down. "Are the eggs still overcooked this term?" he asked Rohan.

"Unfortunately," Rohan said, and Henry frowned as he swallowed a mouthful of perfectly cooked eggs.

Two seats down, Theobold grabbed for the saltshaker and tipped it over his plate. The cap flew off, landing in his tea. A mountain of salt emptied onto his breakfast.

James's shoulders shook as he held back laughter. Rohan nearly choked on a sip of juice. Adam grinned broadly and asked Edmund to please pass the last of the eggs.

"You should finish the sausages. They're excellent

this morning," Edmund said, dumping the remainder of the hot breakfast onto Henry's plate while Theobold fumed.

Medicine was the first class of the morning.

Ever since Sir Frederick's betrayal, the classroom had felt sinister to Henry—haunted, almost, by horrible memories. But that morning the eerie atmosphere seemed to have gone. Winter sunlight flooded through the latticed windows, and the radiator in the corner clanged impatiently. The shelves behind the master's desk, which had once housed human skulls and rolls of bandage, were now crowded with jewel-stoppered apothecary bottles, upright magnifying glasses, and a rather battered set of scales.

Henry, Adam, and Rohan chose seats in the middle. All around them students whispered about the new professor:

". . . a knight detective, I heard."

". . . graduated in my cousin's year. Top of the class."

". . . can't be more than thirty."

Henry had just removed a fresh notebook from his satchel when their new professor limped into the room carrying a black medical bag with a dozen brass buckles, and leaning on a worn mahogany cane. His master's gown had clearly been made to fit someone a great deal shorter and wider, and his tweeds, though very fine, were thin with wear. With the help of his cane the new medicine master slowly made his way to the front of the classroom, deposited his bag on the front table, and raised an eyebrow at his students.

"Well," he prompted, "what can you deduce?"

The students stared.

"No need to raise your hands, lads. Just shout it out."

Edmund, who sheepishly raised his hand anyway, said, "Your name is Sir Robert."

"No, no!" their new professor cried. "I did not ask what you already know—what you have been told. I stand in front of you. What can you perceive, here and now?"

No one dared to speak.

Finally Henry cleared his throat and called out, "That gown wasn't made for you, sir."

"Excellent! What else?" the professor asked.

Encouraged, other students began to call out: His cuffs were frayed; his hair was inexpertly trimmed; he favored his left leg.

The professor raised a hand for silence. "Well done, the lot of you! You have keen powers of observation.

And, yes, by the way, my name is Sir Robert." He nodded in Edmund's direction. "You were quite right about that. I am also a knight detective, which means that not so many years ago I, too, attended Knightley Academy." Their new professor took a seat on top of the master's desk, which caused some whispering.

"I sat in the same desks, studied in the same library alcoves, and fell asleep in the same chapel pews, but, like you, I also worried over something of far greater importance.

"At the end of my third year, we began to hear news from the Nordlands, news of a brewing revolution. We watched the rise of the Draconian party with horror, fearing what a similar uprising here in South Britain would mean for our families. Those were dark times, boys. Times of great doubt, and of terrible rumors."

Sir Robert paused significantly.

"Medicine is a practical discipline," he said, "but the skills you learn in this classroom are not limited to the assessment of and defense against disease and pain. Just now you have observed a previously unknown subject—myself. You must learn to observe for yourself, to question the world, and to deduce the partially hidden answers."

Slowly and painfully Sir Robert climbed to his feet.

"Your first assignment," he said, "for I am loath to call it homework, has no due date. If you wish, you may choose to ignore it entirely. Your assignment, lads, is to ponder what you see and challenge what you believe. For under scrutiny you will find that even an open book can have a surprise scribbled in its margins."

With a flourish Sir Robert pulled off his mustache.

"Horse hair and spirit gum," he said, trying and failing to hide a smile. "There. You see, lads? You are dismissed."

That afternoon the great hall was filled with whispers about the new medicine master.

"I knew all along that mustache was a fake," Valmont drawled, picking the crusts off his sandwich. "Rather a showy move, wouldn't you say?"

Edmund, who was seated across from Valmont, shrugged.

"*I* thought he was brilliant," Henry said.

"Well, no one asked *you*, Grim, did they?" Valmont shot back.

"Henry?" Edmund said with a grin. "What did you think of Sir Robert?"

Valmont shot Edmund a nasty glare.

"Actually," Henry said slowly, "I'd never really given it a thought what it must have been like to attend Knightley during the Nordlandic Revolution."

"Me neither," Rohan said, "but everyone must have been terrified. There were so many Nordlandic sympathizers, and all of those riots. . . . Police knights were *killed* trying to break them up."

"Shut your face," Valmont said hotly. "You don't know anything about it."

"Right, because it's *so difficult* to read a history book," Rohan returned.

At that moment there was a burst of raucous laughter from the second-year table. Jasper Hallworth had stuck two sizable carrots up his nose and was apparently imitating some sort of wounded sea creature.

"Really," Rohan said, shaking his head in disapproval, as Adam reached eagerly for two carrots to try it himself.

Military history that afternoon was just as horrible as everyone remembered. Lord Havelock seemed unaware that a new term had begun. He burst into the room, his master's gown billowing, his expression as sour as ever.

Without so much as a "Welcome back," he seized a piece of chalk and began to write out an assignment on the front board.

"You have until the end of class," Lord Havelock intoned, "to demonstrate whether you have completed the assigned reading or whether you had more important things to attend to over the holiday."

At the desk next to Henry's, Adam swallowed nervously and fiddled with his pen.

"If I were you," Lord Havelock said, his eyes glittering as he surveyed the terrified students, "I would be ashamed to hand in anything less than three sheets of paper. Your prompt is on the board, *gentlemen*. You may begin."

He stepped aside to reveal, in spiny, slanted writing, the question: *"What strategies might the French aristocracy have employed to prevent revolution? Would those same strategies have worked against the Draconian party in the Nordlands? Why or why not?"*

With a sigh Henry reached into his bag for his pen and ink. Lord Havelock had been the only professor to assign reading over the holiday—a particularly expensive and hard-to-find book called *Revolution Through the Ages: From Catastrophe to Strategy*. Thankfully, Henry had discovered a copy in Mrs. Alabaster's shop. Whenever business was slow, he'd hidden the book beneath the counter and read a chapter or two.

All around Henry the other students produced copies of *Revolution Through the Ages* from their satchels. With a sinking feeling, Henry turned his attention to the blank sheet of parchment on his desk.

As he finished the first sentence of his essay, a shadow fell over his page. He looked up. Lord Havelock glared down at him with his signature Havelook of Doom.

"Sir?" Henry asked, his throat dry.

"Forgotten something, Mr. Grim?"

"No, sir," Henry whispered. "I read the book. I just—er—had it on loan."

"Couldn't afford to buy one, Grim?" Theobold asked nastily.

Henry bit his lip and said nothing. Lord Havelock hadn't told them to *purchase* a copy, just to *read* it. And yet, though he'd followed the assignment to the letter, Henry still felt as though he'd turned up with his homework unfinished.

"And, Mr. Beckerman," said Lord Havelock. "What is *your* excuse?"

"Er—forgot mine," Adam mumbled.

Belatedly Henry remembered Adam insisting that he'd get around to the reading eventually, probably on the train. And yet they'd read silly magazines and chatted with Edmund and Luther the whole way.

"Such a pity . . . and did you enjoy the engravings, Mr. Beckerman?" Lord Havelock asked innocently.

"Yeah, loads," Adam fibbed.

Henry winced.

"There were no engravings in *Revolution Through the Ages*," Lord Havelock whispered, and the temperature in the room seemed to drop.

"No, sir," mumbled Adam.

"You may leave the room, Mr. Beckerman," said Lord Havelock. "Tomorrow I shall expect a *five*-page essay under the door of my office before chapel. Do I make myself clear?"

"Very clear, sir," mumbled Adam, packing his things.

"And you, Mr. Grim," Lord Havelock continued. "If you will be requiring a *charity fund* to purchase books in the future, I trust that you will notify the headmaster well in advance."

Henry blushed furiously. With enormous effort he turned his attention back to the essay and did not let his mind wander until class was dismissed.

* * *

Henry had been looking forward to visiting Professor Stratford during his hour free, but the moment Protocol ended, Adam whined so piteously about Lord Havelock's essay that Henry found himself agreeing to help—or at least to keep Adam company in the library instead.

"Don't worry about the essay," Henry said as they walked through the first-floor corridor with the suits of armor that grasped for invisible weapons, long since removed. "Lord Havelock just wanted to make an example of you."

"I'm not worried about the essay."

"You haven't said a word since we left Turveydrop's classroom," Henry pointed out.

Adam was suddenly fascinated by a bit of loose thread on his blazer pocket. "I . . . I heard you and Rohan talking last night."

"Why didn't you say something?"

"Dunno." Adam shrugged. "But if that's how Rohan feels about Frankie, he can go off and be friends with Theobold and that lot."

"You don't mean that," Henry said.

"Yeah, I do." Adam glared. "It's as though he wants to forget about everything that happened last term and pretend that our biggest problem was being unpopular."

"Well," Henry said, considering, "Rohan was already back home when everything happened with Sir Frederick. He didn't go up against the board of trustees and tell them the truth about the Nordlands. And he didn't spend his holiday in the city. Maybe he feels as though we're leaving him out and he needs other options."

"That's ridiculous," Adam muttered stubbornly. "And anyway, I've decided to be cross with him no matter what."

"He *did* lend you his copy of *Revolution Through the Ages*," Henry said as they turned the corner and the great wooden doors to the library came into view.

"While he went off to play checkers with *James*." Adam made a face.

"What's wrong with James?"

Neither of them could help it—they burst out laughing. James, while friendly enough, talked of nothing except sports. Ever.

Adam had tested this theory at the end of last term, asking James an innocent question about Latin grammar, which had hilariously started him off on a long-winded metaphor with a central theme of winning at cricket.

Still chuckling, Henry pushed open the door to the library, expecting the place to be empty. However, there was hardly an unoccupied chair to be found. The third years sat hunched over sheaves of notes, intimidating in their blue and white ties. Quite a few of them glanced up as Henry and Adam stood awkwardly in the doorway.

"Well, come on," Henry whispered, prodding Adam.

Adam clutched Rohan's pristine copy of *Revolution Through the Ages* to his chest and vehemently shook his head. "Nope. Changed my mind. Going to study in the er—armory."

Henry was intimidated by the third years as well, but he wasn't going to let it show. After all, he and Adam had just as much of a right to use the library as they did.

"Come on," he insisted, tiptoeing up the spiral staircase to the balcony level while Adam followed like a cringing puppy.

Henry impatiently threw open the door to the study room, and three boys in blue and white ties looked up haughtily from their notebooks.

Henry gulped. "Er—sorry—I thought that . . ." Henry trailed off miserably.

"What appalling manners," one of the third years drawled in an oddly familiar way.

"We're leaving now. Sorry," Henry said, starting to shut the door.

"Did I *say* you could go?" the boy asked.

"No, Arch, I don't think you did," said a larger boy with bushy black eyebrows, who grinned maliciously at Henry and Adam.

"Good heavens," Arch said, raising an eyebrow. "I think we've caught ourselves those little commoners who've been bothering my brother."

Despairingly Henry realized that this had to be Theobold's older brother. They had the same Roman nose, dark hair, and nasty smirk. Behind him Henry could hear Adam edging toward the staircase.

"Get back here, you nasty little heathen," Theobold's brother said sharply.

The command echoed through the library. Henry saw that they'd attracted the attention of the rest of the third years, who were staring up through the gaps in the wrought-iron balustrade. He took a deep breath to steel his nerves.

"As I said before," Henry began in his most posh tones, "we're terribly sorry to have disturbed you, as we'd assumed the room was unoccupied. We'll let you return to your studies now. Good day." Without waiting for a reaction Henry closed the door and scrambled down the stairs after Adam, startled by his own daring.

At the bottom, however, Henry was surprised to see that many of the third years were grinning in his direction, as though they had very much enjoyed watching an ickle first year stand up to their intolerable classmate.

When the peal of bells, signaling half an hour before supper, echoed through the domed library, Adam didn't look up from *Revolution Through the Ages*.

The third years noisily gathered their notes, laughing and occasionally staring in Henry and Adam's direction.

Henry glanced up from his back issue of the *Tattleteller*. He'd gotten the idea to dig up old gossip magazines from what Sir Robert had said about the Nordlandic Revolution. So far he hadn't found anything worthwhile, but he had discovered a rather entertaining series of knight detective stories.

"Plan on washing up for supper?" Henry whispered.

"Five whole pages," Adam moaned, propping his forehead in his hands.

"It would have been three if you'd done the reading," Henry said with a shrug. "And don't glare at me like that. You know I'm right."

"I was going to read it tonight—honestly. I didn't think the old vampire would quiz us on the first day back."

Henry raised an eyebrow.

"All right. I *hoped* he wouldn't quiz us on the first day back. Mum nearly disowned me when she saw my marks last term. Go on to supper without me. I'm not leaving the library until I emerge triumphant, essay in hand."

"I'm guessing you want me to smuggle some food back to the room for you?" Henry asked.

"Only if it's too much trouble to smuggle it into the library."

"You're unbelievable." Henry grinned as he shouldered his satchel.

"Unbelievably brilliant, more like," Adam corrected, accidentally dribbling ink onto Rohan's book.

6

THE LORD
MINISTER'S SONS

Henry arrived slightly late to supper and found
Rohan at the most crowded part of the table,
deep in debate with James over fencing grips.
Rohan looked up briefly and then returned to the argument. Feeling slightly hurt, Henry took an empty seat
near Derrick and Conrad, two inseparable boys whose
fathers held prominent positions in the Lords' House at
the Ministerium.

"Hallo, Grim," Derrick said, passing the basket of
rolls.

Henry, who'd barely exchanged two words with
Derrick over the past term, nodded his thanks and took
three rolls, stuffing two into a spare napkin. Conrad and

Derrick pretended very obviously not to notice. Henry realized his mistake immediately.

"Adam's stuck in the library," he explained. "You know—Lord Havelock's essay. Didn't want him to—"

"Right, of course," Derrick said hastily. "Lord Badluck's punishment for skipping the reading."

"Lord Badluck?" Henry grinned.

Conrad leaned in conspiratorially. "It's rather fitting, isn't it? We overheard some second year using the name."

"In any case, we can't let Adam starve in the library stacks, can we?" Derrick said, tucking a spare napkin into the empty bread basket. "I don't think this will be missed. Now, Grim, what did you do with those rolls?"

They cobbled together some sandwiches from the roast beef, and after they'd packed up a neat little picnic for Adam, the boys turned their attention to their own suppers.

Conrad regaled Henry and Derrick with a particularly funny story about his sister's suitors and the overactive bladder of his mother's prized terrier. Henry glanced up, his face red with stifled laughter, and caught Valmont glaring in their direction.

"Speaking of overactive bladders," Derrick said, nodding his chin at Valmont.

"Sorry?" Henry asked, puzzled.

"His room's next to mine," Derrick explained. "Up twice last night, that one."

Henry laughed, delighted. He'd expected Derrick and Conrad to be horribly snobbish, with their plummy accents and the way they always clubbed together, but they weren't at all. In fact, they rather reminded Henry of his own roommates, how they gave nicknames to their head of year and told inappropriate stories.

Henry had always considered the other students largely uninterested in becoming friends with anyone whose family didn't keep a Regent's Hill town house. Now, however, he wondered if his impression hadn't been an unfortunate combination of Theobold and Valmont's bullying and a lot of unsure-what-to-make-of-the-common-students moments in the first few weeks of term.

After all, Rohan, whose perceptions were usually bang on, had named Derrick as one of the boys they ought to be friends with. Henry had instantly dismissed it, but perhaps Rohan had seen what Henry hadn't— that Henry and his roommates weren't outcasts at all. They had simply never tried to make friends.

Derrick offered round the mashed potatoes before

spooning the last of them onto his own plate. "How was your holiday, anyway?" he asked Henry.

"I'm sure it's none of our business," Conrad said with a meaningful glance at Derrick, as though he suspected Henry might be embarrassed to talk about his life outside the academy.

"Oh, I don't mind," Henry assured them. "Actually, I got in a fight with Valmont at Lady Winter's holiday party. Lord Havelock caught us."

"Do tell, Grim," Derrick said gleefully.

And so Henry found himself once again telling the story of the boys down the alleyway, and of Frankie's grandmother finding him in her kitchen, and of his brief but disreputable appearance at the holiday fete. Somehow the tale had become immensely funny, and Henry was aware of quite a few boys laughing along with Derrick and Conrad whenever he performed impressions of Lady Winter, Lord Havelock, and especially Fergus Valmont.

After supper Henry picked up Adam's makeshift picnic basket and made his excuses to Derrick and Conrad—and Luther, who had joined them over dessert.

"Don't be ridiculous, Grim. We'll come with you," Derrick said, clapping a hand to Henry's shoulder.

"Yes, of course," Conrad said, tucking a notebook under his arm and sniffling, in what was undoubtedly a very good impression of someone Henry had never met. "You'll need a knight's escort. Can't have an important political figure such as yourself gallivanting about unprotected in such trying times."

Derrick hooted with laughter, and even Luther cracked a smile. Henry was puzzled, until he realized that every group of friends has their own private jokes and references. Well, at least they wanted to come with him.

They found Adam fast asleep and drooling onto the pages of *Revolution Through the Ages*, which set them all off into hastily muffled hysterics.

Holding a finger to his lips, Henry tiptoed behind Adam and, in a terrifying impression of Lord Havelock, bellowed, "Ah, Mr. Beckerman, does my assignment bore you?"

Adam snapped awake, his face white. He turned around and found Henry, Conrad, Derrick, and Luther doubled over laughing.

"Aaahhhh!" Adam complained. "That was horrible. My heart stopped, I swear it did."

"Brought you something." Henry held out the basket.

"Better be a five-page essay in there, to make up for

that," Adam complained, taking the basket. "Oh, sand-wiches! Thanks."

"No problem," Henry said. "Just dropping them by. Finish your essay so I don't have to bring you breakfast as well."

"That would be a job," Derrick mused, "smuggling scrambled eggs out of the dining hall. Wonder how you'd do it."

"That's easy," Adam said, his mouth full of sand-wich. "Use a teacup."

"Now, there's an idea," Derrick said. "To the common room, lads. This library makes me feel as though I'm supposed to be whispering."

"I think you *are* supposed to be whispering," Luther said dryly as the librarian glared in their direction.

The common room was crowded, the best seats already claimed.

Rohan, who was playing cards with Edmund and James, waved them over.

Henry picked up a chess set with two buttons substi-tuted for missing pawns. "Anyone for chess?"

Everyone was suddenly very interested in staring at either the floor or the ceiling.

"Sorry, Henry," Edmund called, finding the whole thing immensely funny. "But no one likes to be slaughtered."

"I'll give a handicap," Henry bargained. "Let's say . . . a knight."

Luther considered for a moment, and then shook his head. "Both knights. Or your queen," he said.

Henry sighed.

And then a peal of loud cruel laughter came from the best chairs, which had been dragged into a circle around the crackling fire.

"Really, Valmont," Theobold hooted. "There's no need to be so *sensitive* about it. You're like some swooning maiden."

Valmont pushed back his chair, his face blotched red, his glasses flashing angrily in the light. "Shut *up*, Theobold," said Valmont, his hands clenched into fists.

"Make me, you four-eyed charity case," Theobold taunted. "We all know how your uncle had to—"

"Valmont, you interested in a chess match or what?" Henry interrupted.

Theobold stared disbelievingly at Henry, his mouth slightly open. Henry couldn't believe it either—rather, he couldn't believe *whom* he'd leapt in to rescue. The common room was eerily silent for a long moment, and Henry fought the urge to fidget under the combined weight of his classmates' stares.

"All right," Valmont said casually, "but I don't need a handicap to play against you."

"Good, because I wasn't offering," Henry returned.

Valmont took the chair across from Henry, and the other students gradually resumed their conversations. With a dismissive sniff at the chipped paint and buttons for pawns, Valmont began arranging the chess pieces.

"Perhaps one day I'll be able to afford a chess set as nice as this one," Henry joked.

Valmont snorted and continued lining up pawns.

As the game progressed, it became clear that Valmont wanted desperately to win. He hunched over the board with a look of intense concentration, agonizing over each move.

"You're making it easier for me to win, you know," Henry said as he scooped up Valmont's remaining bishop. "Don't second-guess your moves so obviously. It gives away your strategy."

"I don't need your advice," Valmont said, choosing to move a useless pawn. "And since when are you friends with those Ministerium brats?"

Henry glanced toward the nearby table, where his dinner companions had joined Rohan's card game. "Conrad and Derrick? I'm not."

"Looked pretty friendly to me."

"Check," Henry said, "and what does it matter to you, anyway?"

Valmont put a castle in the way of Henry's attacking bishop. "I don't like being made fun of."

"I wasn't making fun of you," Henry said, capturing the castle. "Check, again."

"Yes, you were," Valmont said. "You were doing impressions."

Henry went slightly red. It was true, he *had* been doing impressions.

"Who's winning?" Theobold demanded, interrupting.

"It could go either way," Henry lied as Valmont's king retreated.

"Grim's winning," Argus Crowley grunted, peering at the board.

"Really?" Theobold said, delighted. He leaned in closer, crowding them.

"Do you *mind*?" Valmont said stiffly.

"It isn't as though I'm bothering you," Theobold

said, shifting so that he was leaning into Valmont's back. "Because you'd let me know if I were, right, four-eyes?"

Valmont fumed silently.

Henry waited, expecting Valmont to defend himself, but he merely sat there, his jaw thrust forward, his hands clenched into fists, staring at the chessboard as though he wanted to hurl it across the common room. Henry dragged out his turn unnecessarily, hoping that Theobold would lose interest and wander away. Because what Theobold had nearly said about Valmont was a purposefully off-target hit, the sort that wasn't just rude but often caused injury. They were all students at Knightley Academy, and how they'd gotten in, or where they'd come from, was no longer newsworthy.

"Forgotten how?" Valmont whispered disdainfully.

"Sorry. I was preoccupied," Henry said. "I met Theobold's brother today and was trying to figure out if *everyone* in the Archer family starts to go bald and fat so young."

Henry calmly raised an eyebrow at Theobold.

Theobold's eyes blazed. "I don't know, Grim. How about *your* family? How did mummy and daddy die? Hanged in the gallows as common criminals?"

Henry flushed with anger. After all, he'd been asking for it, but that didn't stop him from wanting badly to punch the smirk off Theobold's face, to hear Theobold's cry of surprise as he hit the floor from the sheer force of it.

The truth was, Henry didn't know anything about his parents. He'd pestered the orphanage matron until she'd gotten cross with him, gone through one of those books that kept track of the aristocracy, dug up moldering copies of the *Midsummer Gazette*, and still, nothing. Anyway, it was better not to know—or so he'd tried to convince himself.

"I say, Archer, that was quite uncalled for," Derrick said, throwing down his cards and pushing back his chair. "We're all rather tired of your attitude."

"Are you now?" Theobold asked, somehow managing to pose the question to the entire common room.

"Yes, we are," Derrick returned. "Especially with— Well, this isn't the time to be fighting among ourselves."

Theobold shot Derrick a look of disgust. "You don't honestly believe that rot about the Nordlands, do you?"

"Maybe I do," Derrick said, raising his chin. "What of it?"

Theobold seemed genuinely surprised at Derrick's answer. He frowned, and the fight went out of his voice as he said, "But your father's the Lord Minister of—"

"The Lord Minister of Foreign Relations. Right," Derrick said calmly. "Saw him about twice over the holiday, what with all those emergency sessions in the Ministerium. Or didn't you notice the lights blazing at all hours from Parliament Hall?"

Henry shook his head in admiration at how neatly Derrick diffused what had quickly been becoming an explosive argument. But even more curious was what Derrick had said about fighting among themselves, and about the Ministerium being worried. . . .

"It's your go," Valmont said roughly.

Henry glanced at the board. "Two moves until I have you in checkmate."

"I know," Valmont muttered.

"Listen," Henry said, forgoing the final blows and handing Valmont back his captured pieces, "I'm sorry about earlier. I didn't mean to make fun of you. I just got carried away when everyone laughed at my story."

"What makes you think I care?" Valmont asked, picking up his queen and examining the chipped paint.

"What does Theobold have on you?"

Valmont's shoulders stiffened. "Why do you think he has something on me?"

"Because," Henry said, "you wouldn't even stand up to him. You don't take bullying like that from anyone else."

"I don't need your pity," Valmont spat, standing up.

"Why would I pity you?" Henry asked, confused.

"Never mind. Just forget it."

"Not likely."

When Henry returned to his room that night, he hadn't forgotten it. Instead he'd forgotten something else.

Tomorrow and tomorrow and tomorrow, Frankie had said, and Henry had laughed and agreed. And sure enough, balanced outside their window, frozen and forlorn, was the cake Frankie had promised.

❖ 7 ❖

THE SUITOR'S BOW

At chapel the next morning Henry squeezed into the pew next to Adam.

"How'd it go?" Henry whispered under the cover of the pipe organ.

"Ahjusurnitin," Adam mumbled, yawning hugely.

Henry pretended to misunderstand him. "You just came from confession?"

Derrick, who was seated in front of them, snorted.

"I just turned it in," Adam repeated crossly, closing his eyes and slouching down in the pew. "Now leave me alone. I'm sleeping."

Henry tried to listen attentively to the service, as he didn't fancy a detention should Lord Havelock look over in their direction, but so much had happened the day before, and he'd barely had a chance to wrap his mind around any of it.

It's a funny thing, the flavor of a new school term; unlike the price of a penny newspaper, it is entirely unpredictable. Back on the platform at Hammersmith Cross Station, juggling his too heavy suitcases, Henry had felt certain that very little would change—his three best friends would be up to their usual mischief, the other students would ignore them, his status as an outsider was signed and sealed.

He'd thought Rohan's idea of becoming friends with the other students was absurd—until he'd tried it. And suddenly he understood. Because smuggling sandwiches out of the library in a diversion of loud, joking classmates had been precisely what he'd hoped school would be like, before the terrible incidents of last term had made him certain that he was, and would always be, an outcast.

But Rohan had been right. They didn't need to walk past when their classmates were choosing teams, pretending they needed to borrow a book from the library. They could join in.

Unfortunately—and this was the crux of Henry's

worries—in order to be included, he'd *excluded* Frankie. Of course it had been unintentional, but that's what had made it even more hurtful—how, in the excitement over fitting in, Henry had forgotten that he'd promised to spend the evening with someone else.

Every time he pictured it, he felt horribly guilty: Frankie, standing outside their window with a cake meant for a celebration, waiting for them to let her in, wondering where everyone had gone, and, finally, giving up.

Henry glanced tentatively toward the front pew, where the headmaster and his family sat. Frankie glared in his direction, and he quickly pretended to be absorbed in the sermon.

"I want to explain," Henry said, approaching Frankie after the service.

He was met with a polite curtsy. "Good morning, Mr. Grim. I hope you're well?" she asked demurely.

"I, er," Henry said, caught off guard.

They never spoke formally. Not unless Grandmother Winter was watching. But the adults weren't paying them any attention. So, then, why was Frankie treating him according to his proper station as a Knightley student, and acting as though he were just another boy in a uniform decorated with an impressive school crest?

"Er, I'm very well, thanks," Henry said stiffly. "And yourself?"

For a moment Frankie seemed as though she wanted to call the whole thing off, drag him outside and loudly accuse him of forgetting their plans.

But she didn't. Instead she giggled and twisted a strand of her hair.

"How kind of you to ask, Mr. Grim. I am also well," she said sweetly, but a slight curl to her lip betrayed the game they were playing and the challenge she'd set.

"I trust you're enjoying the lovely weather, Miss Winter," Henry returned.

At this, Frankie very nearly snorted, as it was slush again that morning, with clouds the color of charcoal. Henry straightened his tie with a smirk. They stood there in stalemate, the chapel emptying out around them.

Frankie's tone was blandly polite, but Henry wasn't fooled. He could see that he'd hurt her, and that she'd rather hurt him back than hear his apology.

"Would it be possible to speak in private, Miss Winter?" Henry pressed.

Frankie fake gasped. "But that would be entirely

improper, Mr. Grim. Whatever would your friends think?"

Henry sighed in frustration.

Fine, then. If she wanted to rub it in that he was becoming a proper student at Knightley, that at any moment she could call off their friendship without warning, he'd do the same to her. After all, he'd earned an "above average" in Protocol last term.

"As you wish," he said, and before he could lose his nerve, Henry reached for her hand, touched it to his lips, and gave a suitor's deep bow. He excused himself to the dining hall, trying not to laugh at the look of outrage on Frankie's face.

By their first lesson Henry was sorely regretting the bow. Rather, he was regretting his classmates' reactions. Edmund had been bouncing in his seat at breakfast with a dozen questions, and Derrick had clapped him on the back in congratulations.

"It was a joke," Henry tried to explain, but how could he tell these boys, whose families had attended Knightley for generations, that he'd only done it to get back at Frankie for acting as though they'd never been friends? It sounded ridiculous even in his head.

"Listen," Rohan whispered during the fencing warm-up, "maybe it's better this way."

"Better how?" Henry returned. "How can we play cards with her? Or even say hello in the corridor? Everyone will talk."

"Exactly," Rohan said smugly, executing a perfect practice lunge. "I suppose we'll just have to spend all of our free time with the other boys in our year and *not* get expelled for having a girl in our room."

Henry settled into the on guard position, lowered his back arm to signal an attack, and glared.

"*I* liked her first," Adam complained on the way to languages.

"It didn't mean anything," Henry repeated uselessly. "You know how Frankie is. *She* started it."

"Well, you certainly *finished* it," Rohan put in, gloating.

Adam glowered. "It isn't fair," he grumbled.

"*Adversus solem ne loquitor,*" Henry said with a shrug, taking his usual seat.

"There was reading for languages, too?" Adam looked scandalized at the injustice.

"No, it's Latin for— Never mind," Henry said as

Edmund, James, Luther, Derrick, and Conrad piled into the surrounding seats and Professor Lingua waddled into the room.

The weather had warmed slightly, and the ominous clouds had retreated, giving way to a surprising late-afternoon sunshine that flooded through the windows of Professor Lingua's classroom. Everyone was bent over his Latin exercise—except for Henry, who had finished early but was trying to look as though he hadn't. Which was why he noticed when James discretely passed a note to Rohan.

Rohan slid the note under his desk and tried to open it without glancing down. His hands fumbled, and the note slipped to the ground. He went grayish and twisted in his seat in a panic, nearly giving himself away to their professor.

Henry scribbled *"Reach down for a spare pen and put the note in your satchel"* on the edge of his notebook and tilted it toward Rohan.

Rohan nodded slightly and did as Henry told him.

At the end of the lesson, James sauntered over. "Well?" he prompted.

"Sorry," Rohan said retrieving the unread note from his bag. "I didn't have a chance to open it."

"Stop being such a *prefect*, Mehta," James teased. "And anyway, you were meant to pass it on down the row." James took the note and smoothed it onto the table. It was a list of students. For one horrible moment Henry was reminded of his midnight exploration of Partisan Keep—the hidden room filled with illegal weapons, the targets shaped like human torsos, and the lists of Partisan students with their ranks in combat.

But then Rohan read the heading aloud with a grin. " 'Cricket trials.' "

Henry felt ridiculous. Of course it was a sign-up list for cricket. Now that he looked closely, he saw James St. Fitzroy down as captain.

"Who's the other team, then?" Henry asked.

"A group of second years challenged us to a match this Saturday," James said. "Put your names down if you're interested in playing. We're having trials today on the quadrangle."

Rohan scribbled his name at the bottom of the list. "Shall I put you as well?" he asked Henry and Adam.

"I've never played before," Henry said, looking to Adam.

"I'll teach you," Adam offered. "Put us both."

Adam tried to explain the rules on the way over to

the quadrangle, but Henry was hopelessly confused.

"Wait, so who gets run out? Didn't you say something about partners?" Henry asked.

"It makes sense if you see it played."

To Henry's dismay, it *didn't* make sense when he saw it played. He could barely keep the rules straight, never mind the terms for everything. The other boys dashed around the quadrangle, their ties and jackets draped haphazardly over one of the benches, playing seven-a-side as though they were practicing for professional scouts. Henry gave up about twenty minutes in.

"Too distracted to play, Grim?" Conrad teased, nodding toward the rock garden.

Frankie and her chaperone were taking a leisurely stroll through the grounds, clearly spying on the cricket trials. Henry shrugged and tried to ignore them. After all, Frankie had already caused him more than enough trouble that morning.

Henry shuffled over to the sidelines, where he stood watching his classmates and brooding over the recent discovery of his inability to comprehend cricket. He didn't notice Adam's approach until his friend joined him on the sidelines.

"You're not playing?" Henry asked in surprise.

"I'm rubbish," Adam admitted. "I know *how* to play, but I haven't really— I never— I mean, it's not like there are parks in the East End."

Henry sympathized. He'd forgotten that Adam had been to school in the city and lived at home, while most of their classmates had been off at posh academies with private cricket pitches at their disposal.

"Rohan seems to be enjoying himself," Henry pointed out.

"Yeah, he couldn't wait to be shot of us."

"That's not true," Henry argued. "He's just tired of being an outsider. And anyway, I quite like Derrick and Conrad. You should give them a chance."

"I'd rather be friends with Frankie, thanks." Adam folded his arms across his chest and sulked.

"I'm *sorry*," Henry said. "I didn't mean to. She kept calling me 'Mr. Grim' and goading me."

"So you kissed her?"

"I didn't kiss her," Henry hissed. "It was her *hand*."

"You're unbelievable."

"Just admit it. You're cross with me because you like her."

"Of course I like her," Adam said through clenched teeth. "Are you *blind*?"

"No, I'm just a stupid servant boy who doesn't understand upper-class customs. Happy now?"

Adam's face flushed. "I'm sorry," he mumbled, staring at the ground. "I didn't mean—"

Henry never found out what, exactly, Adam didn't mean, as Frankie chose that moment to interrupt.

"Hello. Who's winning?" she asked, innocently twirling a lacy white parasol.

Colleen sighed. "Miss, we should be gettin' back—"

"Nonsense," Frankie said. "Supper isn't for nearly an hour."

"No one's winning," Adam said. "It's trials. There's going to be a match against the second years on Saturday."

"Why aren't *you* playing?" Frankie asked Adam, ignoring Henry completely.

"I'm too skilled a player. Don't want to ruin everyone's self-worth," Adam said.

At this, Henry snickered.

"Oh, hello, Mr. Grim. I didn't see you there," Frankie said coldly.

"Good afternoon, Miss Winter. What a lovely sunshade you're carrying," Henry returned, in the same posh, polite tones that had so infuriated her that morning.

"Perhaps I could escort you for a turn about the garden?"

Frankie fake gasped. "But, Mr. Grim, you're in nothing but your shirtsleeves! It would be a scandal."

"Would you two *stop it*?" Adam fairly yelled in frustration.

Frankie and Henry glared at each other.

"*I* will when *she* will," Henry muttered, looking to Frankie.

"You treated me like a *girl*," she accused.

"You *are* a girl."

Frankie looked like she wanted to slap him. "You're just like the rest of them, given half a chance," she said. "And I know what you were doing last night. I saw you playing chess with Valmont while I stood outside and *froze*."

Henry digested this new piece of information. No wonder Frankie was furious. She loathed Valmont. "I trust you are unwilling to hear an explanation?" Henry pressed.

"That would be correct, Mr. Grim. Good day." Frankie shot Henry a look of pure disdain and whirled around, intent on a dramatic exit. Her parasol, however, was intent on making a dramatic exit of its own. It smashed neatly into the side of Henry's face.

Henry cursed, cupping a hand to his right eye, which throbbed painfully.

Frankie's chaperone was so affronted by Henry's colorful language, and raised such a racket with her gasps and protestations, that everyone stopped playing cricket to watch the spectacle.

"Are you all right?" Frankie asked with genuine concern.

"Just go," Henry muttered, turning away. "Pretend I offended you or something."

"I don't have to *pretend*," Frankie snarled.

Henry waited until Frankie had left before wincing and removing the hand from his face. "How bad is it?"

Adam let out a low whistle.

"What happened to you?" Valmont asked nastily at supper. "Did someone mistake your face for a cricket ball?"

"If you must know," Henry said with as much dignity as he could muster, "I was assaulted by a lace parasol."

This sent everyone nearby into hysterics.

"What did you say to her, Grim?" Derrick asked, delighted. "We're all dying to know."

"I called her a girl," Henry said, shrugging. "And it was an accident."

"You called her a girl by accident?" Edmund asked through a mouthful of potatoes.

"No, it was an accident that she hit me."

"Somehow, Grim, I sincerely doubt that," Derrick said, grinning.

"Tell them, Adam," Henry said. "You were there."

"Yes, and I don't know what you're talking about," Adam said, the picture of innocence. "You asked if she might favor you with a lock of her hair to place under your pillow at night, and she attacked."

The first-year table hooted with laughter.

Henry glared.

"All right, so that didn't happen," Adam admitted. "It was an accident."

"I'm getting a cold compress from the kitchen," Henry said, abandoning his half-eaten meal.

"We'll be in the library after supper," Derrick called.

"I'll stop by," Henry promised.

"Bring your Latin exercise," Conrad said.

"I've already finished it," Henry admitted.

"I figured you had," Conrad said, "which means you can help us."

Henry shook his head. He was still chuckling at Conrad's nerve when he pushed open the door to the kitchen.

Although the main course had already been served, the kitchen was still oppressively hot, steam-filled, and bustling. Serving boys and kitchen maids rushed back and forth at the cook's orders, ladling custard into serving dishes from a large pot on the stove, readying teapots, arranging cups and saucers onto trays, and preparing counter space onto which they could remove the soiled dishes from the tables.

Henry glanced around the kitchen for a moment, still unnoticed. He watched as a skinny serving boy of about thirteen removed a tea towel from a shelf near the larder and wiped some splatters of custard from the counter. Once the boy had gone, Henry crept over to the shelf and helped himself to a tea towel, tucking it absently into his trousers pocket as he tried to guess where he might find some ice.

A half-arranged tea service was on the counter, and he couldn't help but nudge the teacups into place, arranging their handles on a perfect diagonal, as he hadn't done in quite some time. He neatened the stack of napkins and turned around, nearly colliding with the serving boy he'd noticed earlier.

"Er, sorry," Henry said.

"No, sir, 'twas my fault. I di'nt see you there," the

boy muttered, going red in the face. He glanced toward the tea service, noticed it fully arranged, and gawped at Henry.

Henry gave an apologetic smile. "I was wondering if I might have some ice for my eye?"

"Cor, sir. That's a shiner!" the boy said, letting out a low whistle.

Henry followed the boy through a narrow annex and into a pantry, where he spotted a large wooden ice box. "Thank you," he said, crouching down to unlatch the door and scooping up a handful of ice chips. He put them inside the tea towel and pressed it to his eye, sighing at the instant relief.

"Ain't no trouble," the boy mumbled, regarding Henry thoughtfully. "Di'nt you— Ain't you the one who used to be a servant?"

Henry nodded. "I did."

"Is that what you've been fightin' over?"

"Fighting?" Henry was taken aback. "I wasn't fighting."

"Split lip, 'bout six days old, I'd reckon. Fresh shiner."

Henry bit his lip, which was nearly mended. "Four days," Henry corrected. "How could you tell?"

"Had my fair share of 'em boxing down at the Lance.

You could come, if you're keen. Tuppence a bet, pays back triple, an' they're fair about it."

"I'm sorry," Henry said, "are you talking about pub fighting?"

"O' course," the boy said. "If yer fightin', might as well come watch how to do it all proper. Maybe put down a bet or two."

"You shouldn't be fighting," Henry said with a concerned frown. The boy was small for his age, barely old enough to be legally hired. But worse, Henry rather suspected he was taking on much older—and larger—opponents.

"Well, *you* shouldn't be in the kitchens," the boy pointed out. "But ain't neither of us goin' to turn the other in."

Henry laughed aloud, and the serving boy suddenly remembered he was talking to one of the students. "Right, sir. I'll be gettin' back now, but if yeh need anythin' else, just ask for Ollie."

The boy called Ollie dashed back down the corridor, leaving Henry to find his own way back to where he belonged.

8

FLAG TWIRLING
KNIGHTS

The first years were scheduled for drills the following morning with Admiral Blackwood, to meet directly after breakfast in the quadrangle behind the thatch-castle thing. It was a typical blustery January morning, and while a few students shivered inside their coats, the cold felt good on Henry's black eye.

The night before in the library, some of the boys had come up with a dirty Latin translation from one of the exercises, and they now laughingly repeated the joke as everyone waited for their professor to arrive.

Just as Derrick was saying the dirtiest bit rather too loudly, Admiral Blackwood burst out of the back doorway of Throgmorten Hall. His silver muttonchop whiskers bristled, and his black boots were shined to perfection. He wore a safari hat and khaki explorer's outfit that stretched across his stomach, suggesting that he'd been much younger—and thinner—when it had been issued.

"Form a line," the admiral commanded.

Henry and the other first years shuffled into a scraggly line.

"Double time, lads!" Admiral Blackwood ordered, growing red in the face as his orders caused a chaotic scramble, during which Edmund bumped front-on into a freckled, scrawny boy called Pevensey.

"In the future," said Admiral Blackwood, "you shall greet me with a salute and the phrase 'Good morning, Drills Master.' I shall expect to find you at attention, *alphabetically*."

Another frantic scramble.

By the time they had it right, Admiral Blackwood was very red in the face indeed. He made them salute twice before he was satisfied. With a sour frown he paced the line, calling roll. Everyone tried very hard not to fidget, and although the cold weather caused a lot of desperate sniffling, no one quite dared to reach for a handkerchief.

"Grim?"

"Here, sir!" Henry called, saluting smartly.

"How'd you get that black eye, lad?"

"Cricket, sir," Henry fibbed, while the other boys snickered.

The admiral harrumphed loudly and continued with his role call.

For the rest of the morning, Admiral Blackwood had them marching in formation back and forth across the field. Henry, who was stuck in the back of the ranks, tried to scrunch down without being obvious about it, as he was visibly the tallest and didn't fancy being singled out again.

Finally Admiral Blackwood called them back into line outside the thatch-castle thing. "Next time, lads, we'll try you with the flags."

Everyone stared blankly.

"Flags, sir?" asked Derrick.

"You'll be marching in the King Victor's Day parade in the city this April," Admiral Blackwood explained, as though it were obvious. "Three boys leading the drill, three with flags, and the rest with peacekeeper's batons."

At this, Derrick snorted and whispered something

about "flag twirling knights" to Luther, who grinned broadly. Even though Henry also found the idea of their marching in formation and twirling flags to be absurd, it prickled at him worryingly during ethics. Why would a man like Admiral Blackwood come to Knightley to instruct them on marching in a parade?

Frankie pointedly ignored Henry at supper, and disappeared the moment chapel ended the next morning. Well, Henry thought, at least Adam had warmed to the idea of being friends with Derrick and Conrad.

Everyone was relieved to have fencing first thing Friday morning. As Henry helped Adam do up the back of his fencing kit, he noticed Valmont struggling with his own fastenings.

"Do you want help?" Henry asked.

Valmont glared. "Did I ask?"

Valmont scowled, but turned so Henry could fasten the back of his kit.

"You're welcome," Henry said coldly.

The fencing master cleared his throat for attention.

"Last term you were divided into intermediates and beginners," he said. "But I can see that such rankings no longer hold. From now on you are all intermediates. I'll be evaluating individual performances and will reassign the most promising students to an advanced group in a few weeks' time. For today, partner up."

Henry gladly partnered with Edmund, and they were set with practicing the length of their lunges, parrying only when they thought the attacks would hit.

"It's a bit like old times," said Edmund, who hadn't fenced against Henry since Henry's move to the intermediates partway through last term. Forgetting to signal his attack, Edmund stepped into a long lunge, which Henry parried easily.

"Old times, right," Henry said, thinking it was anything but. "Go again, but watch your back arm and mind your seat."

When the fencing master called an end to the exercise, Henry frowned. Surely there was more time left in the lesson?

"Let's discuss the strategy behind that exercise," said the fencing master. "Why is it to your advantage to vary the length of your lunge?"

"It's less work," called Theobold.

"That's not an advantage. That's laziness," said the fencing master.

Henry caught Adam's eye, and they grinned. It was

immensely gratifying to see the fencing master lay into Theobold for his poor form and even poorer strategy.

"An advantage?" the fencing master continued. "Marchbanks?"

Derrick ran a hand through his dark hair thoughtfully. "Well . . . your opponent is never quite certain from how far away he might be attacked," he said.

"Excellent, Marchbanks," said the fencing master. "You retain the element of a surprise attack. You can catch your opponent off guard. You undermine his confidence in his defenses. Is he out of range? Or have you merely orchestrated it so that he thinks this is so?"

Theobold scowled.

"St. Fitzroy, mask on," called the fencing master. James nervously tugged on his mask and took his place on the demonstration piste across from the fencing master.

The fencing master drove James backward across the piste with a double advance and a lunge that stopped half an arm's length short of a hit.

"You see? He panicked when I made a short lunge. Watch again." The fencing master resumed his on guard position. He advanced quickly, and then made a lunge identical to his first. "Now St. Fitzroy is convinced that he knows my attack distance. At that range he does not expect to be hit."

Again the fencing master faced James across the piste. This time he followed his double advance with a longer lunge, his foil striking cleanly against James's chest before James could react.

"Short lunge," said the fencing master, demonstrating. "And long lunge. It is up to you to decide whether you want your opponent to know and fear your attack distance, or whether you want to mislead and surprise him. Class dismissed."

Frankie apparently decided that she was speaking with Henry again that night, as he was leaving supper with Derrick and Edmund and discussing the next morning's cricket match.

"Cover your eyes, lads. The deadly sunshade approaches," Derrick noted dryly.

"Hello, Miss Winter," Henry said, flashing his most winning smile, noting with satisfaction that Frankie looked upset at his black eye.

"Professor Stratford wants you to come for tea tomorrow," Frankie muttered.

"Oh, er, right," Henry said, guiltily remembering

that it had been nearly a week since he'd last seen his former tutor. "Of course. Tell him I'll be there."

"He said to come by at noon," Frankie said.

"All right," Henry said. An awkward silence passed. Henry was painfully aware that Derrick and Edmund were standing there, waiting for him.

"Anything else?" Henry asked coolly.

"He said to invite your roommates as well. Good evening, Mr. Grim, Mr. Merrill, Mr. Marchbanks." Frankie gave a pathetic curtsy, and then flounced away as though delivering the message had been some sort of traumatizing ordeal.

"Ugh," Henry said as they headed toward the common room. "*Girls.* They just stay mad at you, don't they?"

"I wouldn't know," Derrick said. "I've never been unlucky enough to upset one."

The maid frowned at Henry and Adam when she opened the door to the Headmaster's house.

"Is someone expecting you two?"

"Yes, we're here to see Professor Stratford," Henry said.

"Well, come on, then," she said, and sniffed, acting

rather put out. She marched through the foyer and made a sharp left, leading them up a servants' staircase.

Henry rolled his eyes, and Adam pulled a face at the maid's back. There weren't many students who turned up at the headmaster's front door, and apparently Ellen didn't appreciate the interruption—or the mud that Henry and Adam tracked in from crossing the quadrangle, no matter how carefully they wiped their feet. Hence her insistence on sending them up the servants' staircase.

With a satisfied grin Ellen straightened her apron and knocked on the door to Professor Stratford's study.

"Come in," the professor called, but when he saw Henry and Adam, his eyebrows knitted together in confusion. "Good heavens, is the cricket match over already?"

"It just started," Adam said. "Rohan's playing."

Professor Stratford extracted his pocket watch from beneath an overturned—and, thankfully, empty—teacup on his desk, and frowned. "You're two hours early."

"Frankie told us to come around noon," Henry said, realizing belatedly that she'd given him the wrong hour on purpose, knowing that Henry would miss cheering on his friends' cricket match, and that Rohan wouldn't be able to come.

"We could, er, come back later?" Adam suggested.

"No, no, I wasn't doing anything of great importance," Professor Stratford said, closing a thick book on his desk. "Thank you, Ellen, and if you could bring up the tea?"

With an indignant sniff the maid slammed the door behind her.

"She thinks I'm messy on purpose," Professor Stratford said sheepishly. "Because she ruined my best jacket in the laundry."

"She thinks we track in mud," Adam said, shrugging.

"We *do* track in mud," said Henry. Adam shot him a look.

"Well, don't just stand there," Professor Stratford said, waving toward the two squashy horribly floral armchairs across from his desk. "Sit down and tell me everything."

Henry removed a stack of magazines from one of the chairs and placed them on the corner of the professor's desk. Professor Stratford *was* messy, but it was an absentminded, endearing sort of chaos. He lost track of things—newspaper articles he meant to save, teacups, cuff links. Remembering these quirks, Henry realized that he missed his former tutor immensely.

"I should have come round sooner," Henry mumbled.

"Nonsense, my boy. It's only Saturday. Although I'd like to hear an explanation for that bruise."

Henry reflexively brought his hand up to the fading purple patch beneath his right eye. "It was an accident," he said, shrugging.

"An accident like what happened down that alleyway near the bookshop?" the professor asked mildly.

"No!" Henry said. "She didn't mean to . . ." Henry trailed off, miserable at having given away the identity of his assailant.

"I see," Professor Stratford said, the corner of his lip twitching as though he found the whole thing just as funny as Henry's classmates had.

"Did you know that we're quite popular now?" Adam asked eagerly.

Professor Stratford raised an eyebrow and turned to Henry for confirmation.

"It's true," Henry said. "Rohan's been on a quest for us to become friends with the other boys in our year. He's tired of being an outsider."

"And how about you boys? Are you tired of being outsiders as well?" asked Professor Stratford.

"I'm not certain," Henry answered truthfully. "I thought I liked everything the way it stood, but then I had supper with Derrick Marchbanks and Conrad Flyte and it felt as though I were truly a student at Knightley, not just someone allowed to attend classes."

Professor Stratford nodded, his expression thoughtful. "Marchbanks and Flyte?" he murmured. "Where have I . . . Oh, yes, the lord ministers' sons."

"Valmont called them 'Ministerium brats,'" Henry said. "What does it matter what their fathers do?"

"Well," Professor Stratford hedged, "their families are responsible for the laws that forbid combat training."

"What?" Adam asked, scandalized.

Henry stared at the professor in shock.

"Hadn't you realized?" Professor Stratford asked. "Ah, apparently not. The title of 'lord minister' is hereditary, passed on through the generations along with the responsibility of the post. Lord Marchbanks is the Lord Minister of Foreign Relations, and Lord Flyte is the Lord Minister of Ways and Means, just as their fathers were before them, and just as your friends will be. Ah, come in, Ellen."

The maid entered with the tea tray, which clattered loudly as she placed it on top of the precarious stack of magazines on Professor Stratford's desk. Henry leapt up and only just rescued a wayward platter of scones as it surged toward the carpet. Henry gave her a disdainful look as he placed the scones back onto the tray.

"I'd like to see *you* try breakin' yer back haulin' tea services up three flights o' stairs," Ellen muttered.

At this, Henry, Adam, and Professor Stratford collectively snorted. Ellen bristled, not understanding the joke, and flounced from the room as though she strongly suspected they were making fun of her.

The tea was lovely, though—fresh hot scones with strawberry jam and clotted cream, and a pot of chamomile tea with honey. Adam munched his way enthusiastically through a second scone while Henry filled Professor Stratford in on their first week of classes. When he reached the part about Valmont and Theobold in the common room, the professor seemed oddly troubled by Theobold's behavior.

"I'm proud of you for that, Henry," Professor Stratford said, absently stirring his tea with the jam knife. "It is a good man who stands up for his friends, but an honorable man who stands up for his enemies."

"Who said that?" Henry asked with the hint of a smile, recognizing his old tutor's trick of sounding as though he were quoting.

"I did, just now," Professor Stratford returned with a lopsided grin. "And I know you've had your differences with Valmont, but he could use some friends."

"He *has* friends," Adam muttered through a mouthful of scone.

"Is he playing in the cricket match?" Professor Stratford inquired.

Henry frowned, realizing that Valmont had been absent from trials. James hadn't invited him.

Professor Stratford nodded knowingly at the boys' silence. "With popularity comes responsibility," Professor Stratford said.

"I know," Henry said miserably, recounting to the professor how he'd accidentally ignored Frankie, and how she'd refused to accept his apology. Adam interrupted a few times, mostly to accuse Rohan of enjoying the debacle. And though Henry was careful to avoid accusing Frankie of deliberately giving them the wrong hour for that afternoon's visit, Professor Stratford seemed to guess.

"I can tell this is something neither of you wants to hear," Professor Stratford said, leaning back in his chair, "but allowances are made for those who *need* them. If you have become friends with your peers, one might wonder why Frankie is still climbing through your dormitory window—and, yes, I know that's what she was doing."

"I . . . well . . . ," Henry began, at a loss for words.

"It was noble of you three to be her friends last term," the professor continued, "but you need to think carefully here. Do you want to seize this opportunity to fit in, or do you want to mark yourselves as permanent outsiders? Frankie won't be around forever, but friendships forged during one's school days are everlasting."

"You're on Rohan's side," Adam said despairingly.

"There are no sides. There's only what you choose to do," Professor Stratford gently corrected.

"No, Adam's right," Henry said, upset by Professor Stratford's urging for them to abandon, rather than mend, their broken friendship with Frankie. "There *are* sides, and this isn't about Frankie. You want us to stay out of trouble and ignore everything that happened last term."

Professor Stratford pressed his fingers to his temples and closed his eyes for a moment. When he opened them, he looked tired. "Henry, you are not responsible for what you saw in the Nordlands."

"I thought the truth was supposed to set you free,"

Henry returned. "But all I see are chains. Don't be friends with Frankie. Stay out of trouble. Keep to the path and make good marks in school and let the grown-ups handle things."

"Those are the best things you can do right now," Professor Stratford said. "Truly, my boy, I have your best interest at heart. There is nothing preventing you from earning your knighthood. You have this incredible opportunity before you, and I don't want you to lose it chasing after shadows and rumors."

"You didn't seem to mind it last term."

"Last term, someone was trying to sabotage your every move. You needed every ally you could get, and you had no choice but to fight back."

"Just because you think you're out of range doesn't mean you can't still be attacked," Henry said. "It's like what the fencing master said: The unbeatable attack comes when you imagine yourself to be safe, when you've been tricked into letting down your defenses."

Professor Stratford blanched. "I think you need to tell me what else your professors have been saying," the professor said, suddenly wary.

"Oh, good. Does this mean you two are no longer fighting?" Adam asked hopefully.

"Barely," Henry said, his voice strained. "And if you must know, Admiral Blackwood has us doing marching drills for some bloody parade, Lord Havelock's doing a study of failed revolutions, and Lingua has us reading about Troy."

Professor Stratford ran a hand over his face and stared solemnly at Henry and Adam. Henry could see that his former tutor was very troubled by this news indeed, and that, in his own excitement over becoming friends with the other boys in his year, Henry had ignored hints of something quite serious.

"It seems I owe you an apology," the professor said slowly. "I didn't realize it had already progressed this far. I didn't know they were preparing you for . . ."

Henry raised an eyebrow, waiting for the professor to say that horrible, forbidden word.

A knock sounded at the door.

They all jumped.

"Professor? Is my poetry book on your desk?"

"Er, no, Francesca, I don't see it," Professor Stratford called back.

"You never *look* properly," Frankie complained, pushing open the door. When she saw Henry and Adam, she stiffened. "Oh, it's you two."

"Good afternoon, Miss Winter," Henry said, trying to pretend that they'd been having a pleasant, light conversation, possibly about the weather.

"There!" Frankie fairly yelled, pointing an accusing finger at Henry. "You see? *Exactly* like that." She looked to Professor Stratford, who was suddenly quite preoccupied with his pocket watch.

Henry glared. "Don't talk to him about me," he said hotly.

"Don't make me want to hit you," Frankie returned.

"Go ahead," Henry challenged. "Hit a knight. That's a brilliant plan."

"You're not a knight," Frankie practically screamed. "You're just an infuriating little boy."

"Blimey, someone laced her corset too tight," Adam muttered.

"Stop!" Professor Stratford said sharply.

Henry flushed guiltily. He hadn't meant to quarrel in front of the professor, but now that he thought about it, he couldn't remember why he'd ever wanted to be friends with Frankie in the first place. He didn't understand her at all.

"You've been brought up to behave better than this," Professor Stratford said, and then, with a glance in Henry's direction, he winced a bit at his choice of words. "No more yelling, no more fighting. I don't care who did what—"

"He kissed my *hand*," Frankie complained.

"She gave me a *black eye*," Henry accused.

"I don't care," Professor Stratford continued mildly, daring them to interrupt him again. "This is not how ladies and gentlemen conduct themselves, and it needs to end now, before you two wind up scandalizing each other's reputations and are forced into an ironclad engagement."

Adam choked.

Henry's teacup clattered loudly against his saucer.

Frankie pouted.

"I'll take your silence to mean that everything is forgiven and behind you," Professor Stratford said with a sense of finality. "And now, Francesca, would you care to join us for a short and pleasant visit before our guests depart?"

Frankie shook her head. "No, I'll— Er, I have some French to finish. Sorry about your eye, Henry."

"It was an accident," Henry muttered diplomatically.

"And, Adam?" Frankie said, her hand on the doorknob. "If you ever accuse me of being laced too tightly again, you'll wish you didn't sleep in the bed right next to that ground-floor window. . . ."

With a wicked grin at the look of horror on Adam's face, she slammed the door.

9

THE MYSTERIOUS MAP

For the remainder of the weekend, a dismal atmosphere settled over the dormitory. The first years had lost appallingly at cricket, and, to make matters worse, Jasper Hallworth had taken bets on the match.

Henry tried to listen sympathetically to Rohan's outraged play-by-plays, as he felt guilty for missing it, but by Sunday afternoon his sympathy had worn thin. As soon as lunch ended, Henry ducked off to a quiet corner of the castle, built himself a fortress out of his textbooks, and settled in for an afternoon of reading.

Twenty arduous pages of Latin later, Henry abandoned the dry recounting of the Trojan War and stared across the way at the antique suits of armor, idly wondering if knights really had worn them in battle.

Well, they certainly weren't an art installation, he thought, noticing one suit of armor that would have easily encompassed even Professor Lingua's enormous girth. But if there were so many suits of armor, what had happened to the weapons? Henry frowned, remembering his visits last summer to the Royal Museum. He didn't recall any collections of antique halberds and crossbows, although he *had* seen a prototype of an ancient firearm—nonworking, of course—beneath a thick panel of glass. He'd been fascinated, as firearms were known to be the most evil weapon ever invented, although he suspected Frankie would have argued a fair point for corsets or irregular verb conjugations.

Verbs. Henry sighed, staring down at the dense print of his Latin textbook. He returned to his homework until the sun was slanting through the latticed windows and his legs had gone stiff from sitting.

To everyone's horror they had drills first thing Monday morning. Admiral Blackwood spent a painful hour rotating the students alphabetically as drill leaders, all the while scribbling notes on a clipboard.

When it was Henry's turn, he couldn't quite bring

himself to shout orders at his classmates. "Er, halt," Henry mumbled, embarrassed.

Conrad, who was leading the drill along with Henry, snorted. "You have to be more forceful, Grim," he said. "First years! Halt!"

Everyone came to a neat stop.

"Good, Flyte!" called Admiral Blackwood, scribbling a note. "Now swap out, lads. Next three!"

Conrad, Henry, and Pevensey jogged back into formation.

Finally the last of their classmates had rotated through commanding the drill, and Admiral Blackwood called them all back to the thatch-castle thing.

"Right, lads. Let's see how you do marching with flags."

Two school servants struggled into the quadrangle, carrying a dozen heavy wooden poles between them. Each pole ended in a sharp point, like an old-fashioned jousting lance, and featured a dingy flag made from what looked suspiciously like a mended tablecloth.

Derrick snickered and muttered something to Luther about knights waving table linens.

"These are practice flags," Admiral Blackwood said, hefting a pole from the top of the pile and unhooking the tablecloth. "A bit sturdier than the real thing, I daresay. Good for building muscles. You'll be learning the basics first, but I suppose an advanced demonstration couldn't hurt." Admiral Blackwood began to whirl the practice flag with surprising agility for a man of nearly sixty. Henry and the other first years watched in awe as the drills master went through a complicated series of twists and turns that were anything but laughable.

Henry had been half-expecting a feeble display of flag waving, but Admiral Blackwood's demonstration was far tougher and more intimidating than he'd imagined. It was almost . . . warlike. As soon as he thought it, Henry realized why Admiral Blackwood had *really* come to Knightley Academy. On the first night of term, Headmaster Winter had warned them about changes to the curriculum. Henry had thought Headmaster Winter had simply meant that the professors would be teaching them about war, but this was far more serious than the fencing master's offhand lesson about the strategy behind an attack. Because Admiral Blackwood wasn't preparing them to march in a parade any more than Professor Lingua was preparing them for a fulfilling career composing Latin verse. No, Admiral Blackwood was instructing them in combat—combat disguised as flag twirling.

Henry watched Admiral Blackwood whirl the pole through an elaborate defensive pattern and knew that he was right. He glanced over at Derrick, who was no longer snickering or making snide comments about flag twirling knights. Derrick's expression was quite sober indeed.

By Monday afternoon a full-blown cold front settled over the school, and the eaves dripped with icicles.

"It's nearly February," Adam complained at supper.

"I thought you liked the snow," said Rohan.

"This isn't snow," Adam pointed out. "It's ice and slush."

He was right. It *was* ice and slush, and rather a lot of it. The threat of snow hung over the castle's thatched roof and clung to the turrets of the surrounding cottages, but each morning brought nothing more than frigid wetness.

No one ventured outdoors if he could help it, and drills were canceled for the rest of the week, much to the chagrin of Admiral Blackwood. The fencing master grudgingly allowed students use of the armory for open bouts during the afternoons—but of course the second and third years quickly laid claim.

And so Henry and his friends spent a few restless afternoons playing cards and checkers in the cramped common room before Derrick suggested they explore the castle. Conrad, who was good at art, copied maps of the main building from a book he'd found in the library.

"We've got two maps," Derrick said, taking charge as usual. "I'm claiming the upper floors and towers. Who's coming with me?"

"I will," Henry said, and was surprised when Rohan decided to join them.

They spent the better part of an hour following the map through the upper classrooms. More than once their conversation lapsed into uncomfortable stretches of silence. Henry wondered how Conrad, Edmund, and Adam were fairing.

And then Rohan opened the door to an odd tower classroom, and they stepped into what appeared to be an immense wardrobe. There was an entire shelf of nothing but top hats, ranging in material from the most expensive silk to the cheapest felt. Below that was an assortment of spectacles: half-moons and pince–nez and wire-framed with the lenses tinted bottle green. A rack of opera capes sat next to a selection of worn traveling cloaks, and one table was covered with pots of what looked suspiciously like ladies' cosmetics.

"Brilliant," Derrick said, scribbling a note on the map.

"What is this place?" Henry asked, fascinated.

Rohan had wandered over to the cosmetics table and was frowning at the jars of pigment.

"You know how we choose a specialty at the end of our second year?" Derrick began.

"We don't truly choose," Rohan corrected. "They make us sit an exam."

"Of course," Derrick said with a dismissive wave of his hand. "But it's supposedly rather obvious which answers correspond with which specialty. Anyhow, I'd wager this is for those studying to become knight detectives. Looks like the art room."

"As in 'art of disguise'?" Henry asked, holding a fake handlebar mustache above his lip.

"Precisely," Derrick said, laughing. "And you should hang on to that one, Grim. It makes you look like a dishonest barkeep." Even Rohan grinned.

"Do you reckon we can get in trouble for being up here?" Henry asked, swapping the mustache for a bushy gray beard.

"Since when are classrooms off-limits?" Derrick threw an opera cape lined with crimson silk around his shoulders and admired it in the glass.

"I suppose that's true," Rohan said, cheering visibly. "Look at this."

Henry looked up, still wearing the beard.

"It's got instructions for painting on real-looking smallpox." Rohan held a jar of paint with a handwritten label.

"Into your pocket with that one, Mehta," said Derrick. "We can use it for getting out of drills."

"Exactly what I was thinking," Rohan said dryly, putting the jar back where he'd found it.

By the time they left the disguise classroom, the three boys were laughing and joking. They wandered into a few more rooms, which disappointingly housed nothing more than desks and chalkboards.

"Reckon it's time to head back?" asked Henry.

"In a moment." Derrick frowned as he stared back and forth between the end of the corridor and the map.

"What is it?" Rohan asked.

"Am I imagining things, or is there a wall where the map shows a staircase?"

"Maybe Conrad copied it wrong," said Rohan.

"Maybe the tower collapsed ages ago," said Henry. "I mean, this school's ancient."

"Maybe," Derrick called over his shoulder as he approached the offending wall at the end of the corridor.

It was an ordinary trophy case with a glass front, although instead of trophies the case housed mostly cobwebs. A pair of forlorn oil paintings resided on either side, depicting serene landscapes that looked to be the work of a student rather than a master. It was the most deeply uninteresting wall Henry had ever seen. Which was why it gave him pause. The trophy case was old, but not as old as this section of the castle. However, it seemed to be built into the wall.

With a frown Derrick rapped smartly against the wall with his fist. There was an echo. All three boys exchanged an uneasy glance; the wall was hollow. Derrick examined the stretch of wall behind one of the oil paintings, but it was entirely unremarkable.

So, Henry thought, *if there is a way through, it must have something to do with the trophy case.* He ran his hand around the edge of the trophy case, looking for some sort of latch or hinge.

"We should head back," Rohan said suddenly.

"I'm not going anywhere," said Derrick.

"Henry—," Rohan began.

"If you don't want to be here, you know how to get back to the dormitory," Henry said, tugging at the lock on the case.

"Can you pick the lock?" Derrick asked.

"With what?"

Derrick patted his pockets and then shrugged.

"We can come back after dinner," Henry suggested.

Derrick agreed.

"Hold up," Henry called, jogging to catch up with Rohan. Derrick joined them, rolling the map into a cylinder and playfully thwacking Henry and Rohan with it.

"Listen," Derrick said, "we shouldn't say anything about the wall. Not until we know if there's anything behind it."

"Or if there's a way in," said Henry.

"Exactly." Derrick dashed ahead of them on the staircase, brandishing the map as though it were a sword. "On guard, Nordlandic scum!" he cried, fighting off an invisible assailant.

Henry shook his head, laughing. He rather suspected Derrick had been the one to start everyone fencing with rolls of paper last term.

10

THE FORGOTTEN CLASSROOM

Conrad, Adam, and Edmund had discovered the way into the private corridor Headmaster Winter used to enter the dining hall. They were chattering excitedly about it when Henry arrived slightly late to supper, his hair still damp. Snug in his blazer pocket were a few lengths of wire, two matches, and a candle stub.

"It runs parallel to the corridor with the suits of armor," Conrad was saying through a mouthful of peas. "We think it used to be an escape route, in case the school was under siege."

"An escape route with a lovely mauve carpet." Adam snickered.

"A mauve carpet? Really?" Derrick asked, delighted.

"Why, what did you lot find?" Adam asked.

Henry and Rohan exchanged a brief glance before Henry cleared his throat and said, "There's this brilliant classroom for the knight detective students . . ."

It was easy to break away after supper. Derrick asked Henry a question about the Latin, and Henry invented a book in the library that he'd used to make sense of the ablative form.

"It's really dull," Henry warned.

"Not as dull as my summer holiday will be if I don't earn an 'excellent' in languages," said Derrick.

They were halfway to the library before Derrick frowned and whispered, "You do know I wasn't serious about the ablatives?"

"Of course," Henry whispered back.

"So why are we going to the library?"

"You'll see."

Henry led Derrick into the study room on the balcony level, shut the door, and pushed the panel on the shelf that revealed the passageway Adam had discovered the previous term.

"Where does it lead?" Derrick asked, his eyes bright with excitement.

"To the hallway below Lord Havelock's classroom."

"But that's a shortcut."

"Exactly," Henry finished. "Come on."

The staircase was just as dark as Henry remembered, and just as steep. Both boys were out of breath when Henry pushed aside the creepy unicorn tapestry and they climbed out onto the dimly lit fourth-floor corridor.

If anyone had thought Henry and Derrick were up to anything, they would have seen only that the boys had entered the library, exactly where they'd claimed to be going.

The hallway with the trophy case was on the other side of the castle, in the older part of the school. As they walked, Henry noticed the overhead beams become black with age and the floor grow slightly uneven. They approached the trophy case, and Henry removed the bits of wire from his pocket, kneeling as he fitted them into the lock.

"That's a useful talent," Derrick said, craning his neck to see what Henry was doing.

"Not really. I'm rubbish at this sort of thing."

Henry wiggled one of the bits of wire, getting a feel for the mechanism. Thankfully, the lock was old, which meant it would be easier to open.

"How did you learn?" asked Derrick.

"At the orphanage," Henry admitted, and then, because he was concentrating on the lock, he continued without thinking. "I was eleven. They never quite gave us enough to eat, particularly that summer. It's criminal, I know, but my stomach was growling so loudly that I couldn't sleep. It took two nights before I figured out how to pick the lock on the cupboard, and—"

He broke off, embarrassed. He'd just told Derrick Marchbanks, who had attended a secondary school so posh that even the composition books were embossed with gold leaf, how he'd practically been starved as a boy.

"I used to sneak down to the kitchens myself," Derrick said. "Less of a challenge when the school servants let you take what you want, though."

Henry bit his lip in response and gave the thicker piece of wire a satisfying twist.

The lock clicked open.

"This is why I like you, Grim," Derrick said as they tugged open the great glass door to the trophy case. "Conrad would have gotten scared like your friend Rohan did."

"Rohan doesn't like to break the rules," Henry

said as they scrutinized the inside of the trophy case. "Especially after being expelled for something he didn't do."

"Hmmm," Derrick said absently, pressing on a circular piece of paneling. "Conrad's the same. Scared of getting into trouble and having it become a problem when we start at the Ministerium. Ugh. Why won't this push *in*?"

"Maybe it twists," Henry observed.

Derrick twisted, and nearly lost his balance. The trophy case was a door—or, rather, it had been built over a door. One that led, sure enough, up a twisting stone staircase.

"Dare we, Grim?"

"We're not very well going to shut it and go down to the common room to play checkers," Henry said, taking the candle stub and a match from his pocket. He struck the match against the stone floor and quickly lit the candle, passing it to Derrick.

"It was your map," said Henry. "You can do the honors."

"Trying to save yourself by going last, eh, Grim?" Derrick joked, but Henry could see that through the bravado Derrick was just as nervous as he was about what they would find. However, the staircase was perfectly ordinary. A bit dusty, but ordinary nonetheless.

"What do you think is up here?" Henry asked, brushing aside a cobweb as he followed Derrick.

They stood at the entrance to a tower classroom. A few desks were cloaked with white sheets, and a Gothic bookcase stood against the far wall, its shelves home to a thick layer of dust and cobwebs. Beneath the grimy window were three moldering steamer trunks.

Derrick held his candle stub to one of the wall sconces, lighting a cluster of tapers that burnt a sulfuric green.

"Why go to all of that trouble to block off a classroom?" Derrick wondered.

"Maybe it's haunted?" Henry joked.

"Must be. Or else this was the suicide tower for everyone who earned a 'dreadful' in military history."

Henry walked over to the window and looked out. Beneath them, dark and vast, were the woods at the border of the school grounds.

"Did they even teach military history back then?" Henry asked. "I mean, this classroom was abandoned a long time ago."

"Not abandoned," Derrick corrected, wandering

over to the bookcase and extracting the few remaining volumes. "Closed off. And I wish I knew what for!" He placed the books onto one of the desks, and brushed off the coating of dust.

"What subject are they?" Henry asked.

"Don't know. But this one looks like Latin," Derrick said, passing it to Henry. Burnt into the parchment cover was the word "*Pugnare*." The book was written in painstaking illuminated hand. Henry squinted at the words in the dim candlelight.

"*Si caballus pugnare possent,*" he murmured, and then nearly dropped the book.

"'*Caballus*'? That's something about knights," Derrick replied.

"'If knights should be able to fight,'" Henry translated, flipping through the book, past careful drawings of horses and knights, diagrams of battle formations, and charts of constellations.

"That can't be—"

"It is," Henry said.

The two boys stared down at the ancient training manual, a relic of the old Knightley Academy, where pupils studied fighting rather than French, and where aristocratic boys learned to lead common soldiers into battle.

The rest of the books were thankfully in English, except for one collection of outdated maps with legends written out in Old French. Battle strategy, combat, navigation . . .

Henry stared at the stack of texts, realizing that the books had been hidden for good reason. They were full of ideas that everyone was too scared to ponder. Full of ways to kill boys in battle who fought for the opposing side. Full of plans for the impossible.

"Up for a bit of light reading?" Derrick joked, but his expression was quite serious.

"What good are books?" Henry asked. Unlike Derrick, he didn't find the stack of forgotten texts anything to joke about. "No, I mean it. Suppose that there's a war coming. Suppose that all boys over the age of thirteen will have to fight. What good is it to know the names of ancient battle formations if the only weapons we've ever held are blunt-tipped practice foils?"

"Books are better than nothing," muttered Derrick.

"Not to me," Henry said fiercely. "When I worked in the kitchens, I had loads of books. Traded a few hours' sleep for a few hours in the library. But sitting and wishing for everything to be different only makes you bitter. Memorizing books can't change the way things are."

"So you think we should put these back on the shelf and go down to the common room?"

"No, I think we should learn to fight."

Derrick stared at Henry in shock, and then laughed hollowly. "And how do you plan to do that?"

"The Lance," Henry said. He'd been thinking about it ever since that evening in the kitchen, but he hadn't dared to admit it. Too late now. The words were out, and Derrick was waiting for an explanation. "One of the kitchen boys mentioned this pub, down in the village. They take bets on boxing. We could learn to fight there."

Derrick snorted. "You'll get yourself killed. Or expelled. Probably in that order."

"Well, there has to be *some* way. If the Partisan students can prepare for war, so can we."

"What are you talking about, Grim?"

And so Henry explained about what he had seen in the Nordlands, and how no one had believed him without proof. When Henry finished, Derrick stared thoughtfully at the copy of *Pugnare*, tracing the letters with his fingers.

"That's what *we* need," Derrick said. "A combat training room."

"I think we're standing in one," Henry noted.

"Yes, but this doesn't count," Derrick said. "It's just an ordinary classroom. You said it yourself, we have nothing but some old books."

"And four desks, a bookcase, and three trunks," Henry pointed out, as though it made a difference.

"Hmmm." Derrick sized up the steamer trunks, and then got to his knees, prying open the latch on the largest one. The lid creaked open and Derrick held the guttering candle aloft, peering inside. "Grim. Come look."

Henry put down the stack of books and went to see what Derrick had found.

The trunk was filled with shields. Some were ancient, cast from heavy bronze, with fierce spikes. Others looked like hammered silver. Most were dented, and many were cracked. Together there must have been more than a dozen.

Wordlessly Henry and Derrick each threw open one of the two remaining trunks. Henry's was filled with quivers of practice arrows and ancient longbows. There was even a target, worn nearly to dust from hundreds of punctures. Derrick's trunk contained an assortment of things: two crossbows, a scythe, the metal tip of what might have been a gisarme, a broadsword, a sabre covered in what the boys dearly hoped was rust, and a case of daggers, their points dulled with age.

Henry and Derrick exchanged an uneasy glance. Now they knew why this classroom had been sealed off and forgotten. Back when Knightley Academy had closed down its archery ranges and tilting courses, the weapons hadn't been destroyed. They had simply been left to gather dust—until needed.

Derrick reached into the trunk and took out the broadsword, examining a dull black stone at the hilt. Henry removed a circular shield and the rusty sabre, guessing at the correct grip, since they weren't due to learn the weapon until second year.

"Well, have a go," Henry urged, and Derrick stared at him in shock. "Go on. Haven't you always wondered?"

"Not really, no," Derrick said nervously, glancing back and forth between the broadsword in his hand and Henry's shield. "Maybe we shouldn't have come up here."

"It's too late now." They both knew that Henry wasn't talking about their explorations of the school.

"You could get hurt," Derrick said.

Henry shrugged. "I've seen you fence. We're about

the same level, and that sword looks three times as heavy as our practice blades."

Derrick hefted the weapon. "Four times," he admitted.

"If you land a hit, we'll stop," Henry promised.

Derrick gave Henry a dubious look and began to settle into his on guard position, before realizing that the broadsword was too heavy to be handled like a foil. With a frown he choked up on the grip using both hands, as though it were a cricket bat.

Henry gulped and positioned his shield, giving a couple practice slices with the sabre.

"I can't," Derrick said, putting down his sword.

"How can we lead the others if we can't do it ourselves?"

"Lead the others?" Derrick blanched.

"You know, run a combat club—group—whatever you want to call it."

Derrick laughed hollowly, setting his weapon back in the trunk. "I can't be in charge of something like that. Be serious, Grim. My father's the Lord Minister of Foreign Relations. Can you even imagine the scandal?"

"So what *was* all of this?" Henry asked angrily, his shield clattering to the floor. "Just a game? We're too far in to stand around and laugh."

"Maybe *you* are, but I can't tarnish my record with something like this. Imagine if word got out—a future lord minister running an illicit combat training ring."

"But—," Henry said, his brain spinning to make sense of what had just happened. He'd thought that Derrick was different from the other boys, that Derrick was adventurous and daring and unusually perceptive. But when it came down to it, nothing bad or out of the ordinary had ever happened to Derrick Marchbanks.

"I'm not questioning whether or not it's a good idea," Derrick quickly amended. "I mean, we seem to have opened Pandora's box here, and I'd be bloody glad of some weapons training should this problem with the Nordlands continue sliding toward war, but I have obligations to the Ministerium. My place isn't leading the rebellion; it's fixing the problem."

"So go fix it, then!" Henry nearly shouted.

"You know I can't!"

They glared at each other, no longer in agreement, or able to see eye to eye. Henry couldn't believe how wrong he'd been about Derrick. And then the guttering candle died, leaving Derrick holding a lump of faintly smoking wax.

"We should go," Henry said, wrapping his blazer

around the stack of books. "The others will start to get suspicious."

It was surprisingly easy to make the trophy case look, once again, as though it were part of a long-neglected wall of a rarely explored corridor. In a rather sour silence the two boys headed back toward the dormitory.

"You're clever, Grim," Derrick said, breaking the silence as they passed the hall of armor on the ground floor. "You could do it, you know."

Henry shook his head. "Not by myself. You saw how I was at drills. I can't give orders."

Both boys paused, staring at the suits of armor, a row of unarmed ghostly sentinels. Now Henry knew exactly where their weapons had gone.

"I want to tell Conrad what we saw," Derrick admitted.

"Fine," Henry said coolly.

"Unless you think—"

"Do what you want, Marchbanks." Henry quickened his pace and, ignoring the commotion in the common room, threw open the door to his room. He dumped the stack of books onto his bed, and then picked up the training manual and tried to think what to do. With a tinge of regret he tore the cover off one of the mystery novels Mrs. Alabaster had given him for Christmas and placed it over the training manual. He hid the rest of the books under his bed.

As Henry carried the training manual into the common room, he realized that, despite the eight months that had passed since he'd last mopped a corridor, nothing had really changed. He was still that odd serving boy who stole books and dreamed of a different world, and, despite the events of the past two weeks, he was still very much an outsider.

11

THE TRUTH
ABOUT VALMONT

Y ou should have told us earlier," Rohan said the next
morning as they got ready for chapel in the
gray dawn. "Although I did wonder what you
were doing with your nose buried in that detective story
all night. You just finished it last weekend."

Henry shook his head at Rohan's sharp observation.
Somehow he wasn't quite as upset with Rohan anymore.
At least Rohan had refused to participate from the out-
set, rather than giving flimsy excuses at the last possible
moment.

And anyway, ever since the disastrous cricket match,
Rohan hadn't been quite so keen on his friendship with
James. James had acted as though he'd lost a dear relative

to an unexpected tragedy, rather than a friendly game to a group of older boys who were predictably better at it.

"I know, and I'm sorry," Henry said.

"It's all right." Adam plucked the book from beneath Henry's pillow. "Oi, you never said it was in Latin."

"The rest are in English."

"Just once I'd like to find a book in the library written in Hebrew." Adam knotted his tie shorter than regulation and tucked the skinny end into his shirt, in the way they weren't really supposed to.

"I didn't know you read Hebrew," Rohan said, fastening his cuffs.

Adam shrugged. "This is actually the first year my textbooks are in English," he admitted, shouldering his satchel. "Everyone ready?"

Henry stared at Adam in surprise. No wonder his friend always seemed to finish the reading ages after everyone else.

"How come you never said anything?" Henry asked.

"I went to the yeshiva," Adam said. "I thought you knew."

"But that's just the name of a school, isn't it?" Henry frowned.

"It's a type of school," Adam clarified. "And it

isn't important. Did you really mean it about learning combat?"

"I did."

Rohan gave them both a severe look. "Breaking school rules isn't enough? Now you want to break the law?"

"It isn't illegal to study combat, technically," Henry whispered as they joined the other students on the way to chapel. "It's illegal to be instructed. So if no one is teaching us . . ."

"I don't like this," Rohan said, shaking his head.

"None of this would have happened if you hadn't been dead set on no longer being friends with Frankie," Adam pointed out.

"Do shut up, Adam," Rohan said primly.

Henry snorted. He'd missed his friends terribly.

At supper that evening the first years were unusually subdued. The second years bent their heads and whispered furiously. The third years alternated between silence and bursts of heated debate. And the fourth-year table sat empty, as it had all week; the boys were off serving apprenticeships. But Henry suspected they too were sitting around the dinner table trying to make sense of the news.

That morning the gossip rags had run another staggering headline: POLICING AGENCY QUESTIONS NORDLANDIC HOUSEHOLDS. Dimit Yascherov, the head of both the Partisan School and the Nordlandic Policing Agency, had issued orders for household inspections. Every home in the Nordlands was to be visited and checked, its inhabitants catalogued and assessed. Those deemed to be fit for certain government projects would be transferred immediately to a new work detail.

"Maybe they're building roads," Edmund said, passing the basket of rolls. "Or hospitals."

"Be serious, Merrill," Derrick scoffed. "It's most likely just an excuse to scare everyone into following the laws."

"How do you figure that?" Rohan asked.

"It's like that prison Sir Franklin mentioned in ethics today. I forget the name."

"The Panopticon," Henry said.

"Right, the Panopticon," Derrick continued. "If you think that a police agent could arrive on your doorstep at any moment and assign you to an unnamed work detail, you're going to be terrified to do anything wrong, because you feel like you're being watched."

"That's not really what Sir Franklin was talking

about," Henry argued. "He was saying how if watchmen can't be seen, they don't truly ever have to be on duty, and society governs itself."

"Not society," Derrick returned. "Prisoners. They've already been caught by the law once. They already know what it's like to be scrutinized by these watchmen or whomever. So the threat works because they know what to fear."

"Maybe," Henry said.

"Not maybe," Derrick argued. "I'm right."

"Sorry, Henry, he is," Rohan mumbled.

Henry glanced curiously at Rohan—was that why he'd become so fanatical about following the rules? Because he knew all too well the consequences of breaking them?

And then a fierce argument broke out at the third-year table between Theobold's older brother and a tall, confident-looking boy with an earring. The boy with the earring hauled back and punched Arch square in the jaw.

Sir Franklin and Lord Havelock hurried over and pulled the boys apart.

"Nordlandic sympathizer," Arch spat, rubbing his jaw.

Back at Henry's table Edmund had gone quite pale.

Theobold, however, was seething. As the professors marched the two third years out of the dining hall, they passed by the first-year table.

"Peter—," Edmund began.

The boy with the earring shook his head. "Don't worry about it, kid," he called over his shoulder.

Henry and Adam exchanged an amused glance, even though it was anything but funny. Who would have thought that shy Edmund's older brother was so, well, *daring*?

"I can't believe we're doing this," Rohan muttered as he, Henry, and Adam crept through the corridor. They had just half an hour until lights-out, but Henry had insisted on waiting for Adam to finish the reading for Medicine.

"There better be leftover trifle," said Adam.

"You ate enough of it at supper," Rohan said.

"There is no such thing as enough dessert," Adam protested.

They were on their way to visit Liza and Mary, two kitchen maids who in addition to knowing where the leftover deserts were kept, also happened to be a wealth of knowledge about anything and everything printed in the gossip rags. If anyone knew what was really behind that morning's article about the Nordlandic police inspections, it was Liza and Mary.

But as Henry and his friends reached the bottom of the servants' stair that led to the kitchens, they stopped short. Ollie, the serving boy who had given Henry the ice, was gingerly dragging a mop across the floor, wincing as he clasped his left hand to his side. His right hand was badly bandaged with a scrap of washrag, and his cheeks were shadowed with bruises.

Henry, Adam, and Rohan exchanged an uneasy glance.

"You'll need to bind those ribs tighter," Henry said.

Ollie stared at him in surprise.

"Your ribs," Henry said. "The way you're holding the mop gives it away. Come on. Put that down and let me see what you've done to yourself."

Ollie cringed and eyed Henry and his friends doubtfully. "I tripped, I promise. I wasn't doin' nothing wrong."

At this, Adam snorted.

"We're not going to tell anyone," Henry reassured the boy. "These are my friends. We can help patch you up."

"We can?" Rohan asked, raising an eyebrow.

"Of course," Henry said with far more confidence than he felt.

Ollie shook his head. "I can't. I ain't finished mopping the corridor."

"You shouldn't be doing that," Henry said, holding out his hand for the mop. "You could puncture a lung or something. Give it here."

Ollie passed Henry the mop. The boy really was small for his age, Henry observed, rolling up his sleeves. "So how'd you get hurt?" Adam blurted.

"Pub fighting." Ollie lifted his chin, and then realized what he'd said and blanched. "I mean, I was watching pub fighting an' I fell."

"Pub fighting!" Adam scoffed. "You're about twelve!"

"No, I'm thirteen!" Ollie said fiercely.

"My mistake." Adam smirked.

Henry wrung out the mop and nearly jumped when Rohan appeared at his side. "Listen, Henry," said Rohan with a disapproving frown. "I don't think you ought to be doing that. It isn't your place."

"A knight must help 'those in need, whether of common or noble breed,'" Henry quoted, daring Rohan to object.

"All right," Rohan conceded. "What should we do?"

"Take him to the infirmary. Say that he was attacked by bandits—I don't know, make it believable. If sick matron won't help, we'll need a roll of bandages."

"And how am I supposed to get—" Rohan gave Henry a sharp look when he realized what Henry was asking.

"Look at him," Henry whispered. "If he were your younger brother, could you stand it?"

Rohan pursed his lips in disapproval. He clearly didn't see why Ollie had been fighting at the pub in the first place. But Henry could venture a guess. The boy was either desperate for the extra money or needed very badly to learn how to fight. And neither option was reassuring.

"Come on," Rohan said to Adam and Ollie. "We're going to the infirmary."

"I'll be along in a few minutes," Henry called after them.

When everyone had left, Henry stood there in the darkened corridor, rhythmically pushing the mop along the baseboards and trying to remember the last time he'd done such a thing. He was so lost in thought that he didn't hear anyone approaching.

"Ollie Twisp, you better not be daydreamin' again!"

Henry turned. At the other end of the corridor, Liza shrieked in surprise. She stared at Henry in a panic, her washrag fluttering to the floor.

"Master Henry, what're you doin'?"

"Hallo, Liza," Henry said, retrieving her washrag and offering it with a polite bow. "How are things?"

Liza regarded him doubtfully. "You ain't answered my question."

"I sent Ollie to have his injuries bandaged up," Henry explained as the mop made a hideous squelching noise. "I do hope I haven't missed a spot."

Liza frowned at the wet corridor, and then at Henry, uncertain whether or not he was joking. "You're taller," she said. "How old are you?"

"Fifteen next month." Henry's birthday had always been a bit of a guess, but he'd gotten used to thinking of himself as a year older around March fifteenth. "Say, Liza, you haven't heard anything about the Nordlands lately, have you?" Henry leaned forward on the mop handle, in the way he had never dared back when he was a servant.

"O' course I been hearin' things. I got eyes, don't I?" Liza retorted.

Henry tried not to grin. "My mistake," he mocked, favoring the kitchen maid with another bow. She blushed, pleased.

"I heard they're truly searchin' fer plots against the government. Secret organizations an' hidden schools an' stashes of weapons."

"But why have news of it in the papers?" Henry asked. "They lose the element of surprise."

"Ain't no sense in bangin' on someone's door and catchin' them unawares. Chancellor Mors wants 'em scared. He wants 'em knowin' that someone's comin' to get 'em." Liza paused, giving Henry a dark look.

"So how will they find these secret plots and the like?" Henry asked, playing along. He didn't really believe Liza's theory, or Derrick's, for that matter.

"Don't matter if they find 'em. It's easier to do a scare. Poisons 'em from the inside. No one wants to be punished for doin' nothin' wrong, see? The innocent turn in the guilty so's *they* don't get shipped off to some government project."

Henry stared at Liza in surprise. That was actually quite a valid point.

"Did *you* come up with that?" he asked.

"Not me, Master Henry," Liza admitted. "Overheard that Sir Robert talkin' about it with Lord Havelock when I brung tea to his office."

"Really? Do you remember which one of them said it?"

"Lemme see now," Liza said, pursing her lips as she remembered. "Must've been that Sir Robert. Lord Havelock don' want nothin' to do with 'servant gossip' such as he calls it, the high an' mighty louse."

Henry snorted at Liza's colorful description of Lord Havelock, but he was deeply troubled by what he'd just learned. The schoolmasters were talking about this latest news from the Nordlands. And not just the schoolmasters but Lord Havelock and Sir Robert—both of whom were members of the board of trustees!

Henry resumed mopping, and Liza stood there, watching and shaking her head.

"Ollie didn't look well," Henry insisted after a stretch of uncomfortable silence.

"His da beats him sometimes," Liza said. "Not enough to eat, so's he has to find a reason to send someone to bed hungry."

"That's horrible."

"That's the way o' things, Master Henry. Some are too scared o' bein' caught breakin' the law to do anything, and others are too sure no one's lookin' that they do as they like. An' that's somethin' I came up with meself."

After he finished mopping the corridor, Henry returned the bucket and mop to a broom cupboard he found just outside the kitchen. He caught sight of a clock and made a face; the hour was far later than he'd thought, and students were supposed to be in bed long before now.

But still, he'd promised. And so he took the stairs that led to the infirmary rather than to the first-year corridor. But the infirmary, when he reached it, was locked, the lights off.

He supposed he should go to bed. Adam and Rohan were probably back in their room, waiting impatiently. He could tell them what Liza had overheard Lord Havelock and Sir Robert discussing. He yawned and headed back toward the dormitory, reviewing Liza's borrowed theory about the Nordlands. He was so lost in thought that he almost failed to notice a dark shape creeping down the corridor in his direction. But at the last moment Henry *did* notice. His heart pounding, he pressed himself flat against the wall between two suits of armor.

Fergus Valmont paused as he left the first-year corridor, looking extraordinarily guilty. He glanced over his shoulder, as though afraid of having been followed, and then made his way to an ancient window seat that no one used, due to its being a favorite haunt of the castle's largest spiders.

Henry watched as Valmont lifted the lid off the window seat, removed a large and rather lumpy canvas rucksack, and slung it over his shoulder. With a final backward glance, Valmont crept down the hallway, passing right by Henry, who pressed himself even harder against the wall, holding his breath. After Valmont had passed, Henry silently counted to ten, relaxed, and then considered what he should do.

It was very late, and the door to his room was right there. No doubt his roommates were waiting for him, worried because he hadn't joined them at the infirmary. But he wouldn't be able to sleep unless he knew what Valmont was up to. The sneaking, the stashed rucksack, the nervous glances over his shoulder—Valmont clearly didn't want to be followed.

And so Henry decided to follow him.

Valmont snuck through the corridor that lead to the Great Hall, and then made a sharp left up one of the staircases. Henry hung back, following only when he was certain Valmont wouldn't see. At the top of the stairs, he panicked, thinking he'd lost Valmont. But then he heard a creak down the corridor that led to the armory and rounded the corner just in time to see the door to the armory creak shut.

What was Valmont doing in the armory, in the middle of the night, with a bag he'd hidden outside their dormitory?

Henry took a step toward the armory, and then stopped. He'd just meant to follow Valmont, not to confront him. What if Valmont went to Lord Havelock and claimed that he'd caught *Henry* sneaking around out of bed?

But he couldn't turn back now. Not after tailing Valmont halfway through the school. And so with a deep breath Henry threw open the door to the armory.

Valmont looked up in horror, scrambling to hide the contents of his bag. But it was too late; Henry had already gotten a look. Henry stared at Valmont, his eyes wide.

"What are you doing here, servant boy?" Valmont snarled.

Henry shut the door behind him, thinking how that nickname was oddly fitting after he'd spent the evening mopping the servants' corridor. "I followed you," Henry said coolly. "What's in the bag?"

"Nothing. Go away."

"Not likely." Henry folded his arms, leaning casually against the door.

"I'm going to murder you for this, Grim."

"Really?" Henry asked. "With your broadsword, and me unarmed? Or perhaps you'd be kind enough to lend me your shield?"

Valmont spluttered.

Henry smirked.

"So turn me in, Grim, if that's what you're meaning to do. You were out of bed as well."

"I'm not going to turn you in," Henry said, realizing as he said it that he truly wasn't.

Valmont gaped. "But—"

"Can you use it?" Henry asked curiously.

"Well enough to cut your bowels from your belly," Valmont said, recovering his bravado.

Henry realized with a shock that this wasn't the first time Valmont had spent the midnight hour in the armory. This was, however, the first time he'd been caught.

"How long have you been coming here?" Henry asked.

Valmont scowled. "Not that it's any of your business, Grim, but all term."

All term! For nearly two weeks Valmont had been

sneaking out of the dormitory at night to practice combat while spending his days as Theobold's lackey.

"I don't understand," Henry said.

"Are you dense? There's a war coming. And I'm not going to wind up with my name chiseled into the side of a monument as one of the brave dead."

"But Theobold—," Henry began.

"Is about as clever as a ham sandwich. And he'd sooner believe the Nordlands are planning something than he'd believe form matters in fencing."

"I didn't realize you loathed him."

"Not everyone here is bestest chums like you and your ragtag band of misfits," Valmont mocked.

"Can you show me?" Henry asked, ignoring Valmont's taunt.

"I only have one broadsword."

"I know where we can get more," Henry admitted.

Valmont raised an eyebrow. "What makes you think I'll teach you?"

Henry thought for a moment. Finally he said, "Because you can't go it alone. And because I know where you hide your rucksack."

Valmont considered this. "Grab a sabre," he said, throwing open the door to the weapons cabinet.

Henry took the left-handed sabre and reached for some padding. They fastened each other's kits in silence.

Henry took his guard with the unfamiliar weapon and expected Valmont to walk to the other end of the piste and salute. "Well," he said, gesturing toward the piste.

"You wanted to learn to fight, not to fence," Valmont returned. "No rules, no off target, no salute, and no priority. Let's go, Grim."

Valmont lowered his mask and rushed toward Henry, sabre extended.

Henry gulped. Even though they were using blunted blades and padding, it was still terrifying.

Their blades clashed, and Henry had to force himself not to think about who had the priority, or which hits would land off target. Valmont disengaged to the inside and raised his weapon, bringing it down on the top of Henry's mask with a resounding clank.

"That's my head!" Henry protested in surprise.

"On guard," Valmont called in response, attacking again, this time aiming for Henry's knee. Henry leapt out of the way, curling his blade around and striking Valmont on the back.

"Parry *neuvième*," Henry said, with the faintest trace of a smirk.

Valmont stopped cold. "Where'd you learn that?"

Henry shrugged. The truth was, he'd gotten it out of *Pugnare*.

Valmont took his guard again, and Henry used his left-handed advantage to cut with the edge of the blade against Valmont's forearm. Valmont recovered quickly, slicing his blade through the air, forcing Henry into a retreat with overhead blocks, until a slice landed on Henry's right shoulder.

Five relentless minutes later they were sore and thoroughly out of breath. Henry tore off his mask. "Don't strike," he gasped, putting his hands on his knees. "I need to breathe."

"I've already killed you about ten times, anyhow." Valmont shrugged, pulling off his glove. They regarded each other warily.

"Not bad," Henry said after an interminable stretch of silence.

"We could—I mean, if you want—we could go again tomorrow night," said Valmont.

A horrible thought occurred to Henry, and he quickly pushed it out of his mind. "Maybe," he said, "but my roommates would notice. How come yours hasn't?"

"My room's a single." Valmont didn't sound pleased.

"Listen," Henry said, because the horrible thought had come back. "What if it wasn't just the two of us who wanted to learn how to fight?"

"I doubt the fencing master would agree to teach an illegal course on combat."

"Er, I was thinking more along the lines of not involving any of the professors," said Henry.

Valmont frowned. "With two broadswords and the blunted second-year sabres?"

"I know where we can get more weapons," Henry said. "Training manuals, shields, swords. Arrows and crossbows as well."

"I'm listening," Valmont said, crossing his arms.

"Derrick and I found a whole cache of things left over from before the Longsword Treaty. And you must have noticed the way our professors are changing their lessons, making them more, well, *applicable* to current events." Henry said. "There must be a dozen students at least who would want to learn."

"So you and Marchbanks can go off and form a club," Valmont said sourly. "Invite your friends. Just like you did with the cricket match."

"That wasn't me. That was *James*. But Derrick won't do it. He's too afraid. I just thought that, after tonight, maybe *you* would," Henry finished.

"Me?" Valmont pushed his glasses up his nose and glared. "Whatever gave you that impression?"

"I have no idea," Henry snapped. "Sorry to have annoyed you. I'll let you get back to fighting your invisible opponent." Henry threw down his sabre and headed for the door.

"Wait," Valmont said.

Henry turned.

"So this fight club," Valmont mused. "We'd *both* be in charge of it. Because I'm not answering to *you*."

"I'm not asking you to," Henry returned. "And 'fight club' is a ridiculous name. It's more of a . . . battle society."

"A secret battle society," Valmont agreed.

"So you'll do it?"

"Tonight was the best training I've had in three weeks." Valmont nodded.

"There's just one catch," Henry said coolly.

"We are *not* inviting the headmaster's daughter."

"Definitely not," Henry said with feeling. He could just imagine what a disaster that would be: Frankie hiking up her skirts and challenging Valmont to a duel. "As I see it, you still answer to Theobold. What's to stop you from telling him everything—or from having me expelled in order to save yourself?"

"That's just a chance you'll have to take, Grim."

"Actually, it isn't," Henry said. "Before I show you where the weapons are hidden—before I try to convince my friends to join us—I want some insurance. I want to know what Theobold has on you."

"That's absurd."

"Is it?" Henry challenged.

Valmont's eyes narrowed, and he scrutinized Henry, as though trying to decide whether or not Henry could be trusted. "Don't make me regret telling you, servant boy."

Henry sighed at the mention of his old nickname, but nodded anyway.

They put away their kits and blades and closed up the weapons cabinet. Henry sat down with his back against the cabinet door and waited. Valmont sat next to Henry, staring straight ahead at their dim reflection in the mirrors that lined the opposing wall. From far away they almost looked like friends.

"My father was a police knight," Valmont said finally.

"Was?"

"He died in the riots during the Nordlandic uprising. He was sent in to break up the riot in Whitechapel Market. Took a blow to the head and was trampled in the panic. I was a baby."

"I'm sorry."

"He was stupid," Valmont said. "Rushed in before the rest of the guard and got himself killed for it."

"That's not stupid. That's brave."

Silence.

"So that's what Theobold has on you?" Henry asked finally. "That your father died as a hero?"

"No," Valmont muttered. "Don't you understand? My father was a lord. When he died, everything went to his younger brother, Gideon. The title, the estate, the town house. And Lord Gideon—he threw my mum out."

Henry stared at Valmont in surprise. "Where did she go?" Henry asked.

"Moved in with her brother."

A horrible thought occurred to Henry—had Valmont been raised by *Lord Havelock*? No wonder Valmont had been so certain back at the Midsummer School of the family connections that would land him a place at Knightley. And no wonder he'd been such a horrible bully—it was so no one would taunt him. But Theobold had found out.

"I don't understand why it's such a big secret." Henry shrugged.

"You wouldn't," Valmont said darkly.

"So you were raised by your horrible uncle. It's not as though he treated you like a servant."

"Right, because being the poor relation of the most loathed professor at Knightley isn't bad enough." Valmont pushed his glasses up his nose and glared.

"*That's* what Theobold has on you? That your father died a hero and your uncle raised you instead?" Henry shook his head in disgust. Why did Valmont care so much?

"I'm not a charity case like *you*, Grim," Valmont said hotly. "I attended the Midsummer School. I had servants to cater to my every whim over the holidays."

"I believe you," Henry said.

"I'm not some freak with a dead parent who needs to join your poor orphans club."

"I never said you were." *But Theobold clearly had,* Henry thought.

It was then that Henry realized he actually felt sorry for Valmont. Fancy being so ashamed of where you came from that you'd become Theobold's lackey just to keep it a secret! Henry shook his head, and then stifled an enormous yawn.

"Coming back to the dormitory, Grim?" Valmont asked, picking up his rucksack.

"Er, yeah," Henry said, giving the armory a final glance over to make sure everything had been put back into place, and then falling into step beside Valmont.

12

THE SECRET
BATTLE SOCIETY

Y ou and Valmont?" Adam scoffed. "You'll murder
each other first chance you have. We won't
learn a thing except how to dispose of your
corpses."

Rohan's frown deepened at the mention of corpses.
"I think the whole thing sounds like a dreadful plan.
You'll get caught. You'll get expelled. It isn't worth the
risk."

"It is to me," Henry said quietly. He was lying on
his bed, *Pugnare* propped open against his knee. "Something terrible is brewing up in the Nordlands. We should
know how to defend ourselves. Just because the professors can't teach us, doesn't mean it's wrong."

"I'm with you there, mate, but I can't stand Valmont," Adam said. "Sign me up to show off my skills with a sword, but I'm not spending any more time than necessary with that smarmy little arse-toad."

"I—actually— Valmont isn't so bad," Henry said, shrugging.

Adam and Rohan both stared at Henry as though he had gone quite mad.

"He isn't," Henry insisted. "And if I tell you, you have to promise you won't tell anyone else."

"You know we won't," Rohan said impatiently.

And so Henry told them about Valmont's father dying in the riots, and Lord Havelock taking him and his mother in, raising Valmont out of charity, and about Theobold's blackmail.

"There are some things for which a tragic childhood is an excuse," Rohan said. "Being Fergus Valmont is not one of them."

"I don't know. I think he's turned out rather well, considering," Adam said. "Imagine being raised by *Lord Havelock*."

The three of them shuddered at the thought of it.

"How's Ollie, by the way?" Henry suddenly remembered.

"Matron bandaged his ribs, said he'd live, and sent him home," Rohan said.

"That's good," Henry said.

"He shouldn't have been fighting in the first place," Rohan said harshly.

"His father beats him. He just wanted to learn to defend himself," Henry said.

"There are better ways," Rohan returned.

"Such as?" Henry challenged, raising an eyebrow.

"Flag twirling?" Adam struggled to keep a straight face, and Henry couldn't help but laugh.

Henry and Valmont sat hunched over a chessboard in the common room for the next three nights, planning. Their first meeting was to be that Thursday, and so much had to be done before then.

Henry spoke with Derrick, who agreed to cautiously spread the word among the first years, and he spoke with Jasper Hallworth, asking him to invite any second years who might be interested. He read well past lights-out, squinting at his copy of *Pugnare* in the contraband candle-light and planning what he wanted to say. He snuck off to the armory one more time, where he and Valmont practiced their first lesson. And he spent an exhausting night bringing the contents of the weapons trunks down to the basement with Derrick and Adam.

The battle society had decided to meet in the abandoned storeroom in the basement, which Adam, Conrad, and Edmund had discovered during their explorations. There was no electricity, so everyone would need to bring lanterns and candles, but the room was large and unused and without windows. In short, it was nearly perfect.

The newspapers continued to taunt them with stories of Nordlandic inspections, and of something new. A train departing from the town of Forecastle, just fifteen kilometers south of the Nordlandic border, had derailed. None of the passengers was badly hurt, but even so, Henry couldn't entirely dismiss the story, especially when Derrick wordlessly passed him an article over breakfast the morning of their first battle society meeting. Police knights had found evidence that the tracks had been tampered with, and were turning the case over to the local knight detectives.

A few hours before the first battle society meeting, the common room hummed with an unmistakable air of anticipation. Henry and Valmont sat in an out-of-the-way corner pretending to play a game of chess while they went over some final preparations. But whenever Henry glanced up, he felt as though he and Valmont were seated upon a stage; far too many of their classmates were throwing glances in their direction. For the first time Henry wondered just how many students would turn up for the battle society.

Henry and Valmont arrived early. Henry held a candle to his notes, reading them over and over while Valmont paced.

He knew that Adam, Rohan, Derrick, Conrad, and Edmund were coming, and possibly Jasper, though he'd laughed when Henry had mentioned it.

Sure enough, Adam and Rohan were the first to arrive. Rohan put his lantern down at the base of the stairs and wandered over to examine the weapons.

Next came Derrick, followed by James, Edmund, and Conrad. After them came Luther Leicester, and then Jasper Hallworth and three of his friends from second year, and then Edmund's friends from the choir, and the two altar boys called John and Paul who were cousins, and then Edmund's brother, Peter, and two enormous boys from third year, and after that, Henry was so overwhelmed by the continuous arrival of students that he scarcely would have noticed had Sir Frederick himself come bursting through the doorway.

Gradually the room became bright, filling with lanterns and candles. They flickered merrily, some from the bottom of the stairwell, others from the tops of crates, and still more from the tarnished wall sconces. Henry surveyed the two dozen students, panic rising in his throat. He hadn't expected so many, and certainly not *third years*.

"Go on," Valmont muttered, clearing his throat with impatience. "We should start."

"Er, hello," Henry said meekly. "Thank you for coming. For those of you who don't know us, I'm, er, Henry Grim, and this is Fergus Valmont." Henry closed his eyes for a moment, took a deep breath, and then looked down at his notes, only to find that he'd inadvertently memorized them.

"You're all here because you are free thinkers," Henry recited, pleased to hear that his voice no longer sounded shaky or unsure. "Because you've questioned flimsy explanations, noticed the warning signs that are so easy to miss, or read the gossip magazines without scoffing at the stories contained within their pages. You're here because the Nordlands are plotting something dreadful, and because you are no longer content to sit and wait for their inevitable attack.

"As the ancient Greeks said, 'To rebel in season is not to rebel.' Gentlemen, we are here to prepare ourselves to fight. We are here so that Yurick Mors does not emerge victorious. And we are here because we are knights, and knighthood is not Latin verbs and history essays."

At this most of the first-year students clapped loudly. Henry's cheeks reddened. His half was over. Now it was Valmont's turn.

"Grim and I have weapons and training manuals. We're not experts, and Grim here isn't even an advanced fencer—"

"Right, thanks," Henry said, rolling his eyes as everyone laughed.

"But if we can do it, there's no reason you can't learn as well," Valmont continued. "However, we come here with great risk. And so, if anyone should ask, this society doesn't exist. Any bruises and scrapes you might earn are because you tripped and fell." Valmont stared out at the sea of students, making sure they understood what he was saying.

"There's a suit of armor," Valmont continued, "posted just outside the dining hall. On its breastplate is a fleur-de-lis. If the fleur-de-lis is upside down at breakfast, there will be a meeting that night. This way we don't raise suspicions with a regular meeting schedule, or whispering among ourselves to spread the word. Does anyone have any questions?"

"Yeah, kid, I've got one." It was Edmund's brother, Peter. "Where'd you get all of those weapons?"

"Henry and I found them," Derrick said.

"We did," Henry confirmed. "Inside of a closed-off classroom with some old books." Peter nodded, apparently satisfied.

"If there aren't any more questions," Valmont said, "we'll move on to demonstrating a blade-to-blade disarming technique—"

"I have a question, actually," a huge boy from second year called. "You seem a bit too certain that the Nordlands are preparing for war. There's undoubtedly something odd happening up north, but maybe it's not what we think. Maybe it's nothing to do with us."

The room filled with whispers.

Henry and Valmont exchanged an uneasy glance. He would have to tell them, Henry realized.

"Do you remember when we all went up to the Partisan School?" Henry asked. "I got lost one night and wound up in a room full of weapons and combat ranking charts."

More whispers.

"The Nordlands have violated the Longsword Treaty," Henry continued, and a few students exchanged skeptical glances. "Headmaster Winter believes it, but without proof, we have nothing. The room disappeared. The board of trustees won't listen. Everyone knows war is coming, but no one wants to cry wolf."

"Well, what I want to know," another third year called, "is why *you're* in charge. You're first years."

Henry blanched. "Er," he said. "Well, if you want to vote—"

"I vote for Henry," Derrick called. "Because I can barely keep up with my lessons as it is, and he managed to put all of this together and still check my Latin homework."

"Valmont did most of it," Henry muttered, even though it wasn't true. Valmont had refused to do any of the grunt work, retorting that he'd do as he pleased and would be damned if he took orders from a former servant.

"If someone else wants to be in charge for the next meeting," Valmont said loudly, "he should raise his hand now."

Everyone shifted nervously but no hands raised.

"Look," Henry said, "these weapons belong to the school. If you come down here and practice on your own, that's fine. We just wanted to get everyone together, and Valmont and I had been planning to follow the training manual in order."

"What manual?" James asked.

Henry removed the copy of *Pugnare* from inside his blazer and handed it over.

James frowned. "But this is in Latin."

"I know," Henry said patiently. "Most things were, back then. I've been translating it in the evenings, and it's giving me a bloody headache figuring out some of the terms."

"We'll answer any further questions after the meeting," Valmont cut in, daring anyone to interrupt as he calmly fastened his glove. "I think we've talked enough, and I want to make sure everyone has time to learn the basics of disarming."

"Does anyone already know how?" Henry inquired.

Silence. Everyone looked expectantly at Henry and Valmont.

Henry picked up his blade and took his guard.

"Right," Valmont said. "Lesson one, disarming your opponent. It's extraordinarily useful and not too hard to learn. Watch as I disarm Grim, and stand back if you don't fancy catching a sabre to the face."

Everyone backed up uneasily. Valmont made a flashy cut with his blade before settling into the on guard position.

Their blades clashed, and Valmont let Henry drive him backward. The distance between them closed. Henry lunged into an attack. At the last moment Valmont parried to the inside with a forward recovery, wrapping his blade vertically around Henry's.

With Henry's sword still in the bind, Valmont lifted upward. The pressure on Henry's thumb was too much; his blade went flying.

Henry retrieved the blade while his classmates whispered about what they'd seen.

"What just happened?" Valmont asked.

James called out the moves as though he were referee at a fencing match.

"That's right," Valmont said. "However, in nonfencing terms, I waited for his attack, captured his blade to the inside, and levered it out of his grip using pressure against the natural bend of the thumb."

Henry and Valmont went through it step by step, with Henry fencing three more demonstrations, swapping swords to fence two of them right-handed.

"We'd like you to partner up and try it yourselves," Valmont called. "You'll have to take turns with the sabres." Half of the students took their blades and spread out. The others watched eagerly. Henry and Valmont walked around the room, watching and making corrections if needed. Most of the second and third years got it immediately, and Jasper laughed loudly as he disarmed a freckled boy called Geoffrey with far too much force, sending Geoffrey's weapon halfway across the room.

"Careful!" Henry cautioned. "You don't want to hit someone—or knock over a lantern."

Jasper made a face, but his next go was much more subdued. Satisfied, Henry moved on.

Edmund was struggling to perform the move against scrawny Percy Barnes, and Valmont impatiently corrected Edmund's forward recovery in a manner nearly as terrifying as that of Lord Havelock.

"Could you be a bit nicer about it?" Henry whispered after Valmont had moved on to the next pair.

"Why? He got it right in the end, didn't he?" Valmont snapped.

"Fine. Do what you want," Henry snarled in return.

By the time everyone was reasonably sure that they

could disarm an opponent, it was so late that it was actually rather early. Henry began to gather the sabres.

"Not too shabby, Grim," Jasper said, handing Henry his blade. "I have to admit, I came mostly just to see whether or not you could pull it off."

"Really?" Henry asked with a grin. "Is that why you brought along three friends?"

"Pure entertainment value," Jasper said, waving his hand dismissively.

"Right," Henry said with a knowing smile.

"Oi, Henry, are these from the armory?" Adam called across the room. He had an armload of sabres, and Rohan stood next to him with the gloves.

"You don't have to help," Henry said, walking over.

"Well, you've done enough," Rohan put in. "It can't have been light work, organizing this."

Valmont broke away from his conversation with Luther and noticed that Henry, Adam, and Rohan were carrying most of the equipment.

"Here you are, Grim," Valmont said with a brutal smile, dumping five more blades into Henry's arms and picking up the lantern at Adam's feet. "I'll see you at chapel."

"Oi, that isn't fair!" Adam complained.

Henry sighed. He should have seen this coming.

"I don't mind," Henry said, in a tone that suggested he minded a great deal.

"You see? He doesn't mind," Valmont gloated.

"Give me that," Rohan said, snatching the lantern. "If you insist on being rude, you could at least have offered us the lantern."

"That's not how being rude works," Adam explained patiently.

Henry stifled a laugh. "See you at chapel, Valmont," he said coolly.

With a huff Valmont felt his way up the dark staircase.

"No sense giving him any lamplight after pulling a dirty trick like that," Rohan said primly.

Once they were certain Valmont had a long head start, they set off to return the equipment to the armory.

"Do you know," Adam whispered thoughtfully, "you and the arse-toad actually make a decent team."

"I thought it was useful," Rohan whispered. "Since disarming doesn't count in a bout, I've never been allowed to try it before."

Henry bit his lip at the unexpected praise from his friends.

After depositing the equipment in the armory, they

crept back to the dormitory in silence and changed into their pajamas.

"This might really work," Henry whispered, half to himself. A few days before, he hadn't even dared to think those words, but now he was confident of their inherent truth. The battle society would make a difference, somehow. It would change things.

And, strictly speaking, Henry was not wrong. But secrets, shameful or otherwise, have a way of getting out. Like wild animals captured and caged, they cannot be kept easily, for their dearest ambition is to run free.

13

SNEAKING
AND SECRETS

O ver the next two weeks the battle society met
regularly. Henry or Valmont would flip the
fleur-de-lis before chapel, and when they'd
arrive at breakfast, there would be an indefinable change
at the first-year table—a sort of smug knowingness that
put Theobold on edge and made Argus Crowley's face
take on a pinched expression, as though someone had
slipped a dung beetle into his tea.

"You didn't slip a dung beetle into Crowley's tea, did
you?" Rohan whispered to Adam on the morning of
what was to be the fourth battle society meeting.

"It wasn't me," Adam promised. "That's just how his
face looks."

Henry snickered.

"You shouldn't make fun of people's faces," Rohan snapped.

"I wasn't," Henry replied. And then, because he couldn't resist, he said, "I was laughing while Adam did."

"Hey, Henry?" It was Edmund, his face pale and his eyes shadowed.

"What's wrong?" Henry asked, shifting his grip on his satchel so he could turn the fleur-de-lis back to its normal position.

"I don't think I can make it to—well, *you know,*" Edmund admitted miserably.

"Why not?" Henry asked, falling into step with Edmund as they headed toward their fencing lesson.

"Theobold suspects something. He's being even worse than usual. I think he wiped his boots on my pillow. Well, I hope it was his boots."

"That's awful. I'm really sorry, Edmund." Henry certainly sympathized. It couldn't be easy having Theobold as a roommate, especially after Edmund's brother had gotten into a fistfight with Theobold's.

"You should go down to the laundry and ask for another pillowcase," Henry suggested.

"I will."

"Actually," Henry said, holding open the door to the armory and dropping his voice to a whisper, "when you have a moment, could you ask Peter if he'd show us how to throw punches?"

"He'd be delighted," Edmund said dryly. "He's wild about boxing. Spent one summer traveling around on a caravan playing his fiddle with the gypsies and starting alehouse brawls."

"No!"

"That's where he got the earring." Edmund said. "Our father wanted him betrothed to some girl who did nothing but embroider his initials onto handkerchiefs, and he ran off to create an enormous scandal so her family would refuse."

Henry shook his head in awe at Peter's nerve, as the fencing master strode into the room. They went through the usual warm-up stretches and lunges before the fencing master cleared his throat and removed a foil from the weapons cabinet.

"We're learning the *flèche* today, gentlemen," he said. "Kit up and choose a partner."

"Henry?" Derrick said, and at the same moment Pevensey caught Henry's attention.

"Partners?" Edmund asked cheerfully, tossing Henry the left-handed glove.

Henry snorted in amusement. He hadn't anticipated that after three meetings of the battle society everyone would want to be his partner in fencing. He looked over to Valmont, who was handling the same problem with apparent relish.

"Er, right, Derrick," Henry said. "And Edmund can go with Pevensey?"

Edmund shrugged.

"Why not?" Pevensey said, passing Edmund a blade.

"I thought you were rubbish at giving orders," Derrick whispered.

"Guess I'm getting better at it," Henry whispered back, trying to pay attention to the fencing master's explanation of how to transfer one's weight onto the front foot and cross the back leg over, simultaneous with an attack.

"Do you know," Derrick said sadly, "this move isn't really my forte."

Henry snickered at the pun.

"Gentlemen!" the fencing master called.

"Sorry, maestro," Henry and Derrick chorused.

* * *

The fourth battle society meeting brought with it two more students from second year. Following the chapters in *Pugnare*, they practiced falling so as not to get hurt, slapping the ground as they went down to make it look as though they'd sustained a greater injury. Peter taught everyone how to set an opponent off balance and burst his eardrums by cuffing him around the ears. He showed them how to deliver an elbow to the chin and temple, and how to break an opponent's nose with the palm of your hand. And despite his earlier worries, Edmund crept in only a little late, grinning triumphantly at his escape.

There was no denying it—the battle society was a success, but not only in the way Henry had thought. Jasper and Geoffrey had taken to the role of mischievous older brothers, tousling the first years' hair in the hallways and shooting contraband peas at their backs in the library. Edmund's fencing improved, and Henry noticed new friendships forming among the first years. Theobold was so baffled by the subtle changes among his classmates that he sometimes forgot to order Valmont around the way he had at the beginning of term. And when the newspapers carried a troubling piece of news from the Nordlands—the public hanging of a corrupt government official—the first years discussed the news openly, debating theories over breakfast and hastily pulling down their sleeves over fresh bruises from weapons practice.

"I think we should start archery," Henry whispered to Valmont after chapel one morning.

"Absolutely not," Valmont snarled, pulling Henry into a corner so that they wouldn't be overheard. "We've barely begun the broadsword."

"But the broadsword has a limited range," Henry argued.

"I thought we were following the book, Grim," Valmont retorted.

"We don't know how much time we have," Henry pressed. "We could be found out at any— Oh, no."

Frankie had caught sight of them. She flounced over in a horribly impractical dress composed mostly of ruffles.

"Be nice," Henry muttered to Valmont.

Frankie had been largely ignoring Henry and his friends ever since the incident in Professor Stratford's office, and the truth was, Henry had been so caught up with the battle society that he'd scarcely noticed her absence, although Adam was forever whining about how much he missed beating her at cards.

"Well, if it isn't the most popular boys in first year," said Frankie.

"I haven't a clue what you're talking about," Henry returned.

"Don't you?" Frankie asked, blinking her wide blue eyes at him, a picture of innocence. Henry realized with a sinking feeling that perhaps they weren't being as discreet about the battle society as he'd hoped.

"Er, how's your French coming?" Henry asked, trying to change the subject.

"I'm actually doing Greek," she said with a grin.

"Greek!" Valmont scoffed, and Henry elbowed him.

"She isn't really," Henry patiently explained. "She just wants you to say something horrible so she can feel superior. Isn't that right, Frankie?"

Frankie made a horrible face. "I'm not the one who has a problem with feeling superior," she shot back. "You two are hiding something, and I'm going to find out what it is."

"Ooh, I'm terrified," Valmont mocked.

"You should be," Frankie warned. Without giving either boy the chance to respond, she stomped away, leaving Henry to brood about her threat for the rest of the morning.

"Frankie thinks I'm hiding something," Henry complained to Adam as they slipped into their seats in Medicine.

"That's because you are," Adam whispered back.

"Should I be worried?" Henry asked.

"Nah." Adam wasn't very convincing.

Henry brooded some more as Sir Robert explained the purpose of a tourniquet and asked Conrad to help with the demonstration.

Conrad went pale. "Can you do someone else, sir?"

Sir Robert nodded. "Adam Beckerman, you're up, lad."

Adam gave a weak smile. "Don't suppose I could pass as well, sir?" he asked hopefully.

"Nonsense!" said Sir Robert. "Roll up a sleeve and get going. We haven't got all morning."

"Of course, sir," Adam said as he walked to the front of the room and rolled up his left sleeve. His arm was mottled with bruises, one of them a particularly lovely shade of mustard, the rest in varying tones of purple.

"What have you done to yourself, lad?" Sir Robert asked with genuine concern.

"I, er, tripped," Adam said.

Sir Robert didn't look for a moment as though he believed it. "The other arm, then," he said.

Adam rolled up his right sleeve. There was a large fading bruise along that forearm as well. "Cricket, sir," he said sheepishly.

Sir Robert shook his head and continued with his demonstration.

After the lesson Conrad caught up with Henry and Adam. "Sorry, Adam," Conrad said. "I was practicing extra falls last night, and my arms are frightful. He wouldn't have believed I'd tripped."

"I don't think he believed me, either," Adam said.

"Well, really," Henry admonished. "*Cricket?* No one's played in weeks. The grounds are covered in ice."

"Oh, right." Adam said.

Before the students knew it the half-term exams were upon them. Everyone crowded miserably into the library and hunched over thick stacks of notes, muttering terms and verbs and dates.

"What's an example of a passive periphrastic?" Adam whined.

Henry looked up from his protocol notes. "Sorry. What?"

"Passive periphrastic," Adam repeated.

"Er, how about *'Nordlands delenda est'*?" Henry suggested.

Across the table Derrick and Rohan collectively snorted into their own Latin books.

"I wish you'd stop making jokes in Latin," Adam muttered.

"Would you rather I made them in French?" Henry asked.

For a moment Adam thought Henry was being serious.

"Sorry," Henry said quickly. "But that was a real example. You can substitute any name. It's just the *'delenda est'* part that you need to know." He turned his attention back to his protocol notes and was trying to decipher a hastily scribbled line that couldn't possibly say something about fish custard—although it certainly looked as though it did—when a whispered argument broke out at a nearby table.

Theobold and Crowley were trying to get a look at Valmont's military history notes. "Bugger off!" Valmont whispered. "Look at your own notes."

"But yours are so much more complete," Theobold said with a grin. "I think we should trade."

"I don't," Valmont returned.

"Maybe you didn't hear what Theobold said," Crowley spat. "Hand them over."

"Go rot, Crowley," Valmont said, slamming his notebook.

Crowley looked furious, but Theobold merely held up a hand. "I don't know what's gotten into you lately, Fergus," Theobold said icily. "Maybe you want to call off our deal?"

"Maybe I do," Valmont muttered, but he sounded unsure.

"Don't be hasty now," Theobold said. "Think it over. You have until supper."

Crowley grinned and kicked the side of Valmont's chair with his boot. Valmont fumed silently.

When Henry crept down to the battle society room after supper for a spot of target practice, he found Valmont already in the room, landing blow after blow to the sack of flour they'd strung up as a makeshift punching bag.

The battle society was coming along better than Henry could have hoped. Meetings were far less formal now; students worked on archery, broadsword, or hand-to-hand combat as they chose. Gone were the easy nights in the common room, the free hours spent exploring the castle or watching cricket practice.

And when Henry did have a spare moment, he mostly used it to peruse the books he'd rescued along with *Pugnare*. One book in particular was filled with oddly useful tidbits. Henry was reading it the night before the military history exam when he came across a note on how coins could be used as throwing darts if their edges were sharpened against a whetstone.

"Hmmm," Henry said aloud.

"What?" Adam asked, looking up from his bed, where he was sprawled on his stomach and glaring at his military history notes.

"Nothing. Sorry," Henry muttered. He supposed he ought to be studying for Lord Havelock's examination, but he'd already memorized his notes, and anyway, there were only twenty minutes until lights-out.

He pulled on his boots.

Rohan glanced up from his desk, where he'd been sitting and writing out practice essays, an exercise that Henry considered unnecessarily torturous. "Going to practice?" Rohan asked with a frown.

Henry shook his head. "Kitchen."

"Bring me back something?" Adam asked hopefully.

Henry snorted.

"What do you want?"

"Another orange. I ate mine," Adam admitted.

"You're not supposed to eat them," Henry said.

"I was hungry," Adam protested.

Henry paused with his hand on the doorknob. "I'll see if they have something chocolatey as well," he said.

Adam grinned triumphantly.

The oranges had been Conrad's idea, actually. The fencing master at Easton had made the boys sit and manipulate oranges with their fencing hands as a way to strengthen their grips. Conrad had mentioned it in an offhand sort of way over lunch two days before, when everyone had been fretting over the languages exam.

The moment the exam had been over, Henry had gone to the kitchens and begged a bowl of oranges. He felt rather silly sitting and turning an orange around in circles, but it wasn't difficult to do while studying.

The kitchen, when he reached it, was freshly scrubbed, the lights dim. Liza sat with her stocking feet propped upon a stool, reading the *Tattleteller* and eating a chocolate biscuit with apparent relish.

"It's just me," Henry said, but Liza jumped anyway.

"Master Henry, you gave me a fright!" she said, putting her hand to her heart as though checking to make sure it hadn't quietly stopped working.

"I'm sorry," Henry apologized with a deep bow, knowing how much Liza enjoyed it. "I just came to see if you'd heard any more gossip—and to use the whetstone."

"O' course I heard more gossip. I'm always hearin' things. But what I'm hearin' ain't always worth repeatin'."

"Tell me the best of it, then," Henry said, locating the whetstone and taking a handful of pennies from his pocket.

Liza watched suspiciously as Henry wrapped a tea towel around his hand and began to sharpen one of the coins. "Wha's that for?"

"Er, extra credit for Medicine. It's just an experiment to do with, er, scalpel width," Henry fibbed, gingerly touching the edge of his sharpened coin. It drew blood.

"Oh," Liza said, suddenly disinterested. "Have you 'eard about the medical experiments?"

"Medical experiments?" Henry asked, sharpening another coin.

"In the Nordlands. People keep disappearin', an'

when they come back, they ain't right. They're missin' fingers or toes or worse."

"You think people are being kidnapped and experimented on in the Nordlands? Why would anyone do that?"

Liza took a bite of her biscuit and sighed with annoyance. "Ain't no need for a *reason*."

"Actually, there is," Henry argued. "Experiments have a *purpose*. Otherwise it's just torture." Henry carefully put the sharpened pennies into his pocket.

"Do you have any more oranges, Liza?" he asked.

Liza huffed and pretended to be annoyed, but told Henry he could help himself to the fruit in the larder. He took a few pieces and wrapped them in his blazer.

"An' you can take these back for yer friends," Liza said testily, handing Henry a stack of chocolate-covered biscuits.

"Thank you," Henry said.

"Get out of here," she muttered, but her frown quickly gave way to an indulgent grin.

Henry walked back down the darkened corridor with his armload of oranges and biscuits, hurrying because of lights-out. He wondered what made Liza so certain that the Nordlands were carrying out medical experiments.

Experiments needed motive; they were for building or developing something. Henry was suddenly reminded of the series of articles about the Nordlandic mental asylum and how the patients had been found with their tongues split down the middle—torture, or another medical experiment?

No. Henry shook his head and told himself to be reasonable. But the more that he thought about it, the less far-fetched it seemed that the Nordlands were working on something very sinister indeed.

"Caught you!" a voice called, and Henry nearly cried in fright before realizing that he wasn't doing anything wrong. He turned.

Frankie sat on the bench outside the archway to the first-year corridor, with a dark lantern at her side and a triumphant grin.

"Doing what?" Henry asked mildly.

"Sneaking," Frankie said. "I knew you were up to something, and I told you that I'd find out sooner or later."

"I wasn't sneaking," Henry said. "It isn't even lights-out."

At that moment Lord Havelock emerged from his room wearing a spectacularly mauve dressing gown emblazoned with golden lions. Henry gulped and squeezed himself onto the bench next to Frankie, hoping their head of year couldn't see around the corner.

"Shut your lights, gentlemen," Lord Havelock ordered, flipping the switch that dimmed the electric wall sconces in the corridor to a dull flicker.

Thankfully, their head of year disappeared back into his room. Henry breathed a sigh of relief. And then realized that he was sitting uncomfortably close to Frankie. In a dark hallway. Alone.

He scrambled to his feet and regarded Frankie coldly. She scowled up at him.

"I have to go," Henry said. "I have an exam in the morning."

"Not until you show me what you're hiding in your jacket," Frankie said, making a grab for Henry's school blazer. She caught the sleeve, and oranges bounced everywhere. The biscuits dropped to the floor and crumbled. Frankie turned bright red.

And then Lord Havelock's door opened.

"Quick!" Henry cried, pressing Frankie back onto the bench. Neither of them dared to breathe. Henry was suddenly quite aware that Frankie was—well, a girl. Their biggest problem wasn't being caught in the corridor after lights-out. It was being caught in the dark together on a bench.

Frankie clung to him, her eyes wide with fright.

After an eternity Lord Havelock's door creaked shut.

Henry breathed a sigh of relief, but he didn't feel relieved at all—he'd done nothing wrong. Frankie was forever getting him into trouble by acting as though she were one of the boys.

Henry shot Frankie a brutal glare and gathered the oranges. "Come on," he whispered, opening the door to his room.

Adam and Rohan were both in bed, although Adam was trying to study beneath the covers, which he'd pulled into a tent over his head.

"Frankie!" Rohan exclaimed, none too enthusiastically.

Adam emerged from the tent and waved hello. "Oh, good," he said cheerfully. "Are we friends again?"

"Definitely not," Henry said.

"Not a chance," Frankie retorted at the same moment.

"Two things," Henry told her. "The first is that I want an apology. You had absolutely no right. And the second is that you're leaving through the window. It'll only cause more trouble if you're caught wandering around the school corridors at this hour."

"Fine," Frankie mumbled. "I'm sorry. I made a mistake."

"Obviously," Henry said. "What did you *think* I was doing?"

"I don't know," Frankie muttered. "I thought— I—I'm sorry, all right?"

"I suppose," Henry said, shrugging.

Frankie boosted herself onto the window ledge. "Nice pajamas," she called, grinning at Rohan, who gave a long-suffering sigh.

"*Good night*, Frankie," Rohan said pointedly.

Frankie hopped out the window and then leaned her head back in. "One last thing," she said. "Just because you weren't sneaking tonight doesn't mean I was wrong about your sneaking."

14

THE UNFORGIVABLE
WORDS

*S*upper *the next evening felt like a celebration, as half-*
term exams were over. The tension that had built
over the previous two weeks magically evapo-
rated, leaving a gloriously free weekend in its wake.

Henry meant to shut himself in the now empty
library and finish translating *Pugnare* after supper. But
as he was leaving the dining hall, someone called his
name.

Professor Stratford was hurrying toward him across
the crowded dining hall.

"Hallo," Henry said, trying to calculate how many
weeks it had been since he'd paid his former tutor a visit.
Too many, he realized belatedly.

"Don't suppose you've forgotten about me?" Professor Stratford joked, but Henry wasn't fooled. He could see the professor was hurt, and he felt awful about it.

"Sorry," Henry muttered. "There were exams—"

"Oh, I know," Professor Stratford said dryly. "I haven't missed the celebrations."

Henry grinned. Peter had led some of the third years through a boisterous round of raunchy pub songs over supper until Sir Franklin had shushed them.

"I'd enjoy having you over for tea tomorrow afternoon," Professor Stratford persisted. "Bring your friends, if you'd like. New friends, even."

Henry's smile faded. How could he go to tea and lie to the professor about what he'd been up to? Because he certainly couldn't tell Professor Stratford that he and Valmont had been using a cache of weapons and gathering students to train in combat.

"I, er, don't think I can make it," Henry said miserably. "I'm, er, feeling ill. I should probably stay away. Wouldn't want you to catch it."

The professor frowned. "As you like. But if you feel better, I really am most curious to know how things are going."

Henry blanched. Did Professor Stratford suspect

something? *He must,* Henry thought as he muttered a flimsy excuse and left the dining hall, taking the corridor that led to the library.

Once he had settled into a seat in the abandoned library stacks, Henry considered confessing everything to Professor Stratford. After all, the professor was a friend. He doubted Professor Stratford would approve, but then, it wasn't as though the professor could reprimand Henry for the battle society. After all, the professor certainly believed that sinister things were happening up north, and had for some time. And he knew about what Henry had seen in the Nordlands, and about the slight but ultimately useless changes to the boys' curriculum. . . . Perhaps . . . No. Henry firmly pushed the thought away and opened his copy of *Pugnare,* feeling as though he had deeply disappointed Professor Stratford, and hoping that the damage wasn't permanent.

When Henry's vision began to blur from squinting at the pages of *Pugnare,* he put the book back into his satchel and made his way down to the basement, keen to clear the Latin from his head with some target practice, and maybe to try out his new penny darts.

Henry had taken to the bow and arrow in a way he'd never expected; archery cleared his head somehow and made everything simpler. There was less to concentrate on—just his form and his breathing and the target. It wasn't nearly as exhilarating as fencing, but he preferred it that way. It was easier to imagine an opponent than to see one rushing toward you with a blade poised for attack.

Henry opened the door to the basement and then paused at the top of the landing, listening. Someone was already down there.

"Valmont? Conrad?" he called, as they were the most likely suspects. Everyone else would be off enjoying the freedom of the night after exams.

And then someone yelled out as though in pain. Henry's heart pounded. "Are you all right?" Henry shouted, taking the stairs two at a time.

The basement came into view, and he stopped and stared.

Frankie stood calmly in the center of the room, holding their best broadsword. She made a fairly decent pass with the weapon and grinned at Henry.

"Oh, help! Help!" she called, throwing in a fake gasp for effect.

"Very funny," Henry said sourly. "What are you doing here?"

"Followed Conrad after supper and waited until he left," she bragged. "I knew you lot were up to something, and now you *have* to let me join in or I'll tell."

"You're not joining," Henry said, clenching his fists.

"Yes, I am," Frankie insisted.

"This isn't a few of my friends having a laugh," Henry retorted. "There are more than thirty of us. Second and third years, even. I'm sorry, but they'll never agree."

"How do *you* know?" Frankie shot back. "It isn't as though you're in charge."

Henry bit his lip. Frankie stared at Henry in surprise.

"You *are* in charge."

"Maybe," Henry said coolly. "Maybe Peter Merrill is, or Geoffrey Sutton. That is, if they're even members."

"Oh, is it a secret society now?" Frankie retorted. "How adorable."

"You're just jealous."

"Why would I be jealous?" Frankie shot back. "You're the ones who are going to die in a war."

Henry winced.

Frankie's eyes widened as though she'd immediately

regretted saying it, but too late, the words were out there, floating dangerously.

"I'm sorry," she muttered, dropping the broadsword, which clattered noisily onto the stone floor.

"Be careful with that," Henry snapped, retrieving the weapon. "It's an antique."

They regarded each other, Henry standing there holding the sword, Frankie nearly in tears. "What happened?" Frankie managed. "How did things get so . . ."

"Complicated?" Henry supplied.

Miserably Frankie nodded. And with tears spilling down her cheeks, she fled.

Henry watched her go. And then he looked down at the sword he was carrying. When it came to weapons, he thought sadly, sometimes words could be just as hurtful, and just as forbidden.

Adam congratulated himself on successfully begging the last of the chocolate biscuits off Liza. He crammed one into his mouth as he left the kitchens.

"Hmmpgluhh!" Adam called, spotting Frankie coming the opposite direction down the main hallway. He'd meant to say hello, but coherent speech is considerably difficult when one's mouth is full.

Frankie didn't say hello back. In fact, she looked horribly upset.

Adam swallowed thickly. "Er, Frankie?"

She glanced up, and Adam could see that she'd been crying. "What?" Frankie asked, giving him a fierce glare.

"Are you all right?"

"No, I am *not* all right. I loathe being stuck at a *boys'* school."

"Technically you don't go here," Adam said helpfully. Her expression plainly showed that it had been the wrong thing to say.

"You're right. I don't. And clearly no one wants me around."

"Well, I do."

Frankie laughed. "You don't count."

"Oi, how come I never count?" Adam asked indignantly.

"Because you're *part* of it," Frankie accused. "You and Henry and *Valmont*, I'm sure of it. Oh, I could just scream."

Before Adam had a chance to react, she flounced away, sniffling. "Girls," Adam muttered, shaking his head and cramming another biscuit into his mouth.

They were absolutely impossible. Always talking nonsense and getting upset without bothering to explain the problem.

Adam munched the third biscuit slowly, making it last. He'd seen Henry go off to the library after supper. How anyone could spend that much time studying when they already knew all of the answers was completely beyond him. Maybe Henry knew what was the matter with Frankie. And even if he didn't, he probably wouldn't mind the interruption.

But when Adam reached the library, Sir Robert was just leaving, his arms full of books.

"A good evening to you, Mr. Beckerman."

"Good evening, sir," Adam said. "Er, would you like help with those books?"

Sir Robert smiled. "That would be most welcome. Walk with me, lad."

Sir Robert's cane was glossy mahogany that evening, with a brass handle shaped like a dragon. It tapped an echoing staccato down the hallway as they made their way to his office. Adam was so busy admiring the cane that he hardly heard what the professor was saying.

"I'm sorry, sir?"

"I was just saying that Sir Franklin speaks very highly

of you. He says you have a natural talent for ethics."

"Thank you, sir," Adam said, flushing from the unexpected compliment.

Sir Robert didn't say anything else as they crossed the quadrangle.

To Adam's dismay, Sir Robert had taken over Sir Frederick's former office. Thankfully, though, the office had been transformed. The shelves were crammed with brass scales, pots of paint, and jars of strange powders. A marble bust of King Victor wore Sir Robert's fake mustache—and sported an elegant silk top hat tilted at a rakish angle. A large desk was littered with sheet music, rumpled newspapers, and a rather battered violin.

Making a face at the mess, the medicine master removed a violin bow from one of the chairs and tossed it into a nearby umbrella stand. "Sit, sit," he said, motioning toward the chair. "If you don't mind, I'd quite like to have a little chat."

Adam frowned as he took a seat. Professors rarely wanted to speak with him. His marks were average, his penmanship sloppy, and the cleverer students like Henry and Derrick usually beat him to answering the questions he did know.

"No, sir, I don't mind," Adam said.

"I haven't been able to forget those bruises on your arms the other week," Sir Robert remarked, and although his tone was pleasant, his eyes were sharp. "They didn't look as though you'd tripped."

"I did, sir."

Sir Robert shook his head. "Let us be *honest*, Mr. Beckerman. The coloration, size, and placement of those bruises are not consistent with *tripping*." Sir Robert paused and raised an eyebrow. "I would deduce that you had been in a fight and taken repeated falls—very neatly, I'll credit. You distributed your weight over the forearms quite correctly."

Adam turned crimson. "But—" Sir Robert had it all wrong, Adam thought wretchedly. He tried again. "But, sir, I haven't been in a fight. I was, er, practicing. Just in case."

Sir Robert gave him a very severe look. "Practicing for fights? Someone must have threatened you quite roughly, to prompt that."

"Oh, not at all, sir," Adam quickly amended. "I'm always talking without thinking. Bound to put my foot in it one day, you know."

But the medicine master didn't look convinced. Adam nervously reached for the charm around his neck—a cheap Whitechapel Market replacement of the heirloom *chai* he used to wear.

"Hmmm," Sir Robert said. "I've seen you taking notes in class, lad, with your pen poised over the right side of the page. You studied at the yeshiva, I presume? Reading the Torah and the Talmud?"

Miserably Adam nodded.

"Your English is quite good," Sir Robert remarked, watching Adam carefully. "Perfect, in fact. I'd place the dialect as East London."

"Baker's Green, sir," Adam mumbled, nodding. "And we speak English at home, not Yiddish. Please, sir, you've got the wrong idea. No one is giving me a hard time about anything."

"Not even your roommate, whom I seem to remember sporting a black eye and a split lip earlier this term?" Sir Robert asked mildly. "Possibly your doing?"

"Henry? He's my best friend! We were, er, practicing for fights together."

"Ah, then it seems I'm mistaken," Sir Robert said, inclining his head in apology but keeping his eyes trained on Adam. "Although I can't imagine where you learned that falling technique. Or what possibly prompted the two of you to practice it quite so . . . thoroughly."

Adam sighed. He'd just *had* to go see what Henry was up to in the library. And although Sir Robert was clearly just trying to be sympathetic, the new medicine master was far too observant for comfort.

"Just a bit of fun," Adam said unconvincingly. "And Theobold hates us on principle, so you never know when it could turn out useful."

Sir Robert raised an eyebrow and steepled his long, pale fingers. "I was at your expulsion hearing, you know," he said.

"I remember, sir." Adam dropped his gaze and began to fidget nervously.

"Perhaps I've been paying attention to such things because I was most interested in what you said about the Nordlands," Sir Robert continued. "It takes extraordinary bravery to tell an adult something they don't want to hear, especially when there is little chance of being believed."

Adam continued to fidget with the tassels of his scarf, unsure of how to respond.

"Do you have family in the Nordlands?" Sir Robert inquired.

"Cousins." He hadn't told anyone, and instantly regretted the confession. "We don't really— I mean, it's difficult to know how they're doing, since Chancellor Mors stopped letting post through the border."

"But probably not well," Sir Robert finished.

"Probably not well," Adam agreed. "But that can be said about anyone who doesn't fit the chancellor's idea of 'pure Nordlandic stock.' I mean, it's bloody horrible up there, sir. Doesn't matter if you're Jewish or believe in the thirtieth flying prophet or have skin the color of cabbage."

"Do you know what I think, Mr. Beckerman?" Sir Robert mused. "I think you are going to be a very unusual knight, and I also think that there's no possible way you and Mr. Grim were practicing to fight anyone at this school. You carry the marks of rebellion, boy. Hide them well, and cover your tracks. Something to think about, hmmm? Now off with you."

When Adam returned to his room, Henry was just unpacking his satchel.

"Where's Rohan?" Adam asked.

"Common room," Henry said, and then looked up and caught Adam's expression. "What's wrong?"

"Sir Robert wanted to have a talk with me." Adam made a face. "Seemed to think I was a long way from the yeshiva and getting beaten up by my classmates."

"Beaten up?"

"The bruises. You know." Adam shrugged. "But now I think he's on to us, with the battle society. I think he's glad."

"Glad?" Henry kicked off his boots and flopped onto his bed, not bothering to remove his jacket or tie. The commotion in the common room seeped through their door, filling the silence.

"He's a strange bloke, that Sir Robert. I think he wants to help."

"Well, he can't," Henry said sourly. "And we don't need a mentor. Remember what happened last time?"

"Sir Robert isn't Sir Frederick."

"For all that *we* know," Henry said darkly.

"He was concerned!" Adam shot back. "My arms were all banged up. He just wanted to make sure I wasn't being bullied."

"Or so he said."

"Oi, what is your *problem* right now?"

"Nothing. Sorry." Henry ran a hand over his face. "Frankie. I don't know. Nothing."

"What *about* Frankie? Is that why she was crying?"

"She was crying?" Henry asked.

"Why, what did you say to her?" Adam asked suspiciously.

"Nothing! It's what *she* said to *me*. I found her down in the basement, swinging around a broadsword."

Adam snorted. "You're joking."

"Wish I were," Henry said. "She'd followed Conrad and wanted to join the battle society. I told her she couldn't."

"Why'd you say that?" Adam asked indignantly.

"Because she can't!"

"I bet no one would mind. And she's bloody good with a sword."

"With a *foil*," Henry returned. "She'd get in more trouble than the rest of us if she joined, and really, who would throw punches or swing a sabre at Headmaster Winter's sixteen-year-old daughter?"

"So you told her no."

"Of course I told her no. And then she told me that we were all going to die in a war," Henry said sourly.

Adam winced. "I think I liked it better when she climbed through our window with cake wanting to play cards," he reflected.

"I did too, but Rohan seems to think we're getting too old for that sort of thing."

"What does age matter?" Adam retorted. "Boys of thirteen used to be drafted to fight, if you haven't forgotten."

Henry went pale. "What did you say?"

"Nothing," Adam muttered.

"No. You said that boys of thirteen used to be drafted to fight," Henry said, his voice rising excitedly.

"Well, *you* said it after the Inter-School Tournament." Adam shrugged. "Something about no one having changed the conscription laws. Although they'll probably want to fight anyway. I mean, just think of Ollie."

Henry cringed at the memory of the scrawny serving boy mopping the corridor with one hand pressed against his cracked ribs.

"I *am*," Henry said. "Don't you see? That law can be changed. It has nothing to do with combat training or the Nordlands. It's simply an outdated piece of legislature, left over from the days when boys in the slums were lucky to see eighteen."

"Yeah, well, it's not exactly easy to change a law, mate," Adam reminded him.

"Conrad's father is the Lord Minister of Ways and Means," Henry pressed. "If Conrad could make him listen—just think of the good it would do!"

Henry's mind raced with the implications of what it would mean to change the conscription laws—everyone's little brothers safe at home and away from whatever was coming. No knights knocking on doors and taking away schoolboys who still played marbles, handing them swords and telling them to kill grown men.

"Conrad's father barely speaks with him. He's too important or busy or something," Adam said, and then he saw the look on Henry's face. "It's worth a try, though."

Henry gave Adam a grateful smile. "It would be so nice," Henry said tiredly, "to see some good news in the papers. To have a cause to celebrate even the smallest thing."

Until that moment Henry hadn't considered what it meant to be a Knightley student. He'd thought only of war and fighting, not of command. But they *would* be commanding common boys, the same way that police knights directed the common policemen. In a war they'd be ordering squadrons of little Ollies to march bravely to their deaths.

The weight of the last few weeks pressed down on him, and he was suddenly exhausted. Henry shielded his eyes with his forearm, lying there on top of his covers, thinking of conscription laws and boys like Alex from the bakery who hero-worshipped Knightley students, and of Frankie wielding a broadsword as though she thought that if she asked nicely, she too could play.

15

TAKING
THE FALL

Henry dreaded the next meeting of the battle society. All through drills he barely listened to Conrad's orders and nearly marched straight into James's back. During Protocol, he used the wrong form of address to a hypothetical foreign diplomat. And he only just caught a glaring translation error in languages as he was about to turn in the assignment.

Henry's mind was in a lot of places, but mostly he was distracted by worries. What if Frankie showed up at the meeting? What if his idea of changing the conscription laws was met with stony silence? But he kept these fears to himself, and they worried away at him, snatching his attention from whatever task was at hand.

He supposed he could have spoken with Conrad privately, but everyone had seemed so elated to be rid of exams, and he hadn't wanted to mar their celebrations. So he had sat and fretted quietly and studied in vain and tried not to think about how, on top of it all, he was also avoiding Professor Stratford.

It seemed the battle society meeting had scarcely begun when Henry glanced at his pocket watch to find that curfew had come and gone and midnight was fast approaching. The boys began to gather their things, and Henry briefly debated not mentioning it, but as Valmont gathered his satchel, Henry finally gathered his courage.

"Er, sorry," he said.

A few boys glanced over.

"Sorry," Henry said again, this time louder. "I was just wondering whether any of you lot have given much thought to the conscription laws?"

"Ancient history," Peter called, cracking his knuckles in a way that made Edmund shudder.

"Actually, mate, they're not," Adam corrected.

Now everyone was staring curiously at Henry. "It occurred to me," Henry continued, "that if—er, when—we go to war with the Nordlands, everyone over the age of thirteen will be required to fight."

"Thirteen?" Geoffrey scoffed. "I have a brother who's twelve. He comes up to my waist."

"Here's the other thing," Henry pressed. "Laws can be changed. I can think of a few students who wouldn't be here if change were impossible, myself included. So there's no reason why the conscription laws can't be abolished. I just know that year sevens shouldn't be made to kill grown men, especially without training."

"So why do we have these laws in the first place?" Luther asked.

"They've been around for hundreds of years," Derrick said, shaking his head. "Boys used to be apprenticed off at eleven or twelve to ancient knights. They already had combat training by thirteen, and were entering tournaments to fight one another for fun."

"Glad I wasn't alive back then," Rohan muttered.

Henry snorted. Secretly he agreed. Because from what he'd learned translating *Pugnare* and paging through the other books he'd found in the forgotten classroom, ancient knights had fared far worse than their modern counterparts.

"I only brought it up," Henry continued, "because I thought it was important. We should be able to discuss things here. After all, battles aren't won by skill but by strategy."

"My strategy is to *be* skilled," Jasper called jokingly, making a neat pass with a broadsword.

"This isn't a joke," Derrick said to Jasper. "Henry's right about that law needing to change. I have a younger brother as well. I don't want any of you lot handing him a crossbow in the near future—or any Partisan students aiming one in his direction."

"It's a dashed good idea," Conrad piped up, and everyone turned, knowing that it was Conrad's father who needed to be convinced. "But it won't work. My father wouldn't listen. And even if he did, changing an ancient and technically useless law without reason isn't exactly a priority at the Ministerium. Not to mention that we need the support of a majority of the House of Lord Ministers to have the law brought up for review. Getting enough signatures could take ages."

Henry's spirits fell. He'd been so certain that this was one thing they could really do—that finally the headlines would speculate on something good for a change. But he hadn't thought about getting signatures, or any of the procedures involved in changing a law. It was far more complicated than he'd imagined.

Everyone drifted out of the basement training room a little less hopeful than before. What good was learning to fight if they were going to lead one another's younger brothers and cousins onto the battlefield?

Henry gathered the sabres and waved good-bye to the other battle society members, wondering bitterly if it was even worth trying. He asked Adam as much while they gave the room a final sweep for armory blades.

"It's always worth trying if you feel strongly enough," Adam said, shifting his armload of sabres. "That's why we took the Knightley Exam, isn't it?"

"I suppose," Henry said, unconvinced.

And then a deep voice made them stop cold.

"Francesca?"

Henry and Adam exchanged a look of panic before realizing that they were halfway down the corridor from the stairwell to the armory door and had nowhere to hide. *Please be Professor Stratford,* Henry thought desperately.

But it wasn't. Headmaster Winter, in his dressing gown and worn-through bedroom slippers, had reached the top of the stairs. He frowned at Henry and Adam in the feeble circle of light from his lantern.

"Ah," Headmaster Winter said unhappily. "You two."

Henry gulped. Adam cursed under his breath.

"Good evening, sir," Henry mumbled.

"If you'd be good enough to return those sabres to the armory," the headmaster said mildly, "I'll be here when you return."

Numbly Henry and Adam pushed open the door to the armory.

"Bloody hell," Adam whispered as they opened the weapons cabinet. "We're in for it."

"No, *we're* not," Henry whispered fiercely. "*I'm* the one who started this. Just agree to whatever I say, and you'll be fine."

"Absolutely not," Adam protested. "I'm just as guilty as you are. I've been hauling weapons all over the school."

"Well, we can't tell him that!" Henry returned.

"Boys?" the headmaster called. "I think you've had enough time to put those blades back in their proper place."

"Yes, sir," they chorused miserably, shuffling back into the corridor where Headmaster Winter was waiting at the top of the stairwell.

No one said anything on the way to the headmaster's office.

The silence remained as Henry and Adam nervously settled onto the sofa across from the headmaster's desk, extracting a rather horrible piece of orange knitting that had wedged itself between the cushions. Henry gingerly placed the knitting onto an arm of the sofa and tried not to despair at what was to come.

Headmaster Winter smiled sadly. "Not the most innocent of circumstances in which to be caught out of bed after lights-out."

"No, sir," Henry and Adam mumbled.

The headmaster leaned back in his chair and scratched thoughtfully at his patchy beard. "I don't suppose there's a truthful explanation either of you boys would be willing to share?"

Henry and Adam exchanged a glance, and then shook their heads.

"Hypothetically, sir," Adam piped up, "we might have found the sabres sitting somewhere and then decided to return them to the armory."

Henry elbowed him.

"If that were the case," Headmaster Winter continued, the corners of his mouth twitching with amusement, "you boys would be commended for your chivalrous efforts."

Adam went smug.

"However." The headmaster paused, letting the word linger in the air. "It would also make necessary a thorough investigation into what, exactly, is happening at my school. Because I would clearly have no idea."

Henry blanched. They were already done for, he realized. Nothing good could come from this conversation. They'd been caught out of bed after lights-out, their arms full of school property. And it wasn't as though this were their first offense. Even worse, no one was out to get them, as the case had been last term.

No, they'd blatantly disregarded the Code of Chivalry, even if it had been for a good reason. The least they could do, Henry thought dejectedly, was tell the headmaster the truth.

"You're right, sir," Henry said bravely. "We didn't find the sabres. I borrowed them because I wanted to learn how to fight."

"With a dozen blades? Sounds more like you were practicing to join the circus as a juggler."

Henry's cheeks went red.

"Well, the idea became, er, popular," Adam confessed.

"How popular?" Headmaster Winter asked.

"About a quarter of the school," Adam admitted.

Headmaster Winter's eyebrows shot up. "Really?" he mused. "A quarter of the school?"

"More now," Adam said, and Henry realized with

a start that Adam was right. There were thirty-one of them.

"Well, that is certainly curious," Headmaster Winter said thoughtfully. "Although I'm not sure what, exactly, so many boys were aiming to learn by practicing with only a dozen sabres."

"We had other equipment," Henry admitted. "We found some old trunks full of neglected, er, things."

For some reason Henry couldn't bring himself to be the first one to say "weapons" or "combat." Not when the headmaster was avoiding the words so deliberately. Neither of them quite dared to admit what the boys had been doing, because that was the same as acknowledging what exactly was at stake.

"Ah," Headmaster Winter said, his tone still light and informal. "I had suspected there might be some antiques sitting around the castle."

Henry frowned. The headmaster wasn't just avoiding the words, but also the accusation. By all rights Headmaster Winter should have been furious, but he wasn't even upset. A small part of Henry hoped that perhaps they wouldn't be expelled after all.

"It isn't that I *don't* approve of such late-night activities," the headmaster continued, "but that I *can't* express my approval, because that would mean I not only knew what you boys were doing, but that I allowed such things at my school. Do you understand?"

"I think so, sir," Henry said, and he was beginning to understand what else the headmaster deliberately wasn't saying.

"Yes, we'll stop, er, hypothetically having late-night sabre tournaments," Adam put in.

Henry kicked him.

"A quarter of the school," the headmaster repeated, half to himself, and then his contemplative expression was replaced with one of anguish. "I don't suppose my daughter has been a part of this?"

"No, sir," Henry said. "Never."

"Is that why you were looking for her?" Adam asked.

Henry stared at Adam in surprise. He'd forgotten, but that was right. The headmaster *had* been looking for Frankie.

"It is," Headmaster Winter said gravely. "Francesca has made herself and a few of her belongings scarce."

Henry and Adam exchanged a look of shock. Frankie was missing? No, not missing. She'd run off—without saying good-bye.

The headmaster massaged his temples and shook his

head, as though finally defeated by Frankie's misbehavior. "I'm sorry, boys. I just can't summon the requisite anger to deal with you two at the moment. Come and see me tomorrow after your lessons. We'll all fare better when we've had some sleep—and some answers."

"Yes, sir," Henry and Adam mumbled, rising to their feet.

"One more thing," the headmaster said, his tone sharp. "You wouldn't happen to know anything about Francesca's latest stunt, would you?"

"No, sir," Henry said truthfully.

"Not me," Adam said.

"If I find out that you're lying about this—," the headmaster threatened.

"Please, sir," Henry broke in. "We've barely spoken with her in weeks."

The headmaster scrutinized Henry and decided he was telling the truth. "Off to bed with you," he said gruffly. "And don't forget to see me the moment your lessons are through."

"We won't, sir," Henry promised.

When they were safely in the corridor, Henry glared. "Did you have to say that?"

"Say what?" Adam asked innocently.

"Any of it." Henry shook his head.

"Well, I didn't know Frankie was missing!" Adam said. "I'm worried. What if she's run off to become a stage performer or something?"

"I expect she'd be much happier than she was here," Henry said bitterly. It was strange, how knowing that Frankie might have run off without saying good-bye had left him feeling hollow, as though she'd secretly packed a piece of him in her bags.

"Maybe we can find her," Adam joked. "Once we're expelled and shunned from polite society for our grievous rule-breaking ways."

Henry didn't say anything more until they'd reached the dormitory. He was too busy thinking about Frankie, and wondering what had finally driven her to run off.

Rohan was awake, pacing the room in candlelight, his arms folded across the front of his silk dressing gown. "Where were you?" he snapped. "I was worried!"

"Er," Henry and Adam said, neither wanting to be the one to admit what had happened.

"I knew it!" Rohan cried sanctimoniously once Henry had finished explaining what had happened. "I knew it was a bad idea."

"It was a good idea," Henry argued. "And I don't

think we're going to get expelled. I mean, there are thirty-one of us."

"No, there are *two*," Rohan said primly. "You and Valmont. And you better not take the fall for that insufferable butt trumpet."

Adam snickered at the phrase "insufferable butt trumpet" but was met with such a stern glare from Rohan that his grin quickly faded.

"Sorry," Adam muttered.

"I'm not taking the fall for anyone," Henry said. And then, because he couldn't resist, he said, "No matter how insufferably their butts might trumpet. Is that the right grammar? I'm rubbish with the conditional."

Adam dissolved into hastily stifled laughter. Even Rohan's frown threatened to disappear.

"I don't think the headmaster was upset," Henry persisted. "I know that he was distracted because of Frankie, but even so, he said that he couldn't *be seen* approving, not that he didn't approve."

"If the headmaster wasn't upset, that's even more worrying," Rohan said with a frown.

"*He's* the one who prompted this," Henry said, "hiring Admiral Blackwood to teach us 'flag twirling,' and talking about defying authority in his welcome speech."

"Next you'll say he prompted Frankie to run off as well," Rohan said, and sniffed.

"No," Henry said darkly, "that was me." After all, Frankie had been talking of joining the battle society. It was only after Henry had refused that she'd run off. And he didn't completely blame her for wanting to leave. It couldn't be easy, watching her friends find their place at school, making friends with their classmates while she was stuck with a chaperone, learning embroidery.

Henry felt horrible, replaying all of their squabbling that term, from that ill-fated suitor's bow to Frankie's lying in wait outside the first-year corridor, determined to catch him sneaking.

"I hate to be the one to say it," Rohan said, "but perhaps it's for the best that Frankie has run off."

"Watch it, mate," Adam warned.

"She's scandalized herself now, and frankly it's a relief. None of us will have to carry the blame for ruining her reputation."

"No," Henry muttered. "We'll have to carry the guilt for driving her to do it."

"Speak for yourself," Rohan said primly. "I never gave her the impression that I wished us to be friends."

"That's rubbish, and you know it," Adam said. "You

begged her to help pull a prank on Valmont last term."

Rohan's cheeks colored. "I'm going to bed," he huffed, pulling back the covers, lying down, and clamping his pillow over his head, effectively ending the discussion.

❖ 16 ❖

A QUESTION
UNASKED

Alll through chapel the next morning, Henry couldn't
shake the thought that he was forgetting something important. It wasn't until he wrote the
date at the top of his notes in military history that Henry
realized it was his birthday. He was fifteen.

Lord Havelock was talking about germ warfare, and
how early colonists had given native populations blankets that carried diseases, under the guise of giving presents. "Military technology need not be sophisticated,"
Lord Havelock said. "It need only be innovative. Anything can be a weapon if its effect is harmful enough."

Derrick raised his hand, and Lord Havelock stopped
talking, as though unsure what was happening; it was

rare for anyone to ask a question in Lord Havelock's class.

"Yes, Marchbanks?"

"Well, sir, I was wondering if you truly believe that. For example, can newspapers be weapons? Or what about laws?"

Lord Havelock shot Derrick a Havelook of Doom. "That is a stupid question, boy. Mr. Grim, please explain to Mr. Marchbanks why I shall not deign to answer his inquiry."

Henry gulped. "Er, well," he spluttered. "We're talking about military technology, correct? So newspapers and laws might have a harmful effect, but they're not run by any, er, wartime authorities, so they can't be considered military technology."

"Passable, Grim," Lord Havelock said.

Derrick shrugged and returned to sketching a caricature of Lord Havelock as a vampire bat, which he and Conrad were passing back and forth beneath the table.

But before Lord Havelock could resume his lecture, Adam raised his hand. Lord Havelock's mouth twisted into a scowl. "You'll have to hold it, Beckerman," he snapped. "I do hope it isn't an emergency."

Adam blushed. "I wasn't asking to use the toilet."

"No?" Lord Havelock asked disdainfully.

"No, sir," Adam said. "I just wanted to point out that in the Nordlands, Chancellor Mors runs the newspapers and makes the laws. So, well, in the Nordlands, Derrick would be right, and they *could* be considered military technology."

Everyone gaped at Adam, who was forever giving the wrong answer or forgetting his textbook.

For a moment Lord Havelock had no response, and then he cleared his throat, shuffled his lecture notes, and said, "Obviously."

Adam's smugness on the matter carried on through fencing, where he offered to have a go against James St. Fitzroy, who admittedly beat him, but only by one touch.

Henry originally fenced with Conrad, but for the second bout he partnered with Valmont for the first time since they'd begun the battle society. They hadn't fenced foil against each other in ages.

Henry made sure his mask was fastened tightly as he returned Valmont's salute and took his guard on the opposite end of the piste.

Valmont shot forward with a feint, which Henry anticipated.

Henry tried to free his sword to the outside, but Valmont was expecting this and executed an overhead block at precisely the right moment.

Henry shook his head as he pulled back, surprised at how in tune he and Valmont were with each other's fencing styles. Taking a deep breath, Henry tried a short lunge with a forward recovery, followed by a *coupé*. They'd just taught the same move to the battle society two meetings before.

Their blades locked again, and without thinking Henry disarmed Valmont, sending Valmont's foil into the air. Henry caught it neatly, choked up on the foible, and presented it back to Valmont grip first. It wasn't until Valmont pushed up his visor as he accepted the blade, his expression full of warning, that Henry realized they'd gained an audience.

"Quite an interesting show, Mr. Grim, Mr. Valmont," the fencing master said, raising an eyebrow.

Henry bit his lip. "Sorry," he apologized, and then scrambled for an explanation. "We were just talking about the theory behind disarming during lunch."

"I was referring to your pattern there, the short lunge and *coupé*. Would you mind demonstrating it for the class?"

Henry shook his head and adjusted his mask. He

performed the move again, with Valmont making the necessary blocks.

"I'd like you all to try that," the fencing master called, addressing the class. "As an exercise. Partners facing the mirror will lead. Don't expect to have it on the first try, now."

The pairs of students adjusted their distances accordingly and did as the fencing master asked.

Henry shot Valmont a brief but uneasy glance as the eighteen members of the battle society in first year—discounting Henry and Valmont—executed the move perfectly. The fencing master stared as though unable to believe what he was seeing. He shook his head as if to clear it.

"Can I have that again?" he asked weakly.

Again, nine of the pairs performed the maneuver flawlessly. Theobold, who'd always had trouble with forward recovery, threw down his mask and glowered. "Impossible," he muttered to Crowley, with an accusing glare in Henry and Valmont's direction.

When classes were done for the day, Henry and Adam returned to the headmaster's office.

Henry knocked, but no one opened the door. He

knocked again, this time louder. Still no answer.

"Do you reckon he's forgotten about us?" Adam asked brightly.

"He's not *that* scatterbrained." Henry sighed. "I suppose we could wait here."

"In the corridor?"

Henry shrugged. What else could they do?

Thankfully, Headmaster Winter rounded the corner at that moment. He wore his best suit and a remarkably crisp cravat. Walking alongside him was a tall perpetually startled-looking gentleman in a somber black suit, a notebook tucked under his arm. Headmaster Winter paused halfway down the corridor to finish his discussion, and Henry overheard the name Lord Priscus and something about Throgmorten Hall before the headmaster bade farewell to his companion and hurried the rest of the way down the corridor.

"Sorry, boys," the headmaster called in a way that suggested he'd endured quite an exhausting afternoon. "Quite a full afternoon, you know. Running a bit behind, but it couldn't be helped. You should have let yourselves in."

"Into your office, sir?" Henry said with a frown. "It didn't seem right, since you're supposed to be punishing us for theft."

"Eh?" Headmaster Winter said distractedly. "Ah, right. That. You boys had better come inside." A collection of teacups and saucers had gathered on the headmaster's desk overnight, and sure enough, Henry could make out faint purplish bruises beneath the headmaster's eyes, betraying his lack of sleep.

"Have you found Frankie, sir?" Adam asked as he and Henry took seats on the sofa.

"Not yet," the headmaster said with a forlorn sigh. "And it's really the worst possible time for her to pull a stunt like this."

"I'm sorry, sir," Henry said. "I hope you find her soon."

"As do I," Headmaster Winter replied. "But the matter at hand is not Francesca, but what, exactly, I'm to do with the two of you."

"A crime without a victim is a crime best overlooked?" Adam suggested.

Henry elbowed him. The headmaster regarded them sternly.

"Sorry, sir," they mumbled.

"As I see it," said Headmaster Winter, "since the sabres were put back with no harm done, you boys were simply caught wandering the corridors after curfew.

Unfortunately, as first years, this is an expellable offense. The final decision shall be made by your head of year."

"It's up to Lord Havelock?" Henry asked despairingly. Well, he thought, this was it. They were done for. Because Henry remembered all too well his run-in with Lord Havelock at Grandmother Winter's holiday party, and Lord Havelock's subsequent warning for Henry to stay out of trouble.

Perhaps if he explained that Valmont had been part of it . . . No, he couldn't. Betraying the battle society for leniency was the same as declaring their preparations for war nothing more than a game. The battle society was worth more than a shot at keeping his place at Knightley.

An impatient knock sounded on the door of the headmaster's office. "Come in," Headmaster Winter called.

The door burst open to reveal Lord Havelock, wearing his best pin-striped suit without his master's gown. He brandished a handful of telegrams and an air of dreadful news.

"Ah, Magnus," Headmaster Winter said. "What news?"

"The Nordlandic envoy is short-staffed," Lord Havelock reported, as though Henry and Adam weren't in the room at all, "and it is doubtful that suitable replacements can be found in time. Mr. Frist neglected to consider the servants' absurd superstitions, and the date has them all seeing death omens in the tea."

"Yes, yes, beware the ides of March and all that," Headmaster Winter said with a dismissive wave of his hand. "This certainly is a problem."

"It would be a grave misstep for the envoy to leave without a proper serving staff," Lord Havelock continued. "I'm certain Yascherov would be all too eager to lend us a few of his own loyal young men." Lord Havelock's tone conveyed what an utter disaster that would be.

Headmaster Winter frowned. "How long do we have to find replacements?" Lord Winter asked.

"The envoy leaves at dawn tomorrow. The train is scheduled to depart Avel-on-t'Hems at six exactly."

"Perhaps," Headmaster Winter mused, "there are a few serving boys at the school whom no one has thought to ask." The headmaster's gaze fell upon Henry, and Henry's eyes widened, wondering if the headmaster meant him. But no, that was absurd.

"Er, should we go, sir?" Adam mumbled, fiddling with the strap on his satchel. Henry stared at him in surprise. "Into the corridor to let you and Lord Havelock speak in private, I mean?"

"Yes, perhaps it would be best if you boys returned to your dormitory," Headmaster Winter said distractedly, his attention going back to Lord Havelock. "Has Mr. Frist inquired down in the village for boys?"

Adam opened his mouth as if to ask another question, but then thought better of it and shouldered his satchel instead. Henry followed Adam out of the headmaster's office past Lord Havelock, who shot the boys a withering glare before slamming the door behind them.

"Let's go," Henry muttered, trying to ignore the muffled but insistent rise and fall of voices coming from behind the closed door.

As they walked toward the quadrangle, a burst of hesitant late-afternoon sunshine made the cold air unexpectedly bearable. Henry noticed with surprise that the skeletal trees were coming back to life, proudly displaying tiny green buds and freshly sprouted leaves. Had winter truly passed without his noticing?

Adam pushed up the sleeves of his jacket and squinted up at the sky. "Why aren't we in trouble?"

"I don't know," Henry said. "I think the headmaster's distracted by a lot of things at the moment."

"Such as Lord Priscus being here, you mean," Adam muttered.

Henry frowned.

"The last headmaster," Adam explained. "Ancient bloke. James mentioned it during fencing."

"Hmmm," Henry said, processing this new piece of information. "I suppose. Maybe he's here for that envoy Headmaster Winter was talking about."

They passed the rock garden and neared the quadrangle, where a crowd of third years were enthusiastically playing cricket in the patchy sunshine. Stephen, who was in the battle society, caught sight of Henry and waved.

Adam waved back, but Henry was lost in thought. "That was so strange," he said, thinking aloud. "It was almost as though Headmaster Winter . . . Never mind."

"As though Headmaster Winter what?" Adam pressed.

Henry shook his head.

"Oh, you mean how it seemed like the headmaster wanted us to go on that envoy as spies," Adam said casually.

Henry stared at Adam in surprise. "Actually, yes," Henry admitted. "But that's absurd."

"Not really," Adam said. "If our punishment for breaking curfew is up to Lord Havelock, we're as good as expelled. It's not as though we have anything left to lose if we go."

"Would you really go?" Henry asked.

"Of course," Adam said without pausing to consider.

"But we hardly know anything about it. They could be staying for weeks. It could be dangerous."

Adam shrugged. "We could ask Derrick. It's a diplomatic envoy, right? His father's a diplomat."

A moment of silent agreement passed between the two friends, and without another word they hurried back to the first-year corridor.

Derrick was in his room when Henry and Adam knocked.

"To what do I owe the pleasure?" he asked, ushering them inside.

Henry quickly explained how the headmaster had caught them in the hall outside the armory the night before, and what he and Adam were thinking. Derrick frowned and picked up a small golden clock from his bedside table, absently winding it as he told them what he knew. It was a monthly envoy to visit Dimit Yascherov, who headed both the Nordlandic Policing Agency and the Partisan School, acting as the chancellor's right-hand man. The envoy flew under the guise of fostering discussion, but really it was the Ministerium's way of reminding the Nordlands that they were watching.

"Watching for what?" Henry asked, and at the same moment Adam said, "So they've gone before?"

"I don't know *what* they're watching for," Derrick said. "New technologies? The obvious answer would be violations to the Longsword Treaty. And, yes, last month was the first envoy. I know because my father's secretary went."

"Why didn't you tell us?" Henry asked.

Derrick shrugged. "It's not important. Just a load of old diplomats flexing their muscles and sneering, then bowing politely and returning home at the end of the weekend none the wiser."

"But they're definitely going to Partisan Keep?" Henry pressed. "And just for the weekend?"

"They're going to see Yascherov," Derrick said. "I'd assume so."

"These men work at the Ministerium, right?" Henry said slowly. "If we showed them evidence of Partisan students being trained in combat, wouldn't that make changing the conscription laws a priority, if nothing else?"

Derrick looked up from winding the clock in surprise. "Do you know, it actually might," he said. "It's worth a chance."

"Really?" Adam asked eagerly.

"So if we went to the Nordlands," Henry said,

"we could be the spies that Lord Havelock was afraid Yascherov would have. We could find evidence of combat training, and even if the envoy refused to believe us about a war, they'd at least feel unsettled enough to change the conscription laws."

"You'd actually go?" Derrick asked in surprise, but the answer was plain on Henry's face.

"We're done for anyway," Adam said cheerfully. "Lord Havelock will expel us for wandering the school after hours. Maybe he'd reconsider if we came back as heroes. And if not, well, if we're serious about preparing for war, how could we not go? All we have to do is convince someone called Mr. Frist that we're servants tomorrow morning."

Derrick shook his head incredulously. "I could cover for you," he offered. "So that no one knows you're missing. Perhaps spread the rumor that you've taken ill."

"That would never work," Henry said. "Sander—this other serving boy at the Midsummer School—used to try it all the time. We have to *show* everyone that we're ill."

Adam let out a convincing groan and doubled over in an excessively theatrical coughing fit.

Henry rolled his eyes. "It sounds like you've been smoking Jasper's pipe."

"Oi, then you try it," Adam retorted.

Henry frowned, thinking. And then he remembered the collection of jars in the back of their medicine classroom, one in particular.

Excitedly Henry began to explain his plan.

While Adam went to get the bottle from Sir Robert's classroom, Henry went to visit Professor Stratford. He owed the professor that much, and anyway, joining the diplomatic envoy in the guise of servants was dangerous, and someone had to know where they were going—someone besides their classmates, anyway.

Henry knocked on the door of the headmaster's house, and the butler opened it with a look of distaste.

"Er, where's Ellen?" Henry asked.

"If you've come to see staff, you should use the staff entrance," the butler intoned, making to close the door in Henry's face.

Henry wedged it open with his boot just in time. "Er, sorry," Henry tried again. "I was just wondering. I'm actually here to see Professor Stratford."

"Ah." The butler sniffed. "In that case may I have your card?"

"I don't have a card," Henry pressed. "I'm a student here. Can't I just, er, go upstairs?"

"As you wish, sir," the butler said disapprovingly. "And since you asked, the junior staff is out searching for Miss Winter."

Henry followed the balding, bland butler up the grand staircase and down the hall. The butler threw open the door to Professor Stratford's book-strewn study and announced Henry's arrival with thick sarcasm before bearing a stately retreat. Henry shook his head at the ridiculous formality, assuming it was because of the presence of the diplomatic envoy. Before he could recover, Professor Stratford had crushed him in an enormous hug.

"Happy birthday, my boy!" Professor Stratford said with a broad grin.

"Oh, right," Henry said, grimacing. With everything else that had happened that day, turning fifteen had slipped his mind. "Thanks."

"Well, sit down and open your present." Professor Stratford handed him an expensive-looking parcel tied with a silk ribbon.

"You didn't have to," Henry mumbled, embarrassed.

"Nonsense. I wanted to," Professor Stratford said, leaning back in his chair and lighting his pipe. "Go on, open it."

Henry untied the ribbon, feeling anything but festive.

He'd come to tell Professor Stratford of his plan to sneak off to the Nordlands for the weekend, not to have a carefree birthday party. But he couldn't bring himself to disappoint the professor, and so he forced what he hoped was a convincing grin, opened the parcel, and peered inside.

The parcel contained a pair of striped pajamas, a bottle green dressing gown, and a pair of matching bedroom slippers. It was a thoughtful present—Henry had often been embarrassed of his own pair of ragged pajamas, or gone barefoot to the common room after supper, but he'd had enough trouble affording a new school uniform on his wages from the bookshop. He bit his lip, horribly ashamed at how rarely he had visited Professor Stratford that term.

"Don't you like it?" Professor Stratford frowned worriedly. "I thought you might have outgrown your old ones, but if you'd rather pick out a new pair yourself . . ."

"No, I—," Henry said, at a loss for words. He began again. "This is too much. I can't accept it."

"Nonsense," the professor said. "I want you to have it. In fact, I insist."

"But—," Henry began. Professor Stratford had given him an extravagant present for Christmas as well—his first proper suit. And while Henry was beyond grateful, he wasn't used to receiving presents, much less expensive ones.

"Thank you," Henry said finally. "Truly, it's just what I needed."

"You're welcome," Professor Stratford said. "And now that I have you here, I'd very much enjoy hearing what's going on in your life."

Henry winced. "Er, well," he said, trying to stall as much as he could by retying the ribbon around the parcel.

But Professor Stratford wasn't fooled. His expression turned serious. "I know you well enough to know that you've been avoiding me. So I'm certainly eager to know what, exactly, you've been up to."

Henry sighed and told the professor everything. He began with the forgotten classroom and the trunks of weapons and ended with what Headmaster Winter had said about needing extra servants to staff the envoy to the Nordlands.

"Absolutely not," Professor Stratford said sternly. "You are *not* going to the Nordlands, of all places. You've misunderstood. Certainly the headmaster can't have meant for you to go."

"You weren't there," Henry said coolly. "Because if you were, you wouldn't say that."

"Henry, it's a noble thought, but your place is here with your friends. And your only responsibility is to earn good marks in your classes."

Henry sighed. "I thought you'd be proud of me," he said. "For starting the battle society. For finding a way to prepare the other students for war, and for wanting to help when everyone else is too afraid to even acknowledge the problem."

"I *am* proud of you, Henry, more than you'll ever know. But all isn't lost. You have no call to go running off to the Nordlands just because of a few complications."

"How can you say that?" Henry retorted. "I'm as good as expelled. And now Frankie's gone, and it's all my fault."

"You can't blame yourself for Frankie," Professor Stratford said sadly. "She might come to her senses and return home."

"She won't," Henry said. "She's always talked of running off. I just never thought she meant it. And what's to become of you if she never returns?"

"I'll manage," the professor said. "I always do. But, Henry, please—don't put me in this position."

"If you're so keen to stop me, feel free to tell Lord Havelock what we're planning," Henry retorted.

Professor Stratford frowned and chewed nervously on the corner of his mustache, briefly considering. And then he put his elbows on the desk and rested his head in his hands. "Please don't ask this of me," the professor mumbled.

"I'm not asking for permission," Henry said firmly. "I'm going. I wanted you to know because I hate that I didn't tell you about the battle society. I'll be back on Sunday night." He pushed back his chair and picked up the parcel, ashamed to accept such a gift after what he'd just said. But leaving the package behind would have been even worse manners.

"Thank you for the birthday present," he said gingerly. And as an afterthought he said, "Oh, and whatever happens at supper, it would be best if, er, you just went along with it."

Feeling as though he had deeply betrayed Professor Stratford, Henry slunk from the room and let himself out of the headmaster's house.

17

THE MASQUERADE
BEGINS

A dam made a face and peered skeptically at the bottle of medicine. "How much should we take?" he asked.

Henry glanced up from his desk, where he was flipping through the index to their medicine textbook. "I don't know. I can't find anything about emetics in here."

"A sip should do it," Rohan said in a rather long-suffering manner. "I had to take some when I ate poisonous berries off Father's estate as a child. Although I should warn you, you'll feel horrible after."

"That's the plan," Henry said, closing his textbook.

"Is this really necessary?" Rohan asked.

"Yes," Henry and Adam said.

"No, not the ipecac syrup," Rohan said. "The envoy. What if Lord Havelock's there? What if someone recognizes you?"

"No one's going to recognize us," Henry said confidently. "Servants are as good as invisible. Besides, Adam and I were banned from the Inter-School Tournament last term, so no one should know us at Partisan, either. I hope."

"Just because Frankie's run off doesn't mean you should as well," Rohan said, and sniffed.

"This isn't about Frankie," Henry said. "It's about doing what we can to prevent a war, or at least to prepare for it."

"I'm with Henry, mate," Adam said. "No one ever won a war by sitting and waiting for it to happen."

"Do what you wish. I want no part of it," Rohan said primly, standing up. "I'm going to supper before anyone thinks I've caught what you two have."

"What?" Adam asked, and then helpfully pantomimed vomiting. "You mean that?"

"Actually, I was referring to your ridiculous need to meddle with things that are better left untouched." And with that, Rohan slammed the door.

Henry bit his lip. He'd thought Rohan would come

around, like he always had. It hurt that Rohan didn't approve of their plan, but then, Rohan rarely approved of anything these days besides cricket or schoolwork.

"Do you think we're making a mistake?" Henry asked.

Adam shook his head. "No, but I think Rohan is. He should support us. We're his friends."

"It doesn't feel like it," Henry said dryly.

"He's probably just upset at being left behind."

"We can't take him to the Nordlands," Henry said. "And it's not as though he's begging to come."

"Actually, mate, I meant if Lord Havelock expels us."

"Oh," Henry said. "I didn't think of that."

But now that he did, it made an odd sort of sense. He could just imagine how much Rohan would loathe being the lone commoner at the academy, especially considering how sensitive he was about the label.

"We should probably, you know," Adam said, nodding toward the bottle of ipecac syrup.

"Right." Henry twisted open the bottle. "Bottoms up," he muttered, taking a swig. He made a face and passed the bottle to Adam.

"L'Chayim," Adam said, swallowing. "Ugh, that's awful."

"Not as awful as what's to come," Henry said darkly, fumbling to remove his tie and roll up his shirtsleeves. "Come on, before it kicks in."

Twenty minutes later Henry picked himself up from the floor of the toilets with a groan. He was pale, clammy, and shaking.

"Adam?" he croaked.

"Worst idea ever," Adam whimpered, hugging the sink for dear life. He looked even worse than Henry felt.

"Come on," Henry said weakly. "We have to go to supper."

"Don't mention food," Adam moaned. "I hate food. I hate the way it tastes . . . coming up." He shuddered at the memory.

Henry swallowed thickly, hoping neither of them would be sick again as he held open the door to the hallway. Somehow they made it to the dining hall.

But the dining hall was oddly subdued, the students acting as though they were at a formal supper rather than laughing and joking per usual. Henry winced as he and Adam crept to the first-year table and slid gratefully into their seats, pale, sweating, and exhausted.

"Are you two all right?" Conrad asked, looking back

and forth between Henry and Adam with genuine concern. The boys seated nearby shot one another nervous glances before scooting as far away from Henry and Adam as the benches would allow.

"Yeah, I'm fine," Henry said, pouring himself a glass of water. His hands shook as he hefted the pitcher, and water splashed onto the table. "What's going on?"

"My father's here," Derrick muttered, nodding toward the High Table.

Henry looked. The High Table had been extended to allow for eight guests. No wonder everyone was acting as though they could be expelled for dropping a fork.

"I heard there's flu going around," Rohan commented loudly, with a pointed look at Henry and Adam. "You've looked off all afternoon."

Henry shrugged, his attention still on the High Table. Lord Havelock scowled back at him for a moment before turning his attention to the ancient gentleman on his left. And then Edmund passed Adam the basket of rolls, and Adam went green. He clapped his hand to his mouth and rushed from the dining hall.

Henry wearily watched him go. "Actually," he admitted, "maybe I *am* feeling a bit off." He took a small sip of the water. It made his stomach roll.

"You look awful," Edmund said. "Maybe you should go to bed."

"Yeah," Henry said, climbing to his feet. "Must have caught that flu."

"Feel better," Derrick called.

Henry dragged himself from the dining hall. As he crawled into bed, he wondered worriedly how long it would be until the effects of the emetic wore off.

An hour later he was feeling much better. He sat up, running a hand through his mussed hair.

Adam was curled up in a ball on the floor and clutching their wastebasket, which was thankfully empty.

"Adam, get up," Henry said.

Adam moaned. "I'm dying," he whispered.

"You're not," Henry said. "I feel loads better. I think it's wearing off."

Adam sat up gingerly. "Oh, you're right," he said sheepishly. "I do feel better."

Henry rolled his eyes. And then a knock sounded at the door.

"Act like you still feel poorly," Henry whispered, and then raised his voice. "Come in."

Valmont pushed open the door to their room. Adam

loudly faked being sick into the wastebasket.

Henry's stomach lurched at the sound, and he swallowed.

"What are you doing?" Valmont asked, narrowing his eyes.

"What does it look like?" Henry retorted. "Lying in bed and being ill."

"You're pretending," Valmont said. "You were fine earlier."

Valmont looked around their room, his gaze lingering on Henry's book-strewn desk, Adam's messy half-open drawers, and Rohan's tidy work space.

"We got caught," Henry admitted. "After the battle society meeting last night. Headmaster Winter saw us with the sabres."

"What did you tell him?" Valmont demanded.

"I didn't turn you in, if that's what you're wondering," Henry said sourly, swinging his feet over the side of his bed and briefly explaining the situation. "And everyone's too distracted by our esteemed guests to deal with us. Maybe if you spoke with Lord Havelock over the weekend, he'd go easy on us."

"Are you mad, Grim? That's the same as turning myself in."

"But he'd listen to you," Adam said indignantly.

"Right." Valmont sneered. "That's likely."

"We're going to the Nordlands," Henry admitted. "And you can't tell anyone."

"That's impossible," Valmont said. "You can't get across the border."

"Actually, we can." Henry quickly told Valmont why the gentlemen at supper were there, and what he planned to do about it.

"You're going as servants?" Valmont hooted. "Oh, that's priceless."

Henry shot him a dark look.

"Sorry," Valmont muttered.

"It's just for the weekend," Adam said.

"That's why you're faking ill?" Valmont asked, and then his gaze fell on the bottle of ipecac syrup on Henry's desk. "Oh, very clever."

"Want to try some?" Adam asked brightly. "I bet it works even better after you've eaten a large supper."

Valmont shot him a disgusted look.

"Just keep quiet about this," Henry warned.

"I'm not Theobold," Valmont said angrily. "I'm not going to turn you in for trying to do something that benefits us all."

Adam looked up in surprise. "Really, mate?"

"I'm not your mate," Valmont returned. "But, yes, I think it's a good idea—mostly because I'll thoroughly enjoy my weekend knowing that you two are off scrubbing the floors like the commoners you are."

"Careful," Henry said dryly, "or someone might think you actually mean it."

Valmont huffed and slammed the door.

Henry couldn't sleep that night. He stared at Adam, who was dead to the world, and Rohan, who had clamped a pillow over his head to drown out Adam's snores, and he wondered where Frankie had gone, and if she was wondering after them as well. Not that it mattered what Frankie was thinking.

But mostly Henry thought about how strange it would feel to play the role of the servant again, even if it was only for the weekend.

When it was time, he woke Adam.

"Ready to go, servant boy?" Henry joked, buttoning his most ragged shirt. He pulled on his worn boots and hunted up a plain necktie from the bottom of his drawer.

Adam yawned hugely and staggered to the wardrobe, his blankets wrapped around his shoulders like a cape.

"Should we bring this?" Henry asked with an uncertain frown, holding up the bottle of ipecac syrup.

"Nah." Adam yawned again. "Pour the rest of it onto Rohan's toothbrush."

Henry snickered at the thought.

"I *am* awake, you know," Rohan said primly, rubbing the sleep from his eyes. "Are you two leaving now?"

Adam finished buttoning one of his spectacularly rumpled shirts and nodded.

"Don't forget to make your beds look as though they aren't empty," Rohan said with a sigh, "in case anyone should check."

"We were already planning on it," Henry said, retrieving his battered old satchel from beneath his bed.

"Don't mind me, then, if you've already thought of everything," Rohan said stiffly.

"I thought you didn't want to be involved with this," Henry said.

"I don't," Rohan said, watching as Henry placed an armload of clothes beneath his blankets so that it looked as though he were still asleep.

"Valmont thinks it's a good idea," Adam said.

"You told *Valmont*?" Rohan accused. "Does everyone know?"

"What does it matter?" Henry asked. "Since you're not involved."

"You're right, it doesn't," Rohan said firmly. "I'll see you on Sunday night. Try not to make too much noise, as some of us are *actually* trying to sleep."

Adam caught Henry's gaze and shrugged.

"Ready to go?" Henry whispered.

"In a moment," Adam said, unfastening his necklace. With an apologetic grimace he placed the charm into his desk drawer. "How do I look?" he asked, straightening his shoulders.

"Very, er, nondenominational," Henry said.

Adam ran a hand through his hair and took a deep breath.

"Take care of yourselves," Rohan mumbled.

"We will," Henry said, shoving a few last-minute provisions into his satchel. "And we'll be back tomorrow night."

Adam shouldered his own bag and followed Henry into the shadowy hallway, with its lamps burning low and the sky dark through the windows. When they reached the kitchens, Henry found Liza and Mary hard at work preparing an enormous hamper of food for the envoy.

"Stop lingerin' in the doorway, you two," Liza said without seeming to turn around.

Henry and Adam guiltily shuffled into the kitchen. "Good morning, Liza," Henry said.

"Not really," Liza grumbled. "Got half the staff carryin' luggage down to the train station, an' the other half lookin' for Miss Winter. An' who's stuck in the kitchen doin' all the work? Little ol' Liza, tha's who."

"We're sorry, Liza," Henry said, "and I hate to bother you, but we need a favor."

"Please say yes," Adam put in.

"An' what sort o' favor do you need?" she asked, wiping her hands on her apron and spinning to face them. She clucked as she surveyed the boys, taking in their plain clothing and bed-ruffled hair.

"Spare uniforms," Henry admitted.

"We don' keep student uniforms here," Liza said with a frown.

"Er, actually, I meant staff uniforms. We need to go with the envoy this weekend, but they can't think we're students here," Henry pleaded.

Liza stared at Henry and Adam in shock. "You're meanin' to go to the Nordlands?"

"It's important," Henry said simply. "We have to."

Liza nodded slowly, accepting this as an answer. "Well, then," she said, "uniforms are kept back in that cupboard past the larder there."

"Thank you, Liza," Henry said with a small bow, and then he elbowed Adam.

"Yes, thank you," Adam mumbled, following Henry to get changed.

When they returned to the kitchen, Mr. Frist was already there, his black suit impeccably crisp, his mustache bristling. "Are these the provisions?" Mr. Frist sniffed, peering at the hamper.

"Yes, sorr," Mary said. "All packed and ready to go."

Mr. Frist made a note in his leather-bound book and then sighed. "Yes, well, that seems to be in order, at least. A shame no one could scare up any extra staff."

Henry took a deep breath. It was then or never. "We'd be willin' to go," he said, making his voice gruff.

"To the Nordlands?" Mr. Frist pressed, as though he couldn't believe his luck.

Henry shrugged. "Extra pay's extra pay. Don' much hold for no superstitions."

For a moment Mr. Frist looked like he might hug them.

Liza frowned, but set her mouth into a tight line and kept quiet.

"You're in charge of bringing the food down to the station," Mr. Frist continued. "I'll be along presently. Can you boys see to that?"

"Yes, sir," Henry and Adam chorused, a little too smartly. Henry winced, but Mr. Frist didn't seem to notice.

"Here yeh go," Liza said gruffly, latching the hamper shut and giving it a slap. "Mind yeh don' shake the contents none." But despite her tone Liza's eyes danced with amusement, and she was biting back a smile. Henry rather suspected that she'd always wanted to give orders to the students, and was finally having her chance.

"Yes, ma'am," Henry said, playing along.

He and Adam hefted the enormous hamper, each seizing hold of one of the thick leather straps and carrying it between them. They struggled out the back door of the kitchen, the servants' entrance, and onto the school grounds.

It was still dark outside, the sky a sulky shade of purple that began to lighten as they staggered alongside the road that lead down to the village.

"That was easy," Adam commented, nearly dropping his side of the hamper as he tripped over a stone.

"Careful!" Henry warned.

"Sorry," Adam said contritely. "But it *was* easy. Good thing for Liza."

"We're not even on the train yet," Henry reminded him.

"I know," Adam muttered. "I'm just saying."

"This is going to be difficult," Henry warned. "We have to be careful we don't give ourselves away, like back in the kitchen."

"What are you talking about?" Adam asked.

"I don't think we're very convincing servants," Henry admitted. "There's the bowing, for one thing. Remember how Professor Turveydrop could tell the difference? We have to be rough about it, no matter if we're bowing to a lord minister or just Mr. Frist."

"Okay," Adam said slowly. "What else."

"No saluting," Henry continued. "And if you have to serve tea, stand by the door until you're dismissed."

Adam nodded.

"And speaking," Henry went on, suddenly realizing how very many things had the capacity to go wrong. "We have to sound a bit, you know, *uneducated*. Ugh, this is going to be a disaster."

"But you've done all of this before, mate," Adam reminded him.

They paused for a minute to rest their hands from carrying the hamper, and a crowd of serving boys in Knightley school livery trudged past them on the other side of the road, heading back up to the school. Henry and Adam ducked their heads. When the boys had passed, they picked up the hamper and continued on.

"Yes, but I had nothing to hide," Henry explained. "So what did it matter if I sounded a bit posh? It's not my fault the orphanage priest drilled elocution into me with a birch rod." Henry bit his lip, realizing what he'd just shared. "And if we have to eat with other members of the serving staff, roughen up your manners," he said as an afterthought.

"I think I'm getting a blister," Adam complained.

"Good," Henry said. "We could use some of those."

"You're mental sometimes, you know that?" Adam muttered.

Avel-on-t'Hems was a small, quaint village left over from medieval times, with a narrow street of disreputable shops and a crumbling, dingy church that made Knightley's chapel seem like a cathedral in comparison.

The train station was across from a rather seedy pub with two ancient jousting lances crossed over the front door and three tall, crooked chimneys. The Lance,

Henry thought, the pub where Ollie went to fight.

Henry and Adam straggled onto the platform and eagerly set down the hamper, which felt as though it were filled with encyclopedias, not tea and sandwiches.

"Worst morning ever," Adam complained, picking at a rapidly forming blister.

"Don't," Henry chided. "That only makes them worse."

The platform was empty, but a small gleaming steam engine chortled on the tracks.

"I'm starving," Adam said. "Seeing as how we missed supper." Henry opened his mouth to protest, but Adam grinned and continued, "But I guess that a growling stomach adds to the charade?"

Henry grinned. And at that moment a stocky, disheveled lad of around sixteen poked his head out of the door to the station. Through the door, Henry could just see a small waiting area lined with benches.

"You boys with the envoy?" the lad demanded.

Henry nodded.

"Well, come inside an' wait with the rest of us," the boy said, holding open the door.

Henry and Adam exchanged a nervous glance and then followed.

"I'm George," the boy said.

"Er, I'm Henry and this is Adam," Henry said, and then wondered belatedly if they ought to have given false names.

"Well, it's goin' to be a bloody 'orrible train ride," George said over his shoulder. "I went on the last one. Best drink yer fill before we're off."

George settled onto a bench near another boy around their age, who had a face like a rat and was nursing a silver flask. George grabbed the flask from the boy and took a swallow before holding it out to Henry.

Henry and Adam exchanged an uneasy glance.

George laughed uproariously at Henry's and Adam's expressions of panic.

"Aw, Jem an' I are just makin' fun of ya," George said. "Here, take it."

He thrust the drink at Henry, who took a cautious sniff and then grinned. It was coffee. Even though Henry didn't particularly feel like sharing a flask with Jem and George, he knew better than to refuse. He forced himself to take a sip, and then passed it to Adam. "Want some?"

Adam made a face.

"It's coffee," Henry said.

"Nah," Adam mumbled.

"Aren't we supposed to wait on the platform?" Henry asked.

George shrugged. "Mr. Frist can't leave without us. Relax, Knightley boys."

Henry and Adam jumped. "Sorry?" Henry asked, hoping he'd misheard.

"Yer uniforms," George said. "Yer from up at that fancy school."

"Er, right," Henry said.

"Dunno how you stand it, servin' boys yer age wot never had to lift a finger in their lives," Jem said.

"It's not so bad," Adam said. "They mostly ignore us."

Jem and George were both from the village. George did odd jobs at the Lance, and Jem was a shop boy for a local boot maker. It would just be the four of them, and Mr. Frist, who was in charge.

"Course some o' the gen'lmun will have their personal valets, but they're senior staff so we'll be servin' them, too," George said as Mr. Frist pushed open the door, tapping his pen impatiently against his notebook.

"Hurry up, boys," Mr. Frist snapped, turning on his heel. "Keep to schedule."

George and Jem hurried after Mr. Frist, and Henry and Adam followed nervously.

"Managed to get four, have we?" Mr. Frist muttered, making a note.

"Yes, sir," the boys chorused, Henry and Adam a bit too posh once again.

Jem and George snickered, and Henry elbowed Adam, who shrugged.

"George," Mr. Frist snapped. "You know the drill, so you're in charge of the others. Make certain everyone changes into their livery before the train leaves the station."

"Yes, sir," George said.

"Now stow your things in the servants' car and get to work," Mr. Frist ordered, closing his book with a resounding *thwack* and stalking off to have a word with the conductor.

❧ 18 ❧

THE NORDLANDS
EXPRESS

How do I look?" Adam asked, pulling at his neck cloth.

"Ridiculous," Henry said.

"Oi, you look worse," Adam protested. "At least *my* waistcoat fits."

Henry frowned at his reflection in the window of the servants' car and adjusted his waistcoat, which admittedly was slightly too small, not that it could be helped. It was strange seeing himself dressed as a lackey, with a crisp white neck cloth and silk hose and short breeches.

The livery had come from Parliament Hall, along with Mr. Frist, who was some sort of junior secretary acting as a liaison. It was rather extravagant, Henry had to admit, but then, it was just a show for Dimit Yascherov. After all, South Britain couldn't very well send a political envoy to the Nordlands with servants dressed in mismatched and ragged shirtsleeves. No, South Britain meant to flaunt their class system in the faces of those who had done away with it.

George looked up from where he sat on a crate, carving slices out of an apple with a pocketknife. "Want a piece?" he asked.

Henry's eyes narrowed as he realized what had happened. "Did you get that apple from my bag?" he demanded.

George shrugged and continued carving.

"Don't go through my things," Henry said evenly.

"Oho, th' high an' mighty Knightley servant's givin' me orders," George mocked.

"Listen, Knightley. George here's in charge, an' I think you owe 'im an apology," said Jem.

Henry folded his arms, his too tight waistcoat stretching uncomfortably across his back, and made no move to apologize.

"Just do it, mate," Adam whispered anxiously.

"No," Henry said.

The train rattled noisily over the tracks, but if anything, the car seemed too quiet as Jem reached inside his waistcoat and pulled out a glittering knife. He advanced on Henry with a nasty grin, brandishing the blade. "Sure yeh don' want to reconsider?" Jem whispered, pressing the dull side of the knife to Henry's cheek in warning.

Henry stiffened, realizing what a horrible mistake he'd made.

"Jus' drop it, Jem," George warned. And then the door to their car banged open and Mr. Frist stood there gaping at the scene before him.

Jem scowled and lowered the knife.

"What's going on?" Mr. Frist demanded sharply.

"Nothin', sir," Henry answered before George could speak up. "Just cuttin' a loose thread on my waistcoat."

George regarded Henry suspiciously, and Henry held back a smirk.

"Got it," Jem sneered, snapping his knife closed.

"Give that 'ere, Jem," George said, holding out his hand for the knife.

Jem scowled but gave George the knife.

"The train's ready to depart," Mr. Frist said, consulting his ever present notebook. He assigned each of the boys a car to serve. Adam was given Lord Priscus's car; Jem got the two secret service knights, Sir Fletcher and

Sir Alban; and George was assigned to someone called Lord Hugh.

"And you, what's your name?" Mr. Frist asked, pointing to Henry.

"Henry, sir."

"Your waistcoat's too small," Mr. Frist snapped.

"I know, sir. This one fit the best."

Mr. Frist frowned. "Very well. You'll take the front car containing the Lord Minister Marchbanks, his secretary, and their valet."

Henry paled.

"Is there a problem?" Mr. Frist snapped.

"No, sir," Henry said despairingly. It was just his luck to get stuck waiting on his friend's father all weekend.

When Mr. Frist left, everyone breathed a sigh of relief, and Adam shot Henry a mournful look, as though he rather thought he'd gotten the worst of it, serving the former headmaster.

"Why didn't yeh turn me in?" Jem demanded.

Henry shrugged. "Better friends than enemies?" Henry suggested.

"Poncy Knightley servant." Jem shook his head in disgust.

By midmorning the train was hurtling through the towns on the outskirts of the city, their buildings dense and their church spires competing to see which could stretch higher.

Henry hobbled toward the train's galley in his ridiculous buckled shoes that, just like his waistcoat, were half a size too small.

Thankfully, Lord Marchbanks was too busy speaking with his secretary to pay much attention to Henry. Lord Priscus was another story, however. The retired headmaster kept Adam dashing about for extra cushions or hunting up a copy of the *Royal Standard*, which never printed stories about the Nordlands.

As Henry took down a tea service and began to arrange it on the narrow counter, the door slid open to reveal a rather frustrated Adam.

"How's it going?" Henry asked, folding napkins.

"That man is a nightmare," Adam moaned. "And he's half-deaf to top it off. Thinks my name is Autumn, like the bloody season."

Henry snickered.

"Oi, it isn't funny!" Adam protested. "He's worse than Lord Havelock. And he keeps ordering cushions."

"Sorry," Henry said, wincing in sympathy.

"Well, he wants tea now," Adam whined.

Wordlessly Henry pulled down a second tea service and began to arrange it.

"Thanks, mate," Adam said, reaching to help with the napkins as Henry positioned the teacups so their handles all faced in the same direction.

"Give me that." Henry grabbed the napkin. "You fold them in thirds. They aren't socks."

"Lord Priscus wouldn't notice if they were," Adam muttered.

Henry grinned, but then his expression turned serious. He took the tin of tea leaves from the hamper and drummed the lid nervously. "I'm worried," he admitted.

"What about?" Adam asked. "Jem and his bloody huge knife?"

"No," Henry said. "Although that's certainly a problem. As is George's fondness for rifling through our things. I meant the envoy. Derrick didn't know his father was coming, and this can't be good. The Lord Minister of Foreign Relations is really important."

"Well, so is Dimit Yascherov," Adam said. "I looked him up, and he's a right terror."

"You looked him up?" Henry asked skeptically, letting the tea steep.

"Oi, don't look so surprised. It was that night I stayed in the library writing Lord Havelock's paper about revolutions. He was Chancellor Mors's right-hand man even during the rise of the Draconian party. Rounded up and killed dozens of aristocrats—well, ordered them killed anyway."

Henry frowned. "And now he's ordering household inspections to round up anyone who might challenge the chancellor," he said half to himself, before remembering the tea. He finished with the two tea services and handed one to Adam.

"I hope he thinks it's a pillow and sits on it," Adam muttered.

Henry hefted his own serving tray with a grin. "Deliver your tray and then meet me in the servants' car. We should find somewhere to stow our bags before George decides to go through them again." They stepped out into the corridor and went in opposite directions, but as Henry neared Lord Marchbanks's car, he caught sight of Jem lounging against the door.

Jem saw Henry's tea service and grinned. "I'll take that."

"You will not," Henry said, pushing past him.

Jem grabbed Henry's shoulder, and Henry flinched.

"There's somethin' funny about you," Jem hissed, his breath hot and rank on Henry's cheek.

"You're imagining things," Henry snapped.

"Am I?"

"Let me go, Jem. Unless you want to explain to Lord Minister Marchbanks why his tea is down the front of your uniform."

Jem released Henry's shoulder. "Nice accent, Knightley," he spat as Henry knocked.

Adam was waiting for Henry in the servants' car, holding both of their satchels. "Oi, what took you so long?" he asked.

"Jem." Henry sighed. "And Lord Marchbanks's insufferable valet."

"Lord Priscus was asleep," Adam said proudly. "I just dumped the tray and left. Hope he's not dead."

"Suffocated by too many pillows?" Henry asked with a grin.

"Passed on in his sleep, from a combination of old age and bitterness," Adam returned.

They shared a laugh.

"I'll be glad when we're off this train," Henry said, with his hand on the door to the next car. "Reckon they'll look back here?"

"What's back there?"

"Storage?" Henry shrugged and pushed open the door. The car was filled with crates and boxes, with loops of rope dangling overhead like vines. Henry picked up the corner of a tarp and stashed his satchel beneath it.

"What did you bring, anyway?" Adam asked.

"Some school books," Henry admitted.

"You're joking," Adam said.

"We have reading due Monday, providing we aren't expelled."

And then the tarp in the far corner moved. Adam stiffened. "Did you see that?" he whispered.

"Probably mice," Henry said. "Is there food in your bag?"

"No," Adam said nervously.

The tarp moved again.

"Maybe," Adam admitted. "Blimey, that's some mouse."

Henry held a finger to his lips. He crept toward the tarp and pulled back the layer of sheeting, hardly daring to breathe.

Frankie sat there, rumpled and miserable, glaring up at them. "What are *you* doing here?" she demanded, and then she took in their ridiculous livery and snorted. "And *what* are you *wearing*?"

"Us?" Henry retorted. "What about *you*?"

Frankie stood up and brushed some of the wrinkles from her dress with a scowl. "What does it look like? I'm running away to the city," she replied.

"Er," Henry said, exchanging an uneasy glance with Adam.

"What?" Frankie demanded.

"Diplomatic envoy," Henry said. "This train is express to the Nordlands."

Frankie paled.

"Didn't you know?" Adam asked.

"No," Frankie said. "I was hiding from Father's search party in a room at the Lance and saw this train come in from Hammersmith Cross. I figured it was heading back."

"So you stowed away?" Henry asked.

"I'm not telling *you* about it," Frankie snapped.

Henry sighed. "Look, I know we were fighting back at school, but we have to get past that. In a few hours this train is crossing border inspection into the Nordlands."

"You weren't joking?" Frankie asked, sitting down on a crate. "This train is really bound for the Nordlands?"

Henry sat down on a crate across from Frankie and massaged his temples for a moment, trying to think. But Frankie wouldn't let him.

"Are you going to tell me why *you're* here, then?" Frankie snapped. "Or why you're dressed like fancy footmen?"

Henry sighed and explained.

"But that doesn't make any sense," Frankie said when Henry had finished.

"What doesn't make any sense?" Henry asked irritably.

"There's no way Father meant for you to go to the Nordlands. He's terrified of Yascherov."

"If you hadn't run off, you might have been able to tell us that *before*," Henry said.

"Ooh, my sincerest apologies if I've inconvenienced you, Mr. Grim," Frankie shot back.

"I thought we weren't fighting," Adam interrupted.

Frankie scowled at him.

"Adam's right," Henry said. "This isn't the time or the place. And we have to figure out what you're going to do. None of us has any Nordlandic money."

"Not to mention," Frankie said, motioning toward her frock. Henry didn't see the problem. Frankie sighed and clarified. "Women dress differently in the Nord-lands. Honestly, don't you *read*?"

"Not *fashion* magazines." Adam made a face.

"Er, we should get back," Henry said. "I don't want Jem or George to come looking for us and, well . . ."

"You'll have to stay hidden here," Adam said.

"For how long?" Frankie asked.

"Until tomorrow night."

"Absolutely not," Frankie said, horrified.

"What else can we do?" Henry put in. "Jem and George aren't exactly the sort of boys who would go along with this."

"Not to mention," Adam said, drawing a finger across his throat.

Henry shot him a look.

"What?" Frankie asked.

"They carry knives," Henry admitted. "Like pirates."

"What am I supposed to do?" Frankie wailed.

"You could read textbooks," Adam suggested help-fully. "Henry has a few in his bag. And there should be an orange in mine if you're hungry."

"Starving," Frankie said dryly.

"We'll bring our luncheon back here if we can," Henry promised. The boys stood up.

"Don't leave," Frankie said, her voice trembling. For the first time Henry realized how scared she must be, despite all of her bluster. She'd been hiding on the train for hours, and being discovered as a stowaway bound for the city was one thing, but being a stowaway on a diplomatic envoy to the Nordlands was quite another.

"Sorry, but we have to go," Henry said. "We're servants, remember?"

"With those outfits, who could forget?" Frankie muttered.

Henry bowed sarcastically. "Will yeh be requirin' anythin' else, miss?" he asked.

Frankie shook her head and grinned in spite of herself.

"Right, miss. We'll be off, then," Adam said, joining the pantomime.

Still laughing, Henry and Adam returned to the servants' car. But as soon as Henry closed the door, his smile faded. "This is awful," he whispered. "What if Frankie's caught during the border inspection? She'll have us discovered as well."

"That would be a nightmare," Adam said. And then

he put on a rather poor imitation of Rohan. "Imagine the impropriety of us all running off together."

Henry shook his head. "It's worse than that. It would look as though Knightley were purposefully sending spies to Partisan—as though it were Headmaster Winter's doing—or Lord Havelock's. We *can't* be caught."

"I know, but at least now we know that Frankie's all right," Adam muttered.

"True enough," Henry said, tugging impatiently at his waistcoat. "It is nice that we got to see her again. I was worried she'd disappeared for good."

"What do you care?" Adam asked. "You're not the one who likes her."

"How could I?" Henry retorted. "She's completely insufferable."

Henry nervously stared out the window of the servants' car as the train hurled through the northern reaches of the country. The train had veered inland long ago, racing beyond the remains of old military fortresses and rumbling past rocky, still frozen fields. Up ahead Henry spotted a squat gray building, the only building he'd seen for a long while.

His heart hammering nervously, he slid open the

door to the storage car. "Er, Frankie?" he called.

"Let me guess," she said, climbing back under the tarp. "Border inspection."

"Sorry," Henry apologized.

"It's not your fault," she said, her voice muffled. "Can you see me?"

"No," Henry said. "It should be all right."

He lost his balance for a moment as the train slowed. "Er, I should—," Henry began.

"Go," Frankie called. "I'll be fine."

Henry made sure the door to Frankie's car was shut tightly, then decided that it looked suspicious, and left it ajar, but that looked wrong as well. Finally he closed the door firmly and raced to Lord Marchbanks's compartment, angrily yanking at his waistcoat, which refused to fit.

He knocked smartly.

"Come in," the lord minister called.

Henry opened the door to the compartment and bowed hastily. "Sorry to disturb you, my lord minister, but we're just reaching the border inspection," Henry said. He was worried about Frankie, and nervous that she'd be caught, and wasn't really thinking. But he realized his mistake instantly. The knock, the bow, the phrasing, even his accent, were all wrong.

Lord Marchbanks and his secretary, Withers, gawped at him. Thankfully the insufferable valet was off somewhere, being insufferable.

Suddenly Lord Marchbanks's face broke into a broad grin. "Oh, that was very good," he said.

"I'm sorry, sir?" Henry asked, his heart racing nervously.

"Someone's taught you to behave properly, boy, though I can't fathom why you've chosen to play the part of a *campagnard* all morning."

Henry frowned as he considered the lord minister's words. He realized the trap almost immediately. "Er, I don't know that word," Henry lied.

Lord Marchbanks raised an eyebrow. "No? It means 'an uneducated country lad.'"

"Well, sir, it ain't English," Henry said.

Lord Marchbanks waited patiently.

"I mean, that wasn't in English, my lord minister," Henry corrected as the train screeched to a stop.

"What do you think, Withers?" Lord Marchbanks asked.

The secretary, who was preoccupied with a stack of papers, looked up and blinked owlishly.

"Never mind," Lord Marchbanks said with a sigh,

and then turned his attention back to Henry. "Here is what I think."

Henry gulped, waiting for it. Because if Lord Marchbanks looked, he'd see that Henry's hair, while mussed, was cut to school standard. That his left hand bore the unmistakable callus caused by too much writing, that his fingernails were square and even, that he did not appear to regularly miss meals.

"I think," Lord Marchbanks continued, "that you've been to school, boy."

Henry nodded. That answer was safe, at least.

"Your accent is not regional but taught. Don't look at me in surprise. I speak with foreigners nearly every day at the Ministerium who have learned English such as yours. A most curious puzzle."

Henry desperately grasped for a plausible story, and borrowed one he'd read in a detective story. "Please, sir, it's not a puzzle at all. I was at school, my father died, and I had to take to working because of my younger brothers. The other boys get on me for the schooling, so I try to sound as though I haven't any."

Lord Marchbanks's frown disappeared, and Henry breathed a sigh of relief. The story was plausible, but more than that, it was boring.

"I'll thank you to speak the King's English from now on," Lord Marchbanks said, losing interest.

"Yes, sir," Henry said as the door to the compartment opened and a Nordlandic patroller stepped inside.

"Inspection," he barked.

Lord Marchbanks picked up his copy of the *Royal Standard* and promptly disappeared behind it.

Henry flattened himself against the wall, realizing that at any moment Frankie could be discovered.

But the patroller, in his thick wool uniform and tall, furry hat, merely glanced at the lord minister, his secretary, and Henry before retreating back into the corridor and slamming the door behind him.

"Well, that was unpleasant," Lord Marchbanks said. "That will be all, er, Harry."

"Yes, sir," Henry said with a polite but carefully unschooled bow.

Once the train was moving again, Henry couldn't help but grin triumphantly, despite his recent humiliation. Frankie had gotten through the border inspection. They weren't caught. Lord Marchbanks thought he was Harry, a down-on-his-luck boy with too many mouths to feed. And in just a half hour more, the train would arrive at Partisan Keep.

Henry ducked back into the storage car, bringing the half of his lunch he'd saved. "It's me," he whispered.

The tarp rustled, and Frankie peered out at him. Her hair was coming down from its neat pins, and she looked pale and frightened. "Are they gone?" she asked. "We've started moving again."

"We'll be there in about fifteen minutes," Henry said.

"That was terrifying," she said. "I thought they were going to find me."

"Well, they didn't," Henry said, sitting down on a crate and passing Frankie the bundle of food.

She eagerly unwrapped it, and then her face fell. "Is this all?" she asked.

Henry winced apologetically. "It's half of mine. Plus two biscuits left from Lord Marchbanks's tray."

At this, Frankie bit her lip. "It'll do," she mumbled. "Thank you."

"Don't mention it," Henry said uncomfortably.

Frankie took a bite of the bread.

"So," Henry finally said. "Are you going to tell me why you ran away?"

"You know why."

"I think I do," Henry admitted.

"Then guess."

"The battle society, and your chaperone, and, well, me."

"Don't flatter yourself," Frankie muttered.

"So I'm wrong?"

"No."

Henry nodded slowly, digesting this piece of information.

"You're the first boy who has ever talked to me like I was a person," Frankie continued. "And then when we started fighting that day after chapel and everything got so complicated, I just thought— Never mind."

"Thought what?" Henry pressed.

"Why are you going out of your way to help me?" Frankie asked suddenly.

"I don't know," Henry said, considering. "I suppose because Adam's practically in love with you."

"Wh-what?" Frankie spluttered.

The train began to slow.

"I have to—" Henry grimaced and glanced toward the door.

"I know."

"I'll be back if I can, but if not, I'll bring food with me tomorrow. Can you manage until then?"

Frankie gave Henry a mournful look, her lower lip

trembling. "Oh, God, I've made a mess of everything, haven't I?" she said as the reality of the situation hit her full force.

"No, not at all." Henry gingerly reached out and patted her shoulder. "You're the only girl Fergus Valmont is afraid of. You can beat some of the best boys in our year at fencing, and you speak Latin. If there's anyone who's brave enough and clever enough to get through this, it's you."

Frankie looked up at him, her eyes brimming with tears. "Do you mean that?"

"It's the truth," Henry said. "I—I'll see you tomorrow."

"Good luck spying," she whispered.

"Thanks," Henry said, retrieving his and Adam's satchels from where they'd stashed them earlier.

"You make a ridiculous servant, by the way," she said. "You're all wrong for it."

"I'd like to see you do better," Henry retorted, closing the door.

❖ 19 ❖

THE *COMMON COMRADE*

The Partisan School was an ancient stronghold left over from the days of the Sasson conquerors, with slits for windows to deflect the course of harmful arrows, and a moat gone to sewage. Instead of modern electric light, Partisan used old-fashioned torches, which lit the way up dozens of sagging stone steps and through an enormous wooden door that rather resembled a drawbridge.

But Henry and Adam didn't enter through the enormous wooden door. Instead they carried the envoy's bags from the train station up through a grubby back entrance to Partisan Keep and deposited them in the east wing guest rooms.

After the third and final expedition, they were exhausted. Adam flopped onto what was to be Lord Priscus's bed, burying his face in the quilt.

"Get up!" Henry whispered fiercely. "What if someone sees?"

Adam whined but slid off the bed, patting the covers straight. "I'm exhausted," he complained.

"Well, we're not getting much sleep tonight." Henry neatened the stack of luggage. "Come on. Time to find out where we *won't* be sleeping."

To Henry's and Adam's horror, their sleeping quarters turned out to be a small, narrow room off the scullery with two sets of bunk beds. Having taken both of the top bunks, Jem and George grinned when Henry and Adam pushed open the door.

"Did yeh have a good time with the bags?" George asked, pillowing his head in his hands. Henry shook his head and angrily slammed his satchel onto the bunk below George.

Adam gingerly approached the bed beneath Jem. "Oi, there isn't a pillow," he said.

"Sorry." Jem grinned nastily. "Borrowed it."

"Hey, Adam," Henry called. "Need me to fetch you some more pillows?"

And even though it wasn't funny, really, the two boys shook with laughter. They ducked into the scullery to get it under control.

"I'm going to kill you," Adam muttered, gasping.

"With what, Jem's knife? Or were you planning to smother me with your pillow?" This set them off again. It felt wonderful to laugh, even for just a moment, at the horrible indignities of their day. After all, they were in the Nordlands, dressed as Ministerium Hall lackeys while the rest of their friends were back at school—except for Frankie.

"Do you think Frankie's all right?" Henry asked nervously.

"She better be," Adam said.

They had the next hour free, as the envoy was sequestered in a meeting room with Yascherov. Henry and Adam had planned to poke around Partisan Keep, but they hadn't bargained for it being Saturday, or the weather turning rainy.

Partisan students choked the corridors and sat on staircases, laughing and joking, playing harmonicas or penny whistles, and flipping through magazines.

When they caught sight of Henry's and Adam's ridiculous livery, they leered.

"Er, maybe this was a bad idea," Adam muttered, admitting defeat. "We're not exactly inconspicuous, mate."

"I know," Henry said, running a hand through his hair in anguish. "Ugh, this is useless." They headed back in the direction they'd come, but as a last-minute thought, Henry held open a door that led out the side of the castle.

"What are you doing?" Adam whispered.

Henry shrugged. "Aren't you curious?"

"About what?" Adam asked.

"Well, this is the capital."

They started down the steps carved into the hill, which took them through a twisting stone passageway flanked by two crumbling watchtowers. The passageway ended abruptly, blocking their path with a heavy iron gate topped in nasty spikes. A hulking boy in a Partisan School uniform, his chest decorated with gleaming badges, peered out of the watchtower.

"Aye?" he called. "Ye want to pass?"

"We've been sent on an errand in the city," Henry called back.

The boy shrugged and twisted what looked like a ship's wheel made of metal, sliding the gate aside just narrowly enough for Henry and Adam to squeeze through.

And just like that, they were in Romborough.

It was an ancient city, with buildings still intact from the time of the Sasson conquerors, and ruins that dated back even earlier. At the bottom of the hill, as if in miniature, they could see the steam engine idling in the station, gleaming alongside two dingy Nordlandic cargo trains.

"What do you want to do?" Adam asked.

"Count the seven pylons?" Henry joked.

Adam snorted. After the Romans had disassembled Stonehenge, seven of the pylons had been erected to form the border of what was now known as the Old City, the most ancient part of Romborough. As they headed down the central road, they passed the first of the pylons, erected outside a rolling and ancient graveyard. Beyond the graveyard was a stone church, its roof perfectly round, its windows simple slits.

Most of the buildings were festooned with the Nordlandic flag, the three serpents and the star, which billowed over the packed dirt road. A horse-driven omnibus clattered past, crammed full of miserable-looking passengers and squalling babies.

Many of the shop fronts bore portraits of the chancellor, with his dark pointed beard and cruel gaze. Still more shop fronts were boarded up, or closed for no discernible reason.

Perhaps because of the gray sky, very few people stopped to linger in the streets. They scuttled along, disappearing into the entrances of the narrow closes—the covered alleyways that lined Cairway Road. Henry and Adam received more than a few odd glances due to their livery, but everyone seemed too afraid to be caught staring.

The road widened the farther they went from Partisan, and stalls began to appear on opposite sides. Barefoot children ran across the road, and vendors cooked sausages and nuts, which everyone stared at longingly, Henry and Adam included. The stalls sold all sorts of things—secondhand clothing, mended crockery, even sullen-looking vegetables that had refused to grow to their full potential.

A few ragged girls sold matches on the doorsteps, and other things, perhaps, though Henry didn't care to find out.

At the end of the market, they reached a square where a more prosperous market bustled with patrons. In the center of the square stood an enormous bronze statue of Yurick Mors waving his serpent flag, dressed in the defiant long coat and armband of the revolutionary he had once been.

"'Yea though we roar with the fire of a mighty dragon, we are but its scales, all cut from the same mold, and of equal worth,'" Henry quoted, nodding toward the statue. It was the refrain of the revolution, a verse used long ago to open the clandestine meetings where Mors and his associates had plotted to overthrow the monarchy and publicly behead all aristocrats who would not renounce their titles and land at his behest.

And then the piercing cry of a newspaper boy made Henry jump.

"*Common Comrade*! Get yer free Nordlandic news!" he cried. The newsboy stood cheekily at the base of the statue, waving an armload of newspapers.

"Want one?" Adam asked.

"Do you even have to ask?"

The newsboy balked at the sight of them, but Henry smiled and held out his hand.

"We'll each take one," Henry said.

The newsboy hesitated a moment, deliberating, and then handed over the papers.

"Is this the only newspaper in the city, or are there others?" Henry asked.

The newsboy scowled. "Ain't nothin' aside the *Comrade*."

With the newspapers under their arms, Henry and Adam hurried back toward the castle.

The kitchen bustled with the Partisan School staff in their thin, plain uniforms when Henry and Adam arrived, out of breath, having just stashed the newspapers under their mattresses, but something seemed wrong somehow.

Henry puzzled over this, his stomach growling as he watched the serving boys arranging platters of food, and kitchen maids preparing dessert, their hair twisted up into tightly knotted kerchiefs. He remembered what Frankie had said about women dressing differently in the Nordlands, and he supposed the hair scarves and loose, long dresses with high collars were a bit different from the aprons and mobcaps Liza and Mary wore.

And then Henry realized what was bothering him. "They're not making enough food," he whispered to Adam.

Adam's stomach grumbled loudly in response. "When do *we* eat?" he whined.

"After we serve the envoy," Henry whispered back.

Across the kitchen Henry caught sight of Jem, who

made a show of reaching into his pocket, removing his knife, and flipping it open with a grin.

"Excuse me," Henry said to one of the Nordlandic servants who passed by.

The boy turned, terrified.

"Is this the only kitchen?" Henry asked.

The boy shook his head. "We cook fer the teachers an' visiting compatriots," he snapped.

Henry raised an eyebrow at this news. For a country that prided itself on equality, it didn't seem fair, and it certainly didn't seem in line with the motto of a "common good," if the people who preached such things had a private kitchen where their meals were prepared separately. But, then, many things in the Nordlands were contrary to the values that they preached. At least the kitchen seemed familiar, despite the strange uniforms and the unfamiliar foods.

Henry and the other boys with the envoy waited to be handed serving platters to take to the sideboard in the private dining room where Yascherov was entertaining the guests.

And then a serving girl who was grating potatoes dropped one, and it bounced across the kitchen, coming to a stop near Henry. He bent to retrieve it, and the girl rushed over. When Henry caught sight of her, he nearly lost his hold on the slippery potato as well.

It was Frankie.

Henry nudged Adam, but Adam had already noticed. His eyes were wide and frantic.

"What are you doing here?" Henry whispered, handing her back the potato.

Frankie grinned and shook some potato peelings from her smock. "Well, I wasn't going to wait in the storage car all weekend," she whispered back fiercely.

Henry shook his head in annoyance and glanced at the rest of the kitchen to see if anyone else was watching. Jem and George were.

"Can we help with the potatoes?" Henry asked in a low tone.

Frankie nodded, and they followed her to the mound of potatoes, forming a circle around the peelings bin.

"Well," Adam said, "this is a surprise."

"And by 'surprise' he means 'horrible idea,'" Henry whispered.

"What's horrible about it?" Frankie retorted. "I signed on as a maid, and I'll sneak away tomorrow to meet the train. In the meantime I'll have proper meals and a bed to sleep in, and a bath, thank you very much."

"This is really dangerous," Henry pressed. "What if someone finds out who you are?"

"In the next twelve hours?" Frankie asked with a derisive snort. "No one suspects anything. Besides which, it's just supper, then some cleaning and then bed."

Henry had to admit that she had a fair point.

"Why didn't you tell us what you were planning on the train?" Adam asked.

Frankie scowled. "Because I knew *he'd* be against it." She pointed her potato accusingly at Henry.

"Of course I'm against it," Henry said. "You don't know the first thing about being a maid. You could complicate everything."

"Well, I won't," Frankie said.

"You might." Henry glared.

"Stop it," Adam said. "Listen, Frankie, we're going to have a look around the castle tonight. Can you meet us outside the kitchen at midnight?"

"I'll try," Frankie said, and then shot Henry an enormous mocking grin. "If I haven't blown all of our covers by then."

"You're unbelievable," Henry snapped, slamming a perfectly peeled potato into the basket.

* * *

"I can't believe you invited her," Henry accused.

Adam shrugged and continued transferring dirty plates onto the serving trolley. The envoy had just finished supper, and before Henry and Adam could eat, they had to clear plates.

Jem and George were serving brandy and cigars in one of the reception rooms, and thankfully, supper had passed without incident.

"Why shouldn't I have invited her?" Adam retorted.

"Don't stack the plates that high. They'll fall," Henry chided. "And I can think of about a hundred reasons."

"Well, sorry, but I'm too hungry to think," Adam shot back.

"Here," Henry said, passing Adam half a roll that had been left on the table.

Adam stuffed it into his mouth. "What do we do now?" he asked thickly.

"Dishes," Henry said, nodding toward the cart piled high with soiled serving platters and dirty plates.

"Oh," Adam said, his face falling.

Back in the kitchen the rest of the servants were eating supper together at the long wooden table by the fireplace. Stools and overturned crates were crammed together, and everyone ate silently, hungrily piling food into their mouths. No one looked up when Henry and Adam came in. Next to the sink were four meager plates of food, meant for them.

Henry rolled up his sleeves to scrub dishes, but his gaze fell on the salt and pepper shakers sitting among the dirty serving platters, and he grinned.

"Do we get to eat now?" Adam asked hopefully as Henry picked up the salt.

"Even better," Henry said, handing Adam the pepper. "We get to enact our revenge." Henry liberally tipped the salt over two of the plates of food.

Adam grinned, enthusiastically adding pepper.

"I do hope Jem and George don't mind a bit of extra flavor," Henry said with mock concern.

"What do you mean, 'extra flavor'? This is how food tastes in the Nordlands," Adam said innocently, with another vigorous twist of pepper.

Henry shook his head, his grin stretching wider. "We should probably eat ours before they make us swap."

Adam gladly picked up the slice of rough bread topped with meat and gravy and enthusiastically took a bite, gravy dribbling down his chin. Henry dug into his own supper with equal enthusiasm.

They were just finishing the dishes when Jem and

George sauntered into the kitchen and seized their plates of food. Henry waited, casually wiping a tea towel against a gravy dish that had long since dried.

"Ugh!" Jem said, making a face. "This is disgusting."

"I wouldn't insult Nordlandic food if I were you," Henry said, holding back a smile.

"*You* did somethin'," George accused, pointing a finger at Henry.

"Maybe," Henry said coolly. "An' maybe I'll do it again, if yeh don' start pullin' yer weight."

George scowled.

Jem glared.

"Whaddaya want?" George demanded.

"What's fair," Henry said. "Adam wants his pillow back. An' tomorrow you lot are haulin' the bags back to the train, seein' as how we brought them up."

"I don't really need my pillow back," Adam muttered.

Henry elbowed him. Jem and George exchanged a glance.

"Done," George said.

Henry put down the gravy dish and pushed past them. Adam followed.

"Oi, why did you tell them it was us?" Adam whispered.

"If we didn't admit to it, they would have punished us for the prank," Henry returned. "That's how you handle boys like them—show them you're not afraid to retaliate."

"I suppose," Adam said, "although you might have asked for a top bunk rather than my pillow."

"Bottom bunks are better," Henry said, pushing aside the heavy wool blanket that had been strung across the entrance to their room in place of a proper door. "We can sneak out more easily."

"I knew that," Adam muttered.

It seemed as though Jem and George would never go to sleep. Jem dangled his legs over the side of the bed, his unwashed feet in Adam's face, torturing everyone with hideous harmonica playing for an age.

Henry and Adam read the Nordlandic newspapers they'd gotten earlier, looking for anything important or suspicious. But the newspapers were disappointing and filled with propaganda stories such as "Five Ways to Show Your Support for the Chancellor," or inventive recipes that could be cooked with the standard food rations. At this, Henry snorted. It was a crime in the Nordlands to teach women to read, and then they put recipes in the paper.

He flipped to the next page, an illustration of how

to recognize different types of "heathens," with grossly drawn caricatures and a list of places where heathens had been recently spotted.

There was an article on Morsmas, the upcoming holiday celebrating Chancellor Mors's birthday, and one on appropriate ways to celebrate, and an interview with a woman whose town had been recently searched as part of the policing agency's new initiative.

Twyla Ulkins, 47, was delighted when a policing agent came to search her quiet suburban neighborhood of Little Septimus, South Nordlandshire, under the new laws.

"Now I feel safe," said Miss Ulkins, a washerwoman. "I never know what my neighbors are up to—some could be hiding heathens in their basements! But after that nice young policing agent came to inquire, I can sleep safely with the knowledge that there's nothing to fear here in Little Septimus."

Finally Jem and George dropped off to sleep. Henry and Adam changed into their plain, rumpled clothing and crept out into the hallway.

"I've never had a strong opinion on the harmonica before tonight," Adam mused. "But now I bloody loathe the thing."

Henry snorted. "Do you know what time it is?" he asked.

"No pocket watch." Adam shrugged.

"Me neither," Henry said.

They tiptoed past the scullery and into the kitchen. It was nearly midnight. The kitchen was dark, the fire in the hearth banked and flickering feebly. A wooden stool was pulled up in front of the fire, and a fat bald man sat upon it, snoring loudly, with a mangy dog at his feet. A set of keys dangled from the man's belt, stamped with the Partisan School insignia.

Henry made a face and tiptoed past. Adam did the same, edging toward the wall and away from the dog, which opened one eye and growled in warning at the two of them. They stepped out of the kitchen and into the corridor beyond, where they were to meet Frankie.

Henry leaned back against the cold stone wall and breathed a sigh.

"There's nothing in the newspaper," Adam complained.

"I know," Henry said. "And that's what worries me."

"How do you mean?"

"It's obvious that anyone with a brain isn't relying on the *Common Comrade* for their news."

"Do you think there's some sort of secret newspaper?" Adam asked.

"I'm certain of it," Henry said. "And I want to know what it says."

"Know what what says?" Frankie asked, startling them. They hadn't heard her come around the corner.

"Blimey, don't do that!" Adam complained.

Frankie wiggled a stockinged foot at them. "All the better to sneak with. And at least *I* thought to bring a candle."

Henry had to give her that.

Frankie grinned, tossing her braid over one shoulder. She still wore the modest maid's outfit, and without her shoes she seemed smaller somehow, and more delicate, as though she needed protecting.

"What are we looking for, exactly?" Adam asked.

"Anything suspicious," Henry said. "Combat training rooms, weapons, odd books, secret newspapers. I'm not really certain what. Just something that we can bring to the lord ministers as proof that the conscription laws need to be changed, or that the Nordlands have violated the Longsword Treaty."

The three of them followed the twisting dark corridor until it deposited them in the main entrance hall, at the foot of an enormous staircase that branched in two directions.

"Any preference?" Henry asked.

"Let's go to the left," Frankie said.

And so they went to the left, which led them to a corridor of classrooms.

"You reckon we should look in the classrooms?" Adam asked.

Henry shrugged, and they did, but the classrooms turned up nothing out of the ordinary. Neither did a series of study cubicles—which Henry strongly suspected used to be weapons closets—or a particularly suspicious-looking doorway that led to a cupboard full of lab coats.

The second floor was no better.

They were just about to give up when Henry spotted a landscape painting hanging above a stair that looked oddly familiar. "I know where we are!" Henry whispered triumphantly. "Come on!"

Adam, who was shuffling sleepily behind Frankie, yawned loudly in response.

Henry shot him a look.

"Sorry," Adam said. "I was up before dawn."

"We all were," Frankie put in. "Stop lagging, Adam. You're rubbish as a spy."

"Well, you're rubbish as a runaway," he shot back.

"At least I can peel a potato," Frankie retorted.

"Shhh!" Henry warned, his heart pounding. "Nearly there."

He turned a corner, and there—just before a narrow stairwell—was the fish statue, and the entrance to the secret training room.

"That's it?" Adam wrinkled his nose, unimpressed.

But Henry paid him no attention. He put his ear to the door and listened. Silence.

And then, with a deep breath he pressed the bit of decoration in the wall paneling.

Nothing happened. Henry frowned and pressed harder. Still nothing.

"Frankie, can you hold your candle closer?" he asked. Frankie stepped next to him, the loose sleeve of her dress brushing against his arm as she held the candle aloft.

"Er, thanks," Henry said, uncomfortably aware of their closeness.

"What's wrong?" Adam whined.

"I don't know," Henry said. "Maybe it's locked." He frowned at the wall for another minute, but finally had to admit that they weren't getting in.

"Let's check the towers," he said, trying not to let his disappointment show. But the first tower they checked yielded a collection of telescopes and a large astronomy chart. The second was filled with herbs drying from the ceiling, and a dozen tables, each set with a mortar and pestle.

"We're not going to find anything," Adam said with anguish.

Henry bit his lip. He'd always thought he would luckily stumble upon something the way he had during the Inter-School Tournament, and he'd never pictured the reality of finding nothing. He had no idea what to do. He just knew that there was no possible way he could return to Knightley empty handed.

"I suppose we could give Lord Marchbanks the newspaper," Henry said.

"What does that prove?" Adam asked, at the same moment that Frankie demanded, "What newspaper?"

Quickly Henry explained.

"But you said it yourself," Frankie said. "It's a perfectly innocent paper."

"It proves there's some other newspaper out there, filled with incriminating articles," Henry argued.

"Maybe," Frankie said, her hand on her hip. "Or maybe it proves that no one in the Nordlands is interested in politics. They just want to be left alone to enjoy their quiet, boring, equally equal lives."

"She does have a point there," Adam said.

Henry shook his head angrily. "No. There has to be something. We're just not looking hard enough."

"We could check the armory," Adam suggested.

Henry considered this. It wasn't a bad idea. But by the time they found the armory, even Henry was yawning, although he forced himself to keep going.

The equipment room was dark, its cupboards looming. Adam grabbed the handle of one of the cupboards and yanked. "Locked," he moaned.

Henry bent down to inspect the lock, and then took a few lengths of wire from his pocket. "Can either of you . . . ?" Henry asked.

"I brought my own," Frankie said, smirking as she removed a hairpin from her braid. She set to work on one of the cabinets, and Henry set to work on another.

"Don't mind me," Adam said. "I'll just sit down here on this nice bench and have a nap."

"You will not," Henry said. "Someone has to have a look at the armory." Adam sighed and trudged through the archway into the armory.

Henry gave the bit of wire a sharp twist. He heard part of the mechanism click.

"I could have a look around the maids' quarters in the morning," Frankie offered.

"Thank you," Henry said, frowning at the lock and giving the wire a final twist. The cabinet clicked open. But it was full of disappointingly ordinary practice foils and sabres with blunted bits on the end.

Frankie managed to open her cabinet a moment later, but it contained nothing more than masks and gloves. "Maybe there's a false back?" Frankie asked.

Henry glanced over. "There isn't enough depth," he said, sitting down on the bench and putting his head in his hands. "I was so certain," he mumbled.

Frankie quietly closed the cupboards and sat down next to him. "I'm sorry," she said.

"So we're going to be expelled." He hadn't truly believed it until that moment, but the more he thought about it, the more obvious it became. They'd been caught wandering Knightley after lights-out, had faked ill, and had run away to the Nordlands to prove the unprovable—to say nothing of the battle society.

"I could go back with you," Frankie said, so softly that Henry thought he'd misheard.

Henry looked up. "What?"

"Instead of going off on my own, I could go back with you and Adam, to Knightley. You'd be quite the heroic young knights, returning from your quest to rescue the foolish young maiden from the clutches of an evil foreign ruler." Frankie bit her lip.

It was a generous offer, Henry had to admit. And it was certainly a sacrifice on Frankie's part—one he'd never considered asking her to make. But returning to Knightley with Frankie in tow would certainly give Lord Havelock pause in expelling them.

"Saying that we've found you doesn't change anything that really matters," Henry pointed out.

"It changes your being expelled, and that matters," Frankie said. "Besides, I can run away again if I feel like it."

Henry sighed. Maybe Frankie was right. After all, they had to make the best of their situation somehow. And then Adam appeared in the doorway.

"Find anything?" Henry asked.

"No," he said, shuddering. "Unless you count a bloody huge spider."

"Let's go to sleep," Henry said. "Whatever this school is hiding, we're not going to find it."

"I'll see you in the morning," Frankie promised as they closed the door to the armory.

"It *is* morning," Adam complained, yawning.

20

THE EMPTY
COMPARTMENT

By the time Jem and George began to carry the luggage back down to the train, Henry was ready for the day to be over. Mr. Frist had woken the boys unforgivably early, filled their morning with the small but hideous tasks of ironing cravats, waking the members of the envoy with fresh jugs of water and towels for their nightstands, and bringing up tea. He then left them at the mercy of the valets while the rest of the envoy closed themselves once again in a meeting room with Yascherov and his men.

Henry ached from lack of sleep and too little food, but he knew that Adam was fairing even worse.

They'd caught sight of Frankie in the kitchens when

they'd returned the tea services. She was being sent on some errand to Romborough and had winked at them as she'd picked up an enormous wicker basket. At least she seemed to be doing all right.

Henry and Adam gave the guest rooms a final sweep for personal effects left behind and, finding none, returned to the kitchen, where the cook was packing the food hamper for the journey.

"Off with ye," he said without even so much as a glance at Henry and Adam.

Somehow downhill wasn't quite so bad as up, and they managed to wrestle the hamper down to the train station without too much of an ordeal—although Adam did whack his shin rather hard a few times.

Steam billowed impatiently from the train as Henry and Adam deposited the hamper in the kitchen car. They could hear Jem and George arguing over the luggage, which had apparently gotten jumbled up. Henry grinned.

"Shall we stash our bags?" Adam asked.

"Might as well."

They passed Mr. Frist, who called after them, "Train's leaving in three minutes, boys!"

Henry slid open the door to the servants car and

then knocked on the door to the storage car, sliding it open. "Frankie?" he called.

There was no answer.

"Are you there?" Henry called, lifting up the corner of the tarp to reveal her hiding place.

It was empty.

The train whistle shrilled, making Henry jump. "She's not here," he said, trying to think.

"Well, where is she?" Adam asked.

"She was sent on an errand," Henry realized with a gulp. "I don't think she came back."

"What do you mean, you don't think?" Adam accused.

Henry closed his eyes, trying to remember. "The basket she took wasn't back in the kitchen when we got the hamper," Henry said finally.

"What do we do?" Adam asked, panicked. "The train's about to depart!"

"We can't leave her!" Henry said.

"Well, we can't stay in the Nordlands, either! What about school? What about money?"

"I'm not stranding her here," Henry protested. "We'll figure something out if we stay. There will be another envoy next month."

Adam went white. "A month," he moaned. "My

family would panic. Not to mention, I'm a rubbish servant, and Jewish to top it off."

"You go back with the envoy," Henry said quickly. "Tell the headmaster what happened. I'll stay with Frankie."

Adam shot Henry a look of pure anguish as the train whistle sounded again. "Henry, you can't leave me! They'll ask questions!" he wailed.

Henry grimaced at this. "Cover for me as long as you can. Say I'm feeling poorly."

"Wait!" Adam cried, but the carriages had already begun to groan at their couplings.

Henry stepped onto the hitch between the cars. "I have to go," he said. "I'll sign on as a servant at Partisan. It'll be fine."

"It won't!" Adam exclaimed. "I'll be expelled if I turn up at school without you! And what if the headmaster doesn't believe me and thinks you two have run off together?"

Henry gulped. He hadn't thought of that. The compartment shuddered as the train began to roll forward. "I don't know what else to do!" Henry cried in exasperation. "I'm sorry. I can't leave her." And with that he jumped onto the tracks.

"Henry!" Adam called, and then took a deep breath to steel his nerves. "Wait! I'm coming with you!"

As they watched the train depart without them, Henry was struck with the horrible realization of what they'd just done. They were stuck in the Nordlands—for a month. The three of them.

Henry bit his lip and brushed off his livery. "We should get out of here," he said.

Adam groaned. "I just jumped off a moving train. Give me a minute."

"It wasn't moving!" Henry protested.

Adam glared.

"It wasn't moving that fast," Henry amended.

Adam climbed to his feet and shouldered his bag.

"I can't believe you stayed," Henry said.

"Neither can I," Adam said, and snorted. "The starvation must be making me mental."

"Well, mental or not, I'm glad you're here," Henry admitted. "Come on."

They changed from their livery in the train station and trudged back up the hill to the Partisan School wearing their raggedy shirts and trousers. Their hands were blistered and raw from scrubbing dishes and soft rains had come overnight, dampening the soil, which clung desperately to the soles of their old boots. They looked tired and wan, with circles under their eyes and stomachs rumbling with hunger.

Somehow, Henry thought wryly, he didn't anticipate problems convincing anyone that they were down on their luck and desperate for work.

He was right. No sooner had they turned up at Partisan and inquired after serving work than they were standing once again in the staff kitchen, being scrutinized by the large-bellied man they'd seen sleeping in front of the hearth the night before.

He didn't seem to recognize them, and Henry tried a bit of a Nordlandic accent, explaining that he and his cousin had been living in South Britain before Mors closed the border, and they had some experience with serving work.

The man scratched the side of his stomach, sized the boys up, and asked them to follow him. He lumbered out of the kitchen and down the corridor, twisting down a narrow passageway that barely allowed for his girth. The passageway deposited them in a much larger and far shabbier kitchen.

"Cook?" the man yelled. "Got ye some new lads."

Cook, a man with an enormously drooping mustache and biceps like hams, looked up from the rind of cheese he was slicing. "What's yer names?" Cook asked.

"Henry, er—Gray. And this here's me cousin Adam, er—Beckham," Henry said nervously.

"We've been wantin' some lads in the staff kitchen, but let's see how ye do here first," Cook said with a scowl.

"We're hired?" Adam asked.

"Aye," Cook said. "May I not live to regret it." He sniffled loudly, wiped his nose on his sleeve, and pulled a string that connected to one of the dozen bells on the wall.

"Sit ye down and wait," the cook said, pointing his knife toward a rickety wooden table with a dreary collection of wobbly stools. Half a loaf of bread sat on the table. Adam's stomach growled loudly as he stared longingly at the bread.

"Please, sir, is there something we might eat?" Henry asked.

"Yesterday's bread's on the table. Take a slice fer yer luncheon if ye've had none," Cook said.

Adam was already cramming the bread into his mouth with enthusiasm. Henry rather suspected that when they got back to school, Adam wouldn't be nearly so much of a picky eater as before.

School. Henry's stomach lurched at the thought. They were to find out the results of their half-term exams that week. He pictured Rohan and Derrick and everyone going to class without them, Rohan alone in their triple room, and Valmont left with running the battle society. Professor Stratford, worrying. Adam's parents.

After a few minutes a no-nonsense-looking young man of around nineteen appeared in the doorway, entirely unruffled.

"Ye rang fer me, Cook?" the young man asked, raising an inquiring eyebrow.

"Got ye some new serving boys, Compatriot Garen," Cook said.

"Thank the chancellor!" the young man said. "We've been understaffed fer a week!" The young man straightened his waistcoat and glanced toward Henry and Adam. "I'm Garen," he said. "You boys can come with me."

Henry and Adam numbly followed Garen, who kept up a steady stream of chatter as he led them through the castle. They were expected to report to the kitchens by six every morning, to clean the school between meals, to shine the boots of the senior-ranked students two nights a week. The list of tasks went on exhaustively.

"Any questions?" Garen asked, pausing at the bottom of a steep and precarious stairwell with stone steps so worn that they appeared to sag.

"Sorry—senior-ranked students?" Henry asked.

"Those with white stripes on the arms of their jackets," Garen clarified.

Henry bit his lip. He'd meant to ask how students were promoted to different ranks, but Garen had misunderstood. Not quite daring to rephrase his question, Henry followed Garen and Adam up the ancient stairwell. The stairwell led to the castle's attic, a haphazard honeycomb of low-ceilinged rooms.

Garen pointed out the latrine, the serving girls' bedchamber, the cleaning cupboard, and the cupboard with staff uniforms. He stopped at the last, sized up Henry and Adam, and then ducked inside, returning a minute later with a bundle of clothing.

"If they don't fit, ye can swap them yerselves," Garen said. "And here we are. Serving lads' bedchamber. Any of the cots here are free."

Henry frowned. There had to be at least four empty beds. And Garen had said something earlier about being short staffed. Granted, it didn't seem the best of jobs, but something about the way Garen was so eager to have them on staff worried Henry deeply. He dropped his satchel onto one of the cots, and Adam chose the cot next to Henry's.

"Get changed, and then ye can start with an easy enough task fer the afternoon. The spare silverware needs polishin'. Cook can set ye to it. Ye'll keep to his orders in the kitchens and mine otherwise, mind."

"Yes, sir," Henry said.

"It's 'Aye, Compatriot Garen,'" Garen corrected firmly, turning on his heel and closing the door behind him. Once Garen had gone, Adam held up the staff uniform shirt and made a face.

"What are we, vicars?"

The shirts were collarless, with tight high buttons around the throat. But the worst bit were the suspenders, which fastened inside the waistband of the trousers.

"At least we don't have to bind up our hair," Henry pointed out as they headed down to the kitchens.

Cook showed them to a storage pantry with a discouragingly small slat window. "Ye better not scrimp the silver," Cook warned, showing them where the polish was stored and then slamming the door.

Henry explained to Adam what they were to do, and

the boys set to work. "Did you catch that bit about the school being understaffed?" Henry asked.

Adam looked up from the spoon he'd been attacking with the polishing cloth. "What?"

"Why do *you* think Partisan is understaffed?" Henry pressed.

"Dunno. Maybe it's just a rubbish job." Adam shrugged.

"Maybe." Henry was unconvinced.

"All right. Let's hear it," Adam said. He admired the spoon he'd just polished, then hung it from his nose.

Henry laughed. "Don't," he said. "Someone has to eat off that."

Adam removed the spoon. "Smells like polish anyhow," he muttered. "All right. I'm ready for your absurd theory."

"It isn't absurd," Henry protested. "And I don't have a theory—yet. I just know that those empty cots are far from the worst beds in the room, and Garen said they've been understaffed for a week, which means that no one on staff claimed the beds."

"Could be," Adam said.

"I'm right," Henry argued. "Everyone avoided those beds after their occupants left. The school is desperate for staff. And the boys who served the envoy last month wouldn't go a second round."

"George did," Adam pointed out.

"Well, not everyone at Partisan quit either. Just some," Henry returned.

"So now that we're stuck here, you think there's something horrible happening?" Adam whimpered.

"Not necessarily horrible," Henry said. "It just seems like people have been spooked by something."

"Maybe they're just spooked because the students are being trained in combat?" Adam suggested.

"Maybe," Henry said doubtfully.

They didn't see Frankie again until much later that night, as they were returning to the servants' quarters after mopping the dining hall. She paused a moment at the bottom of the stairs, yawning.

"Frankie," Henry whispered fiercely.

She turned and gawped at them. "What are you doing here?" she asked, grabbing Henry and Adam by their sleeves and dragging them farther down the corridor. "I thought you'd gone."

"You didn't make it back to the train," Adam accused.

"I got lost in Romborough," Frankie said. "On that

dratted errand. I was so certain you'd left. I've been in a panic all afternoon."

"Sorry," Henry said. "We were stuck polishing silverware."

Frankie sized up their staff uniforms and nodded. "Common kitchens," she said.

Henry's eyes widened with surprise. "How can you tell?"

"No waistcoat," she said as though it were obvious.

"Oh," Henry muttered.

"So here's some bad news," Adam said brightly. "We're stuck here for a month."

Frankie went pale. "A month?"

"That's when the next envoy is due to arrive," Henry said, shrugging.

"B-but—," Frankie spluttered.

"Fear not, fair maiden. We're here to rescue you," Adam said. "And by 'rescue' I mean 'endure a month in the Nordlands at your side.'"

"I—" Frankie shook her head slightly as if to clear it, and then began again. "You chose to stay here for a month because of me?"

Henry and Adam exchanged a glance. "We couldn't leave you here," Henry said with a shrug.

"But what about school?" Frankie pressed.

"I have some textbooks in my bag," Henry said, frowning. "I suppose we could try to keep up with the reading."

"Blimey, I sure am glad you brought those textbooks now," Adam said with a snort.

Frankie grinned, and then noticed Henry's scowl. "Sorry," she muttered.

"Does anyone know you're here?" Henry asked.

"No!" Frankie retorted. "Did *you* tell anyone where you were going?"

"Actually, yes," Henry admitted.

"Rohan," Frankie guessed.

Henry nodded.

"Professor Stratford?" Frankie continued. "Anyone else?"

"Well," Adam hedged. "Derrick. And Valmont."

"You told *Valmont*?"

"It's complicated," Henry muttered.

"What's complicated about it?" Frankie accused. "You chose to be friends with him and pushed me away for no reason."

"Then why am I here now?" Henry challenged. "Why did I jump off a blasted moving train to spend a month polishing boots in the Nordlands?"

Frankie turned crimson. "Sorry," she murmured.

"I jumped off a moving train too," Adam put in.

"Ooh, aren't you a gallant young knight," Frankie taunted.

"Shhh!" Henry said, glancing around. "We shouldn't talk like that here. It isn't safe."

"I should get to bed anyhow," Frankie said. "We can talk in the morning. I don't think it would draw any suspicion . . . unless it's improper?"

"It isn't," Henry confirmed. "The serving class do as they wish, at least back home. But it wouldn't hurt for us to make certain we know the customs here."

"I'll see you in the morning," Frankie said primly, heading back in the direction of the servants' quarters.

"Er," Henry said pointedly.

"What?" Frankie asked.

"Boys' bedchamber is just across the way from the girls'," Henry said.

At this a slight blush colored Frankie's cheeks. "Well, come on," she snapped.

At the top of the stairs she regarded the two boys thoughtfully. "Servants can do as they wish?" she questioned.

Henry nodded.

Frankie gave each of them a quick hug. "Thank you for coming back for me," she whispered before darting into the girls' bedchamber.

Adam stood there, grinning ear to ear.

"Wipe that grin off your face and come on," Henry said.

"Did you know," Adam said thoughtfully as Henry forcibly steered him into the boys' bedchamber, "that girls don't wear corsets in the Nordlands?"

"I'd imagine not. It must be impossible to scrub floors if you can hardly breathe," Henry returned, and then he realized that Adam had been talking about Frankie. He blushed, but thankfully, it was quite dark inside the boys' bedchamber.

By the small amount of light that spilled in from the hallway from a low-turned gas jet, they changed into the nightshirts Garen had provided for them. The other boys were already asleep, the room buzzing with their soft snores and the occasional cough or sniffle.

Henry was exhausted, but even long after Adam's snores joined the rest, he stared up at the low ceiling, unable to sleep.

Somehow he'd wound up back in the attics, a serving boy at a posh boys' school. He wondered if he'd ever have the chance to be a student at Knightley again, or if the opportunity had rushed past him, like a missed train.

And then he wondered why his heart had lurched at the thought of Frankie being left alone in the Nordlands—why he'd leapt off the train to stay with her. And finally he wondered after the strange happenings he'd noticed in the Nordlands. The propaganda-filled newspapers, the missing servants, the beds that spooked the other boys.

Perhaps they could redeem themselves after all—return to Knightley triumphant, having successfully rescued Frankie, and bringing with them the evidence that would prevent a war, or at least help everyone prepare for one.

21

THE UNCLAIMED
LUGGAGE

Rohan woke on Monday morning with a start. He listened to the peal of bells, feeling as though he'd fallen asleep waiting for something, and was waiting still.

And then he glanced toward the two empty beds and tried very hard not to panic. Henry and Adam had been due to return the night before. He'd tried to wait up for them but had fallen asleep.

Their absence threw him. Had something happened?

Rohan dressed quickly and sat with James at chapel, trying to ignore the questioning glances from Derrick and Valmont. Did they know? Apparently so, as both boys ambushed him the moment the service ended.

"What's happened?" Derrick asked.

"I don't know," Rohan said tersely.

"Maybe the envoy is late," Valmont said.

"How the devil did *you* get involved in this?" Derrick asked Valmont.

"I might ask you the same," Valmont returned.

"Be involved in it together, then," Rohan said. "I wanted nothing to do with it from the beginning." And with that he quickened his pace toward the dining hall.

Even though saying that Henry and Adam hadn't gotten up for chapel and were currently indisposed wasn't truly a lie, Rohan still felt as though it were. It wasn't until whispers started circulating that the search had been called off for the headmaster's daughter that Rohan decided to abandon his self-imposed silence.

He approached Derrick and Conrad after languages that afternoon.

"Want to know how we did on the midterm?" Conrad asked, as they had just gotten their marked translations back at the end of the lesson.

"No," Rohan said. "I, well, I've been hearing whispers that they've found news of Miss Winter."

"So have we," Derrick said.

"Well, do you know anything more about it?" Rohan pressed.

"Not a thing," Derrick said. "It's servants' gossip anyhow. But if I were you, I'd be concerned with your roommates. They can't stay ill forever."

"I told them I wasn't a part of this," Rohan muttered.

"No use bemoaning it now," Derrick scolded. "Man up."

Man up? Rohan thought bitterly. And do what? Confess to Lord Havelock that he'd stood idly by while his roommates ran off to the Nordlands?

Well, he reasoned, it was a servants' envoy. If anyone would know whether the envoy had come back the night before, it was the servants. Rohan shouldered his bag with a sigh and headed in the direction of the kitchens.

"Where are you going?" a voice drawled. Valmont leaned casually against the wall, a cold smile playing over his face.

"To the WC, if you don't mind," Rohan snapped.

"Wrong direction," Valmont said, his smile stretching wider.

Rohan glared.

"The way I see it," Valmont continued, unruffled,

"is that we've both been left with a rather unpleasant mess to clean up. I'd prefer we handled it together, if that's all right with you."

Rohan considered the proposition. It was a bit of a sticky situation, and he could do worse than ally himself with Lord Havelock's ward and nephew.

"Come on," he said finally.

Valmont fell into step. It didn't dawn on him where they were headed until Rohan paused at the top of a servants' staircase. "Keep your opinions to yourself, if you don't mind," Rohan snapped.

"Suits me," Valmont said coolly.

The kitchen was bustling, with the staff already hard at work preparing supper. A few serving boys and maids glanced up when Rohan and Valmont appeared in the doorway. "Er, excuse me," Rohan tried, a bit nervously. He'd never ventured to the kitchens by himself, and rarely accompanied Henry and Adam, who were veterans at coaxing biscuits and tarts out of the softhearted maids.

"Yes, sir?" one of the newer maids said, flouncing over and bobbling a curtsy. "Anythin' I can 'elp with?"

Rohan shot Valmont a warning glance. "Er, is Liza here?" he inquired.

The maid tittered.

Rohan turned crimson at the silent insinuation. "Just fetch her, will you?" he ordered imperiously.

"No need fer that, deary," Liza said, sauntering over as she dried her hands on a tea towel. "I'm here now." She stared at the boys, as though expecting a bow, but that would have been absurd, Rohan reasoned. He was the son of a duke, and he had no call to humble himself in the presence of school servants.

"Has the envoy returned?" Rohan demanded.

Liza pressed her lips together and continued drying her hands on the ragged tea towel.

"It's rather important," Rohan continued. "You see, my friends were on it—and they've left me in quite a pickle this af—"

"Come with me," Liza interrupted, seizing Rohan by the sleeve and towing him into the hallway. Valmont followed, snickering at the injustice.

"Now listen 'ere," she scolded, poking him in the chest with a finger. "Yeh can be polite about comin' down where yeh aren't wanted nor allowed an' demandin' answers."

Rohan blanched, and then with a sigh he favored the maid with a stiff bow. "My apologies, madam," he tried. "I'm quite out of sorts this afternoon. You see, my roommates are missing."

Liza, who'd been mollified by the bow and flowery language, suddenly paled. "Whatchoo mean, missing?"

"They've yet to return," Rohan clarified.

"But the envoy came back las' night," Liza said.

"Without them?" Rohan pressed.

Liza shrugged. "No one much noticed nothin' besides the carpetbag."

"The carpetbag?"

"Found it back in the storage car, they did. Full o' the belongings o' one Francesca Winter."

"What?" Rohan thundered.

"Shouldn't a told yeh that." Liza sulked. "The 'eadmaster don't want it gettin' out."

"Wait, I don't understand," Rohan said, frowning. "So where's Fra—er, Miss Winter?"

"Either she stowed away on that train fer two days an' then hopped off in the city with them fancy lords, or . . ."

"Or?" Rohan urged.

Liza grinned and leaned in close, relishing the dramatics. "She's in the Nordlands."

"But why would she get off in the city without her bag?" Rohan frowned.

"Tha's what I said!" Liza crowed. "But if Master Henry and Master Adam ain't returned neither, tha's a whole 'nother kettle o' kippers."

Valmont loudly cleared his throat. "Can we go?" he demanded.

"In a minute," Rohan snapped. "Hold on."

But Liza had slipped back into the kitchen, as cool as you please. The door slammed shut in their faces.

"You bowed to a servant," Valmont crowed.

Rohan glared. "Well, it got the job done. Now we know what's happened."

"Maybe," Valmont said. "Or maybe Grim ran off with that improper little lady friend of his and Beckerman's too much of a coward to come back here with the news."

"If you really think that, I have nothing more to say to you," Rohan said primly, hurrying up the staircase.

"What?" Valmont snapped. "Oh, very well. I was just being callous. I didn't mean it. Satisfied?"

"Hardly." Rohan waited for Valmont to catch up.

"Where are we going now?" Valmont asked.

"To see Professor Stratford," Rohan said tensely.

"Out of the question."

"Why?"

"Go by yourself, Mehta," Valmont spat, stalking off in the opposite direction.

"No," Rohan said. "You wanted in, and you can't very well dump this on me because you suddenly feel like it." Rohan crossed his arms and tapped his foot impatiently.

Valmont glared.

"What the deuces is your *problem*?" Rohan asked, and then he realized why Valmont had balked at the mention of where they were going. Professor Stratford had been Valmont's teacher back at the Midsummer School.

"Oh. Sorry. I'd forgotten the two of you are already acquainted," Rohan muttered.

Valmont scuffed the toe of his boot into the ragged carpet and was quiet for a long while. "Did you believe that serving girl?" Valmont finally asked.

"I wouldn't think there's a need to see Professor Stratford if I didn't. Besides which, he already knows most of it. I want to know what he's thinking."

"I cannot believe I'm doing this," Valmont said under his breath. "Lead the way."

Professor Stratford glanced up mournfully as the two boys hovered in the doorway to his study. The maid hadn't wanted to let them in, but Rohan had insisted. Now he wished he hadn't.

He barely knew Professor Stratford, and the professor looked terrible, his hair drooping forward and shading his brows, dark circles beneath his eyes, and the beginnings of a patchy beard.

"Oh, Rohan, I wasn't expecting you, lad," Professor Stratford said with an unconvincing smile. "And, my goodness, Valmont."

"Hello, Professor," Valmont mumbled.

"Sorry to interrupt," Rohan said with a solicitous bow. "Would you be able to spare a moment, sir?"

"So formal," Professor Stratford said, shaking his head. "Take a seat, boys, and tell me what I can help you with."

Rohan and Valmont exchanged a nervous glance as they settled into the chairs across from the professor's book-strewn desk. Headmaster Winter's house carried an air of misfortune, and the tragedy was thickest there in the professor's study.

"We've heard the news about Frankie's bag being located," Rohan said.

Professor Stratford bit his lip.

"Sir, what do you think has happened?" Rohan pressed.

But the professor said nothing. A silent war had broken out between Professor Stratford and Valmont—a staring match, of sorts. The professor steepled his fingers and waited.

Valmont cracked first. "You have my word that nothing will leave this room," he said sourly. "Grim and I haven't always gotten along, but we had an understanding, and he honored it when he could have betrayed me, so I owe him enough to keep quiet about whatever's happened."

Rohan stared at Valmont in shock. That was actually rather decent of him, and Rohan hadn't previously counted decency among Fergus Valmont's qualities.

"Thank you for the assurances, lad," Professor Stratford said, his mustache twitching as he attempted, and failed, to deliver yet another reassuring grin. "I hear your battle society has been quite the success, actually."

"Do you and your roommates tell him everything?" Valmont demanded, turning to Rohan.

Rohan shrugged. "He's a friend."

"You're *such* a trio of do-gooders," Valmont muttered.

"Well, we *are* knights in training," Rohan returned.

"Boys," Professor Stratford said, massaging his

temples. "Honestly you two are as bad as Henry and Frankie."

Valmont went cold. "Excuse me?" he asked icily.

Rohan couldn't help it—he burst out laughing. "Sorry," he said, still chortling. "Frightfully improper of me."

"Are Henry and Adam coming?" Professor Stratford asked. "Or are they resting? I'd imagine they're exhausted."

Rohan and Valmont exchanged a look of horror. The professor didn't know?

"B-but—," Rohan spluttered.

Professor Stratford frowned. "You're not here about Frankie," the professor said evenly.

"No, sir," they chorused.

"Henry and Adam never came back," Rohan admitted.

Professor Stratford went white, and then gray. His hands began to tremble. "Impossible," he breathed.

Rohan felt as though he ought to do something to comfort the professor, but he had no idea what. He shifted uneasily in his chair as Professor Stratford slowly processed this news, and its implications. And then the professor's eyes narrowed, and his attention came to rest on Rohan and Valmont once again.

"Who knows about this?" the professor asked.

"Us," Rohan said. "Derrick Marchbanks, sort of, but he encouraged them. And that kitchen maid who's always trying to fatten Adam up."

The professor snorted at this. "You're certain they didn't return?"

"Positive," Rohan said. "Do you think they were caught?" he asked.

Professor Stratford shook his head. "I hope not. Henry's a clever lad, and adept enough as a serving boy that they wouldn't suspect anything."

At this, Valmont snorted.

Rohan kicked him.

"There's only one explanation for it," Professor Stratford continued. "The boys must have discovered Frankie as a stowaway. If she left her bag, it was because she couldn't take it where she was going—a destination she hadn't originally intended."

"So you think she meant to go to the city and wound up in the Nordlands?" Rohan pressed.

"I do," Professor Stratford said. "I'd wager the three of them got stuck in the Nordlands somehow, and I hope it wasn't because they decided to go off chasing evidence of that infernal combat training Henry's so convinced the boys up there are learning." The professor thumped his fist against his desk, losing his calm demeanor. His shoulders trembled, and for a moment it seemed as though he might go to pieces in front of them. But then he took a great, shuddering breath and composed himself.

"I'm sorry, lads," the professor said. "It's just that I blame myself. I didn't stop them, and now they're in who knows what sort of danger."

"Can't we get them back?" Rohan asked.

"Not right away," Professor Stratford said sadly. "The border is closed, and it would be unwise to draw attention to the situation. But this isn't your concern. I'll bring this matter to the headmaster myself."

"Thank you," Rohan said.

"Yes, thank you, sir," Valmont echoed.

"I'll be as tactful as possible," the professor promised. "You boys weren't involved in this."

As they hurried from Professor Stratford's office, Rohan sighed with relief. It was no longer their problem. The adults would handle everything, the way things should have been done in the first place. After all, they were still just first years. What cause did they have to get involved with politics or even to challenge school rules? Systems worked, and authorities were to be obeyed, and if you forgot that, you wound up with a disaster like the Nordlands.

The next morning at breakfast someone had flipped the fleur-de-lis. The first-year table buzzed with whispers.

"Grim and Beckerman are missing, I've heard . . ."

". . . left all of their things behind."

"Do you think their roommate knew?"

"What about the headmaster's daughter?"

Rohan bristled at the gossip about his friends, but he was even more bothered by the undercurrent of excitement for the first battle society meeting in nearly a week.

"I say, that was in rather poor taste," Rohan whispered to Valmont on the way to Medicine that morning.

"What are you talking about?" Valmont snapped.

"The fleur-de-lis. You know," Rohan said.

Valmont stopped short in the corridor, forcing Edmund and Luther to have to walk around him.

"That wasn't me," Valmont whispered. "I thought it was you."

Rohan shook his head and held open the door to their medicine classroom. "Well, we'll find out who called the meeting soon enough," he said.

The twenty-nine remaining members of the secret battle society milled around the basement room, whispering nervously. Lanterns and candles flickered from the stairwell, creating a cascade of light and cloaking the room with eerie shadows.

With a sigh and a pointed glance at his pocket watch, Valmont cleared his throat and stepped to the front of the room. "Thank you for coming," he said. "Will whoever called this meeting please step forward and explain?"

It took all of his nerve to stand there calmly, staring out at the sea of incredulous students, at the center of a situation completely beyond his knowledge and control.

And then Derrick Marchbanks, hands in his pockets, strolled out from the crowd, as cool as you please.

"Right, gentlemen," Derrick said. "I didn't call you here to train but to talk, and if you'd rather head on back to your beds, I won't keep you. Although I think you'll be interested in what I have to say."

A couple of boys shifted restlessly but kept their places.

"We've all heard the rumors," Derrick continued. "Grim and Beckerman are quite obviously missing, and have been for four days. I think it's time to set the record straight about where they've gone."

"Can I talk to you? *Now?*" Valmont snarled, grabbing Derrick by the arm.

"Be a sport. This won't take more than a few minutes," Derrick returned, calmly removing Valmont's hand from the sleeve of his jacket.

And then Geoffrey cleared his throat and called, "I think we all know what Grim is doing." Jasper laughed uproariously at this, and a handful of second years snickered.

"And what would that be?" Derrick asked coolly.

"I'll spare you innocent first years the details. Don't think Sir Robert has explained them to you yet." Geoffrey made a lewd gesture and then added under his breath, "The lucky sod."

Valmont's face soured.

Rohan sighed.

"Oh, how droll," Derrick said dryly. "That's precisely the sort of rumor I want to make certain no one walks out of this room believing. Because we owe it to them to be gentlemen about what's happened, not to mock them behind their backs. You see, Grim and Beckerman took the fall for us, lads."

"What do you mean, 'the fall'?" Edmund called.

"They were caught returning the sabres to the armory after our last meeting," Derrick clarified, and then he continued to tell the tale, explaining how he'd encouraged Henry and Adam to join a short-staffed envoy to the Nordlands. He explained how they'd expected to find proof of preparations for war, or at the very least, something they might use in order to have the conscription laws repealed immediately.

The members of the battle society listened, and even Valmont had to admit that the Ministerium brat had a way with words. "I know that rumors spread treacherously, and I felt as though everyone in this room deserved to know the truth," Derrick continued. "No matter what cover story Headmaster Winter or our heads of year are going to come up with, that's what happened."

After Derrick had finished, the room was silent, everyone considering what they'd just heard. And then Edmund raised his hand as though in lecture.

"Yes, Merrill?" Derrick called.

"What are we going to do about it?" Edmund asked.

"Beg pardon?" Derrick frowned.

"We're still here, the lot of us. There has to be something we can do," Edmund said.

"What, like hop on the next train to the Nord-lands?" a third year asked.

"No," Edmund retorted. "Like keep the battle society going."

Headmaster Winter announced that Henry and Adam had taken seriously ill and had been sent to a hospital in the city, but no one believed it.

Rohan watched the students file out of the chapel that morning, and more than once he caught the eye of another member of the battle society, but no one stopped to speak with him. He asked Derrick about this at breakfast.

Derrick topped off his tea and shrugged. "Well, everyone might be thinking that you're a bit of a coward," Derrick admitted.

"A c-coward?" Rohan spluttered.

"Your friends all went off to prevent a war and change the laws, and you sort of . . . stayed here and disapproved."

"*Of course* I stayed here and disapproved. It was the only sensible option," Rohan returned. "I didn't think everyone would consider them heroes for behaving recklessly." And then he caught sight of Theobold, who was straining to hear their conversation from the other end of the table.

Theobold grinned. "Feeling a bit under the weather, Mehta?" Theobold asked loudly.

"Not at all," Rohan said.

"If I were you, I'd be terribly nervous about coming down with that awful illness your roommates seem to have caught," Theobold continued, and then he raised his voice even more, to make certain everyone would hear. "I do hope you're not contagious."

Rohan took a bite of a scone, trying to ignore Theobold, who was still watching him with narrowed eyes—or rather, watching Derrick and James, who sat on either side of him. They sighed and tried to ignore Theobold as well. Rohan realized their mistake almost at once, and paled.

"Interesting," Theobold remarked, "how Marchbanks and St. Fitzroy don't seem to think you're contagious." He paused and took a sip of his tea before ominously adding, "Or maybe they know where your nasty little roommates have really gone."

Later that afternoon, during the hour free, Rohan took a walk around the school grounds. The trees were beginning to blossom, and the weather was, if not wholly pleasant, at least tolerable.

After breakfast they'd had drills for the first time that week, and Admiral Blackwood had pulled aside Conrad and James, the drill leaders. When the boys had returned, they'd shifted the formation, closing the gap in the ranks caused by Henry and Adam's absence. Rohan had pressed James about this at lunch, but James had only shaken his head and shrugged. "Blackwood didn't say why. I think he's nervous because the parade is in three weeks."

But Rohan wasn't sure. Had Admiral Blackwood simply wanted to patch a hole in the formation should Henry and Adam not return in time for the parade, or did he know that they weren't coming back?

Rohan agonized over this as he tramped along the perimeter of the quadrangle, soiling his boots and wishing he weren't stuck with the largest and loneliest single room on the first-year corridor.

He was fretting over the indignity of Adam having left his things a mess, when a chauffeured automobile pulled up to the front of the headmaster's house. Rohan stiffened and thought to turn back the way he'd come. But then the chauffeur hopped out and ran around the brass front of the car, opening the door and extending an arm to the passenger.

It was Grandmother Winter.

22

LIFE IN THE NORDLANDS

First days can be disorienting. They are rather like skipping ahead in a trusted textbook, only to find the material impossible to grasp. And yet with perseverance you will wake up one day and find yourself staring at what had once seemed so baffling, and without quite knowing what has changed, you will understand it all without a second thought.

Such went life for Henry, Adam, and Frankie in the servants' quarters and kitchens of the Partisan School. The days fell into a routine of tasks: They polished boots, prepared and served meals, washed dishes, scrubbed floors, brought coal for the schoolmasters' fireplaces, and did any other odd jobs that might be sent their way.

Henry and Adam were frequently set to the same work, which was fortunate, as Adam was rather hopeless. Although, to his credit, he did try. And though Henry and Adam spent their days assigned to the same tasks, Frankie worked separately, in the staff kitchens and the laundry. Oftentimes they saw one another only in the evenings and, of course, at night.

The three friends met after the other servants had gone to bed, despite their own exhaustion. For the past two nights they had explored the castle systematically by candlelight, starting with the attics. They were determined to find evidence of combat training— the dummies with targets painted on, the halberds and crossbows, the equipment Henry had seen all those months ago, during the Inter-School Tournament.

And yet they had discovered nothing, except a mutual distaste for missed sleep. By Wednesday morning everyone was in low spirits.

"I think I'd rather sleep tonight, if you don't mind," Adam said after breakfast while they scrubbed the tables in the dining hall.

Henry wiped his hair back with his sleeve and continued scrubbing. "Fine," he said.

"What do you mean, 'fine'?"

"If you don't want to come, don't. And by the way, you've missed a spot in the corner there."

"Blast the spot!" Adam said.

Henry couldn't help it, he grinned. "You sounded like Derrick."

Adam went over the spot he'd missed, and both boys were quiet for a long time, as scrubbing and thinking go well in hand.

"I miss school," Adam admitted.

Henry glanced around nervously, but the other boys cleaning tables that morning were at the opposite end of the hall.

"Me too," Henry said. "And I keep wondering after our marks on the half-term exams."

"I don't," Adam said with a shudder.

"I thought you were doing better this term." Henry wrung out his washrag.

"I am. I was hoping for an 'excellent' in ethics," he confessed. "Sir Franklin's never read the Talmud. He thinks I'm a bloody genius."

Henry snorted.

"I've been thinking," Adam went on, "about what I'm going to do if we're expelled."

"You'll go home to your family, I'd expect," Henry said sourly.

"Are you mad? After a disaster like this?" Adam dropped his voice to the barest of whispers. "They'll send me back to the yeshiva. No more fencing lessons, but extra mathematics and private Torah study to make up for the year at the goy school."

Henry winced in sympathy. He hadn't thought about what would happen to Adam if he went home, about what it meant to have a family that expected things of you.

"That won't happen," Henry said with as much confidence as he could muster. "Tell them you want to try for a scholarship somewhere for next year."

"It's not about that," Adam said. "I took the exam behind my parents' backs, and when they found out about Knightley, they said I wouldn't last a year. If they're right, I'll never hear the end of it."

"It could be worse," Henry said.

"Worse how?" Adam asked.

"You could be Rohan." Henry tried very hard to keep a straight face. Though he felt awful about it, he couldn't pretend that it wasn't funny. He could just imagine Rohan's panic at having two missing roommates and only Valmont and Derrick to confide in.

"Reckon he's upset?" Adam asked innocently.

"Nah," Henry said. Both boys grinned.

As they dumped the dirty buckets of water outside the kitchen, Henry took a good look at Adam. They were both exhausted, but it showed more on Adam somehow, the lack of sleep and irregular, meager meals.

"Are you still looking forward to going to bed early tonight?" Henry asked.

"Would you be upset?"

"What? If you were tired, or if you left me alone with Frankie?"

"Oh, that's right. You two loathe each other."

"We don't loathe each other," Henry snapped. And then he couldn't resist adding, "She's far more tolerable now that she's stopped wearing a corset."

One of the serving boys was missing.

This was all anyone talked about in the kitchen that afternoon. Henry and Adam silently sliced beetroots, listening to the news pass worriedly among the kitchen staff.

"Maybe he's run off," someone said.

"He ain't. He's been taken."

"Be careful, talkin' like that, or the doctor'll getcha."

"'S the truth," one of the younger boys protested, wiping his nose with the back of his hand before going back to the dough he was kneading. "He went out, and then he never come back. Same as the rest."

At this, Henry's stomach lurched, and not from the delicious aroma of raw beetroot.

This was the reason he and Adam and Frankie had been hired so quickly. The reason there were empty beds and the other servants seemed spooked to go outside after dark, even just to the coal stores or the pump.

"Same as the rest," Henry whispered to Adam.

"I bloody loathe beetroot," Adam muttered in response.

"One of the boys is missing," Henry whispered, pulling Frankie aside. He'd volunteered to run to the staff kitchen for some onions.

"Cort, wasn't it?" Frankie whispered with a superior smirk. "I found out hours ago. One of the girls is sweet on him, and she's been sobbing into the butter churn all morning."

"We have to find out what's happened to him," Henry said. "Everyone keeps saying that he's disappeared 'same as the rest,' as though this has happened before."

Frankie sighed. "I'll ask some questions," she promised.

"Thank you," Henry said.

"Now take your onions and get out of here. Common kitchens and staff kitchens don't mix," Frankie joked.

"You say that"—Henry put his hand to his heart as though wounded—"but when *I* disappear, it'll be you sobbing into the butter churn."

Supper that evening was a solemn affair. Cort still hadn't returned, although one of the boys had optimistically set the table for fourteen, which left an empty place, where everyone tried very hard not to look.

As Henry had been sweeping one of the hallways that afternoon, he'd overheard two of the students talking. They had been laughing and joking the same as the boys at Knightley, but the words had been different, and worryingly so. One of the boys hadn't written his essay for their history course, which was due the next day.

"Ye should buy a paper off Carrow down at the Dragon's Inn. Graduated last year. Keeps a collection o' the things."

"Wouldn't Erasmus know the difference?"

"He might, but d'ye think he'd say anythin'?"

"S'pose not. But I'm not goin' down to Romborough meself, not after dark."

"What's the matter, think the doctor's gonna get-cha?"

"Shut yer mouth, Soren."

The students had drifted away after that, ribbing each other and joking, without so much as a backward glance at the boy their age who had been sweeping the corridor.

As Henry slowly worked his way down the corridor with his broom and dustpan, he'd puzzled over that conversation. The boys back in the kitchen had said the same thing. "The doctor's gonna getcha." At first he'd thought it was a servant's superstition, but then he'd caught sight of the white stripes on the boy called Soren's sleeve, and the badges gleaming on both boys' coats.

The white stripes, Henry knew, marked the senior-ranked students—those boys who had earned distinction at sport or academics, and were granted certain privileges because of it. They were the boys whose boots Henry shined, the boys who left such a mess in their private study room in the library, and who spent Friday nights eating in the staff dining room with the professors.

And though the Nordlands pretended not to keep a

class system, even after four days, Henry could tell you that they did. Men whom Yurick Mors had put in power gave power and privileges to others for dubious distinctions, and denied it to others for reasons just as murky.

Henry was still puzzling over this at supper, as they bent their heads and Cook recited a prayer over the meal. After the prayer everyone bit hungrily into hunks of coarse bread, their eyes avoiding the empty place at the table the same way passersby would avert their gaze from a drunkard on the city streets.

They talked of the weather (overcast and gloomy as always) and of the students (haughty but manageable) until finally the conversation turned sinister.

"Happens without warnin'." Cook growled, his mustache dripping with purple soup. "One day yer there, and the next, no one's seen 'ide nor 'air of ye."

"They always go out to Romborough first," the youngest boy, who was called Isander, said. "An' then they never come back. That's what happened to Becky and Parl."

Everyone at the table stiffened at the mention of those names.

"Becky came back," a burly lad called Brander grunted.

"Missing a finger an' with her toes all black!" Isander shrilled.

At the mention of black toes, Adam shuddered and looked down at the purple soup as though just remembering that he disliked it.

"Did she say what happened?" Henry asked.

Brander narrowed his eyes at Henry.

"Aye, she said," he grunted. "Said the doctor came for 'er, and it was him that did it, writin' down note of her ev'ry scream."

At this, everyone shifted uneasily.

"The doctor?" Henry asked with a calculated frown, hoping for an explanation.

"Aye, you know the legend. He come for those unfortunates out after curfew, and when he's done, they scream instead of sleep, and can't bear the dark, and some are missin' fingers or toes, an' some are blackened or blistered, an' no one knows why, but it's the doctor that done it," Brander said, and then he raised his bowl of soup to his mouth and slurped it like coffee.

"So if she came back, where is she?" Henry asked.

"Quit after a couple days," Brander said. "No one had the heart to give 'er the boot, though she worked none and sat by the fire all night so close she nearly burnt the tip o' her nose."

Even though Henry was bursting with questions, he

forced himself to keep quiet. After all, tension was running high at the moment, and he didn't want to draw any unnecessary attention. That was all he needed, to be suspected of being an outsider. But there was something oddly familiar about what Brander had said . . .

And then it came to him, and he nearly dropped his spoon into his soup in surprise. Back in the kitchens at Knightley, Liza had talked about medical experiments in the Nordlands. What was it she'd said? Henry frowned, remembering: *People keep disappearin', an' when they come back, they ain't right.*

Well, that settled the question of what had caused everyone to be so spooked. Henry had to admit, he was a bit unsettled himself. No wonder the servants at Knightley had been too afraid to go on the envoy.

As Henry and Adam collected the boots that night from outside the doors of the senior-ranked students, Henry mentioned what Liza had said about medical experiments in the Nordlands.

"So there's a creepy bloke doing creepy things," Adam said. "If you ask me, we should stay well away from it."

"I know," Henry said, grimacing over an absolutely

filthy pair of boots that he was forced to toss into the basket by their laces.

"Good," Adam said. "Because I don't want to wind up like that bloke from our expulsion hearing."

Henry stopped short. "What?"

"You know," Adam said with a shrug. "That viscount who came up here after we told him about that combat training room."

Henry stared at Adam in shock but couldn't deny that Viscount DuBeous *had* gone up to the Nordlands in search of combat training rooms, and had come back with rope marks around his wrist, refusing to say what had happened.

The boys heard footsteps behind them and stiffened. Henry turned.

It was Frankie. She pushed back a few strands of hair that had escaped from her kerchief, and wrinkled her nose at the basket of boots. "Who's been mucking around in the stables?" she asked.

Henry glanced at the basket and sighed. "Everyone, from the looks of it. You'd think they'd be afraid to go outside, what with the doctor on the loose."

"So you've heard the stories too?" Frankie asked, joining their procession down the hall. They quickly compared notes.

"Is it possible," Frankie asked thoughtfully, as they reached the end of the hall, "that what you saw last term was a torture chamber?"

"I think I can tell the difference," Henry snapped, and then he frowned, considering. No, that was impossible. The room he'd seen had been filled with weapons, but also charts, ranking the students in armed and unarmed combat. Besides which, torture wasn't a violation of the Longsword Treaty, strictly speaking. But combat training was. Why disguise a room as the far more dangerous choice?

Henry explained as much.

"I was only supposing," Frankie muttered.

"And torture isn't the same as medical experiments," Henry said, nettled. "Medical experiments are investigative."

"Maybe someone wants to investigate how much it hurts to chop off people's fingers?" Adam asked.

Henry snorted. And then Adam gave a tremendous yawn, nearly dropping the basket of boots. Guiltily Henry remembered his promise to let Adam get some much needed rest.

"I can do the boots myself, if you want to get to bed early," Henry offered.

Adam brightened and then, as though it pained him to do so, shook his head at the offer. "You've been cleaning up after me all week."

"I didn't think you'd noticed," Henry admitted, embarrassed.

"Well, I didn't want to boast about it," Adam said. "Might give you a complex."

"A complex?"

"That I'm so much better suited to the loafish lifestyle of the aristocracy," Adam said.

Henry swung the basket of boots at him, and Adam ducked out of the way, grinning.

"Boys," Frankie said, rolling her eyes. "If you're quite finished?"

"Sorry," they chorused.

In the end Adam did go up to bed, and Frankie kept Henry company in the scullery as he scrubbed and polished. She craned her neck at Henry's task. "How can you stand it?"

They sat side by side on the stone steps, and Henry was scrubbing patiently at a boot that strongly wished to remain soiled. They were alone, aside from the beetles that scuttled along the floorboards. The castle was dark and quiet, and there was a sort of peacefulness to the rhythm of the task that Henry found oddly comforting.

"Because I've done it before, I suppose," he said.

"I just can't picture it," Frankie pressed on. "I've spent five days in the company of the other servants, and all I keep thinking is, 'How did Henry grow up doing this?'"

He shrugged. "I didn't, really. It was only a year at the Midsummer School after I left the orphanage. And it wasn't long before Professor Stratford started giving me lessons."

"A year is a long time," Frankie argued. "Think where we might be a year from now."

Henry grimaced.

Frankie winced slightly and picked at a stain on her skirt. "I didn't mean it," she said. "Back at Knightley, about your dying in a war."

"I know. But at least you were brave enough to say the words. No one else seems to be able to."

Frankie nodded. She stared at Henry, who was intent on scrubbing the muck off those old boots, as though the task was in no way beneath his dignity. His hair was falling into his face again, but then he looked up, shook back his hair, and grinned, showing that all was forgiven.

"I don't know how we're going to stand a month here," Frankie said.

"It could be less. You *did* leave your bag on the train. Someone might have found it. Maybe the board of trustees is arranging a rescue mission at this very moment."

"Or an engagement party, more like," Frankie said mischievously. "I wonder, which of you boys should I claim as my corrupter?" She'd started off joking, but somehow the cold seeping from the basement walls and the way they had unconsciously sat so close to each other on the stairs made the joke into something quite serious.

"Are you finished yet?" Frankie asked with a pout.

"Almost."

"I think Garen sounds perfectly hilarious when he speaks," Frankie insisted a bit too loudly, scooting over on the step so that her skirts weren't quite so near to Henry.

Henry considered this as he buffed a pair of boots. "You're right, actually. It's like his grammar is studied, but backward."

"Backward?"

"He's deliberate about his mistakes, not their corrections."

"I just meant that he sometimes bleats when he's nervous," Frankie said.

Henry grinned. "That, too."

"Well, *you* can do a Nordlandic accent perfectly. I've heard you speaking to the other serving boys," Frankie said.

"I pick up languages quickly." Henry shrugged. "Accents, too. Adam's been ribbing me for spending too much time around Derrick."

Frankie snorted. "Oh, frightfully sorry," she said, her blue eyes mocking. "Please forgive that hideously improper lapse in behavior."

Henry shook his head. "He doesn't sound as bad as that."

"Who said anything about Derrick? I was doing an impression of you," she said innocently. "And how do you find the weather, Mr. Grim, this time of year?"

Henry threw a rag at her.

She spluttered indignantly before realizing it was one of the spares.

Henry finished with the boots soon after. His back ached as he stretched, and he wanted to do nothing so much as crawl into bed, but Frankie was wide awake, her blue eyes shining in anticipation of that night's adventure.

"I have an idea," Frankie said as Henry scoured his hands in the scullery sink.

"Just for the record," Henry stated, "I have come to fear all of your ideas in advance, simply from having endured enough of them."

"Be glad you weren't on the receiving end," Frankie said with an evil grin. "But I think you'll like this one. I propose that before we spend another night aimlessly wandering the castle, we go to the library and see if we can find some blueprints."

Henry stared at Frankie in surprise. That wasn't a horrible idea at all. In fact, he should have thought of it days ago.

"You don't think Adam will be disappointed that we went to the library without him?" Henry asked with a hint of a smile.

"Oh, he'll be furious." Frankie grabbed Henry's hand. "Come on."

The library, when they reached it, had closed for the night. The gas jets were turned low, thrusting the contents of the bookshelves into shadow. But even in the dimness Henry could tell that the library was a disappointment. Without standing on tiptoe he could reach the top shelves, and the room was anything but cozy.

There were two long tables where students could study, and uncomfortable-looking chairs pockmarked with graffiti. On the wall across from the study tables was an enormous oil painting of a glowering Chancellor Mors.

"Come on," Frankie said, pulling Henry over to the card catalogues, past a trolley piled so high with unwanted books that it looked ready to topple. "We need books on the school."

They looked up the section number, and then squinted at the shelves, searching for the section. When they found it, Henry turned up the nearby gas jet.

"You don't think anyone will see, do you?" he asked nervously.

Frankie shook her head. "There aren't any windows."

She sat down on the floor, her back against a collection of farmer' almanacs, and began to page through one of the most likely volumes. Henry sat with his back against the opposite shelf, his legs cramped by the narrowness of the aisle.

He'd forgotten how hard it was to sit and read books at the end of a long day's work. He didn't know how he'd done it every night back at the Midsummer School.

"I loathe this thing," Frankie said, taking off her kerchief. "It makes me feel like a country milkmaid."

"Those poor cows," Henry said, picking up the next volume in the stack and flipping to the index. They sat for a few minutes, paging silently through their books.

"Here, I've found a map," Henry said, spreading the volume, a bulky folio, across his knees.

Frankie scooted closer to have a look.

"This is the hidden room where I saw the weapons last term," Henry said, tracing the corridor with his finger.

"How can you tell?"

Henry quickly explained about the hidden door.

"I just look for a room that has a door pretending to be a wall?" Frankie asked, and Henry nodded.

She scowled at the book on Henry's lap, her hair falling forward over her shoulder. Henry gulped.

"There," Frankie said, pointing.

"Hmmm." Henry frowned at the page. "I think you're right. Where is that?"

"Looks like it's near the library, actually," Frankie said.

"Do you reckon we should take a look now? Or should we wait for Adam?"

"He'll never forgive us," Frankie said solemnly.

"No, he won't," Henry replied just as seriously.

And before either of them knew what was happening, they were kissing.

Kisses are powerful things, easily underestimated because they can seem so small. And yet, though it may feign innocence, the kiss is a deceptive creature that delights in causing trouble. Such was the kiss that Henry and Frankie shared—small and fleeting, yet deeply troublesome.

The kiss lasted just a moment, and then Henry pulled away. "I'm sorry," he mumbled. "I shouldn't have— I didn't— I mean—"

"You mean what, exactly, Mr. Grim?" Frankie demanded, grinning. "To apologize for kissing me or for waiting so long before you did?"

Henry stared at her in surprise.

"Ugh, you're insufferable sometimes," Frankie went on. "Head filled with books and conspiracies, and not even a second thought that there might be a reason it scandalized everyone to see us speak with such familiarity back at school."

"I was helping you with your French!" Henry retorted.

"I didn't need the help! I just wanted to hear you recite poetry." Frankie blushed at the confession.

"Poetry?" Henry asked, baffled. "Whatever for?"

"It was rather dashing," she admitted. "You were so earnest about it."

"Well, I wanted you to earn good marks."

Frankie found this hysterical.

"Of course, I didn't know at the time that you were planning to run away and join the circus," Henry continued, "or else I needn't have bothered."

"I only left because I thought you hated me," Frankie said.

"You said you were sick of your chaperone!"

"Oh. Well, yes, but I wouldn't have tolerated being stuck at a boys' school nearly so long if I hadn't met a young knight who didn't mind if I climbed through his window." And with this, Frankie kissed him again.

Upon consideration, Henry decided that first years were not, in fact, too young to kiss girls. He rather wished he'd come to this conclusion sooner, as it would have saved him quite a bit of confusion over why Frankie had become so upset when he'd jokingly played the role of a suitor that fateful morning after chapel.

And upon even further consideration, Henry realized that he was going to be in a load of trouble with Adam. But the way Frankie was gazing at him, he felt as though he could take on the chancellor himself. . . . Or perhaps that was just because the portrait of Chancellor Mors was watching them with an accusing glare.

In a rather loaded silence they memorized the location of the strange room on the map, replaced the books on the shelves, and tiptoed out of the library.

When they reached the servants' quarters, Henry hesitated for a moment, uncertain of what he was expected to do. And then, with the faintest hint of a smile, he gave a suitor's bow, took Frankie's hand in his, and gently raised it to his lips.

"Good evening, Miss Winter," he said. "I hope you sleep well."

"Oh, very funny," Frankie muttered, but Henry could see that she was blushing.

❖ 23 ❖

AN AWKWARD
CONFESSION

Henry was nervous that Adam would suspect something the next morning, but a decent night's
sleep had greatly improved his mood.

"How was it, then?" Adam asked as they removed
dirty breakfast plates from the dining hall.

"How was what?"

"Your night with Frankie."

Henry nearly dropped the stack of dishes before he
realized what Adam meant. "Fine," he mumbled. "We
found a map in the library. There's some sort of hidden
chamber on the second-floor corridor."

"Did you go without me?"

Henry shook his head.

"I have a good feeling about tonight," Adam pressed on.

Henry sighed. "Listen, Adam, there's something I should tell you," he began, and then he stopped, as the room had become oddly silent.

One of the Partisan students, a scholarly-looking boy with the white stripes of senior rank on his uniform stood frowning in the doorway. Henry realized miserably that he was the closest to the door. "Aye, compatriot?" he asked.

"I'm looking for Garen," the boy said haughtily.

"I can fetch him for ye," Henry said, carrying the stack of plates into the kitchen as the boy followed. Henry yanked the cord that rang for Garen, and then stood there awkwardly, not knowing the protocol. Should he have led the boy into the kitchen? Was it allowed, or was it some egregious breach of etiquette? If anything, the boy was looking around the kitchen in fascination, taking in the stacks of dirty dishes and the efficient line of girls who were scrubbing them. He watched Henry add his own plates to the girls' pile.

"Ye look familiar," the boy said, and Henry stiffened. "Were we in the Morsguard together?"

Henry shook his head.

"No, I think we were," the boy continued. "What village are you from?"

"Er," Henry stalled, his heart hammering as he tried to remember the name of a Nordlandic village. And then he recalled the newspaper article he'd read that first afternoon. "Little Septimus."

"Really?" the boy said. "But yer accent sounds south-westerly."

Henry blanched, as he'd been unaware that there were regional differences. Well, he thought, he'd need to find a map in the library and memorize the name of a village in the southwest region. "Moved around a lot," Henry finally answered.

And then he noticed that the boy was playing nervously with a ring he'd absently removed from a trousers pocket. Henry caught a flash of the gold band.

Thankfully, Garen dashed into the kitchen, straightening his waistcoat and trying to look as though he had just been passing by. Garen caught sight of the boy waiting for him and frowned.

"Aye, Compatriot Florian?" Garen asked.

The boy merely gave Garen a significant glance and waited patiently for Henry to take the hint.

"I'll, er, take my leave if there's nothin' else?" Henry asked.

"Henry, isn't it?" Garen said. "Can ye read?"

Henry nodded cautiously, hoping that wasn't the wrong answer.

"It would be best if ye took over deliverin' the post to the teachers' offices," Garen said, removing a thin stack of envelopes from his waistcoat. "Names are on the doors. Third floor north. Everyone's at prayer, so just slide 'em under the doors."

Henry accepted the envelopes. "Aye, Compatriot Garen," he said with a curt nod.

As he left the kitchen, he couldn't help but overhear the boy remark, "A servant from Little Septimus who can read?"

Henry hesitated in the hallway, waiting to hear Garen's response.

"Ye shouldn't have come here askin' after me," Garen growled, his voice growing louder as the two boys made for the doorway.

Henry dashed down the corridor, not wanting to be caught eavesdropping. He quickly sorted through the small stack of post as he took the stairs to the third floor. He slid the letters beneath the doors to the teachers' offices, reading their names and subjects off the plaques. He knew that Partisan's curriculum was similar to Knightley's—the two schools had been practically identical before the Nordlandic Revolution.

Henry continued down the corridor, reading the subjects off the plaques in fascination. Music, ethics, languages, law, fencing, drills, history . . . He was so absorbed in thought that he failed to notice that the last door was wide open.

The plaque read ERASMUS MORTENSEN: HISTORY, DEPUTY HEAD OF SCHOOL.

"Is that the post?" a voice called irritably.

Henry jumped guiltily. "Er, aye, Compatriot Erasmus," he said.

"Well, bring it here." The history teacher sat behind his desk wearing a somber suit and a deep frown. His scholar's cap sat upside down on a stack of papers. He was perhaps in his midforties, though the gray streaks through his beard made him seem older. The lights were turned low, and he massaged his temples as though they pained him enormously.

"D'ye need anything fer that headache, sir?" Henry asked, gingerly placing the post on the edge of the desk. The teacher reached for the letters, giving them a cursory glance before placing them beneath his cap, still unopened.

"It will pass," Compatriot Erasmus said. And then he glanced at Henry for the first time, and a flicker of surprise passed over his face. "What's yer name, boy?"

"Henry," he said nervously.

The teacher continued to stare.

"D'ye need somethin' else?" Henry asked, edging toward the doorway.

The teacher shook his head, and then winced, raising a hand to his temple. On his hand was a gold ring.

When Henry returned from delivering the letters, Garen set him and Adam to polishing the banisters for the rest of the afternoon.

"Where were you?" Adam asked, giving the polish a dubious sniff.

"Delivering post to the professors," Henry said. While they polished, he told Adam about the strange conversation between Garen and the student Florian.

"Maybe they're cousins," Adam suggested.

Henry hadn't considered that. It was possible, since the students at Partisan were selected from a sort of student scouts called the Morsguard, but somehow he doubted it.

"They don't look a thing alike," Henry protested. "And he was nervous about something. He kept fiddling with this ring, but he didn't have a mark on his hand from wearing one." Henry looked both ways down the empty corridor and dropped his voice before explaining what had happened when he'd visited Compatriot Erasmus's office.

"It was really bizarre," Henry said. "He acted as though he recognized me. Both of them did. Florian even thought we'd been in the Morsguard together."

"Either they recognized you from the Inter-School Tournament or else you've got a Nordlandic twin," Adam suggested.

Henry grimaced. And then, on some invisible symbol, the doors to the classrooms opened and students spilled out into the corridor, stowing books in their satchels, talking loudly and joking.

One of the boys, who was bespectacled and a bit portly, nearly tripped over the bottle of polish. "Beg yer pardon," he called over his shoulder as Henry lunged for the bottle, catching it just in time.

Henry shook his head at the close call and continued polishing the banister as the students surged past.

"You were about to tell me something earlier," Adam said.

"Oh. Right." Henry supposed that it was as good a time as any. "Don't get upset."

"Why would I get upset?" Adam asked suspiciously. Henry sighed.

"We're stuck here forever, aren't we?" Adam asked.

"No, it's nothing like that." Henry worked furiously to buff a scratch off the banister. "It's to do with Frankie. We, well, . . . Last night, when we were in the library, we sort of kissed." He winced, and then snuck a look at Adam, who had dropped the polish rag.

"You sort of kissed?" Adam said incredulously. "How can you 'sort of' kiss?"

"We kissed," Henry admitted.

Adam went very quiet. He folded the polish rag, and then unfolded it, and then nodded his head. "How was it?" he asked, his voice small.

"Surprising," Henry said. "And then it was really nice—incredible, actually."

"I liked her first," Adam moaned.

"I know. I'm sorry, Adam. It just *happened.*"

"Well, make it un-happen."

"I can't," Henry snapped. "And furthermore, I don't want to."

"So you like her," Adam stated.

Henry nodded.

"Well, you could have bloody said something." Adam snarled.

"I didn't know I liked her until she kissed me," Henry retorted.

"*She* kissed *you*?"

"The second time," Henry confirmed.

"Polish the bloody banister yourself." Adam threw down the rag and stalked off in the direction of the servants' stairs. Henry sighed as he watched Adam go. He'd been afraid Adam would react badly, and he felt horrible, as though he'd betrayed their friendship somehow. He waited a few minutes, giving Adam time to cool off, and then he gathered the basket of rags and polish and went after his best friend.

Adam was hunched over on the stone steps of the servants' staircase, his chin in his hands. "Go away," he muttered.

"No," Henry said, sitting down next to him. "I understand that you had feelings for her, but you keep saying you had this prior claim, that you liked her first, and that's not really fair. I'm the one who met her first, if that counts for anything. And liking someone isn't straightforward. I'd never even talked to a girl before—well, a girl who wasn't a kitchen maid. I didn't even realize we were being too familiar until Grandmother Winter came to stay."

"I bet she liked you all along," Adam muttered.

Henry couldn't resist. "Who, Grandmother Winter?"

Adam snorted. But they both knew what he'd meant.

"She said that she did," Henry confessed. "Apparently she didn't really need help with French. She just wanted to hear me read French poetry."

"Girls," Adam said, shaking his head. "Oh, and one more thing. I am not a chaperone. So no canoodling in front of me. I'll vomit."

"Got it," Henry said, fighting to keep a straight face. "No canoodling."

"Oi, watch it," Adam warned, climbing to his feet. "Because I'm strongly resisting the urge to punch you in the face right about now."

24

THE FIRST
RESCUE

Henry *was setting places in the dining hall when* the tall, formidable woman arrived at the entrance to the Partisan School, demanding to be let inside. He was in the kitchens, slicing meat pies, when Compatriot Erasmus, the deputy head of school, showed the woman into his office, despite his pounding headache. And he was clearing the main course from the dining hall when Compatriot Erasmus followed the woman down the stairs to the foyer, hoping Dimit Yascherov wouldn't blame him for the spectacle.

But news of a spectacle in the castle traveled fast. Henry and Adam had just come into the kitchen to deposit stacks of plates when a maid appeared in the doorway, out of breath and wringing her apron in her hands.

Everyone looked up.

"Ye should come an' see this," the maid said, her cheeks shining. "There's a grand lady in the foyer what wants her runaway maid back. She's a right terror."

Before Cook could protest, the maids and serving boys had abandoned their posts. Henry looked at Adam and shrugged. They might as well go along. After all, they didn't want to draw any unnecessary attention. They trailed after the rest of the serving staff, but when they reached the foyer, Henry wished they could turn around and head back toward the kitchen.

The grand lady raising such a fuss was none other than Grandmother Winter.

"I don't care if she's serving supper to the chancellor himself," she roared. "I want to see her *now*!"

Compatriot Erasmus winced and raised a hand to his forehead. "Madam, please. Perhaps ye might wait? We can have the girl brought to my office."

"I have already seen your office, thank you," she replied haughtily. "Returning to it would be counter-productive."

Henry never thought he'd be overjoyed to see Grandmother Winter, but at that moment it was all he could do to keep from grinning ear to ear. They were going back to Knightley!

He nudged Adam, and the two of them began making their way to the front of the crowd. Everyone let them pass. They were all wary of the imperious Brittonian woman, dressed in what looked to be mourning, radiating silent fury at Compatriot Erasmus.

And then Garen hurried into the foyer with a bewildered Frankie in tow.

When Frankie caught sight of Grandmother Winter, the color drained from her face.

"That's her," Grandmother Winter said, pointing an accusing finger. "That's my indentured girl, Francine."

Frankie gawped as Grandmother Winter shot her a withering glare.

"Two years left in your contract," she thundered. "What do you have to say for yourself?"

"I'm sorry, ma'am." Frankie bobbed a pretty little curtsy, too shocked to do anything but play along.

"You are coming home with me and returning to your duties at once," Grandmother Winter said, grabbing Frankie by the arm. Grandmother Winter pushed her way past an astounded Compatriot Erasmus, dragging Frankie after her.

And then she caught sight of Henry and Adam at the front of the crowd. A flash of recognition crossed her face, but then she narrowed her eyes as if in warning and hurried past.

Henry realized in horror that Grandmother Winter hadn't been sent to get them after all. She had come by herself—to rescue Frankie.

And she was leaving them behind.

Frankie looked back over her shoulder in panic, as it dawned on her that the performance was over and her grandmother had gotten what she'd come for. Her mouth opened, and her face clouded with a storm of emotions as she stared at Henry and Adam.

Henry watched her go. He stood there in the middle of the foyer with Adam spluttering at his side, and he felt for all the world like that scrawny boy back at the orphanage, watching as a family adopted another orphan, and cruel fate had forsaken his happiness once again.

"I suppose we ought to be glad," Adam said dubiously. He sat down on the floor of the stone corridor next to Henry, who was staring at a mop and bucket as though he'd forgotten their purpose. "I mean, we did stay to make certain she'd be all right. I thought the three of us would be stuck here for a month, and no offense, but you two mooning over each other would have driven me mental."

Henry sighed. He felt as though he were leaking despair, poisoning the corridor with his bitterness. He didn't know how Adam could stand it.

"Here," Adam said, tossing a hunk of bread into Henry's lap. "You didn't eat your supper. I think you confused your spoon for a mop."

Henry looked down at the bread and began to eat it without thinking. It tasted as though it had been in Adam's pocket.

Or maybe that was what despair tasted like—the inside of Adam's pocket.

Henry was suddenly seized with a fit of laughter at the thought. He nearly choked on the bread.

Adam thumped him on the back, staring at Henry as though he'd lost his mind.

"Sorry," Henry said. "You're right. We should be happy about Frankie going home." He climbed to his feet and brushed the crumbs from his lap.

"Are you all right, mate?" Adam asked.

"No," Henry said, picking up the mop. "But, then, I'm not the only one having a hideous day."

"Well, look at it this way—nothing worse can happen."

"Never say that," Henry warned.

"Or what? The doctor's gonna get me?"

Adam gave a halfhearted grin and picked up the spare mop. The two boys set to cleaning the corridor in companionable silence. But a new fear was niggling at the dark recesses of Henry's mind, one that demanded attention. Had everything changed now that Frankie had returned to Knightley Academy without them? Would they still be credited as rescuing her, three weeks after her safe return, or had Grandmother Winter effectively taken away the only thing that stood between them and expulsion? Because if they didn't find evidence of combat training, what hope did they really have of becoming knights? Henry wondered if it had occurred to Adam that he might be headed back to the yeshiva after all.

"How do you think I'd do as a patrolman?" Adam asked. "I wanted to be a police knight, but I reckon it's nearly as good." So Adam had been thinking the same thing.

Henry shrugged, not wanting to admit out loud to

the probability of their impending doom. "You'd be all right."

"I'd get bored," Adam said. "It's rubbish work, just patrolling the streets and slapping cuffs on criminals. The police knights get to do the good bits."

Henry privately agreed. "And you'd probably have to answer to Theobold or someone," he said.

"Oi, thanks, mate."

"Sorry. I'm a bit low on optimism at the moment."

They finished mopping the corridor and returned the supplies to the cupboard. With Isander and Polen assigned to scrub boots for the next two nights, Henry and Adam were done for the night.

"That bloke who was with Grandmother Winter," Adam mused as they made their way up to the servants' lodgings, "was he the one who acted funny when you brought the post?"

"Why?"

"Just curious. I mean, Frankie's grandmother is terrifying, and it hardly bothered him. I just got the impression that he used to be a lord or something."

Henry nearly tripped on the stairs. *"What?"*

"You know, before the revolution," Adam said with a shrug.

"But all of the aristocrats were killed. If not in the revolution, then after Mors came to power. He had them hung in a public gallows."

"Not everyone," Adam said. "I had to do those extra pages for Lord Havelock, remember? I looked it up. He gave them a choice: renounce their title and give over their property, or be killed."

"So you think Compatriot Erasmus . . . ?"

Adam nodded. But that still didn't explain why he'd seemed to recognize Henry . . . unless . . . Lord Havelock.

"I'll bet he recognized me from the Inter-School Tournament," Henry said despairingly. "He *does* teach history. He's probably an old friend of Lord Havelock's."

They shuddered at the thought, and then they came to the narrow stairs that led to the attic.

"Are we free for the rest of the night?" Adam asked.

Henry nodded. "Why?"

"I think we should go to the library," Adam said.

"Who are you, and what have you done with Adam?"

"Oi, shut up! I want to see if I can prove it about that Erasmus bloke."

"All right," Henry said. He had to admit that he was curious. After all, he'd grown up in the aftermath of the revolution, hearing news whispered in the streets as Chancellor Mors turned tyrant and enacted horrible laws.

Henry had always thought of the revolution as a marker—the point at which the Nordlands became irreparably different from South Britain. He'd never truly considered what it had meant for the Nordlandic aristocracy after their king was murdered. It was a gruesome choice, to be sure: die honorably for the crime of being born noble, or renounce everything and live in a country built upon the bloodshed and hatred of everything you were.

"Er, where *is* the library?" Adam asked.

Henry shook his head. "Follow me."

When Henry opened the door to the library, he tried very hard not to think about what had happened there the night before. For all he knew, Frankie was on her way to a foreign finishing school, and he'd never gotten the chance to say good-bye.

And if he was kicked out of the academy, there wasn't much of a chance for him as a suitor. It was as good as finished. Professor Stratford had warned him, and he hadn't listened, because he hadn't fully realized what he had to lose . . . or that he'd cared for Frankie as more than a friend, and always had.

"Oi, Henry?" Adam experimentally poked him in the side.

"What?" Henry asked irritably.

"I was just checking."

"Sorry. I know I'm not the best company. I'm a bit off at the moment."

They turned up the gas lamps on either side of the door and headed for the card catalogue.

"What are we looking for?" Henry asked.

"Blimey," Adam said, letting out a low whistle. He nodded in the direction of the enormous portrait of Chancellor Mors that hung on the far wall. "His eyes just follow you, don't they?" Adam made a couple of sudden movements, and then walked in a circle, testing his theory.

Henry nearly laughed.

"What's back here?" Adam called.

"Back where?"

"Restricted reading section." Adam was already behind the librarian's desk, eagerly pushing aside a moldering velvet curtain.

"Wait a moment," Henry said. "Maybe this isn't the best—" And then he ducked behind the curtain, and his mouth fell open.

Elaborately carved bookshelves stretched to the ceiling, crammed with old volumes, some of which looked hand-lettered, and others that glittered with gold leaf. A stained-glass window depicting a knight in old-fashioned armor pulling a sword from a stone reflected moonlight in jewel-colored patches.

On one wall was an enormous tapestry of *The Moste Noble and Ancient City of Romburrowe*. It showed a medieval collection of buildings encircled with seven pylons, all guarded by the stone fortress of Prince Artisan's Keep upon the highest plateau.

In the center of the room was a circular table inlaid with the school crest, an equal-armed cross inside of a diamond. Henry had seen the crest before, but beneath it was etched an unfamiliar motto: *Que mon honneur est sans tache*.

"'Let my honor be without stain,'" Henry translated.

"Does it really say that?" Adam asked. "My French must be getting worse. I thought it was 'My honor is without a mustache.'"

Henry snickered, but then forced himself to be serious, as there was nothing funny at all about the "restricted reading section." Do you reckon this used to be the library?" he asked. "Before the revolution?"

Adam nodded.

"It's brilliant," Henry said.

Beneath the stained-glass window was the perfect bench for reading on a rainy afternoon, and the ceiling was painted with angels and men—scenes from holy Scripture.

The library was a relic of the Partisan School's former glory, and Henry could almost imagine the rivalry between Knightley and Partisan as it had once been: The boys in old-fashioned frock coats competing to see which school had better imparted knowledge to their students. And before that, so very long ago, the boys in bowl haircuts and tunics, breaking their lances in the jousting ring.

Henry examined one of the bookshelves. It held heavy tomes on physick and biologie and astronomye, the spellings as antiquated as the books' crumbling spines.

"Henry," Adam whispered.

"What?"

"Come and see this."

Henry reluctantly left the books to see what Adam had found. It turned out to be a wall of faded tin daguerreotypes, each of them small enough to fit into his hand. They depicted a dozen or so schoolboys standing proudly behind a banner proclaiming them the INTER-SCHOOL TOURNAMENT CHAMPIONS, with the year engraved at the bottom. The last of the pictures was dated just two years before the revolution.

Henry squinted at the pictures in the dimness. Suddenly there was a flare of light.

Adam had found a candle and a match, and he was looking rather pleased with himself as he held the light toward the wall of pictures. Henry stared at the tiny images of the boys—from both Knightley and Partisan, he supposed, though the banner obscured their uniforms.

"Poor blokes," Adam said sadly, shaking his head.

Henry rather agreed. The wall was a haunting reminder of how few of these boys had lived to see their hair streaked with gray.

"Is that? Nah, it can't be," Henry said, squinting at a boy who bore a strong resemblance to Fergus Valmont.

"Well, I think I've found Compatriot Erasmus," Adam said, pointing at a picture in the middle of the collection.

Henry looked. He supposed it could have been, but the daguerreotype was old and faded, and there weren't any names on the pictures. And then another face in the picture made Henry freeze, because the boy holding the left side of the banner could have been his twin.

At first Henry thought he must be seeing things, but the boy in the picture with his old-fashioned slicked-back hair had the same square jaw and large dark eyes as he did. A corner of the boy's mouth was quirked up, as though he'd just thought of something terribly clever and couldn't wait to share the joke.

"Blimey," Adam said, leaning in to investigate. "Is that . . . ?"

"I don't know. Maybe."

Henry's heart pounded. He couldn't look away. The date on the picture was 1871, more than twenty-five years before.

It was possible. Henry held on to this knowledge. When they got back to Knightley, he could go through the class registers for 1871. He could know the one thing he'd always told himself didn't matter—because they'd never come back for him—the identity of his parents.

And then they heard voices in the corridor. Adam cursed; they'd left the lights on in the library. "Come on," Adam said, tugging insistently on Henry's sleeve.

Henry gave the picture one last tortured glance before following Adam back through the velvet curtain and into the dreary library dominated by the portrait of the chancellor.

They each turned down a gas lamp and stood with their backs pressed against the wall, trying to catch their breath.

The voices and footsteps passed.

The boys waited a few minutes, and then Adam opened the door and they crept into the hall. To the left was the main stairs, and beyond that was the servants' stairs, which would eventually take them up to the attic. To the right was a long, dark corridor—and the secret room Frankie had found on the map.

For Henry it wasn't a choice. He nodded in the direction of the corridor.

"Our beds are that way," Adam whispered, pointing in the opposite direction. And then he sighed. "But who needs sleep?"

They headed down the corridor, Adam still holding the candle to light the way. The castle was drafty at night, and the candle flickered, casting wiry shadows along the stone walls.

And then they heard footsteps. Adam blew out the candle, and he and Henry pressed their backs against the wall, trying not to breathe.

It was Garen. He held a dark lantern and wore a dressing gown as he crept down the corridor, passing within an arm's length of Henry and Adam.

They watched as Garen stopped next to an ancient stone fountain carved into the wall of the castle, and reached his hand into the basin. The slab of wall groaned and swung aside, revealing a doorway.

Garen stepped primly through, and the slab of stone swung back into place, once again an innocent decoration.

"Come on," Henry whispered.

"It might be dangerous. We don't know what's behind that wall."

"One way to find out."

Henry laid his ear against the wall, listening.

He heard voices inside.

Was this it? Had the combat training room been moved here?

Henry motioned impatiently for Adam to join him.

Adam sighed and ambled over. And then his toe hit an uneven patch of the stone floor, and the candleholder tipped, spilling hot melted wax onto his hand.

"Aahhh!" Adam cried, and then clapped a hand over his mouth.

But it was too late. The hidden door creaked open, and this time it was Florian who peered into the hallway, holding a lantern.

He grabbed Henry by the arm. "Got ye," he sneered, hanging the lantern from a peg and grabbing a handful of Adam's shirtfront. "Now both of ye come inside and explain yerselves." Florian marshaled them through a short passageway that quickly widened into a large, echoing chamber.

A moth-eaten Partisan School banner hung from the wall, but the chamber held no weapons. Instead there was an enormous round table encircled with a motley assortment of chairs appropriated from different parts of the castle. The table was covered with dozens of candles that formed an equal-armed cross. And seated around this table were Garen, the bespectacled boy who had tripped over the polish bottle, Compatriot Erasmus, and five others whom Henry didn't recognize. Two were teachers, one looked like a member of the serving staff, and two were students.

Henry tried not to panic.

"Found them spying in the corridor," Florian said with a painful twist of Henry's arm. "What shall I do with them?"

Compatriot Erasmus held up a hand. "Search them. And then they will tell us everything."

Adam whimpered at Compatriot Erasmus's statement—or threat. Either way, it sounded ominous.

Before Henry could react, Florian was patting him down, as though suspecting that Henry kept knives sheathed to the backs of his legs. Garen had taken hold of Adam and was roughly doing the same.

"Nothing," Florian said.

Garen nodded in confirmation.

"Henry, wasn't it?" Compatriot Erasmus said. "Have a seat. I dinnae think I know your friend."

"That's Adam," Garen said. "They arrived together."

"Did they now?" Compatriot Erasmus's eyes gleamed at this news as Henry and Adam nervously took seats at the table. "And, Alfrig, can ye fetch a bottle of acid from the science laboratories?"

The bespectacled boy nodded and hurried from the room.

"Acid, sir?" Henry asked weakly.

"Yes, lad. I wonder if ye have ever seen the effect of acid poured onto an open wound. It is not pleasant, but sometimes it is necessary."

Henry gulped.

"Now," Compatriot Erasmus continued, "who sent you?"

"Sorry?" Henry frowned.

"Don't play games with me, lad. Are ye one of the chancellor's men? Do ye report to Yascherov's secret police? ANSWER ME!"

Henry shot Adam a look of horror. They were in far over their heads.

And then Adam put a hand over his face and began to pray. *"Shiyr lamm'aloth esa eynay el-hehariym—"*

Henry elbowed him. Adam gulped and slid down in his chair until his eyes were level with the table. He looked ready to faint.

"Please, sir, no one sent us," Henry said in his true accent. "We're students at Knightley. We came with the envoy last weekend as servants. We'd heard rumors that the boys at Partisan were being instructed in combat and preparing for war, and we wanted to see if it was true. But then we missed the train back and wound up stuck."

"Ye 'missed the train'?" Compatriot Erasmus asked with a deadly smile.

Adam explained about Frankie being a stowaway, and how they'd stayed because of her. "And then her blasted grandmother left us here to rot," he said indignantly. "I knew I didn't like that woman."

At that moment the boy called Alfrig returned with the bottle of acid. Henry noticed a gold ring glinting on his hand as he placed the bottle of acid on the table with a curt bow.

"I believe that is no longer necessary, but I thank ye for gettin' it," Compatriot Erasmus said.

"Aye, my—Aye, Compatriot Erasmus," said Alfrig.

"Ye boys have seen nothing here," Compatriot Erasmus continued, turning to Henry and Adam. "It was an empty room ye found. Ye may leave, provided ye hold your tongues, or else they may be taken from ye as recompense."

"Yes, sir," Henry said. "We understand. Come on, Adam."

Adam pushed back his chair, and Henry could see that he was still praying, his lips moving silently.

"Just a minute there," a boy said. He was older, perhaps eighteen, and terribly good-looking. He spoke as though he expected to be obeyed, and sure enough, every head in the room turned in his direction. "I'm not satisfied that they are who they say. What kind of Knightley students would pretend to be servants? I think they were *sent* to spy on us."

"Who would send us?" Henry retorted. "We're first years and commoners."

"Commoners?" Compatriot Erasmus asked with a frown.

Henry supposed that, with the difficulty of getting anything through the border, news of Knightley's accepting common students had not made it to the Nordlands.

"There are three of us this year at Knightley," Henry said, quickly explaining the circumstances of how he had come to sit the Knightley Exam, and how Adam and Rohan had also been admitted.

"Yer Nordlandic accent was very convincing, lad," Compatriot Erasmus said, his expression inscrutable. "As though you were raised in . . . Manorly, perhaps?"

"Little Hawkshire, more like," Alfrig grumbled under his breath.

"Right, well, we should be going," Adam said nervously. "We'll leave you blokes to your secret society—er, sorry, empty room where nothing at all is happening."

"What kind of secret society do you imagine this to be?" Compatriot Erasmus asked, leaning across the table with a wolfish grin.

Adam gulped. Henry could tell that he was about to start praying in Hebrew again.

"I want them gone!" the older boy demanded. "Erasmus, see to it!"

"Wait!" Henry said. "Can't we join?"

Everyone looked up.

"Join?" Adam asked, as though that were the very last thing he wanted to do.

But Henry pressed on, without quite knowing what he was going to say. The words spilled out, a tumble of everything he'd seen and thought over the past six days at Partisan Keep.

"Adam and I are stuck here for another three weeks. We could help with—well, whatever it is you're doing. You have the school banner on the wall there, with the old motto, so I take you to be honorable men, and perhaps we're after the same thing. Adam and I want to make certain that we are not forced to lead schoolboys off to battle if there's another way. South Britain is afraid of an invasion, of Chancellor Mors seeking to rule not just the Nordlands but the whole of the Brittonian Isles. I saw those pictures in the restricted section of the library, and it was a wall of ghosts. I don't want to be haunted by the ghosts of my classmates, and I don't want to be haunted by the possibility that I didn't do everything I could to find a way for there to be peace."

Henry sat back down in his chair, though he couldn't recall how he'd come to be standing. He was dizzy with the momentum of what he'd just said, and the realization that he'd meant it. His heart pounded like a drum, and the candles flickered in their equal-armed cross, casting eerie shadows across the faces of everyone at the table.

Finally Compatriot Erasmus spoke. "Ye may return here tomorrow night, if ye speak the truth."

Henry shakily climbed to his feet, realizing they'd been dismissed. "Yes, my lord," he said without thinking.

Compatriot Erasmus nodded slightly. "Ah, ye know me. But do ye know yerself?"

❖ 25 ❖

AN UNLIKELY
ALLIANCE

Professor Stratford burst into the sitting room where Grandmother Winter sat calmly drinking a cup of tea and reading that morning's *Royal Standard*. She looked up witheringly and took another sip of her tea.

"I am not entertaining visitors at the moment, Mr. Stratford," she said, returning to her newspaper.

"How could you?" Professor Stratford demanded.

He'd woken in the middle of the night to hear voices in the parlor, and he'd come down the stairs to find the lights blazing and Frankie sitting miserably in a chair by the fire, looking for all the world like a forlorn little kitchen maid.

But his joy at their safe return was short-lived. Now he was furious, and he wanted answers. He glared at the imposing gray-haired woman, not caring that he was overstepping his place or that she'd had him fired once before.

"If you insist upon imposing yourself, take a chair, Mr. Stratford," Grandmother Winter said frostily. "Do not presume that I will be offering you tea, as I do not wish to prolong your presence in my sitting room."

"Your son's sitting room," Professor Stratford said, taking a seat on the edge of the sofa. "This isn't your house, and it wasn't your place to leave those boys behind!"

"Ah," Grandmother Winter said. "I might have imagined you would misunderstand the delicacy of the situation, Mr. Stratford. Francesca's bag had been found—only Francesca's. I did not anticipate needing to forge identity papers for three children, and furthermore, the impropriety of those three running off together is shocking.'"

"I—," Professor Stratford spluttered. "The circumstances are irrelevant. You left those boys there in who knows what kind of danger. They're barely fifteen!"

"They are not my responsibility. Nor are they yours."

Grandmother Winter arched an eyebrow. "I don't seem to recall your having any adopted children, Mr. Stratford."

Professor Stratford glared. He was certain Grandmother Winter knew perfectly well that it was impossible for him to adopt Henry—he was, after all, unmarried, poor, and not yet thirty.

"You're unforgivably heartless," the professor spat. "How you could leave those boys in the Nordlands, scrubbing floors and half-starved, is beyond my comprehension. I bid you good morning." And with that, Professor Stratford stalked from the room. In the corridor he put his head in his hands and tried to regain his composure.

"Professor Stratford, isn't it?"

The professor looked up. Lord Havelock was coming down the stairs with an armload of papers, his master's gown swirling around his ankles.

"Yes, it is," said Professor Stratford.

"I couldn't help but overhear," Lord Havelock said. "I am headed to my office while the students are still at breakfast. If you would care to join me?"

Professor Stratford nodded.

"It is not easy," Lord Havelock continued, "to be

responsible for arrogant boys who do as they please and think you blind to their deception and sneaking."

Professor Stratford realized belatedly that Lord Havelock was, of course, Fergus Valmont's guardian, and that he was speaking of his own experience.

"'Deception' and 'sneaking' are strong words for a bit of boyish rebellion," Professor Stratford said.

"You're a fool, Stratford," Lord Havelock growled. "Both Henry and Fergus have always been trouble. I've tried my hardest put a stop to their schoolboy rivalry, but it seems I've inadvertently inspired them to join forces and drag half the school into a dangerous combat training club."

Professor Stratford winced. "How long have you known?"

"Since the beginning. And of course I looked the other way. It seemed inspired. A good way for the students to work out their frustration and learn to function as an army." Lord Havelock shook his head, disgusted with himself. "I thought, 'Let the boys teach themselves what little they can, before we are shuffling them into ranks and marching them toward the border with their names pinned into their coats, so that we might identify their bodies.'"

Professor Stratford thrust his hands into his pockets, trying to disguise the slump of his shoulders. He felt hollow, not just from Lord Havelock's brazen mention of war, but at the thought that both of them had known all along what the boys were doing and had sat there and done nothing.

"Your silence makes for unfortunate company, Stratford," Lord Havelock said.

"Sorry." Professor Stratford sighed. And then he explained what was troubling him—the knowledge that he had kept to himself, the thought that he'd been protecting the boys, when truly he had sent them to their doom.

When Professor Stratford finished, Lord Havelock simply raised an eyebrow and unlocked the door of his office. The room had only the barest of furnishings, though they were of impeccable quality, and the walls were covered with maps. There were maps of ancient empires and of Roman battle encampments, of sea routes to the American states, and of constellations.

"You're planning to go after them yourself," Lord Havelock said, dropping the armload of papers onto his desk. "I can see it in your eyes."

"I can't live with myself any other way," Professor

Stratford said. "Tutoring Francesca, seeing her every day as a reminder—"

"Enough," Lord Havelock said with an impatient wave of his hand. He settled himself behind his desk and removed a pipe and a pouch of tobacco from a drawer. "You'll get yourself killed if you're not careful about it."

"Then, tell me how it can be done."

Lord Havelock tamped down the bowl and lit his pipe, filling the air with the spicy, sinister scent of his tobacco. He closed his eyes and blew a ring of smoke.

"We shall leave for the city tomorrow morning," Lord Havelock said. "Wear a good suit—if you own one."

26

THE ARISTOCRATS' REBELLION

I can't believe you told them we wanted to join," Adam whispered as they got dressed the next morning.

"What other choice was there?" Henry retorted. "And if joining means answers, I want in."

Adam was about to say something in return, but Henry never found out what, as Garen appeared in the doorway to the boys' bedchamber. Everyone turned.

"Henry, Adam, can I see ye in the corridor?" Garen ordered.

"Aye, Compatriot Garen," they chorused, following him into the hallway.

"Yer promoted to the staff kitchen," Garen said, handing them each a striped waistcoat. This wasn't what

Henry had been expecting, but then, with Frankie gone, he supposed that kitchen was in need of staff.

"Senior-ranked students dine with the staff on Fridays," Garen reminded them, as though nothing at all had happened the night before. "Ye'll be expected to serve a formal meal, and if ye have any questions of the protocol, ask them now. Come with me."

Henry and Adam hurried after Garen. Henry asked a lot of questions, mostly for Adam's benefit. When they reached the staff kitchen, Garen appraised them critically, and then jabbed a finger into Adam's chest.

"Keep the heathen prayers to yerself," he warned. "Ye don't want to find out what happens to those that don' keep the faith of the Nordlandic Church."

Adam gulped. "Aye, Compatriot Garen," he said.

The staff kitchen was rather a welcome surprise. They were given a hot breakfast of porridge and coffee, and then set to folding napkins and arranging coffee and cakes on the sideboard in the dining room.

The rest of the serving staff took Henry and Adam's presence in stride, although one of the older boys made it plain he'd preferred Frankie, or, as he put it, "the wee tasty lass." Henry nearly hauled back and hit him, but mastered his temper and returned to ironing napkins with a sigh.

* * *

When Henry finished delivering the post to the school-masters' offices later that morning, he made the turn that led him back to the main kitchens without thinking.

And there, sitting on a stool in front of the fireplace, was Cort—the boy who had been missing for two days. His lips were a sickly shade of bluish-gray, and he shivered heavily despite the wool blanket wrapped around his shoulders.

"What happened?" Henry asked, gently placing a hand on Cort's shoulder.

The boy continued to stare into the fire as though mesmerized.

Henry frowned, and then bent down until he was eye level with the boy. "Can you look at me?" Henry asked. The boy's eyes flickered toward Henry, but then they unfocused.

"What are ye doing?" a voice demanded.

Henry looked up guiltily. Brander's arms were folded across his chest. He sneered at Henry's waistcoat.

"He's ill," Henry said.

"Aye. The doctor cured his health," Brander said, his lip curling sarcastically.

"When did he come back?"

"Stumbled through the door 'bout two hours ago, while ye were dinin' on yer hot breakfast. Now get ye back to the staff kitchen. Yer no longer welcome here."

Henry made it a point to look in on Cort throughout the day. The boy didn't move from the fire, though his color gradually returned. The maid who Frankie had claimed was sobbing into the butter churn at Cort's disappearance resumed sobbing into the butter churn. The serving boys shot one another dark looks, as though Cort's return had only confirmed their worst fears, and they wondered which of them would be next.

Henry and Adam were made to serve supper along with two older boys. They stood at attention on either side of the door, refilling glasses of cider and wine and whisking away serving platters. There were twenty schoolmasters and twenty senior-ranked boys, but Henry was aware only of the presence of Dimit Yascherov, whom he had been fortunate enough to avoid during his life at Partisan so far.

Yascherov was short and plump, with a heavy beard and wickedly pointed eyebrows streaked liberally with gray. His suit was cut in a military style and weighted down by badges and brocade. He wore no scholar's gown, and his plump fingers were encased with glittering rings. He ate heartily, with a napkin tucked down his front to catch the frequent droplets of food.

From his post by the door, Henry could see Compatriot Erasmus seated at Yascherov's side, sipping a glass of cider and wincing every time Yascherov followed one of his own jokes with a booming laugh. Now Henry rather understood why Compatriot Erasmus was rumored to have frequent headaches, and what's more, Henry didn't blame him.

Thankfully, dinner passed without incident, and Henry and Adam gathered the soiled linens and carried them down to the laundry.

"Do you know," Adam said cheerfully, "this staff kitchen isn't half-bad."

"I'm glad Frankie was assigned here," Henry said. He'd felt awful that he and Adam had been able to spend their days together, while Frankie'd been by herself in a different kitchen, but if she'd had to be alone, at least her work had been far more manageable than theirs. But Henry couldn't shake off the suspicion that their transfer to the staff kitchen had something to do with the secret meeting they'd inadvertently stumbled upon the night before.

The boys ate supper in the staff kitchen that night, and Garen joined them, along with a handful of other staff who otherwise never set foot in the kitchens. Though Henry and Adam were stuck with the dishes, they finished at a reasonable hour and joined a game of cards with the other serving boys.

But on their way back to the servants' quarters, Henry poked his head into the common kitchen, where he found Cort still in front of the fire, an untouched plate of supper at his feet. The boy's face was flushed, and sweat stood out above his upper lip, but he still clutched the woolen blanket around his shoulders.

"It's time for bed," Henry said.

Cort didn't react.

Henry sighed and put a hand on the boy's shoulder to rouse him from his stupor. The boy flinched. "Cort," Henry said, his voice firm. "I need you to tell me what happened."

"Tell ye when I c-c-can't stand it n-n-no m-more," the boy muttered.

"Good," Henry said, although the boy was speaking nonsense. "Stand what? The cold?"

"C-c-cold. So cold," the boy said, and then he tilted his head and stared at the fire, and didn't respond when Henry called his name again.

As Henry and Adam crept past the door to the library that night, they were both caught up in their pwn thoughts. Adam had been grinning all evening, delighted by their new positions. But Henry's expression was quite sober indeed, for he knew that their easier work had been bought, and that they were about to find out the price of the expected payment.

Florian was waiting outside the hidden entrance to the chamber, squinting at a schoolbook by lantern light. He frowned when he saw them. "Dinnae think ye'd be back," he said.

"Well, ye thought wrong, then," Henry returned coolly.

"Drop the Nordlandic accent. It's ridiculous on ye," the boy retorted as he followed Henry and Adam inside.

The room hadn't changed. The banner still hung from the wall, reminding them to let their honor be without stain, and the table was once again quartered with dozens of flickering candles.

Compatriot Erasmus rose from his chair when Henry

and Adam entered the room. "Ah, so ye are men of honor."

"And sons of chivalry," Henry said with a lopsided grin, finishing the quotation.

It was the first line of the Code of Chivalry they'd signed on their very first day at Knightley. Something about Compatriot Erasmus's way of quoting reminded Henry of Professor Stratford, and a lump formed in his throat at the memory of those long-ago days in the old flat above Mrs. Alabaster's bookshop.

"Well spoken, lad." Compatriot Erasmus nodded solemnly. "And do ye both come here tonight to join us out of yer own free will?"

"Aye, Compatr—" Henry began to say, but Garen cut him off.

"We dinnae use such forms of address among ourselves. It's 'Lord Mortensen.'"

Henry nodded. "Yes, Lord Mortensen," he said.

"And what say ye, Adam?" Lord Mortensen asked.

"Yes, Lord Mortensen," Adam said nervously.

Satisfied, Lord Mortensen continued. "And do ye swear to act in the best interest of our order and to speak only truth to its members?"

"Yes, Lord Mortensen," both boys chorused.

Lord Mortensen removed the gold ring from his hand,

clutched it in his handkerchief, and held it to a candle.

"Up with yer sleeves, lads," he said.

"Why?" Adam asked suspiciously.

Garen sighed and unfastened his crisp cuff, pushing back his sleeve to reveal a mark just below the inside of his elbow: an equal-armed cross inside a diamond. Henry bit his lip. He should have known. These men weren't playing, and this wasn't some little club that they could join and then call take-backs a day later. He began to roll his sleeve.

"Henry, be serious," Adam hissed.

"I am," Henry said, holding out his arm.

"Good lad," Lord Mortensen said, pressing the ring into Henry's arm. Henry gritted his teeth against the pain.

Lord Mortensen held his ring to a candle once again.

"You're not coming near me with that thing," Adam said, backing toward the door.

"It's not so bad," Henry said.

"You're mental, Grim, you know that?" Adam said.

Lord Mortensen was suddenly seized by a coughing fit. Henry, remembering the schoolmaster's headache, wondered if the man was ill.

"I'm not mental," Henry said. "It's just a mark. It's meaningless back home. If anything, I think it might find me favor with the ladies."

Adam grimaced at the joke, and then suddenly he brightened. "Do you know, I bet they'd never take me back at the yeshiva with one of those," he said, eagerly pushing up his sleeve. "Do it quickly."

Lord Mortensen, who had regained his breath, pressed the mark into Adam's arm. Adam winced. "Blimey, that stings," he said philosophically, pushing his sleeve down over the mark. Henry gaped at his friend. He'd been expecting a show of dramatics.

"Stop staring," Adam muttered. "I got run through the stomach with a sword last term. I can handle a burn."

"Take yer seats, lads," Lord Mortensen said.

Henry and Adam sat.

Lord Mortensen introduced everyone around the table using titles that were forbidden in the Nordlands. Nearly everyone was "lord," but Lord Mortensen stopped when he got to the handsome older boy, the one who had given orders the night before.

"An' this is Prince Mauritz."

Henry gulped and inclined his head. But Adam snorted. "Sorry," he said. "But wasn't the royal family, well, *killed*?"

"Aye, they were indeed," Lord Mortensen said gravely. "And the dukes and barons and counts, and their wives and heirs. Ye have hit upon why we are here, lad, and what we aim to do."

Henry stared at Lord Mortensen in shock, suddenly understanding everything. "But—," he began.

"Yes, lad?" Lord Mortensen gave Henry an encouraging smile. "Have ye guessed it as well?"

"I think so, my lord," Henry said. "You mean to overthrow Chancellor Mors and to reinstate the monarchy. And if you don't mind my saying, the round table is a nice touch."

"Thank you, lad," Lord Mortensen said. "And that is it precisely. We have seen enough of Chancellor Mors and his absurd and ruthless policies. We have suffered, and we have endured, and we are ready to reclaim this country and return it to the old ways.

"The Draconian party was right to challenge the aristocracy, for we had grown entitled and lazy. But we have learned from our mistakes as well as seen the ill effect of heavy-handed rule."

As Henry listened to Lord Mortensen speak of their plans to rebuild the Nordlands as a fair monarchy, he saw the grief and strain fall from the man's face, to be replaced by hope. And a small spark of hope was kindled within Henry as well, because what Lord Mortensen wanted was to overthrow Chancellor Mors—and perhaps a civil war would happen, but everyone in South Britain would be able to go on with their lives, no longer waking up in fear of an invasion.

What Lord Mortensen was proposing would mean that peace would prevail among the countries of the Brittonian Isles once again. Adam seemed to realize this as well; when Lord Mortensen was finished, he applauded.

"That's brilliant, sir," Henry said. "But what good can *we* do?"

"Oh, I'm certain ye'll find your place," Lord Mortensen said. "Have ye any questions?"

"Only about a million," Henry admitted. "What is this legend of the doctor? I can't seem to figure it out."

"Ah, the mad doctor," Lord Mortensen said. "With his little blue book where he writes down your every scream. Is that the legend you mean?"

Henry and Adam nodded.

"He is one of the chancellor's men," Lord Mortensen said. "This is all we know. The law here is that if ye are claimed to be a criminal, whether that be for breaking curfew or killing a man in cold blood, your body belongs to the chancellor. And so his good doctor performs experiments on these prisoners. I dinnae what the purpose of these experiments may be, but it is a sinister practice, and a newer one. There is an old mental asylum by the town square that was cleared at the start of the year, and the rumor is that he runs the experiments there."

Henry bit his lip, remembering the story he'd read in the *Tattleteller* about gruesome practices in a Nordlandic mental asylum. He just wished he knew *why* the doctor was performing these experiments, and what he was looking to find. Something to do with hypothermia, Henry supposed.

"Is there anythin' else?" Lord Mortensen asked.

"Well, sir," Adam said, absently tracing a finger over the mark on his arm, "we did come here because we were worried the students were being trained in combat . . ."

"Not trained," Garen said with a shake of his head. "But they're learnin'. I hear 'em sneakin' around the corridors at night, and of course the muck on their boots gives it away. Some of the lads were wantin' to learn to fight, should the Brittonian aristocracy invade, an' so they've been practicin' with old weapons out in the carriage house, and punching one another black an' blue in the old stables."

Henry felt as though the chair had fallen out from under him. "They're teaching themselves?" he asked, trying not to panic.

"Aye," Garen said.

Lord Mortensen nodded and leaned back in his chair. "Some of the lads wish a war. They're enjoying the privileges of the Partisan School and the power it affords them. But they are young and full of big ideas. I say let them fight among themselves rather than take their bloodlust to the streets."

Henry put his head in his hands. There was no combat training. The room he'd seen, and the boys who'd whispered of it, were doing the same thing that he and Valmont had done—taking battle preparations into their own hands. It wasn't illegal, and it wasn't a violation of the Longsword Treaty.

They had come all this way for nothing.

No, not *nothing*, Henry corrected himself. There was still this conspiracy, this secret group of aristocrats in hiding. And if these men could overthrow the chancellor, that would change everything.

So there was hope yet.

Henry glanced at Mauritz, the future king, who lounged in his chair, absently playing with the gold ring he wore, which bore the mark of the rebellion, the same mark that Henry now carried.

27

SIR FREDERICK'S REVENGE

R*ohan was asleep when a rock banged against his* window. It was Saturday morning, and he intended to sleep in. He rolled over and promptly ignored it.

And then another rock hit.

He sighed and threw on his dressing gown, opening the window. "What?" he asked.

It was the first time he had seen Frankie since her return. She wore her hair plain, without a silk ribbon, and it made her look older. He bristled, pulling his dressing gown tighter as she stared at him solemnly.

"Hello," she said.

"May I help you with something, Miss Winter?" he asked.

"Professor Stratford and Lord Havelock just got into an automobile together," she said. "I think they've gone after Henry and Adam."

"Are you certain?" Rohan asked.

"No. Maybe they went shopping for some nice lace curtains," she said with a derisive snort.

"Thank you for telling me," Rohan said, and then he hesitated. "Would you like to come in?"

"But, Mr. Mehta, you're wearing pajamas," Frankie mocked.

"Come through the corridor," he said. "I'll be dressed by then."

Frankie knocked as Rohan was fastening his cuffs, and then she barged in.

"I say!" Rohan exclaimed. "I could have been putting on my trousers."

"I would have fainted from the impropriety," Frankie assured him, and then she sat down on Adam's still unmade bed just because she knew it would make Rohan bristle.

Rohan bristled.

"How are they?" he asked. "You were together, weren't you? In the Nordlands?"

Frankie's shoulders slumped. "We were," she said, her voice small. "I— Oh, Rohan, it was terrible. They were exhausted and half-starved. It wasn't as bad for me. And it was all my fault. They stayed because I missed the train back. If it weren't for me . . ." She looked up at Rohan, and sniffed.

He offered a handkerchief.

And then the door to the room burst open. It was Valmont. Frankie glared at him. Rohan sighed. "Is *everyone* going to come and go as they please?" he muttered.

"Uncle Havelock just left," Valmont said. He was still in his pajamas and dressing gown.

"We know," Rohan said. "Go away."

"No," Valmont said. "I'm part of this too. I want to know what you know."

"What darling pajamas you're wearing, Mr. Valmont," Frankie said.

Valmont went red. He removed his spectacles and polished them on a corner of his dressing gown. "Thank you," he said. "And now, if you're quite finishing mocking me, can we please move on to why my uncle just left in a motor car with Professor Stratford?"

* * *

Professor Stratford stared nervously at the identity papers in his hand and fiddled with his borrowed cravat. Across from him in the private train compartment, Lord Havelock dozed, frowning even in his sleep.

The train slowed as they came to the border inspection, and Lord Havelock came awake with a start. Professor Stratford stared out the window at the squat, low building and the six men in the heavy wool uniforms of the Nordlandic Policing Agency who marched smartly in formation toward the train.

"Stop gawking, Stratford," Lord Havelock ordered.

Professor Stratford nodded. He was so nervous he could hardly breathe.

And then a sharp knock sounded on the door to their compartment.

"Come in," Lord Havelock called.

Two policing agents saluted. Lord Havelock returned the salute crisply, and Professor Stratford did his best, trying not to feel like a fraud. He was a terrible liar.

"Papers, please," the policing agents demanded.

The men passed forward their identity papers, showing that they were the Lord Ministers Marchbanks and Flyte, and Lord Havelock handed them a sealed envelope explaining their business across the border.

"Just a minute, compatriots," the larger of the two policing agents said. He and his companion disappeared into the corridor.

Professor Stratford watched through the window as the policing agents marched back into the station. Was something wrong? He nearly mentioned his concern to Lord Havelock, but caught himself. After all, he had never crossed the border into the Nordlands before; perhaps this was normal.

Ten minutes went by, and then twenty. The train still sat at the border, unmoving.

Lord Havelock's frown deepened, and he disappeared behind his copy of the *Royal Standard*.

Finally the patrollers came back onto the train. There were eight of them now.

A knock sounded on the door of their compartment.

Lord Havelock calmly folded his newspaper. "You may enter," he called imperiously.

The patrollers didn't salute. They held their nasty-looking spiked batons in their fists, and they grinned menacingly. "Looks like ye're not who ye claim," one of the patrollers said. "Get up, both of ye."

Professor Stratford stood, and was seized immediately, his arm twisted painfully behind his back, the patroller's baton poking painfully into his kidneys.

"Now march," the patroller ordered.

Another patroller did the same to Lord Havelock. The two men were marshaled off the train and into the border inspection office, where they were thrown into a room that rather resembled a cell. There were no furnishings and no windows.

Professor Stratford sunk to the floor and put his head in his hands. "What went wrong?" he muttered.

Lord Havelock paced for a few minutes and then gave up and leaned against the wall, glowering. "If I knew that, Stratford, we wouldn't be here."

The men waited in silence for an hour, alone together with their thoughts. And then the door opened. Professor Stratford looked up, hardly daring to hope that they were being released.

The man in the doorway wore a pin-striped suit and a triumphant smile. His hands were hidden beneath a pair of white gloves; he carried a medical bag in one hand and a journal in the other, its cover a striking peacock blue.

"Hello, Magnus," he said. It was Sir Frederick.

"Frederick," Lord Havelock growled, "explain yourself at once!"

"Explain?" Sir Frederick frowned and set down his medical bag. "I should think it was obvious." He opened his journal, which was not a journal at all but a cleverly disguised case. He removed a syringe filled with clear liquid and idly tapped his thumb against the plunger, sending a few droplets of the cocktail into the air.

Professor Stratford gulped as he found himself roughly seized by the same patroller who had manhandled him earlier.

Sir Frederick took a step toward Lord Havelock, who was being similarly restrained. "I am here to collect what is due to me, Magnus," Sir Frederick said, sticking the needle into Lord Havelock's arm but hesitating before pressing the syringe, drawing out the horror. "You betrayed me and washed your hands of our alliance, but I have not forgotten how you wronged me back at Knightley, and finally I shall have my revenge."

Sir Frederick depressed the syringe.

"High treason and conspiracy," Lord Havelock said woozily.

Sir Frederick merely smiled. "'Yea though we roar with the fire of a mighty dragon, we are but its scales, all cut from the same mold, and of equal worth.'" He calmly wiped the syringe against his palm as Lord Havelock slumped forward, unconscious.

Professor Stratford swallowed nervously, feeling his knees buckle as Sir Frederick advanced, removing a second vial of clear liquid from his case.

"Ah, Stratford," Sir Frederick said. "A shame for you to have come here. I actually quite liked you. And how is little Henry these days, if I may ask?"

Professor Stratford gulped, realizing that he had to lie. "I wouldn't know," he said. "After the boy was expelled at the end of last term, he blamed me."

"Liar," Sir Frederick breathed. And then he grinned. "But I can make use of you yet, Stratford. I could send word of my triumph back to South Britain. . . . Yes, dread is better than surprise in this case. And you should do nicely."

Professor Stratford felt a sting, and then a rush of coldness in his arm.

"I'll deliver no messages for you," he managed weakly. His heartbeat sped, and his breathing slowed, and spots danced before his eyes.

"As though ye have a choice," Sir Frederick sneered.

And then everything went black.

* * *

On Monday night Henry was seated next to Mauritz in the hidden meeting room, helping the boy with his Italian homework before the meeting. They bent over the slim volume of Machiavelli, frowning.

Henry had warned Lord Mortensen that his Italian was out of practice, but the schoolmaster had thought he was being modest.

"Truly," Henry had insisted, "I've barely even looked at anything that wasn't French or Latin for a year now."

"It will do ye good," Lord Mortensen had said. "Both of ye. He needs the help."

Mauritz *did* need the help. At first he'd tried to demand that Henry do the assignment, but Henry had quickly put a stop to that.

"I won't do it for you. You have to learn this stuff," Henry had said with a sigh.

They weren't making much progress, as Mauritz puzzled over the simplest rules of Italian grammar.

"No," Henry said, biting back his frustration, "look at the words you *do* know. Does anything look familiar?"

"'*Arte,*'" Mauritz grumbled.

"Good," Henry said. "Now underline the words that modify it."

Mauritz hazarded a guess.

"No," Henry said through his teeth. "Look at the pronoun agreement. It's feminine, so you've got 'quella è sola,' see?"

"Just translate it for me, if ye can," Mauritz challenged.

"Fine," Henry said with a sigh. "From the beginning: 'Chapter Fourteen. That Which Is of—no, sorry—That Which Concerns a Prince on the Subject of War.' As I've said, my Italian is rusty. Shall I continue?"

"If ye want to be punched in the face," Mauritz grumbled.

"Sorry," Henry whispered furiously. "This wasn't *my* idea. But I gave my word to help, and if that means forcing Italian grammar down your throat, so be it."

And then Garen burst into the chamber, out of breath and brandishing a copy of the *Common Comrade*.

"My lord," Garen said, with a quick bow in the direction of Lord Mortensen, and a deeper bow toward the table where Henry and Mauritz sat. "My lord prince, there is news. A Brittonian man was caught crossing the border this weekend with forged identity papers. There is to be a hanging tomorrow in the square."

Lord Mortensen frowned. "Let me see that, lad."

Henry craned his neck as the paper passed to Lord

Mortensen. He noticed with surprise that the paper was wet, and in the spaces between the articles, violet letters were cramped onto the page.

"Sir, is that . . . ?" Henry began.

"Only shows up if ye dab it with the right chemicals," Garen said.

Lord Mortensen put down the paper, looking far older and far more tired than he had just moments before. "This could start a war," he muttered.

"What's happening?" Mauritz demanded.

Garen bowed and explained. A man had been caught crossing the border with forged diplomatic papers. He was being held at the prisoner's asylum, and there was to be a public execution at dawn.

"No!" Henry said, surging to his feet. "He was coming to rescue us!"

"Ye don't know that, lad," Lord Mortensen said.

"I do!" Henry cried. "It must be Professor Stratford."

Henry's heart felt as though it might break his rib cage. He couldn't sit. He couldn't stay still. His hands shook as the horror of the situation washed over him.

It *was* Professor Stratford—he was sure of it. And if the professor had been caught, it was all his fault.

Public execution.

The phrase sounded like something out of a medieval nightmare. With a gulp Henry remembered the gallows in the public square, across from the statue of the chancellor. And then he remembered something else—Lord Mortensen's explanation of what the chancellor did to prisoners.

"The doctor has him," Henry muttered.

"Aye," Garen said darkly. "Cure his health before he cure the man of his life."

"Don't say that!" Henry cried, running a hand over his face and trying to think. But all he could conjure up was a hideous image of Professor Stratford, his lips blue and his toes turning black, strapped to a table as a faceless man in a butcher's apron asked him to describe the pain.

"I have to go," Henry said. "We have to get him back."

"That is not possible," Lord Mortensen said sadly, shaking his head.

"Make it possible, then!" Henry retorted.

"I cannae do it, lad. An' where would we hide a fugitive who cannae cross back to his own country? There are greater things at play here, an' the risk is too high. Our rebellion must tread carefully if we are to succeed."

"He's the only family I have," Henry said. "You said the doctor takes his patients to the old mental asylum. I'm going. If I can't rescue him, at least I can say good-bye."

"Stop him!" Lord Mortensen cried, but Henry was already forcing open the door to the hallway, and then he was running down the corridor and out of the castle.

The student guard took in Henry's staff kitchen waistcoat and the expression on his face and pulled back the gate without comment. Henry slipped through, the cold night air of Romborough making him shiver. He passed the graveyard, that ominous place where men became slabs and memories, buried again over time, and he passed the church with its funny circular roof quartered by blackened beams, and the first of the pylons that loomed up ahead, marking the widening of Cairway Road.

The streets were rough at night, with gangs lurking in the entrances to the closes, and ladies calling after him from the skeletons of the market stalls.

And then he was in the square, with the bronze statue of Yurick Mors waving the banner of the revolution. There. The gallows.

Henry saw the gentle sway of the rope in silhouette,

and the gruesome stage, its stains buried deep beneath a layer of sawdust.

No.

This enormous statue of the chancellor couldn't be the last thing Professor Stratford saw. Henry swallowed back a desperate sob as he crossed the square toward the small white building with no windows.

THE PRISONERS' ASYLUM, a sign read, hanging from the rusted gate.

Henry ignored the voice in his head that shrilled for him to turn back toward the castle, toward the hidden chamber where the rebellion convened at midnight, where they sat as old-fashioned knights loyal to the overthrown king, at a round table like something out of legend.

For the place he was about to enter was like something out of his nightmares. He took a deep breath and passed through the gates, but no one stopped him. He opened the door of the prison, where no one stood guard.

And he walked down a hallway with electric lights ablaze, harsh on his eyes after more than a week of old-fashioned gaslight and candles. He squinted, wondering why there were no guards, and then he realized belatedly that those who came here were meant to escape and carry with them the warning of this place.

No, he didn't want this main corridor. He wanted some place far worse. The building was small, and there was only one place he could think to look. The basement.

Or the dungeon, he supposed, for when he found it, the subterranean stone tunnel certainly looked like one. The left wall was lined with cells, and there was no guard, no chance to overpower the warden and wrestle away the key, or steal it from his belt as he slept. The doors to the cells gaped open, as though awaiting the embrace of their future occupants.

But one door at the end of the corridor was closed.

"Professor?" Henry called, hurrying toward it.

"Ah, Mr. Grim," a chilling voice said. Henry looked wildly around the corridor, but could not place the speaker. And then he reached the closed door and gaped in surprise at the occupant of the cell.

"As you can see, Mr. Grim, I have come to rescue you," Lord Havelock sneered. The military history master had deep circles under his eyes, and his cheeks were hard with stubble. His suit was horribly wrinkled, and his left arm drooped as though it had been pulled from its socket.

"Where's Professor Stratford?"

"I don't know," Lord Havelock said. "We were stopped at the border, but he dosed me first. I was here when I woke, and Stratford had vanished."

Henry frowned. "But—"

"A special torture has been reserved for me," Lord Havelock said, answering Henry's unspoken question. "He wishes me to enjoy every last ounce of his revenge."

"He?" Henry asked.

"Dr. Von Izembard." Lord Havelock's brows knitted together. "Of course, you know him by a different name: Sir Frederick."

"Sir Frederick?" Henry didn't think he'd heard correctly.

And then it all made sense. Sir Frederick, who had betrayed them all last term, who had wanted a war so that Chancellor Mors might rule the full of the Brittonian Isles, had talked of opening a hospital. He had asked Henry and Adam to join him.

Just a few months ago Henry had been so certain that Sir Frederick would return to enact his revenge, but he'd never thought that revenge would be meant for *Lord Havelock*.

It made a horrible kind of sense. And news of

Nordlandic medical experiments had surfaced only months after Sir Frederick's disappearance. No wonder he hadn't been apprehended; he had fled to the Nordlands. He had rejoined the chancellor and become something out of a hellish fable: the doctor who cured your health.

"Listen to me, boy," Lord Havelock growled. "You have to get out of here. Tomorrow, after they—after it is over, Sir Frederick will send my body back as a warning. You must get on that train. They are superstitious of corpses here and will not check the compartment carefully. Do you understand?"

"But, sir, I can't. There has to be a way that—"

"There is no hope for me, boy. I have been given my medicine, so to speak. But there is small comfort in knowing that some good may come of my demise."

Henry nodded, not knowing what to say. "Yes, sir," he whispered. "I understand."

"Poor Fergus," Lord Havelock said, half to himself. "The boy's father was one of the first to go in the uprisings. He rushed in to break up a riot and save the children."

"I know, sir," Henry said, his throat dry. "I'm so sorry."

"You shouldn't be here," Lord Havelock said harshly. "You must leave before the doctor returns."

"But, sir—"

"Go," Lord Havelock spat. "Do not make me tell you to get out of here a third time, Mr. Grim."

"No, sir," Henry said with a heavy heart.

As he left the basement, his eyes brimming with tears, a hand closed over his mouth, and his arm was twisted painfully behind his back.

28

THE FUTURE
KING

Henry struggled against his captor until a voice hissed, "Stop that, lad. Ye'll disjoint your arm."

"Lord Mortensen?"

"It's Compatriot Erasmus here," the schoolmaster whispered, releasing him. "Hurry. We must get ye back to the castle."

"I don't understand," Henry whispered, hurrying after the schoolmaster, but Lord Mortensen shook his head and held a finger to his lips. It was only when they'd passed through the gates to the prisoners' asylum that the schoolmaster breathed a sigh of relief.

"What don't ye understand, lad?" Lord Mortensen

asked as they passed by the gallows. He shivered and made the sign of the cross.

"You said it was too dangerous," Henry said. "And yet you came."

"Too dangerous for ye, not for an old man such as myself."

Henry frowned. "But, sir—"

"Don't argue with me, lad. That was a foolish thing ye did. Foolish, yet noble."

"I had to see for myself," Henry said. "I— Oh, God, everything is ruined. I never should have come here."

"Listen to me, Henry," Lord Mortensen said fiercely, putting a hand on the boy's shoulder. They were outside the gate to the graveyard, and the moonlight glittered on the roof of the old church. "Coming here is the best thing ye could have done."

"How can you say that?" Henry asked, angrily brushing the hand from his shoulder.

"Come back to the meeting room, lad, and I shall explain everything."

Adam knew.

That was Henry's first thought when he saw the look on his friend's face. Whatever it was that Lord

Mortensen wasn't saying, he could see the secret threatening to burst from Adam at any moment. Everyone was assembled around the candlelit table, and they went silent as Henry and Lord Mortensen entered. Adam bit his lip and didn't meet Henry's gaze.

Was it that bad?

"Sit, lad," Lord Mortensen urged.

"No," Henry said, folding his arms across his chest.

"Very well." Lord Mortensen gave Henry a grave look, and one by one the men around the table rose, even Mauritz, who shot Henry a reproachful glare.

"Why is everyone standing?" Henry asked.

"Because you stand," Lord Mortensen said.

Henry snorted. That didn't make any sense. Experimentally he took a seat.

"Thank ye, lad. The walk has tired me," Lord Mortensen said, lowering himself into a chair with a grimace.

"Will someone please tell me what's going on?" Henry demanded.

Lord Mortensen reached into his pocket and removed a daguerreotype, passing it to Henry. It was the picture from the restricted library, the one with Lord Mortensen as a boy, and with the youth who looked so like Henry.

"This is my father," Henry said.

Lord Mortensen nodded.

"You knew him?" Henry asked.

Again Lord Mortensen nodded.

"So this was back when he was a student at Knightley," Henry said.

Lord Mortensen smiled sadly and shook his head. "Turn it over, lad."

Engraved on the back of the picture was a list of the champions.

"I don't know his name," Henry said.

"Will," Lord Mortensen said. "Wilhelm."

"But—," Henry began, and then he saw it, like some cruel joke. ORATORY CHAMPION: WILHELM GRIMAULDI. PARTISAN SCHOOL. "What?" Henry said. "No. I can't be Nordlandic."

"I dunno, mate. You are rather tall," Adam said with a shrug.

"Thanks," Henry said, rolling his eyes. He appreciated Adam's attempt to lighten the mood, as he suspected there would be nothing more to laugh at for a long while.

"So my father went to Partisan," Henry said, and then he looked up. "He's dead, isn't he? He and my mum?"

"Aye, lad. I'm sorry," Lord Mortensen said.

"How—," Henry began. "How long have you known who I was?"

"I suspected," Lord Mortensen continued. "They had a son called Henry. He'd be your age, and the resemblance is striking. You're left handed, for one, and that speech you made was so like your father. And the way Adam called you 'Grim.' Your dad went by the same."

"It isn't a nickname," Henry said. "That's my name. It's Henry Grim."

"Grimauldi," Lord Mortensen corrected gently.

"No," Henry said. "I have a birth certificate. 'Baby boy found on church steps' or something."

"Have ye seen this certificate, lad?"

"Well, no," Henry admitted with a frown. "But the orphanage said they had a copy." And then a thought occurred to Henry. "If I'm Nordlandic, why was I brought to an orphanage in South Britain?"

"Ah," Lord Mortensen said, lacing his fingers. "Good, lad."

Henry glanced at Adam, who squirmed in his chair, still unable to meet Henry's eye.

"Your father was a speech writer," Lord Mortensen

continued. "A scholar. He preferred the company of his books to the applause of an audience. Does this sound familiar, lad? We were all fighting against the rise of the Draconian party, but speeches are dangerous things, and words have a way of being traced back to their maker. Before your parents died, they told me they were taking ye where your life might not be touched by the revolution. They were killed just days after they returned without ye. It was a profound loss."

"Thank you," Henry murmured, overwhelmed. He had never known his parents, and yet the story Lord Mortensen told made Henry feel as though he were staring at their freshly packed graves. And then Henry realized why his parents had hidden him away—to save him. After all, Midsummer was little more than an hour's train ride from the Nordlandic border. And if his father had attended the Partisan School . . . If his family had died during the revolution . . .

"My father was a lord," Henry said, looking to Lord Mortensen for confirmation.

"No, lad," Lord Mortensen corrected. "Your father was an earl."

Back at Knightley, Professor Turveydrop had tested them on the different levels of the peerage in a protocol exam. An earl, Henry knew, ranked below a duke but above a viscount.

"But you said that everyone was killed," Henry accused. "The royal family and the dukes and earls and barons and their heirs."

"Aye, and the lesser lords could renounce themselves and live in shame," Lord Mortensen said sadly. "So ye see, lad, we are fortunate ye have come."

At this Mauritz sighed loudly and rolled his eyes once again, and Henry realized with sudden, horrible clarity exactly what was going on.

"No," Henry said, pushing back his chair.

One by one the men around the table did the same.

"Stop that," Henry cried. "I can't— I'm the— No. This is absurd. I spent my whole life scrubbing floors and dreaming of becoming a knight, and I finally got the chance to attend Knightley. Not Partisan. *Knightley*."

Henry sunk back into the chair, burying his face in his hands. He'd worked so hard to learn all he could so that he might have the chance to rise above his miserable lot in life. He'd never even dreamed he would be admitted to Knightley, much less that he would excel at his studies and find friends among his aristocratic classmates.

Even now, the thought of Derrick and Conrad helping him to smuggle a picnic out of the dining hall, of nights playing chess in the common room, of midnight forays to the kitchens with Adam and Rohan, of Frankie climbing through his window—even of Valmont and the battle society. He was painfully aware of how wonderful all of it had been, and how much he didn't want it to end.

"What happens now?" Henry asked dully.

"We go forward in our plans to do away with Yurick Mors and his men. We restore the monarchy," Lord Mortensen said.

"You mean me."

"Yes, lad. Mauritz is the younger son of a minor viscount. You supersede him in his claim as the heir presumptive to the Nordlandic throne."

Henry glanced accusingly at Adam, who shrugged and bit his lip.

"If we are successful in removing Chancellor Mors and his Draconians from power," Lord Mortensen continued, "ye would ascend the throne. And if we are too late, or we dinnae succeed and the chancellor invades South Britain, there would come a great and terrible war, which the chancellor must not win. But do ye think old King Victor would want the responsibility of rebuilding this country? And I dinnae think the Nord-landic people would let him rule in protectorate, when they could have their independence restored under their own monarch."

Henry gulped. He hadn't considered it like that. He was stuck no matter what happened. If there was a way to prevent war, or even if they fought, the goal was the same: to do away with Chancellor Mors and the horrors they had all endured from his bloody rise to power. To reinstate the monarchy—him.

His entire life was crumbling away before his eyes: graduating from Knightley, joining the knight detectives, moving into a flat in the city and spending his days solving crimes and his nights in the Royal Archives, bent over his research. Joining his friends in the drawing rooms of high society, perhaps with Frankie at his side . . .

All of it gone.

If only he'd never gone down the corridor that night during the Inter-School Tournament—if only he'd left that trunk of weapons where Derrick had found it—if only he'd let the envoy go to the Nordlands short staffed—he might have been back at Knightley Academy at that very moment, spending a carefree night with his friends.

Shamefully Henry realized that there were tears on his cheeks, and he wiped them away. He wasn't crying only for himself but for his dead parents and for Lord Havelock calmly awaiting the gallows, and for Professor Stratford, who could be anywhere, enduring who knew what sort of torture.

"Ye could stay, lad," Lord Mortensen said. "In the Nordlands. I could adopt ye, and next year ye could start school at Partisan, if the peace holds till then."

The offer was unexpected. Stay in the Nordlands?

It would be like starting over—being adopted by a kindly schoolmaster, studying alongside the students whose meals he had served and boots he had shined, and knowing that, back in South Britain, life at Knightley went on without him, until it was as though he had never been there at all.

"I can't," Henry said firmly. "I have to go back. Everything's left unsettled, and I gave my word to Lord Havelock. I'm sorry, Lord Mortensen, but I don't belong here."

"An' I am sorry, lad, about your Professor Stratford," Lord Mortensen said kindly.

And Henry realized that he had never explained. He

had simply run off, shouting about rescuing the professor.

"Henry," Adam said suspiciously. "What's happened?"

Henry sighed and explained.

"Blimey," Adam said when Henry was finished. "Sir Frederick. That bloke just keeps coming back to haunt us, doesn't he?"

Henry sighed and shook his head. "I hope Professor Stratford's all right," he said. "He might have been sent back, if it was revenge Sir Frederick wanted. The newspaper said one man had been captured, not two."

"Henry," Lord Mortensen said gently.

"No!" Henry said. "He's fine, I know it. Sir Fr—the doctor—sent him back."

"He may have done, lad," Lord Mortensen said, "but he might still make the connection and come after ye and Adam next. This school is Yascherov's. He would think nothing of handing over two boys to another of the chancellor's men."

Henry related Lord Havelock's plan to the table of men, how he had promised that they'd hide away on the train. They could go back home before Sir Frederick realized their whereabouts.

At this, Lord Mortensen nodded gravely. "It is not safe for you here, lad, with an enemy such as the doctor.

I had wanted ye to stay, but it matters not where ye are, only that ye are kept safe."

And then Adam yawned. "Sorry," he muttered.

"Is that the hour?" Lord Mortensen said, checking his pocket watch. "Off to bed with ye boys, before the dawn catches up with us."

Back in the servants' quarters, Henry and Adam unlaced their boots and changed into their nightshirts. Everyone else was long asleep.

"Good night, my lord prince," Adam joked as he climbed into bed.

"Don't," Henry said tiredly. "That isn't funny."

"Actually, mate, it is," Adam insisted. "I'm rubbish at foreign history, but even *I* know that there have been seven Nordlandic kings called Henry."

"Oh, that's just wonderful," Henry said. "Just what everyone needs. Another King Henry the Eighth."

"You won't be." Adam yawned. "For one thing, he had six wives, and you're hopeless with girls."

"Well, you're rubbish with secrets," Henry retorted. "I thought you were going to burst out with it at the meeting tonight."

"I wish I had," Adam said. "Maybe then you would have laughed."

"Somehow I don't think even *you* could have made it funny," Henry said, pulling up the ragged blanket and closing his eyes.

The hour crept forward, until gray dawn stretched over the city of Romborough. But no one on the streets stopped to wish their neighbors good morning. They kept their heads down in dread of the sight that awaited them in the main square. For there, across from the market stalls, under the stern gaze of the bronze statue of the chancellor, the toes of Lord Havelock's boots made gentle circles in the sawdust beneath the gallows.

The passengers on the platform crossed themselves and averted their gaze from the pine box that the four patrolmen carried.

Henry and Adam stood on the platform as well, dressed in the rumpled shirts and trousers that had sat at the bottom of their satchels for the past week and a half. Lord Mortensen stood between them, a hand on each boy's shoulder, his black suit somber and somehow appropriate as they watched the coffin loaded onto the steam engine.

"Ye have your tickets, lads?"

Both boys nodded. Lord Mortensen had bought them third-class passage to Alberforth, a town they would never see, as by the time the train pulled into Alberforth Station, they were to be hidden away in the storage car.

"Henry," Lord Mortensen said.

Henry shrugged the schoolmaster's hand off his shoulder.

"I have to go," Henry said. "I know, keep out of trouble. And thank you, for everything."

"The offer still stands, lad. I would be proud to adopt ye, should ye find life in South Britain no longer to your liking."

But they both knew that it was hopeless. With Sir Frederick at his hospital of horrors tinkering away at who knows what sorts of experiments, with Yascherov and his secret police keeping a watchful eye over the Partisan students, it was not safe for Henry to stay, even if he had wanted to leave his life behind.

"Take these," Lord Mortensen said, handing each boy a parcel. Henry's was small and flat, while Adam's was lumpy.

"What is it?" Adam asked, giving the parcel an experimental sniff.

"Fish jelly sandwiches," Lord Mortensen said. "For the train."

Adam gulped and smiled bravely. "My favorite."

Night fell as the train traveled through the Brittonian Isles, past the rocky cliffs and wobbling Cotswolds and gleaming city lights. But Henry and Adam, crouched behind crates in the storage car, knew only the jolt of the train tracks and the haunting presence of the corpse inside its pine box.

When the train rumbled to its final stop in Avel-on-t'Hems, Henry roused himself from the melancholy company of his thoughts and whispered, "Are we here?"

"I think so," Adam said.

Both boys climbed to their feet and stretched the stiffness from their limbs. They made their way onto the platform. It was late, and there were just a handful of passengers alighting from the second-class cars. The men went on their way with the brims of their hats pulled low and the collars of their coats turned up against the chill of the night. Beyond the rail station stood a funeral carriage, its driver dressed in mourning, reading the *Royal Standard*. Across the road, smoke curled from the three crooked chimneys of the Lance, and a few drunken patrons exited the pub, their laughter and revelry dwindling as they caught sight of the funeral carriage across the way.

Henry and Adam trudged silently past the Lance, through the narrow village streets, and up the hill to their school. Knightley Academy stood out against the moonlight in silhouette, a ramshackle collection of chimneys, turrets, and gables. Both boys stopped to take in the sight of the manicured lawns and tangled woods, the soaring chapel and ivy-covered brick of the head-master's house. They were home.

For this, Henry felt, was home. Not some foreign castle encircled by guard towers, but this cozy, bizarre assortment of buildings, with its gossiping kitchen maids and eccentric professors and clever students.

They crossed the quadrangle, and Henry took a deep breath before knocking on the door of the headmaster's house. Ellen opened the door with a sniff at the grubby-looking boys who stood there.

"Servin' staff around the back," she said, making to slam the door in their faces.

Henry caught it with his boot.

The maid put her hands on her hips and glared.

"We're here to see Professor Stratford," Henry said, and then bit his lip, waiting in dread of her reply.

"You and the whole Ministerium," she said with a sigh. "Come on."

But Henry had already pushed past her and was running up the stairs to the professor's study.

Ellen called angrily after him, but he didn't care.

"Wait for me," Adam complained as Henry burst through the door.

"Professor!" Henry cried.

Professor Stratford sat at his desk. His face was bruised and his left arm was in a sling. An untouched cup of tea warmed his elbow as he read the latest issue of the *Tattleteller*. He dropped the magazine, gaping at Henry and Adam as though they were ghosts, and then he enveloped the boys in an enormous hug.

"I'm so glad," Professor Stratford said. "I thought— I— It's not important. Now sit down and tell me everything."

It felt strange to settle themselves in the chairs opposite Professor Stratford's desk, to be back in a place so familiar and safe. Henry and Adam exchanged a glance, and then, with a heavy heart, Henry began to tell the tale of their time in the Nordlands. Adam, to his credit, tried very hard not to interrupt.

When Henry got to the part about going to see Lord Havelock in the prisoners' asylum, Professor Stratford went gray. "You shouldn't have done that, Henry," he said.

"I thought it was you!" Henry replied. "What else could I do? Go to sleep and know that in the morning you'd be . . ." Henry stared miserably at his lap, unable to finish the thought.

"Tell him about what happened next," Adam said. "That's the good bit."

Henry sighed. He didn't know if he'd call finding out that he had no choice over his future the "good bit." "Right," he said. "So, I've found out who my parents are. They were Nordlandic."

At that moment a small thump sounded outside the door to Professor Stratford's study.

"Francesca?" Professor Stratford called, narrowing his eyes.

Frankie appeared in the doorway looking guilty. "I thought I heard— Henry! Adam!"

"Hallo," Henry said, grinning in spite of himself.

Frankie padded over to the club chair by the window, arranging her nightgown so that it covered her bare feet.

"Er, Francesca," Professor Stratford began, "I don't really think you're dressed . . ."

"That's all right," Adam said cheerfully. "We all slept up in the attic together."

"Somehow I think that makes it worse," Henry muttered.

"What? It's not like I said how you kissed her," Adam returned.

Henry and Frankie both turned crimson.

"Ah," Professor Stratford said, looking back and forth between Henry and Frankie with the faintest hint of a smile. "So I take it the fighting has ended."

Frankie scowled. "You were just getting to the good part," she said. "About your parents being Nordlandic."

"Thank you, Miss Winter," Henry said dryly, rolling his eyes at her for eavesdropping. And then he told Frankie and the professor what Lord Mortensen had said about his father being an earl, and how they planned to restore the monarchy.

"I just wanted to be a knight," Henry finished. "I didn't ask for this. It's just an unfortunate effect of my being the last one standing."

"You make it sound like you got picked last for cricket, mate," Adam said.

"At least with cricket I can choose to sit out the game and go do something else with my life," Henry snapped. He'd meant to say "something else with my time" but it was too late now.

"Oh, Henry," Professor Stratford said, as though they were back at the Midsummer School and Henry had once again been sent off to bed without any supper.

"Don't," Henry said evenly. "Don't try to make me feel better about it. This is my fault. If only I'd never gone to the Nordlands— If only I'd listened to everyone who said that it wasn't my responsibility, it bloody well wouldn't be!"

"Am I missing something?" Frankie asked. "How is this *your* fault? If anything, *I'm* the one who stowed away on that dratted train and decided not to stay hidden until its return. I'm the one who snuck off to the castle and then made you miss the envoy."

"You can't blame yourself for my doing reckless things because I wanted to rescue you," Henry said.

At this, Professor Stratford coughed delicately, and Henry realized what he'd just said. Because he did blame himself for Lord Havelock's death, in a way, even though there was no way he could have known what Sir Frederick was after, or that he had been lying in wait just across the Nordlandic border all this time.

But a tiny voice in the back of Henry's mind insisted that Professor Stratford was all right, and that Frankie and Adam had returned safely, and that, if anything, he had done what had been needed. It was unfortunate about Lord Havelock, yes, but every war begins with tragic and untimely death. For though Henry hadn't found evidence of a gathering army in the Nordlands, he knew more than enough to explain what was truly happening. Everyone had lived in blind fear for so long, and he could put a stop to it—if only someone would listen.

Chancellor Mors certainly wished to go to war, and was undoubtedly planning his attack, but the country was not yet mobilized to fight. The students at Partisan still spent their time studying Italian grammar, not combat techniques, and though some of them might have been sneaking off to teach themselves to fight in the old stables, Henry couldn't blame them, as he and his classmates had done the very same thing.

But what worried Henry deeply was Sir Frederick; those medical experiments had a dark and sinister purpose, one that Henry knew was undoubtedly connected to Chancellor Mors's plans for war. Perhaps those old rumors about new technologies, about Mors finding a way to attack without violating the Longsword Treaty, were more than just hearsay. . . .

"So," Frankie said, breaking the silence, "just to be clear on this point, you do know that you'd be—sorry, it's just too good—King Henry the Eighth?"

"It's not funny," Henry snapped, as Frankie and Adam snickered.

29

THE PRINCE
AND THE PAUPER

Lord Havelock had not been a beloved professor. He'd been, beyond everything else, unpleasant. He bullied, and he played favorites, and he gave notoriously low marks. But the hastening of death is a melancholy affair, and to treat the abrupt end of a man's life as anything other than tragedy would be unchivalrous indeed.

Because while Lord Havelock had been prejudiced and certainly elitist, he had not been wicked. He had cared for Valmont, raising the boy without complaint and without wanting. He had spoken on Henry, Adam, and Rohan's behalf so that they might not be expelled after they had proven themselves to be apt pupils, and he had looked the other way when the boys had formed their battle society. And, perhaps most telling of his character, he had died selflessly and with honor.

But Lord Havelock's students did not know any of this. They knew only what they saw: the military history master's body returned to Knightley Academy in a pine box etched with the inscription: "Yea though we roar with the fire of a mighty dragon, we are but its scales, shed when no longer needed, and lost without mourning as the great beast marches on."

Valmont had gone white at the news, and then quietly turned and walked back down the first-year corridor, closing himself inside his room. There he stayed for three days, refusing to take his meals in the dining hall or to attend his classes. Ollie was sent up with food, and the first years watched the scrawny serving boy knock repeatedly before leaving the tray outside Valmont's door in defeat.

Henry thought about going to speak to Valmont himself, to explain what had happened, and perhaps lessen some of the unfortunate guilt he, Henry, felt over Lord Havelock's death. But he never quite managed to summon the courage, and even if he had, he wouldn't have known what to say.

Henry and Adam had quietly rejoined their classmates on Headmaster Winter's orders, as though pretending their absence had never happened would make it any less of a curiosity. They spent their nights in the library, making up their missed assignments under the watchful eye of Professor Turveydrop, and trying to repair the distance that had appeared between themselves and Rohan.

For though Rohan was overjoyed to have them back, there was a new coolness to their friendship. Rohan had been left behind twice now, and so many things seemed to divide them—a fear of Sir Frederick, whom Rohan had known only as a kindly professor; the drudgery of serving work; the horrible journey home from the Nordlands in the company of Lord Havelock's corpse.

And then there were the marks on Henry's and Adam's arms. Rohan had balked at the sight of them, claiming such marks were only fit for pirates.

"Really?" Adam had asked brightly. "Girls like pirates, don't they? Do you reckon I should get an earring to go with it?"

"It might clash with your yarmulke," Henry had said, barely able to keep a straight face.

"Oh, right." Adam's face had fallen. "Maybe if I just carried around a sword instead?"

"But then they might mistake you for a knight," Henry had pointed out.

Rohan had shaken his head, left his roommates to their preposterous antics, and gone off to find James.

The morning of Lord Havelock's funeral dawned unseasonably warm. Henry grimaced as he looked out the window at the bright sunlight, wishing the weather might have conducted itself with appropriate decorum.

But it was too late for it now. The students gathered solemnly in the school chapel, and only a few of them noticed that the pine box had been replaced by a fine coffin made of yew.

Valmont sat in the front pew of the chapel, next to a woman in an enormous black mourning hat and veil, whom Henry took to be his mother. She sobbed theatrically through the service in a way that made Henry suspect she had spent the entire weekend shopping for the perfect funeral bonnet.

The board of trustees came, and a handful of lord ministers. They sat somberly in the back, and Sir Robert joined them.

Headmaster Winter spoke, and then Fergus Valmont,

though Henry couldn't have told you what either of them said, just that they both seemed to have experienced a profound loss, which had shaken them to their very souls. He was acutely aware of a number of students realizing for the first time that Lord Havelock had been Valmont's guardian.

Henry stared down at the gold ring he now wore; it had been inside the parcel from Lord Mortensen, along with three letters: one for him, one for Headmaster Winter, and one for Lord Minister Marchbanks. Henry had kept his letter unopened and had given the others to Headmaster Winter, who had revealed nothing of their contents. But then, what could the letters possibly say that he didn't already know?

Henry listened to the dirge of the pipe organ and twisted his ring, reading the inscription etched around its band: *Que mon honneur est sans tache.*

"Let my honor be without stain."

Well, he thought grimly, *it's a bit too late for that.*

The service ended somberly, and as the students spilled out of the chapel, Henry felt a hand on his shoulder. He turned.

Valmont's face was drawn, and purplish smudges

beneath his eyes betrayed his lack of sleep. Unlike the rest of the students, he didn't wear his formal uniform but rather a neat dark suit. He swallowed thickly and glared at Henry through his spectacles.

Henry had been expecting this. He followed Valmont over to a stone bench, but neither of them made any move to sit. They stared at each other, and then Valmont broke the silence.

"You did this," he accused.

Henry merely bowed his head.

Encouraged, Valmont continued. "I wish it had been you instead. You or your precious Professor Stratford."

Henry felt anger welling up inside him, and he struggled to master it. "I'm sorry," he said hotly. "I truly am. I never meant it to happen. I didn't know—I thought Sir Frederick was gone. I thought he blamed me. I never thought it was going to be your uncle in that cell. I tried to save him; it was just too dangerous, and I . . ." Henry trailed off miserably.

"What are you talking about?" Valmont demanded.

Henry frowned. Valmont didn't know? "How Sir Frederick killed Lord Havelock," Henry said.

Valmont paled, and Henry realized that Valmont

had stayed locked inside his room refusing to come out, that he had heard only of his uncle's death, and not of the circumstances.

The one thing Henry remembered about the funeral was that Lord Havelock's death had been called noble, but it had not been explained. Henry had told Headmaster Winter in excruciating detail what had happened, and he didn't think he could bear to tell the tale another time. But then he saw the look on Valmont's face and knew that he had to.

"Come on," Henry said, nodding toward the woods.

"I'm not going anywhere with you, you murderer," Valmont spat, and then he looked instantly sorry.

"Suit yourself."

"Fine. Let's go, servant boy."

Henry told him everything that had happened, up until he'd left Lord Havelock's cell. Valmont was quiet for a long while. He unearthed a half-buried stone with the toe of his boot.

"So you were wrong," he said finally. "There was no combat training."

"No," Henry admitted. "There wasn't. Just another secret battle society."

"I really do hate you, you know," Valmont said.

"Good. You should."

"Good, because I do."

But Henry could tell that Valmont didn't truly mean it. They'd become friends somehow, without their realizing.

When Admiral Blackwood pulled Henry aside and told him that he wouldn't be marching with the rest of the students in the King Victor's Day parade, he wasn't surprised.

"It's the headmaster's orders," Admiral Blackwood said.

"Of course." Henry nodded. "I understand completely."

Which was why Henry stayed behind at school while the rest of his classmates went off to the city for the day, dressed in their formal uniforms and hats, laughing and joking as they crossed the quadrangle.

From the window of his room, Henry watched them go.

He pulled a knight detective novel from his shelf and settled at his desk to read, but it was no good; the story merely reminded him of the career he would have chosen, if the choice were still his.

Henry threw the book across the room, watching it smack into the wardrobe and then flop onto the floor in defeat. He put his head in his hands.

And then, without quite knowing what else to do, he pulled out his ethics textbook and began to study for the end of term exams. Not that they mattered.

Henry glared glumly at the textbook for the better part of an hour, until someone knocked on the door to his room.

"Come in," he mumbled.

It was Lord Minister Marchbanks.

"Er," Henry said, surging to his feet and giving the proper bow. "Good afternoon, my lord minister."

Lord Marchbanks bowed in return, and Henry's cheeks colored as he recognized the bow. It was one Frankie often teased him for using by accident, though he never had. It was the bow used when addressing a foreign prince.

"Good afternoon, lad. May I call you Henry?"

"Yes, please," Henry said with much relief.

"I was wondering if I might have a word?"

"Certainly, my lord minister."

"Come, let us take a walk about the grounds. It is lovely this time of year."

Lord Marchbanks was right; the weather was lovely, and the pathways through the quadrangle were bordered with vibrant sprays of bluebells and primroses. As they walked through the quadrangle, Lord Marchbanks frowned at Henry.

"I really should have suspected," he said.

"Suspected what, my Lord Minister?"

"That you were one of my son's irresponsible friends from school."

"You mean during the envoy," Henry said, cringing.

"Oh, don't get me wrong, lad. You made a very convincing serving boy. I was sad to hear you'd taken ill on the ride back. I had quite a horrible boy who steeped tea as though it were dishwater."

Henry grinned in spite of himself.

"But enough of that," Lord Marchbanks continued. "Let's get down to it, shall we?"

"Down to what, sir?"

"I'll admit the letter certainly shocked me. But then, it is a remarkable fortune. We were all worried they'd scare up someone quite unsuitable—a *campagnard* who could barely read, for example, or else someone horribly spoiled in an exiled court."

"I'm sorry, my Lord Minister, but I don't follow."

"You, lad!" Lord Marchbanks said. "It's perfect. I couldn't have dreamed of someone better—though a few years older wouldn't have hurt, but you'll grow up fast enough."

Henry sighed. He still wasn't exactly following Lord Marchbanks's train of thought, but he could certainly venture a guess. "So you know, sir, about Lord Mortensen and his . . . plan?"

"I suspected. That's why I set up the envoy—so that I might have my suspicions proven and so that I might have an excuse to speak with the man in person. If only that dratted Dimit Yascherov hadn't been keeping an eye on me the entire time, we might have been able to speak at length. Mortensen's letter was quite informative. I thank you for carrying it, Henry."

"Not at all," Henry said, wishing he'd read it. Derrick had mentioned something once about steaming letters open. . . .

"As I was saying, lad," Lord Marchbanks continued, "we at the Ministerium were worried about what might happen in the aftermath of a war with the Nordlands, not to speak of the horrors of the war itself. But if your Lord Mortensen and his men can prevent a war, I would do everything in my power to help them."

"As would I," said Henry.

"Which is why you must stay at Knightley Academy," Lord Marchbanks said.

"Sir?"

"I can see it in your eyes, lad. It is the same hurt that Derrick carries, knowing he must take up my position one day, that he cannot choose to be a secret service knight as he wishes. And yet he took the Knightley Exam knowing his fate. For him, a taste of the life he wishes is preferable to sulking about his obligations in a less prestigious school, or at home with private tutors."

Henry frowned. He'd nearly forgotten, having become friends with Derrick and Conrad over the course of the term, that neither boy could choose his future, that they were both due to inherit their fathers' seats in the House of Lord Ministers.

"I've only ever dreamed of becoming a knight, sir," Henry said honestly. "And that seemed an impossible enough thing to wish for. But what good does it do me to stay here when I'll never live in South Britain? It's as though I'm taking another boy's place, a boy who might actually become a knight. And the professors are already treating me differently. Even if my classmates don't know, it can't be long before they find out." Henry shook his head, angry with himself for saying so much, especially to a man he hardly knew.

"If you truly feel that way, I would be willing to arrange for you to have private tutors."

Henry nearly snorted. Private tutors indeed! Without Knightley Academy, he had nowhere to live.

"Unfortunately, another boarding school would be out of the question, as your enrollment would cause quite the sort of attention we are hoping to avoid." Lord Marchbanks frowned, misunderstanding.

"That's not what I meant, sir," Henry said carefully. "I am a bit lacking in funds, you see. I would need to find a job so that I might pay rent."

Lord Marchbanks let out a sharp barking laugh. "I thought the letter was clear, Henry. You are to be my ward."

"Wh-what?" Henry spluttered. "What letter?"

And then he guiltily remembered the unopened letter from Lord Mortensen, stashed in his desk drawer.

"I'm sorry, Lord Minister," Henry said, "but I never read it."

"There is no need to apologize, Henry. I often vent my frustrations through ignoring the post myself." Lord

Marchbanks's black whiskers twiched with amusement.

"So I have to live with you?" Henry asked.

Lord Marchbanks nodded. "It's best that way. I am the minister of Foreign Relations. You can be Derrick's."

At this, Henry laughed. "Good one, sir."

"I've been saving that one for days," Lord Marchbanks admitted with a chuckle. "But in all seriousness, lad, I will not force you to return to Knightley if you don't wish it."

"No, sir, I do want to come back," Henry said, and was surprised to realize that it was true. Everything was changing, perhaps not the way he'd wished, but not unbearably so.

"I had thought so," Lord Marchbanks said. "You will spend the summer with my family at our town house in the city. But, then, it's all in the letter, should you have a chance to read it."

With that, Lord Marchbanks glanced at his pocket watch, gave his apologies, and walked briskly toward the headmaster's house, where a chrome-nosed automobile waited at the curb. Belatedly Henry realized that, somehow, without his noticing, he had been adopted—out of political obligation.

* * *

Henry couldn't find the letter anywhere. He was certain he'd put it in one of his desk drawers, but the search turned up only pencil stubs, empty ink bottles, and a black checkers piece.

He was still searching for it when Adam and Rohan straggled into the room that evening, loaded down with sweets Rohan had purchased at the train station. "Catch," he said, throwing Henry a large bag of salt-water toffee.

"Thanks."

"Oi, that's no way to treat a foreign prince, throwing food at him," Adam joked.

"I'm not a prince. It's just a courtesy title. Oh, never mind." Henry gave up on explaining and offered round the toffee. "So, how did it go?"

"It was fine," Rohan said cautiously.

"Brilliant!" Adam enthused. "It was really rubbish you couldn't come! We got to meet the king, and everyone cheered the parade, and the police knights came as mounted guards and everything!"

Rohan sighed pointedly.

"I mean it was boring," Adam said. "Absolutely horrible. Especially when Theobold farted."

"You're making that bit up," Rohan said.

"Ask Edmund!" Adam insisted. "We nearly fell out of step, it was so bad!"

Henry laughed so hard he thought he might choke on the toffee.

Henry, Adam, and Rohan spent the rest of the evening in the first-year common room in the company of their classmates. Derrick had unearthed a meerschaum pipe from somewhere and was coughing and spluttering on the thing as he frantically fanned the fumes out the window.

"I say," Derrick choked, "do I look distinguished?"

"Extremely," Henry said dryly, returning to the chess game he was playing against Valmont.

Derrick gave up on the pipe and joined Adam, Conrad, and Edmund, who were playing cards and betting with peppermint candies.

"It's your go," Valmont said.

Henry looked down at the board and moved his knight.

Valmont, a look of incredulous triumph on his face, captured it with his bishop. "Check," he said.

And then a shadow fell over the chessboard. It was Theobold.

"What do you want?" Henry asked irritably.

"Who's winning?" Theobold grunted.

Crowley, who was forever at his side, peered at the game and said, "Valmont."

"Really?" Theobold said delightedly. "Anyway, Grim, thought I'd return this." He reached into his pocket and removed an open envelope with a hastily folded letter stuffed inside.

"Where did you get that?" Henry asked, his hands clenching into fists. He seized the envelope and pushed back his chair.

"Hmmm, now where did we find that again, Crowley?" Theobold mused. "A drawer, wasn't it?"

"You went into my room?" Henry snarled.

"Easy, Grim. I was merely curious. I'd heard you were ill. I was rather hoping you'd succumb to the fever and pass on to the great beyond, but apparently you pulled through. Although not before infecting Lord Havelock with that same deadly illness. I think that's the story we were meant to believe, isn't it?"

"If you ever touch my things again . . . ," Henry threatened.

"You'll do what, you piece of Nordlandic scum?"

And then Valmont pushed back his chair and punched

Theobold in the jaw. It was a solid hit, and Theobold reeled with the force of it.

"What kind of a punch was that?" Henry asked curiously, not caring that the rest of the common room was staring.

"An undercut," Valmont said smugly. They both peered at Theobold, who sat on the floor, rubbing his jaw in shock.

"Works well," Henry said.

"I could teach it to you," Valmont offered.

"Yeah, all right," Henry said.

"There's just one condition."

"What's that?"

"If you ever throw a chess match against me again, Grim, I get to use it on you."

Henry grinned. "Fair enough," he said.

The school term came to a close, as school terms tend to do, though they sometimes seem determined to plod on forever. Students brought their textbooks outside and studied for their exams under the shade of the gnarled old oaks trees, and the heat made it a bother to put on jackets each morning.

Theobold hadn't forgotten that night in the common

room, and he'd taken to referring to Henry and Valmont as "the prince and the pauper" whenever he saw them playing chess before bed. Henry sighed and set his jaw, refusing to let Theobold's taunts goad him.

One afternoon Derrick put together a game of croquet and dared everyone to whack the balls into the boys who were studying outdoors. No one took him up on the dare, although Edmund hit a ball at Geoffrey Sutton by accident.

Henry had never played croquet before, and was relieved to find it far easier to master than cricket. It was strange, thinking that he'd be back. That after the long stretch of the summer holiday, he'd return as a second year, with a room on a different corridor, and with Sir Robert as their head of year.

Sir Robert had been named the new chief examiner, and while the Knightley Exam wasn't open to commoners, the school had decided to reserve the now traditional three places for any fourteen-year-olds who wished to sit the exam in the National Gallery.

Somehow the shock over the passing of Lord Havelock had receded. But it was still there, the hovering ghostly memory of his death, creeping up behind Henry as he studied for the military history exam given by Lord Ewing, the temporary tutor.

The battle society did not meet again before exams, and often Henry saw Valmont slip out to the graveyard beyond the woods before supper, as though he preferred the company of the dead to that of his classmates.

After his last exam, Henry turned up on the doorstep of the headmaster's house. He hadn't visited in ages, but he'd needed the time, both to catch up on his studies and to come to terms with everything that had happened.

Ellen opened the door and curtsied.

"Come in, Master Henry!" she said, ushering him into the foyer. "Can I take yer coat? Will yeh be requirin' tea?"

Henry shook his head. "I'm fine, Ellen. Thank you."

That had been happening more and more. Henry had gone down to the kitchens to ask for some tea and biscuits one evening, and the maids had panicked. Liza had quickly shooed him out of the kitchen with a full lemon tart he hadn't wanted, and not a bit of gossip.

Somehow Henry rather suspected that they knew. Theobold's taunts hadn't gone unnoticed, and though no one dared to ask him directly, more than once a group of students had fallen silent as Henry had walked past.

After all, with the relentless fear of a Nordlandic invasion, it wasn't exactly the best time for it to come out that he was Nordlandic—or for there to be whispers that he'd run off to the Nordlands for nearly two weeks, returning with a coffin containing their head of year. And then there was the way Henry hadn't marched in the parade, and the way he always seemed to set Professor Turveydrop into a panic during protocol. . . .

Sometimes Henry wished that he could explain. But to explain would be to cause the exact sort of attention that Lord Mortensen had cautioned them against. At least he still had the group of friends he'd made that term. And so he had silently endured the changes, and the way so many of the other students, who had once been friendly, now regarded him with suspicion.

Ellen led him up the grand staircase and down the hallway to Professor Stratford's study. There were voices, but she threw open the door anyway.

Professor Stratford looked up. He was evaluating Frankie on a piece of French poetry. She scowled at the interruption and continued with her recitation.

Henry had to admit that, from what he heard, she truly hadn't needed tutoring in French.

"*Formidable, Mademoiselle Winter,*" Professor Stratford said once Frankie had finished. He laid down his book. "*Dix-huit.*"

Frankie flushed at the praise. "Are we finished, Professor?" she asked.

He nodded.

"I've just finished my exams as well," Henry said.

"So you're leaving tomorrow," Frankie said. It wasn't a question.

"Lord Marchbanks is sending his driver. It's a nightmare. No wonder Derrick warned me I'd hate it."

"It'll be good for you," Professor Stratford said. "You'll get to see how the aristocracy live."

"I'd rather work in the bookshop."

"You can come and visit," the professor promised.

"Only for the summer," Henry complained. "And next year— I don't want to lose either of you. It isn't fair."

"My services are no longer needed," Professor Stratford said lightly. "And it's a curious thing, change. You never get used to it, and you're never sure where it comes from—"

"But you better learn to expect it," Henry finished.

Professor Stratford nodded, and Henry could see that he was pleased.

"I know," Henry said. "I just wish it didn't have to be that way."

Henry bit his lip at the thought of Frankie going off to finishing school. He'd known about it for a week, but that didn't make it ache any less to know that the carefree days of Frankie climbing through his window were long gone.

"It's only because of my blasted grandmother," Frankie put in. "She *knows* I loathe finishing school. She's sending me as a punishment for running away."

"Good thing she doesn't know about the kiss, or you'd be sent to a reformatory," Henry muttered.

"Kiss?" Frankie frowned. "Now, Mr. Grim, I don't think I know what you're talking about. Perhaps you ought to refresh my memory?"

At this, Professor Stratford cleared his throat, but he wasn't truly upset.

After all, how could he be? This was the last time Henry would be able to ring the doorbell after lessons, the final trip to the headmaster's house. For in the fall these rooms would be empty. Frankie was leaving for finishing school, and Professor Stratford was moving on, and the triple room on the first-floor corridor would gain new occupants while Rohan went off to room with James. And no matter how hard they pretended it was just the final day of term, it was more than that—it was the end of an era.

Did you **LOVE** this book?

Want to get access to great books for **FREE?**

Join